PRAISE FOR ANDREWS & WILSON

"*Dark Intercept* is a masterpiece of a military thriller with remarkable heart and depth. No one in the genre writes grittier and more authentic action than these two authors, and yet *Dark Intercept* also deals with the intriguing questions of spirituality and the human condition, making it a spellbinding page-turner that will leave you both thrilled and enriched by the experience."

MARK GREANEY, #1 *New York Times* bestselling author of *Relentless* and the Gray Man novels

"A blistering page-turner of a thriller . . . that effortlessly transports the reader from the adrenaline-filled highs of the battlefield to the soul-searching lows that follow."

JOSHUA HOOD, author of Robert Ludlum's Treadstone series

"The characters are unforgettable and unique, promising a blockbuster Shepherds series. Andrews & Wilson write with the authenticity that can only be achieved through boots-on-the-ground downrange experience. Whether you're military connected or not, reading this novel will make you want to enlist with these spiritual warriors. Un-put-downable."

K.J. HOWE, internationally bestselling author of *Skyjack*

"In *Dark Intercept*, Andrews & Wilson flawlessly weave a tale of spiritual and natural warfare as riveting as it is inventive. By combining the grittiness and veracity of their bestselling military thriller series with an unabashed focus on the eternal struggle between light and darkness, Andrews & Wilson inject a shot of adrenaline into faith-based fiction. Frank Peretti has company!"

DON BENTLEY, author of the Matt Drake thriller series

"A thrilling and gripping ride through the eyes of those who strap on the uniform and serve, [this book] helps us see what true leadership looks like. . . . You'll enjoy this crackling adventure and learn some valuable things along the way."

DANIEL DARLING, bestselling author of *The Characters of Christmas* and *A Way with Words*

"Andrews & Wilson strategically position the physical realm with the spiritual in this edge-of-your-seat thriller. . . . This novel captures perfectly the spiritual warfare raging around us, in a way that is both entertaining and chilling. Expertly woven and crafted, *Dark Intercept* is sure to have you view the world around you with a different set of eyes. A must-read!"

EDWIN E., military ministry leader and former Green Beret

"From the jaw-dropping opening chapter to the pulse-pounding climax, *Dark Intercept* is an emotional thrill ride of cinematic proportions. Expect to be blown away and entertained but also left thinking and talking about this book for weeks after you turn the last page. With *Dark Intercept*, Andrews & Wilson usher in a new era of Christian thriller fiction!"

CRAIG ALTMAN, lead pastor, Grace Family Church

"Shifting constantly between the fast-paced thriller and thought-provoking moments of personal challenge, *Dark Intercept* will take you to a new dimension of fiction that changes your reality. Take the journey!"

CHRIS BONHAM, senior executive pastor, Grace Family Church

THE SHEPHERDS SERIES

DARK INTERCEPT

ANDREWS & WILSON

Tyndale House Publishers
Carol Stream, Illinois

Visit Tyndale online at tyndale.com.

Visit Andrews & Wilson online at andrews-wilson.com.

Tyndale and Tyndale's quill logo are registered trademarks of Tyndale House Ministries.

Dark Intercept

Cover designed by Faceout Studios, Jeff Miller

Interior designed by Dean H. Renninger

Edited by Sarah Mason Rische

Published in association with the literary agency of Talcott Notch Literary, LLC, 276 Forest Road, Milford, CT 06461.

Dark Intercept is a work of fiction. Where real people, events, establishments, organizations, or locales appear, they are used fictitiously. All other elements of the novel are drawn from the authors' imaginations.

For information about special discounts for bulk purchases, please contact Tyndale House Publishers at csresponse@tyndale.com, or call 1-855-277-9400.

Library of Congress Cataloging-in-Publication Data

Names: Andrews, Brian, date- author. | Wilson, Jeff, date- author.
Title: Dark intercept / Andrews & Wilson.
Description: Carol Stream, Illinois : Tyndale House Publishers, [2021] | Series: A Shepherd series novel ; 1
Identifiers: LCCN 2021006522 (print) | LCCN 2021006523 (ebook) | ISBN 9781496451347 (hardcover) | ISBN 9781496451361 (kindle edition) | ISBN 9781496451378 (epub) | ISBN 9781496451385 (epub)
Subjects: GSAFD: Adventure fiction. | Christian fiction. | Suspense fiction.
Classification: LCC PS3601.N552625 D37 2021 (print) | LCC PS3601.N552625 (ebook) | DDC 813/.6—dc23
LC record available at https://lccn.loc.gov/2021006522
LC ebook record available at https://lccn.loc.gov/2021006523

ISBN 978-1-4964-5135-4 (softcover)

Printed in the United States of America

28	27	26	25	24	23	22
7	6	5	4	3	2	1

For all those who have been on the pointy tip of the spear, fighting for freedom and all that is good, and have stared down evil in the world. We ask you to remember that while there is no promise of freedom from pain and loss, in surrender to God comes the good that is promised. We thank you for your courage in staving off the darkness.

★

AUTHORS' NOTE

Dark Intercept begins a saga we've had a heart and mind to tell for many years, but only recently did the stars align for us to do so properly. The Shepherds series is more than a series of books; it is a journey . . . one that mirrors the private, personal journeys of countless men and women who have worn the uniform in the service of our great nation. As veterans, we have served alongside countless true heroes—some of whom have made the ultimate sacrifice.

When confronted by true evil, be it during military service or as a citizen navigating the gauntlet of everyday life, a person's perception and understanding of everything he or she took for granted is shattered. Such confrontations force one to seek answers to questions that are difficult and often terrifying to ask—challenging, uncomfortable, raw questions about the existence of God, the nature of good and evil, and things we feel deep in our bones but can't see with our oh-so-rational eyes. And in the asking, we open ourselves up for a truth we weren't prepared to believe or even contemplate.

In this series, we ask these very questions. We explore the idea of spiritual warfare and forces in the world that can penetrate our consciousness and change our lives dramatically—sometimes for the better but sometimes not. *Dark Intercept* is a work of fiction, but it is also a starting point. In turning the page, we invite you to come along on a journey. The characters in this story will ask tough questions about God and faith and evil in the world. And through them, maybe, just maybe, you'll discover answers to some of the questions you've been struggling with yourself but have been too afraid to ask.

SHEPHERD | 'she-pərd *verb*

1 to tend to as a shepherd

2 to guide or guard in the manner of a shepherd

3 colloquial: to serve as a pastor

PROLOGUE

Tactical superiority, courage under fire, and unbreakable brotherhood—these were the traits that defined Naval Special Warfare.

It was a community where discipline eclipsed faith.

Where grit outperformed hope.

Rather than praying for divine intervention, Navy SEAL
Jedidiah Johnson harnessed the cadence of combat to steel his
nerves. As far as he was concerned, God had no place in covert

operations. With his brothers beside him, and a SOPMOD M4 assault rifle in his hands, he could do anything.

Hooyah.

Thigh muscles burning, Jed advanced in a combat crouch. Sighting over his rifle, he methodically swept his targeting laser across the buildings on the opposite side of the dusty street, looking for targets. His green beam crisscrossed alongside those of his teammates—an ever-evolving geometric malice sweeping over the crumbling stucco facades, searching for threats in every doorway, windowpane, and alley. Invisible to the naked eye, the infrared lasers from their PEQ-2 target designators shone bright thanks to the night-vision goggles that hung in front of their eyes like miniature binoculars mounted to their helmets.

Chief Danny Carroll—"Scab" to his teammates, thanks to some long-forgotten story—advanced two paces ahead of Jed. They worked together with silent, practiced precision clearing ahead, behind, and the rooftops above as they moved down the block toward the target house. Upon reaching the corner, Scab held up a closed fist, stopping the four-man fire team. Jed took a knee, his scan now intent on the corner forty-five degrees across the unpaved intersection. On the other side of the block, a second four-man team was converging in mirror image from the opposite direction. They would arrive at the target house simultaneously, one squad breaching from the front and the other from the rear.

Jed slid his NVG-enhanced scan over the rooftop of the building across the street, looking for movement. *That's where I'd put a shooter,* he thought but found nothing of concern.

"Choctaw One is Budweiser," Scab said, reporting his squad making the checkpoint.

After a two-second pause, the other team leader, Morales, answered, "Choctaw Two is Corona," the distant voice perfectly clear in Jed's Peltor headset.

With the checkpoints made, both teams would advance the final stretch to commence the assault on the two-story house where a terrorist bomb maker called Harim al-Abbas and his lieutenants were busy building IEDs to kill American and coalition forces throughout western Anbar.

"Choctaw, Home Plate—you are clear to the target," came the report from their mission coordinator at the tactical operations center back at the forward operating base where real-time imagery was being monitored from a Predator drone in orbit above. "Eagle shows no thermals of concern between you and Miller Lite. Call Sam Adams."

Miller Lite was the target house, and Sam Adams was the call they would make when the bomb maker was either dead or captured and the site had been secured. If they continued undetected and completed the mission without incident—as they nearly always did—then that call would come in just minutes from now.

Scab rose and chopped a hand forward, taking point. Jed fell in behind him, offset his right flank, scanning above and behind as they advanced along the narrow street. Scab vectored left, leading the fire team diagonally across the next intersection to the opposite side of the street toward the building Jed had imagined would be the perfect sniper hide for terrorist sentries. But Home Plate had reported no thermal signatures of concern from the Predator circling silently overhead. Jed felt the subconscious need to shift to Scab's left side and gave his team leader a squeeze on the left shoulder to let him know his position shift as he did. As they closed on the building, the unspoken need to divert back welled up inside him.

There was no voice in his head . . . no burning bush . . .

He just knew.

"Shift left, shift left," Jed called and grabbed Scab by the arm, vectoring back across the intersection.

"On Four," Scab commanded, using Jed's call sign as Jed took the lead to make sure the trailing pair of SEALs understood the redirect. The four-man fire team quick-stepped back to the side of the street where they'd started.

"What did you see?" Scab asked, pressing against the wall and scanning the building they'd been approaching.

"Yeah, bro. What gives?" the SEAL called Reed chimed in— clearly confused at the random, unprompted redirect. No sniper had fired on them; no RPG had streaked over their heads.

Jed felt heat rise in his cheeks. How could he explain it when the knowledge came to him without words? He tried anyway.

"I just—"

The building across the intersection exploded, cutting Jed off midsentence. A storm of deadly shrapnel—glass, wood, and cement fragments—rained down on everything in a one-block radius as Jed and his fellow SEALs got small. A split second later, like a metaphorical exclamation point, what remained of the exploded building collapsed onto the sidewalk where they'd been just seconds ago. If they hadn't been vaporized by the massive detonation, they would have been crushed in the aftermath.

"How did you know?" Reed said through a cough, but Scab didn't give Jed time to answer.

"Up and move," the team leader commanded, surging forward up the street and cutting off Reed's question. "Choctaw Two—go now."

"Two," came the clipped and simple acknowledgment of the order from the Bravo fire team leader on the other side of the target.

Boots churning, Jed and his teammates sprinted north toward the target house, spreading out in a modified arrowhead and scanning every window, rooftop, and doorway as they closed the fifty-meter distance. The sound of a breacher charge going off echoed faintly in the night, confirmation that Bravo element was about to enter the target house from the rear.

"Single tango by the gate," reported the cool voice of their coordinator from the TOC, relaying real-time bird's-eye visuals. "Two has breached. Expect tangos flushing toward the front, One."

"One," Scab answered.

The terrorist sentry stationed at the front gate turned to face them, belatedly realizing what was happening. Eyes wide, the shooter raised his rifle, but Jed had already slid his PEQ-2 green targeting laser onto the man's forehead. He squeezed the trigger, and his M4 burped twice, dropping the enemy guard. Bursts of AK-47 fire reverberated inside the house, followed by more precise, controlled pops of M4 return fire, announcing to all that the fight was on. Jed kicked the iron gate hard, breaking the locking bolt free from the crumbling stucco perimeter wall.

Scab surged through the gate and into the small courtyard at the front of the house. Jed followed, clearing right as his team leader cleared left. His other two teammates shot the gap between them and rushed the front door, which hung open on its hinges.

A backlit al Qaeda fighter stood just inside the doorway, unaware of their presence as he backpedaled, firing his weapon at SEALs already inside the house. Two pops sounded as Reed engaged, dropping the jihadist in his tracks. With his two teammates clearing left and right, Jed and Scab surged up the middle—in a role-reversal instant replay of how they'd breached the courtyard just seconds ago. Jed flipped his NVGs up onto his helmet as he crossed the threshold, since his night vision would be washed out by lights glowing inside the house.

Movement to his left drew his attention and he spun that way, sighting now through the holographic sight mounted on top of his rifle, the green laser no longer visible off NVGs. A bearded man stood on a staircase, and Jed placed his red dot in the center of the terrorist's chest. Instead of engaging, the bearded jihadi terrorist threw his hands up in surrender and his AK-47 clattered down the stairs. Reed ascended the staircase halfway, jerked the terrorist down, and forced the bearded man facedown on the ground. With a knee on the jihadist's neck, the SEAL scanned up the staircase for emergent threats.

"Two is clear in the rear of the house," came the call from Morales. "We have the package. No squirters."

Jed grinned. Mission accomplished—their HVT, al-Abbas, was on-site and had apparently surrendered.

"Five and Six," Scab barked. "Clear upstairs."

The two SEALs nodded and moved quickly up the staircase, scanning over their rifles.

Jed followed Scab to the rear of the house to meet up with Morales. Al-Abbas, whose visage Jed had burned into his memory from photographs presented in their intel briefs, sat silent and still in a wooden chair. Cigarette smoke swirled toward the ceiling from butts burning in three different ashtrays atop a small, square dining table. Jed surveyed the modest kitchen, noting three dead terrorists on the floor and two captured terrorists flex-cuffed and waiting. One fighter leaned against a cabinet in the corner of the room, and the other was on his knees, forehead pressed to the floor, murmuring.

"Five and Six are clear," Reed called in Jed's Peltors.

"Choctaw is Sam Adams," Scab reported, victory in his voice. "Exfil from primary in five mikes."

"Choctaw, Home Plate—copy."

"Choctaw, grab anything of value. We're out of here in three mikes."

Double clicks in his headset told Jed his teammates understood. He and Scab would provide cover on al-Abbas and the captured jihadists while the rest of the team gathered cell phones, computers, and anything else of potential value. Morales, the Bravo fire team leader, began the unpleasant task of photographing the dead terrorists' faces, which they would compare for matches against the database back at the TOC later.

So you are the one who saw me. Interesting . . .

Jed flinched at the voice and flicked his gaze to the bomb maker, al-Abbas, who still sat unmoving in his chair, wrists bound behind his back. Their eyes met and Jed felt a powerful and visceral hate seep into his skin, the way cold ocean water floods a wet suit after the splash.

You might have the gift, but this is our time . . .

Death is my victory.

The voice could only belong to al-Abbas, but it spoke to Jed in English, and the man's lips never moved. Jed felt a lump form in his throat. His trigger finger twitched. And as he stared at the bomb maker, a second visage—distorted and grotesque—appeared superimposed on al-Abbas's face. Then an amber ring, like dying embers in a campfire, flared around the terrorist's dark-brown irises.

"What did you say to me?" Jed said, his breath catching.

"Huh?" Scab said from beside Jed, confusion in his voice. "I didn't say anything, dude."

Jed took a step back and raised his rifle, placing his red targeting dot on the center of the bomb maker's forehead. The demonic double-face smiled at him, and a memory—one he'd spent the past eight years trying to forget—clawed its way into his mind's eye.

This isn't happening, he told himself. *It's not real.*

He pulled tension on the trigger and squeezed his eyes shut for a split second, chasing the horrible memory away.

"Jed," Scab barked, but with genuine concern in his voice. "You good, bro?"

Jed let out a long, shaky breath and eased his finger off the trigger and outside the guard.

"Yeah, man, I'm good," he said, forcing a smile onto his face—a smile that he didn't feel on the inside.

Scab reached to grab the laptop computer resting on the table beside the bomb maker. "Morales is in the other room. Tell him to wrap up. I'm ready to get the hell out of here."

Jed nodded and headed out of the kitchen. Three paces later the voice was back to taunt him in his head. It uttered a single word:

Boom!

Jed whirled and looked at the devil in the chair.

The amber rings in the bomb maker's eyes flared. He smiled at Jed, and the kitchen exploded. The shock wave hit Jed like a semi-truck and blew him backward through the cased opening into the other room. And as he flew through the air, as the black curtains closed all around him, a single thought echoed in his head.

I let it happen again.

PART I

THE TAKING

Stay alert! Watch out for your great enemy,
the devil. He prowls around like a roaring lion,
looking for someone to devour. . . .

1 PETER 5:8, NLT

CHAPTER ONE

VANDERBILT UNIVERSITY BOOKSTORE

2501 WEST END AVENUE

NASHVILLE, TENNESSEE

SATURDAY, 1730 HOURS LOCAL

"'To one who has faith, no explanation is necessary. To one without faith, no explanation is possible,'" quoted Father Philip Maclin, gently tapping his index finger on the wooden tabletop.

"That's easy," said the brown-eyed teenage girl sitting across from him. "St. Thomas Aquinas."

"Okay, smarty-pants, then how about this one: 'If the highest aim of a captain were to preserve his ship, he would keep it in port forever,'" he said with a dose of playful superiority.

"That's the oldest trick in the book," Corbin Worth answered.

"Oh, really?"

"Yes, really."

"Then who said it?"

"St. Thomas Aquinas too."

"St. Thomas Aquinas *two*? Who's that? I only know the first one."

She laughed at this—a real laugh, and by now he could tell the difference. Getting that laugh was always his goal with Corbin. He watched her shoulders sag a fraction of an inch and felt her aura change. Now she was relaxed. Now she could do the thing he had asked her here to do.

It got harder for the kids with each passing year—using their gifts. And like all Keepers, Philip could empathize. For most, the power faded gradually as one grew into adulthood, but not him. A couple of weeks after his eighteenth birthday, it had simply left him. A clean break. Very unusual, Tobias had said. That year had been the most difficult of his life. It was faith that saw him through the storm. But even now, twelve years later, there were times when the emptiness swallowed him. As hard as learning to live with the gift had been—harder because of how young he had been when it arrived—it was much harder still when it disappeared. After a decade of intimate connection to the world, and the people in it, he'd tumbled into a dark pit of isolation, where only his *own* voice filled his head. He'd felt so utterly alone, so disconnected. Paralyzed. But now when the desolation struck him, he would think of Corbin and Josh and Michaela, and one of them would always find him—with a cheerful text or an unexpected phone call—and rescue him from the abyss. Yes, he was their Keeper, but at the same time, they were often his.

When God starts us on a path, He equips us for the journey.

"Ask me another one," Corbin said with a grin. "But by somebody *besides* St. Thomas Aquinas this time."

He feigned consternation. "Okay, one more and then we really should get back to the War of 1812. Try this one: 'We shall steer safely through every storm, so long as our heart is right, our intention fervent, our courage steadfast, and our trust—'" He stopped midsentence. Corbin's expression had changed.

"What is it?" he said.

"She's here," Corbin whispered. "She seems excited."

"Okay, good," he said, hoping his calm would be infectious. Corbin was gifted, and her gift no longer frightened her, but this was something new. "How close is she?"

"Um . . . less than a block away, coming from the west. No, south," she said, squinting. "I can't tell."

"No problem. Locating is difficult, I know."

"Much harder in the field," she said, glancing around the bookstore nervously. "It's different than being in the center. There are so many distractions here. So many other voices, Father."

He admonished her with his eyes and she quickly corrected herself.

"I mean, Phil," she said, dropping the priestly title but still using his fictitious cover name. Her cheeks flashed crimson and she looked down at her notebook.

He liked Corbin. He liked all of them, and not just because he had once been like them. This new generation was better—stronger, more attuned. At first, he thought they were more adept at sifting through all the noise to find "signals" in a world of ever-increasing informational traffic. But it was not their proficiency with tweeting, texting, and social media that made them better . . . The difference was spiritual. These kids took the responsibility that came with their abilities very seriously. More seriously than he had, that was for sure. They believed in the mission, and they courageously volunteered to put themselves in harm's way. He had come to admire them as the heroic youth of the next generation, taking a stand for God and country.

Or maybe it was that they sensed the dark menace in a way he no longer could—creeping, creeping, creeping into the light—and they were afraid.

A phantom itch chased along the line where his collar was supposed to be, reminding him how vulnerable he felt. When he had first been frocked, the stiff, starched fabric had irritated his skin to no end. Then over time, it had become an extension of him. The collar was more than just the uniform of his profession; it was his spiritual Kevlar. Since taking it off two years ago, he felt naked. He scratched his neck out of habit, but it offered no relief.

I am still a man of God, he told himself. *Faith is the only garment I need clothe myself in.*

A group of college girls breezed by their table, laughing as they headed toward the line for the coffee bar. One of the girls glanced in their direction, but the others paid them no mind. To the store's patrons and staff, he and Corbin were just another tutor and student studying in the bookstore.

He glanced at his watch and then at the door behind his protégé.

The girl should be here by now, he thought. *Something's wrong.*

"You think so too?" Corbin asked.

"Don't do that," he whispered.

"What?" she asked innocently.

"You know what," he said a bit more sternly. "Don't read my thoughts in public."

"I thought it was my job," she grumbled at him over her notebook. "And anyway, I was just—" Her voice caught in her throat. She looked up at him, mouth open, all the color drained from her face.

"What is it?"

"They're here," she hissed, her voice a tight, quivering chord. "They're going to take her."

"Close your mind," he said and squeezed her wrist, harder than he meant to. "Stop watching or they'll find you."

"Oh, God," Corbin said through a breath. "She doesn't see them. Oh no . . ."

He shoved Corbin's notepad and history book into her backpack and yanked her to her feet. He glanced around quickly, but no one seemed to be paying them any mind. He lifted her face by the chin and looked into her terrified eyes.

"Don't leave me alone," she said, her voice desperate.

"Listen to me," he said. "It's crowded in here right now. There's safety in numbers and it's easier to hide in the din of many minds. Guard your thoughts as I taught you and listen only for me. They have two unisex, single-stall bathrooms here. Go inside one and lock the door. If anyone tries to break in, call the police."

"Okay," she said. "And what are you going to do?"

"I'm gonna try to save her."

"Alone?"

"Of course not," he said and forced a smile. "I'm calling a team. If I can make a scene and draw a crowd—enough to give the Dark

Ones pause—it might give her a chance to get away. When it's over, I'll come back for you. I promise."

She nodded. "Okay."

"Go now," he ordered.

Corbin did as he instructed, while he retrieved his mobile phone. As he hurried toward the exit, he pressed *1* on his speed dial.

"Operator," a calm voice said in his ear.

"I need Shepherds," he said. "Priority one. My location."

"Identify?" the woman's voice asked with a slight edge to it now.

"Zechariah four-six." He paused at the door, just long enough to scan through the glass panes and verify he wasn't going to be ambushed upon exiting.

"Confirmed," the operator said. "A team will be at your location in nine minutes."

"Too slow. The Recruit is at risk, and my Watcher needs to be secured."

"Stay with your Watcher," the voice instructed.

"I can't do that. In nine minutes, it'll be over." Philip clicked his phone off before the tactical coordinator could object. Then he pushed through the double doors and stepped onto the sidewalk. He turned right, and at the corner he looked down the street toward the Vanderbilt campus. He saw the girl a half block away, her mother walking beside her. He had inhaled to shout a warning when a gloved hand gripped his upper arm.

"You're too late," a raspy male voice hissed in his ear.

Philip turned, his gaze drawn instantly to the faint amber glow around the other man's irises.

"You can't hurt me," Philip said, jerking his arm free.

"You're right. I can't," the Dark One said, taking a step back.

Philip whirled back to face the girl and her mother, who were less than twenty yards away now. He watched a white van pull along the sidewalk next to them and the rear cargo doors swing open.

"Noooooo!" he shouted.

"Watch out!" screamed a woman nearby.

For an instant, he wasn't sure who the woman was calling to, but then he heard the squeal of tires. The black Dodge Charger hit him in the pelvis and sent him sailing backward into the corner wall of the Barnes & Noble. His body stopped, but the Charger kept coming. In the split second before impact, he made eye contact with the driver through the windshield. A college student no older than twenty, who looked catatonic. Philip had seen this look before. Then his entire body erupted in pain as the front end of the car smashed him into the wall. His forehead hit the hood of the car and his nose flattened. His vision flashed brilliant white, and the pain, so loud and all-consuming, suddenly turned off like a switch.

With great effort, he lifted his head and looked at the driver. The young man's expression had changed and was now one of terror and confusion as he registered what he had just done. *Poor kid,* Philip thought. *This will haunt him for the rest of his life. Dear Lord, give him comfort.* He turned his head left as his vision began to bleach gray. He watched the young Recruit's feet kicking wildly in the air as strong arms dragged her into the white van. The girl's mother was screaming, ten feet away and impotent where she'd been knocked to the ground. But he couldn't hear her screams. He couldn't hear anything, except the rasp of breath coming from his crushed chest.

His mind went to Corbin and he prayed she was still tuned in and listening to him.

Stay inside. The Shepherds are coming. Don't unlock the door until they arrive.

Her answer came swift and strong, a scream inside his head. *Where are you? What's happening? Sarah Beth is so scared.*

With all his remaining willpower, he answered her. Just forming the words in his mind was impossibly difficult. *She's been taken. Be brave and remember what I taught you. Find her . . . before it's too late.*

Then he rested.

Corbin would be fine. She was strong . . . the strongest he'd trained.

The world was black now.

He tried to open his eyes but realized they were already open. He felt himself shift.

The tether snapped, and he was adrift.

There was light, though he couldn't see it. But he could feel it, and it was warm and tender.

His lips began to move.

"Bless me, Holy Father, for I have sinned . . ."

CHAPTER TWO

HUI TUNA BAR AND GRILL

2817 SHORE DRIVE

VIRGINIA BEACH, VIRGINIA

WEDNESDAY, 1700 HOURS LOCAL

Navy SEAL Senior Chief Jedidiah Johnson loosened the tie on his dress blue uniform and slid onto a barstool. He raised a hand to the girl behind the bar.

"Hey, Jed," she said and pulled a Corona from the cooler. She slid it to him across the counter. He caught it and then licked some spilled suds off the back of his hand. "Big day, right?" the girl said with a wink and a smile—the same pretty smile that earned her thousands in tips and hundreds of unsolicited phone numbers scribbled on cocktail napkins from the legion of Navy SEALs who called this bar their home away from home.

"Yeah," Jed said. "Big day." He took a long pull on his beer and looked around the bar. In minutes, the joint would be swelling with his teammates—*former* teammates, actually. He would have to get used to the word *former*: former teammate, former Navy SEAL, former senior chief. He sighed and smiled at the bartender. "Whaddaya say we get out of here? Run away to the Caribbean and drink Coronas on a real beach."

"Nuh-uh. No way, Jed," she laughed. "You're not getting out of this one. I promised the boys I'd lock the doors if I had to."

A resigned smile curled his lips and he shook his head. For a Navy SEAL, retirement was as difficult as it was inevitable. Being a SEAL was like being a professional athlete, and the human body, as amazing as it was, could only take so much abuse. At thirty-five, he would still be considered a young man in most professions. But in special warfare, seventeen years of hard service and a shattered hip had left him a bit long in the tooth. After taking a 7.26mm round to the left hip, the docs had said he'd walk with a cane for the rest of his life, but he'd proven them wrong and rehabilitated himself back into fighting form. And yet, it was important to be honest with himself. Could he still do his job? Yes. Could his brothers without chronic pain, scar tissue, and flaring arthritis in their hips do the job better? As much as it stung, the answer was also yes. Retiring with grace was not the same as being retired. Passing the torch was not the same as quitting. These were the things he'd told himself, and they were true . . .

But why didn't it feel that way?

"What's up, Senior?" A voice interrupted his rumination, and the slap on his back sloshed beer onto the back of his hand.

He looked up into the smiling face of a teammate ten years his junior—a lifetime in the SEALs. "Is this a party or a wake?"

"He's right, Jed," a familiar voice beside him boomed, and Jed felt himself reflexively straighten up at the sound of the Group Two Commander, Captain Mike Jared. He had served with the senior officer on and off his entire career. Jared was one of the SEALs Jed respected most, and he was confident the man would make admiral and one day command all of WARCOM. "You okay, Senior Chief? Not having second thoughts, are you?"

"No, sir," Jed said with a forced grin. "I'm good."

"Well," the officer said, "if you change your mind, let me know. I've got enough rank to make your retirement package disappear." Captain Jared smoothed his dress blues as he took the barstool beside his former platoon leader. Like the rest of the SEALs funneling into the room, Jared would be more comfortable in BDUs or blue jeans. In the Teams, the dress uniforms were little more than dust collectors in between funerals and retirements—more of the former than the latter since 9/11.

"I'm sure you could, sir," Jed said. "Like we made that bus disappear in Qatar that one time."

"Easy now," Jared said but laughed at the memory. "We agreed never to speak of that, shipmate."

Jed nodded and took a pull from his Corona. He loved his brothers more than anything in the world. Maybe he was making a mistake. What kind of life could he ever have apart from these men? Then a parade of faces marched past his mind's eye—the brothers lost and the lives he had taken. The same faces that harassed him in his dreams every night.

Jed sighed. *No, it's time.*

"What are you gonna do, Jed?" the younger SEAL asked.

"Still working on that," Jed said and looked away, not sure what else to say.

"My offer stands, Jed," Captain Jared said. "I have a lot of friends at the Agency and others working in contracting jobs. One quick call and I can have you in a six-figure job doing what you do best."

"I appreciate that, sir," he said, feeling uncomfortable now. "I may take you up on it, but I need to look around a little first. My whole life has been Navy. . . . I just need to see what else is out there."

Jared nodded. "Completely understandable. Look around and see what your options are. Just know I'm a phone call away if you need me."

Jed's phone vibrated and then rang in his pocket, giving him a perfectly timed out. He retrieved the phone and checked the caller ID but didn't recognize the number. Nonetheless, he'd take a call from the devil himself to get out of questions about what he planned to do with his life now that he was a *former* Navy SEAL.

"Excuse me a moment, sir," Jed said to Captain Jared and slid off his stool. He walked quickly to the door and stepped outside before pressing the green button on the screen.

"Hello?"

The relative quiet of the outside was shattered by the roar of an F/A-18 fighter jet screaming in from the ocean and then breaking in a ninety-degree turn directly over him before heading toward the runway at Naval Air Station Oceana a few miles away. When the vibration stopped and the ringing in his ears eased, he tried again.

"Say again," he began. "I couldn't hear you."

"I'm sorry. Maybe I have the wrong number?" The voice on the line sounded tight and strained. The owner was clearly under stress—maybe even duress—and Jed looked again at the screen, hoping the seemingly random string of numbers would become enlightening.

He put the phone back to his ear. "Who's calling?"

"Is this Jed?" the voice asked, and Jed suddenly felt something familiar about the voice, but he couldn't place it.

"This is Senior Chief Jedidiah Johnson," he said coolly. "Now who is this?"

"It's David," the trembling voice replied. He thought the man on the other end of the line might even be crying.

"David who?" he demanded.

"David Yarnell," the voice answered, and Jed felt the blood drain from his face. "I'm sorry to call, Jed. I know it's been a long time, but I need your help. I desperately, desperately need your help."

Anger, indignation, and a wave of other conflicting emotions swirled in his mind and made his guts ache.

"How did you get this number?" he asked and instantly realized what a ridiculous and inappropriate question it was. As far as he knew, his childhood best friend still lived in Murfreesboro and David's parents still lived three doors down from the house where Jed had grown up. Even if David had moved, he could still just call Jed's parents to get Jed's mobile number. It had been a long source of strain on Jed's relationship with his parents that they'd stayed in close contact with David all these years, despite his own bitter estrangement from his childhood friend.

"Please, Jed." David's voice choked. "You have to help me. They took her."

Jed felt his chest tighten as if he had just taken a blow to the ribs. "Took who—Rachel? Is Rachel okay?" he blurted.

"No, not Rachel," David said. "Sarah Beth—our little girl. They took my little girl. Please, Jed, you have to help us get her back."

Jed loosened his tie even further and started down the block, walking away from Hot Tuna, toward the corner where he could cross over to the beach side of the road.

"Take a deep breath, David," he said. "Start from the beginning and tell me exactly what happened."

He heard only uncontrolled sobbing from the other end of the line.

"David, listen to me. I can't help you if you don't talk to me."

His *former* best friend coughed and cleared his throat. "Okay . . . I'm okay . . ." David breathed, gaining his composure. "I didn't know who else to turn to. The police are looking for her, but so far they've got nothing. I know you're a Navy SEAL, and I . . . I just thought that if anybody could find my baby girl, it would be you."

Jed swallowed hard, but the lump in his throat persisted. None of the memories swirling in his head were pleasant. Old wounds reopened and the once-extinguished anger at the betrayal he'd suffered rekindled. And then there was the other memory—the one he'd been running from his entire adult life—that usurped all others and filled his mind with dread. He squeezed his eyes shut. How could he possibly go back to Nashville and face all the unresolved matters that awaited him there? And besides, he was a Navy SEAL, not a miracle worker, and he was certainly no investigator. What did he know about finding missing kids? Give him a target package and a location, and he and his team of SEALs could unleash the wrath of God, but what David was asking for was no counterterrorism operation.

"Are you there?" David said.

Jed let out a long, quivering sigh. He felt nothing but animosity toward the man on the phone, a man he'd vowed to never forgive. But this wasn't about David, was it? A little girl was missing. *Rachel's* little girl. And try as he might, he'd never been able to stoke a fire of anger toward Rachel. The connection they'd shared had been powerful and special. He'd never experienced anything like it with any other woman in the years since.

"Jed, please. She's only twelve years old. You have to help us."

The sound of a father weeping for his missing daughter eroded his defenses. No matter what had happened between them, no matter how painful unpacking the past might be, how could he walk away from the man he'd once loved as a brother?

"Okay," Jed said at last. "Tell me exactly what happened, and you have my word I will do whatever I can to help."

CHAPTER THREE

SOUTHWEST AIRLINES BOEING 737

ON APPROACH TO NASHVILLE INTERNATIONAL AIRPORT

THURSDAY, 1015 HOURS LOCAL

Jed looked out the oval window on Southwest Airlines flight 539 as the aircraft banked on approach. He looked south, past the Nashville airport, toward home. Despite the fact that he had only been back to Tennessee twice in almost two decades, the nostalgic pull of Murfreesboro was unsettling. As he looked over the rolling green hills, a deep, powerful longing washed over him.

Followed by regret.

And then anger.

He leaned his head back into the headrest, closed his eyes, and tried to purge the negative feelings from his mind.

This isn't a homecoming, he reassured himself. *It's a mission. As long as I stay in mission mode, everything will be fine.*

He felt the plane flare. A moment later, the tires chirped on contact with the tarmac. He opened his eyes and checked his watch. They were early—ten minutes ahead of their 10:25 a.m. scheduled arrival time.

While the passengers around him squirmed anxiously in their seats, Jed sat perfectly still, trying to decide what he would say to David. Given the circumstances, he saw no point in trying to make small talk. The simplest solution, he decided, was to ask questions and let David do all the talking. The more he minimized face-to-face time, the better. David had offered to pick him up at the airport, but that would have been too much. Not only was the gesture more familiar than Jed wanted, but the looming possibility that Rachel might tag along was more than he could bear. Just the thought of seeing her made his mouth go dry.

The plane settled to a halt at the gate, and the passengers disembarked row by row. When his turn to exit came, Jed stood too quickly, and his hip flared with pain. Cramming his six-foot-four frame into a window seat was partially to blame, but sitting for too long was the primary culprit. He'd meant to get up and move around, but the transit had been turbulent and the pilots had kept them in their seats for most of the flight. Wincing, he straightened up and collected his single dark-gray go bag from the overhead compartment. After a few anguished strides up the aisle, things settled down and he walked without limping up the Jetway. Forty-five minutes later, after a stop at baggage claim to collect his small checked bag with his more "sensitive items" not allowed in his carry-on, he piloted an Avis midsize rental sedan west on I-40. Instead of taking I-24 directly into downtown, he subconsciously took the longer, more familiar southern route on I-440.

He'd agreed to meet David—and *only* David—at the Barnes & Noble on the north side of Vanderbilt's campus. Jed didn't know this incarnation of the university bookstore. The last time he'd been on campus, the bookstore had been centrally located in Rand Hall just off Alumni Lawn. As high school seniors, he and David had occasionally made ill-conceived pilgrimages to Nashville, with David intent on cruising fraternity row and prowling the Vanderbilt campus. With Jed as his wingman, David hoped to charm a hot Vandy coed into thinking they were enrolled as freshmen. Of course these aspirational hookups never came to fruition, as Jed knew they wouldn't, but that hadn't stopped David from trying and Jed from tagging along to keep his buddy out of trouble.

Jed caught a fleeting glimpse of the exit sign for Route 70 in his peripheral vision. Gritting his teeth, he swerved across two lanes of traffic, barely making the exit ramp. Horns blared behind him, and he chastised himself—first for daydreaming and second for reckless driving. He shook his head. Since David's call, his mental focus—the most valuable asset a SEAL operator had—felt like it had been through the shredder. If he were downrange with the Teams right now, he would ground himself before he got someone killed. In seventeen years as a SEAL, he could not remember being so self-distracted.

Leave the past where it belongs. Get your head together, dude. Be a pro.

As he cruised eastbound on West End Avenue, he cleared his

mind with a series of four-count tactical breathing sequences. He needed to chase away the anger and resentment brewing close to the surface, knowing those feelings would color his thinking. Every time a distracting thought about David or Rachel popped into his head, he beat it down, like a game of mental Whac-A-Mole. He passed Vanderbilt University Stadium off to the right—the home of the Commodores football team—so he knew he was coming up on Natchez Trace. The Barnes & Noble was another block up, at Twenty-Fifth and West End. He signaled and steered the rental car into the right lane, then turned in to the long, narrow run of parking spots in front of the various restaurants and shops. He grabbed the first open spot in front of the bookstore, put the transmission in park, and checked his watch. He was thirty minutes early.

His legs were restless.

And his hip was aching.

No point in sitting and obsessing in the car. This is just another brief for another impossible mission.

He climbed out of the rental, locked it with the fob, and walked to the bookstore. The entrance doors were fifteen feet or so from the corner, but just beyond them he noted orange road cones and yellow police tape cordoning off a hole in the corner wall between the large plate-glass windows, which were missing and covered with plywood. A three-foot chunk of the corner facade was missing, and the sidewalk beneath the yellow tape was bleached white compared to the surrounding cement. Jed swallowed hard and wondered what had been scrubbed away. Was this the scene where the kidnapping had occurred? If so, it had ended very badly for someone . . .

He closed his eyes and said a quiet prayer that the someone had not been Rachel's daughter.

Opening his eyes, he suddenly wondered if God still heard his prayers, as infrequent as they came now.

Mine probably go to His spam folder these days.

With a self-deprecating grimace, he pulled the door open and stepped inside the Vandy bookstore. As soon as he entered, he saw his childhood friend, staring absently at a cup of coffee, at one of the mostly empty tables in the café, set off by a half wall from the rest of the bookstore. He should have known David would arrive early and steal that emotional advantage as well as everything else. Despite over a decade and a half having passed, David looked the same—devilishly handsome, with a mouth poised permanently on the brink of a devious smile. He still wore his light-brown hair long, but today it was unwashed and unkempt. Jed closed his eyes, took a long, deep breath, and headed over. His normal practice would be to make a joke, break the ice, and get moving onto business, but right now to do so felt wildly inappropriate. So instead, he cleared his throat.

David didn't look up.

"Hello, David," he said after a beat.

The gray-blue eyes that looked up at him were bloodshot and weary.

"Jed?" the man said, looking him over.

Jed nodded.

David shook his head in disbelief as he got to his feet. "I wouldn't have recognized you if you hadn't found me first. You look like Samson the Nazirite . . . except for the hair, of course."

Jed shrugged his powerful shoulders. "I wouldn't go that far."

His years in the SEAL Teams had transformed his body. He was no longer the skinny teenager who couldn't break a buck fifty on the scales no matter what he ate. Contrary to popular belief, Navy SEALs had a wide variety of physiques. Most of the guys in his unit, despite their incredible level of fitness, looked pedestrian in street clothes. Not Jed. In his twenties, something had clicked, and he'd started packing on the muscle. Now he was a *big boy*, and David's reaction was certainly justifiable.

David stuck out his hand, and Jed hesitated, then tossed off the bitter reluctance and shook it firmly. Being childish would serve neither of them. David gestured to the seat opposite him, and they both sat down.

"So Vandy, huh?" Jed said, awkwardly.

David nodded. "I'm in my last year of seminary—getting my master's at the divinity school over on the Peabody campus. I spent ten years as a lay pastor in the youth ministry, but the church sponsored my seminary application and gave me a scholarship. After graduation, I'll be ordained and get my own parish—as an associate minister with the United Methodist Church."

David Yarnell a minister?

The idea sucked the wind from Jed's soul. His parents had mentioned David working with a youth group, but Jed didn't know it had become a vocation. Under the table, he clenched his fists at the thought that David was living *his* dream. First he'd stolen Rachel, and now he was living the life with her Jed had always imagined for himself . . . a life that had been on track until *that night.*

"Let's skip the chitchat," Jed said. "Tell me exactly what happened."

The words came out more hostile than Jed intended. He saw a flash of anger in David's eyes—reminiscent of the hot-tempered boy his once-best friend had been. An angry, restless soul—driven by thrill seeking, excited by conflict, and perpetually swapping orbits around the rogue stars of Murfreesboro. In high school, Jed had made it his mission to share with David the joy and sense of purpose he found through his faith. David had wanted none of it. But despite their differences, Jed and David had been inseparable. They were yin and yang—opposites lost when separated but in balance together.

Now, it occurred to Jed, the poles had reversed.

"They took her," David said softly after the long pause, peering down into his coffee. "They took my little girl, Jed."

"Who took her?" Jed asked, struggling to soften his voice. The empathy he suddenly felt was competing with his bitterness, and for the moment the former took a slight lead.

"I don't know," David said, his voice cracking as he wiped a tear from his eye.

Jed paused, resisting the urge to ask David how a Navy SEAL could possibly help in this situation. Instead he said, "What about Amber Alerts? Has anybody reported anything? Anything at all?"

David shook his head. "They put out an Amber Alert, and um, there've been a few calls back, but the police are saying that nothing has panned out so far."

"But the police are working on it, right?"

"Yeah, for whatever that's worth. Rachel and I spent all last night and this morning at the precinct. They're trying. Nashville PD has their best people out looking, and the state highway patrol has been involved since the beginning, but I'm just . . .

I'm just so terrified. Rachel looked up the statistics. They're not good, Jed."

Jed nodded. He'd done some homework of his own in the airport terminal before his flight. According to the National Center for Missing and Exploited Children, in nonfamily abductions, 20 percent of the children reported taken were not recovered alive. And 74 percent of abducted children who are ultimately murdered are killed within three hours of their abduction. By his calculation, David's daughter was missing at least eighteen hours, assuming they had called him right away.

"Do they have any suspects?" Jed asked.

"No."

"Any leads at all?"

"No. None."

Jed blew air through his teeth. "Okay, well, let's start at the beginning. Can you walk me through exactly what happened?"

David nodded. "Her mother was walking her to the bookstore— to this bookstore," he added, gesturing around but not looking up.

Jed flinched and wondered if David said "her mother" instead of "Rachel" on purpose. He pushed the thought away as insanely selfish.

"I was running late, and so I was still over on Peabody campus at the time."

"What do you mean? Were you supposed to be here, at the bookstore?"

David's shoulders fell.

"You can't do that, David. You can't blame yourself. It's not your fault," Jed said. "Trust me. I'm speaking from experience on this one."

"How can you say that to me?" David hissed. "You've never lost a daughter."

Jed felt heat in his cheeks from the barb. "No, I haven't, but don't tell me I don't know about loss. Nobody does the job I did and escapes unscathed," he snapped, aware his voice was louder and sharper than he intended. He'd given his soul to his service in the Teams and to the brotherhood. "Believe me when I tell you I've suffered a lifetime's worth of loss. SEALs I loved as brothers, killed while they were at my side because of mistakes I've made . . . instincts I failed to act upon. That's a burden I have to carry with me every day, for the rest of my life."

"I'm sorry, Jed," David said, his voice quiet and conciliatory. "I didn't mean to offend—I'm sure you've suffered too."

An image of Rachel smiling and holding a baby girl in her arms materialized in Jed's mind. In the image, she was holding *his* daughter. Then he imagined that daughter being stolen away from him. A surge of angst welled up inside him. Yes, he had suffered, but David was right. Losing a child was different.

"It's all right," Jed said. "You didn't deserve that. This is not about me; it's about you and . . ." He closed his eyes, not able to say her name out loud. "And your wife and your daughter. Please, go on."

David took a deep breath and exhaled before continuing. "We meet here Saturdays sometimes," he began.

"Wait," Jed interrupted. "Saturday? She's been missing since Saturday?" His mind slipped back to the statistics David had just referred to—grim statistics indeed. And they were well on the other side of the "good outcome" curve now.

"Yes," David said, looking at his hands. "We called you—*I* called you—when we'd all but lost hope." Jed watched the man he'd spent years hating wipe a tear from his face "Anyway, we moved into town when I started seminary and live not far from here, so Saturdays they often do a mother-daughter afternoon—shopping or whatever—while I go in and get some work done on my thesis. Then after, we meet up at the bookstore and have a Frappuccino together. It's just a special little weekend thing we started a couple of months ago. This week, we had a meeting planned with an alumnus and student from a private school we were considering sending Sarah Beth to. I was supposed to be there already, but I was running late . . ."

"You meet here every Saturday afternoon?" Jed started to imagine how easy it would be to surveil that routine and plot a kidnapping, though it hardly answered the "why."

"That's right, but like I said, I was running late. Rachel said she parked down the block, south toward the stadium, and they were walking up West End when the accident happened."

"What accident?" Jed asked, not following David's disjointed segue.

"Sorry; I'm getting ahead of myself." David took a deep breath. "Rachel and Sarah Beth were walking on the sidewalk, and a van pulled up beside them. Two men jumped out the back, shoved Rachel to the ground, and grabbed Sarah Beth. They forced Sarah Beth into the van and drove away. But seconds before they grabbed her, there was a terrible accident. A guy lost control of his car and jumped the curb and crashed into the building. You probably saw the damage on your way in."

Jed had, of course. He pursed his lips. He had learned in his first few years in the Teams that there were no such things as coincidences, and a simultaneous accident and kidnapping was one heck of a coincidence.

"Who was the driver?" Jed asked.

David looked confused. "Of the van?"

"No, the driver of the car that crashed into the wall."

"Oh," David said, shaking his head. "That poor kid . . . he's a Vandy undergrad. He must be a basket case. He cut that guy in half, they said."

Now Jed was really confused. "What guy?"

David sighed and shook his head again as if clearing away cobwebs. "I'm sorry, man. I am so exhausted I can't focus. . . . All I know about the driver is he was a student here. Different detectives are working that case. I heard that the accelerator stuck or something. When the car hit the dude on the sidewalk, it cut him almost in half. The guy died almost instantly."

Causing an accident as a distraction was a plausible theory, but vehicular homicide was another thing altogether. Maybe the accident wasn't related to Sarah Beth's snatch and grab.

"Then what happened?"

"I wasn't here for the accident or the kidnapping," David said, his eyes rimmed with fresh tears. "By the time I got here, it was over and they were gone. Rachel was running down the sidewalk screaming, chasing after them."

"Did she get the plate number?"

"The van didn't have any, but it doesn't matter now anyway because the cops found the van less than three miles away from campus. They dumped it and changed vehicles."

"Are they sure it was the same van?"

"Definitely, because it had Sarah Beth's DNA in it—from a hair, no blood or anything."

"Any other DNA?"

"No, just hers." David suddenly looked on the verge of collapse.

Jed wanted to reach out and squeeze his arm, but he just couldn't do it. "I know it's hard. Take all the time you need."

David looked up. "There's nothing else to tell. Rachel is the only witness because everyone else was fixated on the accident. It's like Sarah Beth disappeared off the face of the earth, and the only record of the event is the one in Rachel's memory."

"How is Rachel?" Jed asked, saying her name aloud for the first time, with some difficulty.

"A mess," David said. Then he thought a moment. "No, not a mess. That would be me. She cries a lot, but these days it seems like she's actually the strong one. I can't—I just . . ."

"I know it's hard, David, but I need you to focus. I want to go back to the guy who got hit by the car."

"What about him?"

Jed shrugged. "Who was he?"

"I have no idea."

"Was he a local?"

It was David's turn to shrug. "Seriously, Jed, I don't know anything about him. Why?"

"Just asking. The more information the better, right?"

"So you think the kidnapping and the accident are connected? Because the police don't."

"No, I'm not saying that," Jed said. "But I'm . . . I'm just not a big believer in coincidences."

David nodded and returned his gaze to the depths of his coffee cup.

They sat in silence for a long minute.

"What about the people you were meeting from the private school?" Jed asked finally. "Did they see anything?"

David looked off in the distance, as if he'd not thought of that. "I . . . I don't know. For obvious reasons, we never met them. I don't even know if they showed up. The whole thing was a little weird, frankly."

"What do you mean?"

"We had a phone interview with the school first and it went well. A face-to-face meeting—with an alumnus and current student—was supposed to be the next step. But we didn't even know the names of the people we were meeting that day. The admissions office said they do so many of these, they usually don't know which interviewer will be assigned until the last minute."

"So you picked the Vanderbilt bookstore café as the location and agreed on a time?"

David nodded.

"Oh" was all Jed could say.

"No point in rescheduling now. If we get Sarah Beth back, I'm never letting her out of my sight. And if . . . if . . . if not . . ." David covered his face with his hands and began to sob.

Jed looked at the weeping, broken man across from him and felt his lips purse again. After all their years apart, and the chasm between them, why would David ask for his help? They weren't friends—not anymore. They didn't even know each other anymore, did they? He looked at David, who was now a million miles away. Empathy finally trumped bitterness, and he squeezed the man's arm.

"David," he said gently, "I'm so sorry you are going through this. I'm so sorry for you and for . . ." He swallowed hard. "Rachel."

The seminarian looked up, his face slack but his eyes grateful for the words.

"But I don't know why I'm here," Jed continued. "I see nothing that I can bring to the situation. It seems to me you'd be much better off engaging a private detective." He wondered if David—like most people—had no idea what Navy SEALs *actually* did for a living. "Why did you think to call me, of all people, to help with this?"

David's eyes cleared, and Jed saw a little fire there. His former friend looked around and then leaned in, his voice hushed. "Because it happened again."

"What happened again?"

"I . . . I don't know. I felt *them*, Jed. At the precise moment when Sarah Beth was taken, I felt the same thing as that night when we saw *it*. That same horrible feeling infiltrated my mind and I knew . . . I knew Sarah Beth was in trouble." David looked him in the eyes. "It was just like the night of the bonfire. The carnivorous hate, the hungry malice . . ."

Jed jerked back in his seat as if he had just touched a live power line. "I don't know what you're talking about."

"You know exactly what I'm talking about," David said, his voice rising, a harsh whisper ripe with desperation and urgency.

"I didn't see anything." Jed pushed his chair back from the table. "And I didn't hear anything." In that moment, his voice sounded like a small boy's—nothing like the battle-blooded Navy SEAL he was.

"You can lie to everyone else, but not to me," David hissed. "We were both there. It happened, Jed. It was real."

Jed swallowed down the vile stomach acid in the back of his throat. "I can't go back there, man," he said, clenching his fists. "No way."

He turned to leave, but the unadulterated anguish in David's voice stopped him in his tracks.

"Please, Jed. She's my little girl."

Jed paused, his back to David and his mind reeling. He felt like a five-year-old kid, deathly afraid of the unseen dark.

"If not for me, for Rachel," David begged.

The hair stood up on the back of Jed's neck.

That was a low blow.

"I'm at the Courtyard by Marriott just around the corner," he said without turning around. "Let me check in, take a shower, and change clothes. I'll meet you in the lobby in an hour."

"Does that mean you'll help us?"

"It means I'm not saying no," he said softly. "Beyond that I don't know what it means."

"Thank you, Jed. God bless you."

The blessing was more than he could take, and he whirled to face David.

"I don't need your blessing, David. And I'm not doing this for you or for your God. I'm doing it for the girl."

With that, he turned and hurried out the door.

For the girl . . . and maybe for Rachel.

CHAPTER FOUR

David's voice played on a loop in Jed's mind:

"You can lie to everyone else, but not to me. . . . It happened, Jed. It was real."

The hot shower loosened his aching muscles and washed away the fog of fatigue, but it did nothing to thaw his friend's chilling words.

"No," he mumbled to himself as he toweled off in the bathroom. "It wasn't real."

Fear plays tricks on the brain, he reminded himself. He'd seen that firsthand in combat with the SEALs. And that day—so many years ago now—his thoughts had been clouded with fear. Fear and rage.

He looked at his reflection in the mirror and for an instant saw that skinny, terrified teenager he had spent over a decade and a half remaking—first disassembling and then painstakingly rebuilding. He balled up his fists and studied the cords of muscle that rippled beneath the heavily veined skin of his forearms. Fear was the architect of this body. Fear was the secret engine that had powered him through BUD/S and SQT and every grueling mission he'd participated in over the years. Fear was his drill sergeant, driving him to become the perfect soldier—the perfect killing machine.

And fear helped him quiet the rage.

He tsked at his reflection and walked out of the bathroom.

After quickly dressing, he glanced at his Suunto watch. He'd burned over half of the hour he'd asked David for. Jed exhaled sharply and looked out the window, trying to think how to help find Sarah Beth. He wasn't a police detective, wasn't an investigator of any kind. He was a *receiver* of intelligence. If only he knew someone with actual experience finding missing persons . . .

Jed opened the Google app on his phone and queried key words pertaining to the events at the Vanderbilt bookstore. Immediately the screen populated with multiple hits about the kidnapping and vehicular manslaughter. Jed systematically opened links to the articles pertaining to the accident, looking for any information he could find about the victim and the driver. Details were sparse, but he found enough to get him started. He jotted notes in the notebook app on his phone as he read, toggling back and forth between the two apps. He winced when he discovered that the car accident victim's home address was in Murfreesboro, which reminded him that he still hadn't called his parents to tell them he was in town. They would be in Florida, where they spent the winters as snowbirds since retiring, for at least another month. Still, if they heard he'd been in town and he hadn't let them know . . .

Jed classified the guilty thought as non–mission critical and pushed it aside. *Later,* he told himself.

He stuck the hotel key card in his left pocket, the rental car fob in his right, and then paused, looking at his large gray tactical backpack, unzipped and flipped open on the bed like a clamshell, with toiletries, personal effects, and electronics secured in one half and clothes stuffed into the other. He reached under the clothes to the bottom of his pack and pulled out a rectangular metal box. He set it on the bed, then pressed a thumb onto the biometric reader, watched the red light turn blue, and heard the click. He opened the lockbox and pulled out the Sig Sauer P229 pistol. Next, he slipped one of the three magazines beside the gun into the butt of the pistol and cycled the slide to advance a round, pulling back to confirm the weapon was charged. After that, he removed the magazine, topped off with one additional 9mm bullet, and replaced it.

He fished the small leather holster from his kit and slid the pistol into it before sliding the whole thing into the right front corner of the waistband of his cargo pants. He dropped the two extra magazines into the interior magazine pockets in the left thigh cargo pocket, then returned the lockbox to his bag. He pulled a KUIU Rubicon jacket on over his head without unzipping it all the way, partly for the chill of the early spring air, but mostly to conceal the pistol in his waistband.

Satisfied, he closed his pack, hung the Do Not Disturb sign

on the exterior door handle, and headed to the lobby. He found David sitting on a sofa, legs crossed at the knees, staring at a flat-screen monitor announcing events at the hotel. David had the same blank expression Jed had seen during their first meeting. Jed plopped down on the cushion beside him, startling his former friend.

"Sorry," he mumbled.

David gave him a pained smile. "So what now, Navy SEAL Jedidiah Johnson?"

"Special Operations Senior Chief," Jed said. He stared at the electronic marquee himself for a moment, as his plan for the day began to gel. He turned to David. "Now I do a little poking around, I guess."

"Where are we going first?" David's face was tight and all business.

"You go home," Jed said. "Go be with . . . with your wife. Keep checking in with the police, just like you've been doing. Keep me in the loop on anything that changes, and I'll circle back in a few hours."

David's face flashed with anger. "You don't think I can handle this, is that it?"

"No," Jed said, shaking his head. "That's not it at all. I just think it would be better if I work alone on this."

"Don't assume that because I'm in ministry I somehow became a wimp overnight. My daughter is missing and I need your help to find her, but I'm not going to stop being her dad. There must be something I can do."

Jed smiled tightly. Then a thought occurred to him. "There is," he said, getting to his feet. "Reach out to the detective in charge of

Sarah Beth's case. Ask if we can meet her later. That way you can make the introduction and get me into the communication loop."

"Okay," David said, but after a beat, he screwed up his face and looked at Jed. "How did you know the lead detective is a woman?"

A very good question, Jed thought. *I didn't know I did.*

He shrugged. "Just a feeling, I guess."

David nodded but looked unconvinced. "What do I tell her about you?"

"Say I'm Sarah Beth's godfather or something and that you asked me to help out with the search. Tell her that you and Rachel are so emotional right now, you need someone with a clear head to be involved and make sure rational decisions are being made."

"That's true, actually," David said, his gaze downcast. "What will you be doing in the meantime?"

"Just looking around a bit," Jed said, holding his cards close to the vest. It would be better if David didn't have anything to pass on to the cops about what he was doing. He had no idea how these investigations worked, but he couldn't imagine Nashville PD would be pleased to have a Navy SEAL with no jurisdiction or authority—and let's face it, no real expertise or experience snooping around their case.

David nodded.

"If I find anything, I'll call you immediately so you can pass it on to the police, okay?" Jed said.

"Okay."

Jed stood and headed for the exit doors.

"Wait," David called after him.

Jed desperately wanted to pretend he didn't hear that, but grudgingly he stopped in his tracks.

"Take this," David said.

Jed looked down at David's outstretched hand. Clutched between his friend's thumb and index finger was a wallet-size glossy photograph of a beautiful young girl with curly brown hair, porcelain-white skin, and glacier-blue eyes.

Jed's heart skipped a beat—the young girl in the picture was a doppelgänger for Rachel the first time he'd met her more than twenty years ago. They'd been in elementary school . . .

"Just so you don't forget, Special Operations Senior Chief Johnson," David said. "This is the mission."

Jed swallowed and took the picture. He opened his mouth to speak, but the words caught in his throat.

"Bring my baby home," David said and then left him standing in the lobby without a backward glance.

CHAPTER FIVE

Jed felt the strong pull of the past as he drove to the home address of Philip Maclin, the man who'd been killed in the car crash during the kidnapping. The wisps of nostalgia he felt as the vibrant-green countryside rolled by outside didn't change the fact that it had been decades since Tennessee had felt like home. His home was in Virginia Beach with his brothers in the Teams—or sleeping under a UH-60 in the middle of the desert on an op—but definitely not here.

Despite his best effort to stay focused, his mind drifted to his youth and the simplicity of those days. He thought of middle school, when he and David and Rachel had been the three amigos, exploring the woods that stretched for acres behind Rachel's house and building a tree house fort. The tree house had been their project and their refuge for two wonderful summers. A simple time, before his romance blossomed with his childhood sweetheart, when they'd just been three friends—young and naive and unburdened—hanging out in the woods.

Then came the high school years—hot summer nights and Friday night lights at school football games. He felt the pull of those days, of Young Life and leading a small group in prayer, of Pastor Tobias, the youth minister who had taught him so much and whom he had prayed he might one day be like. He remembered the look of pride on his mom's face when he had told her he wanted to be a pastor someday. For a moment, the powerful pull of nostalgia beckoned him to drive by the house—just to *see* it. Even with Mom and Dad in Florida, driving through the old neighborhood would bring back such warm memories. Sitting with Rachel on the porch swing—drinking homemade lemonade, holding hands, and their first kiss . . .

Get your head in the game, man, he chastised himself.

He needed to focus on Philip Maclin, the man killed in the bizarre accident that coincided with the kidnapping. The news outlets online had been a source for an address but little else. The press had identified Maclin as a teacher. From what Jed could gather, Maclin wasn't from Tennessee, but none of the news outlets said where he was from. The small local paper in Smyrna said Maclin was from "up North" but didn't say where. These were just little things but contributed to the "something is off" feeling he couldn't seem to shake.

He continued south past the Sam Ridley Parkway exit and then Lee Victory Parkway. A few minutes later he took exit 78A onto Old Fort Parkway and a moment later turned north onto John R. Rice Boulevard and found the entrance to The Reserve at Harper's Point. He drifted past the front office at idle speed and, seeing it empty, looped around to the back of the luxury apartments that formed a circle around the clubhouse, gym, and community pool. He chose a parking spot at the end of the row in front of the last building. The parking lot was nearly empty, which implied most of the tenants were either at work or school.

The fewer watchful eyes, the better.

He slipped his keys into his pocket and made a show of checking an imaginary piece of paper for an address, and then he headed up the nearest flight of stairs. At the third floor, he turned left on the balcony style outdoor hallway and walked until he reached the last door—apartment 301. He glanced around, saw no one, and tried the doorknob. Unsurprised, he found it locked. He pursed his lips. His sixth sense was screaming at him now, and he felt an absolutely overpowering desire—no, *need* was the right word—to get inside Maclin's apartment. He looked at the heavy painted-metal door. He could breach it—he was a SEAL for pete's sake—but he needed something more subtle than his SEAL pedigree could provide. This was definitely not a door-kicking event.

He glanced around again and then pulled out a folding knife from his cargo pant pocket. Just as he was poised to crack the glass on the window beside the door with the hilt of his knife, a woman's voice stopped him.

"Hey there."

He turned to see a heavyset woman with a big smile headed toward him down the hall.

"Hey there," Jed returned, slipping his knife casually back into his pocket. "How are you today?" Courtesy went a long mile here in the real South.

"Glad for the cool weather today," she said, but her eyes fixed on him with real interest—and suspicion maybe. "I'm certainly not ready for the heat to come. Can I help you with something?" She stopped several paces away—out of arm's length—and Jed understood. He was a big guy. "I'm the property manager," she added and folded her arms across her chest.

Jed smiled. "That explains why you weren't in the office," he said, relaxing his shoulders. "I'm Jedidiah. Phil Maclin's brother-in-law. I was hoping to get into his apartment to get a few things. Just some pictures my wife wants. She couldn't bring herself to come."

"Have you spoken to the police?" the woman asked. Her body position suggested she wasn't buying it.

Maybe I should call the police on this guy. Detective Forester at the precinct—or that lady detective from Nashville.

The property manager's voice was clear as a bell in his head, but her lips weren't moving. The last time this happened, he'd been in Anbar province hunting a bomb-making terrorist, and his team leader had died because he had written it off as paranoia. A chill chased down his spine and his trigger finger twitched. He took an involuntary step backward and looked deep into the property manager's hazel eyes for a glow—the color of burning embers. But her eyes were dull and plain and normal . . . beautifully, wonderfully normal.

He relaxed a little and as he did, he felt a shift . . . not inside but not outside either. In the *in between*, if there was such a place. A single name came to him, *Mary*, and he knew—inexplicably but with certitude—that it was hers.

What in God's name is happening to me?

"Sir?" she said, snapping him out of his headspace. "Are you all right?"

He shook his head. "Honestly, no. This whole thing just happened so suddenly, and—I don't know—I'm just trying to get through it. I spoke with the police detective in Nashville, and she told me to look up an Officer Forester here in Murfreesboro, but he wasn't available when I called. The precinct told me to ask for Mary, here at the property. Mary . . ." He looked up as if searching for the surname.

"Dressler?" the woman asked, her eyebrows going up in confirmation.

"That was it," he said, forcing himself to look surprised. "Mary Dressler."

"I'm Mary Dressler," the woman said, clearly relaxing, and extended a hand. Jed shook it. "I didn't know Mr. Maclin was married, though I really didn't know him at all. But they can't be married, right?"

"He wasn't," Jed said, smoothly continuing the lie. "I'm married to his sister, Beverly."

"Of course," the woman said as if she had any clue who Beverly was. She looked Jed up and down. "You're in the military?"

Jed nodded sheepishly. He was wearing an NSW Group Two ball cap and BDU-style cargo pants. "Yeah, I'm the Navy SEAL brother-in-law he talks about."

"Of course," Mary said again, by this point probably even believing she had heard Philip Maclin talk about his sister Beverly and his Navy SEAL brother-in-law. The property manager chewed on the inside of her lip a moment. "I'm really not allowed to let you take anything."

"And I won't," he said. "Not really. There's just this one special picture of Phil and Beverly—when they were kids—that my wife really wants to have for the memorial back home in a couple of days. I won't even take the frame, but she'll be devastated if I don't come home with that picture."

Mary looked conflicted for a moment but then sighed and smiled. "I guess if it's just a picture," she said and pulled a ring of keys out from under her tent of a top.

Jed stepped aside, knowing his size alone could be quite intimidating, and waited while she unlocked the door.

"You're sure it's okay with Detective Forester?" she said, pausing with the door partway open.

"No," he answered. "I couldn't get Forester, but I know it's okay with the Nashville detective." The minutiae of a lie were what sold it.

It was enough for Mary Dressler, who pushed the door open and stepped away, gesturing him in.

"I'll wait out here for you," she said. "Nothing but the picture, okay? I could probably get in a lot of trouble for this."

"Cross my heart," Jed said with his best smile. "Thanks so much, Mary. It will mean everything to my wife. She's just devastated. I won't touch anything else, I promise. I think the police will be releasing everything soon and then we'll come and get all of his stuff, okay?"

"Sure," Mary said. "I was wondering about that. We had no next of kin or anything on Mr. Maclin, so I didn't know what would happen. The man from the diocese or whatever—you know, the other priest, I guess—he didn't say anything about what would happen. Did you talk to him?"

Jed struggled to keep the surprise and confusion off his face.

"Not yet," he said. "What was his name again?"

"Oh, I'm not sure. Father something or other, right? Honestly, I didn't even know your brother was a priest, until that other priest came by and told me. I thought he was a teacher or something, but he didn't talk much. Always super nice, of course," she added, perhaps afraid she might offend the family of the dead man. "Just didn't talk about himself much. But a priest? Well, I had no idea. In my day, they dressed in black clothes and wore those white collar things. I guess times change . . ."

"Brother-in-law," Jed said absently, correcting her mistake while the gears in his head churned.

Maclin was a priest . . . a priest killed seconds before the daughter of a Methodist minister in training was kidnapped. In what universe was that a coincidence? And the cops didn't think the kidnapping and the manslaughter were related? Why didn't David bring this up when they spoke? Was David a suspect?

He shook the questions off.

Later.

Jed smiled. "Thanks, Mary. I'll just be a moment."

"Take your time," she answered and pulled out her iPhone.

Jed stepped into the dimly lit apartment and closed the door softly behind him. To call the room inside spartan would be the understatement of the year. He scanned the walls, which lacked any and all decor. Not one painting or photograph hung. Not one piece of memorabilia or knickknack stood on the mantel or any other surface for that matter. No extra pair of shoes by the door, no sweatshirt on a hook. Even the air felt depleted and lifeless.

He shuddered.

Creepy.

The living room housed a single recliner chair with a floor lamp beside it. He walked over to it and found a leather-bound Bible resting facedown on the seat cushion, since there was no end table nearby on which to place it. Curiosity getting the better of him, he picked up the Bible and opened it to the page where the silk bookmark had been placed in John 12. A specific passage had been highlighted and he read it:

"My light will shine for you just a little longer. Walk in the light while you can, so the darkness will not overtake you. Those who walk in the darkness cannot see where they are going. Put your trust in the light while there is still time . . ."

Jed set the Bible down and couldn't help but wonder if the passage had been prophetic for Maclin. Had the man somehow known his time was short?

Or was that passage meant for me?

He shook off the disturbing thought and walked to the dine-in kitchen, where a bistro table with a single wooden stool sat under a window. A yellow legal pad with a blank top page sat on the table with a single pen. He picked it up and looked across the surface into the light from the window for indented scribble. He sighed—in the movies and on the detective shows, they always found traces of something written on the sheet above and torn away, but Jed saw nothing. In fact, the pad seemed to be new, with no sheets missing. He flipped through the pages, thinking maybe something was tucked inside, but it was empty. He scanned the apartment again. This place reminded him of something, or somewhere, but he couldn't place it.

The bathroom in the short hall proved even less help. A single white towel and washcloth hung from the bar beside a meticulously clean shower. A toothbrush sat lonely in a plastic cup and looked remarkably clean—maybe even new. There was a bar of soap in the shower that looked untouched.

Next he checked the bedrooms.

The first was completely devoid of furniture, and his footsteps left imprints in the vacuum lines of the brand-new carpet. He opened the bifold closet door to reveal a whole lot of nothing. The second bedroom seemed lived in, but barely. With a single twin bed, neatly made with the white sheets folded down over the brown blanket, military style. In the closet hung two pairs of khaki pants and three button-down shirts, identical except for the color. A pair of blue jeans was folded neatly on the shelf above, beside two white T-shirts and two gray sweatshirts, which he already knew would have no logos.

As he headed back to the living room, he finally realized what the apartment reminded him of. He had logged time in a handful of CIA safe houses while conducting joint operations with the intelligence community. They all looked just like this: sterile and nondescript with absolutely nothing identifiable to tie the apartment to anything or anyone.

Jed gritted his teeth and made one final pass through the living room and kitchen, hoping something else would catch his eye but finding nothing. Disappointed, he left the way he had come—with nothing but questions.

"Did you find the picture you were looking for?" Mary asked, waiting dutifully outside the apartment door. He could feel her kind spirit and it warmed him. This woman genuinely cared about people.

"No," he said and closed the door. "I'm afraid not."

"Oh, shoot," she said, mirroring his disappointment. "Your poor wife."

"Thank you so much for helping me try, Mary," he said and returned her sad smile. "You are so kind."

"I'll keep y'all in my prayers," she said. In his heart he knew she would and felt bad for deceiving her, especially since this foray turned out to be pointless.

"Tell me something, Mary. The other priest—did he take anything from the apartment?"

"Like the picture?"

Jed shrugged. "Anything."

"No," Mary said. "He just talked to me and explained that they would let me know about his stuff—where to send it if family didn't come, you know? But here you are."

"Here I am," Jed said. "So you didn't see him pick anything up at all?"

"Oh, we didn't go in the apartment. We just spoke for a few minutes in my office up front."

Jed nodded.

Why come by at all? Maybe the "priest" was keeping her distracted while someone else tossed the apartment? *Or maybe I'm just being paranoid.* Too many years in the Teams, where no one but the brotherhood could be trusted. Maybe Philip Maclin was just a priest, with a side hustle as a teacher who happened to be in the wrong place at the wrong time?

But I know there's more to it than that—I can feel it.

He stared at Mary intently, trying to "hear" her thoughts, hoping to pick up another name or tidbit of information she might be holding back, but nothing came to him. Had he been imagining it before, or had it been real?

I must be losing my mind . . .

"Is there anything else I can help you with?" she asked him with a patient smile.

"I don't think so. Thanks again, Mary," he said and bid her goodbye.

What a waste of time, he lamented minutes later as he drove out of the apartment complex. *I'm going crazy and didn't find a single clue.*

Lips pursed, he tapped the steering wheel with his thumbs as he headed back toward Nashville on I-24. Then suddenly it occurred to him that he *had* found something after all. The apartment itself was the clue. Maclin might have used that apartment, but it certainly wasn't his home. The safe house metaphor was important. There was something else going on here. Father Philip Maclin, if that was his real name, *was* a critical piece in the puzzle.

If I can figure out how Maclin's death is connected to the kidnapping, he thought with renewed hope, *then I'm one step closer to figuring out who took Sarah Beth and why.*

CHAPTER SIX

Sarah Beth Yarnell wiped her sleeve across her cheeks for, like, the millionth time, soaking up the tears. She let out a long, trembling sigh as a fresh tear spilled onto her left cheek, followed by another that ran reluctantly down her right. She looked at the wall beside the head of the bed where she was cuddled up and counted the grooves she'd carved into the wall with the end of the toothbrush they'd left her by the bathroom sink.

Five gouges . . . five days. I made the first mark when the sun came up after I screamed myself hoarse during that first night, which was Sunday. Then one mark for each day after—Monday, Tuesday,

Wednesday . . . which makes this Thursday. My bedroom window looks east and the sun is already past overhead and setting behind the building. I've been missing for five days . . . They probably think I'm dead.

She didn't know why keeping track made her feel better, but it did.

Feeling restless, she crawled out of the bed with its comfortable pink-and-purple comforter and three down pillows and started pacing. Looking for anything that might help her get out of this prison of a room, she conducted an inventory of sorts: *Kid's desk with a journal and colored pens, like I'm going to write anything for them. Stupid shag rug beside the bed with too many colors to be pretty. Dresser with T-shirts, jeans, sweatshirts, and socks—not mine. Underwear drawer, yuck. Wearing someone else's underwear is gross and disgusting and I refuse. Ugly flannel nightgown, which looks like something a grandma would wear, on a hook. TV and remote on the dresser, with no cable channels and only stupid Netflix, so I can't check the news to see if people are looking for me and figure out where I am. Under the bed . . . no monsters, just my sneakers and fluffy pink slippers with a smiling puppy head at the toes. Seriously, people, I'm not four.*

She exhaled with exasperation and sat cross-legged on the floor beside the bed. "Crisscross applesauce," her mom would say— *Mom also sometimes forgets I'm not four*—and the thought brought a smile to her face and then more tears. She glanced at the black things mounted in two of the upper corners of the room—one by the door and the other across from her bed—and noted the little blinking red lights. She knew these were cameras, and she didn't want whoever was watching to see her cry. Suddenly feeling brave, she popped to her feet and stared defiantly at the camera by the door. With great effort, she resisted the urge to raise a middle finger to the camera and the people who watched her.

When I'm rescued, the police will see what I did and probably so will Mom and Dad. They would hate to know I made that gesture— or even knew about it.

Mom would probably be less surprised. The last year, she'd begun to treat her like more of a grown-up—a "young adult," she liked to say—and Sarah Beth loved that. Dad was different. Dad still saw a little girl when he smiled at her. He'd told her so, though she'd have known even if he hadn't.

She walked to the window and looked out the glass and through the black vertical bars that cemented her prisoner status. Long shadows stretched now at an angle across the large green field to the edge of the thick tree line a hundred yards away. The shadows revealed to her that the prison she found herself in was not an old-style hotel as she'd thought at first. This place was built in the woods, on top of a hill or small mountain. Based on the shadows, she'd identified two other buildings around her, even though she couldn't see them directly from her window. One large, long building to the north and a smaller building to the south. It sorta reminded her of a summer camp she'd attended last July— with a bunkhouse for the campers and a main lodge and smaller house where the counselors and staff slept.

I'm in the main building, she decided.

Using the shadows, she made a mental map of the camp and stored it in a little memory box in her brain, feeling like the layout could be important eventually, if she was rescued or got the courage to escape. She opened her eyes and looked across the valley at a taller mountain that had the only distinctive landmark she'd noticed since her arrival. She stared at it now—an odd, conical tower surrounded by a circular fence and regularly spaced poles topped with red lights that glowed at night. The entire top of this peak was cleared of trees and was covered with grass. The strange object on top looked almost like a toy lighthouse, but with no windows and no searchlight on top. The best description was a giant bowling pin. She added this image to the box in her brain. The rest of the mountains around her were covered with trees and looked very much like what she remembered from the daddy-daughter camping trip he'd taken her on when she was seven.

If these are the same mountains, then maybe I'm still in Tennessee.

She closed her eyes and bowed her head in prayer. She'd been praying several times a day that she would be rescued, but this time decided to set her sights lower.

"Father God, please let me still be in Tennessee. And please be with Mom and Dad—they must be freaking out by now. Let them know I'm okay."

A voice answered her, as it sometimes did.

Tell her.

She wasn't sure whose voice this was. She assumed it was God talking to her now, but she also accepted the possibility that the voice belonged to someone else . . . because she heard people's thoughts all the time. The first time Dad had touched her cheek and she'd repeated his thoughts back to him with a smile, he'd turned white as a ghost. The terrified look on his face had seared itself in her memory, so she never did it again. She'd been seven at the time. With Mom it was different. She didn't need to touch Mom. Sometimes they didn't even need to be in the same room together. Once, after one of her terrible nightmares, Mom had lain beside her bed and they'd had an entire conversation in their heads, without their lips even moving. She sometimes wondered if it had been a dream, but in her heart, she knew it wasn't.

The frustrating thing was that she had no idea how thought sharing happened. How far away did it work? A mile? Ten miles? A hundred? She didn't really have a good feel for miles.

I might as well try, she told herself. *Mom . . . Mom . . . can you hear me?*

She waited, but no voice answered her.

Mom . . .

MOM!

She didn't know if screaming in her head worked the same as screaming with her voice, but it couldn't hurt to try.

MOM, IT'S SARAH BETH. I'M OKAY. I'M SAFE AND NO ONE HAS HURT ME, BUT PLEASE, PLEASE COME GET ME! THEY TOOK ME TO A PLACE WITH ROLLING HILLS. TO A CAMP IN THE WOODS. PLEASE HELP ME—

Footsteps on the creaky stairs outside her room snapped Sarah Beth from her headspace and her eyes sprang open.

Her keeper was coming.

The old woman filled Sarah Beth with terror, despite having not laid a finger on her. The woman said very little and always smiled when she dropped off trays of food, but something filled the room whenever she came—a dark energy that made Sarah Beth feel sick to her stomach. Like a horrible smell, but one that she felt rather than inhaled. It all sounded so stupid, but the feeling was real.

A key rattled in the lock.

Instead of scurrying across the room like a scared mouse as she usually did, Sarah Beth said a quick prayer.

God, make me strong.

She stood her ground, gaze fixed on the heavy old door, despite her nauseous stomach and the bile burning in the back of her throat.

Please make me strong.

The door opened.

The woman, who looked like a skinny version of a TV grandma, was dressed in a simple purple dress. She wore an apron tied around her waist, and her gray hair was pulled into a bun atop her head. The tray she carried with her left hand smelled of fried chicken and french fries. In her right, she clutched a small brown paper bag. An old-fashioned metal key hung from a long chain around her neck, which she promptly tucked inside an apron pocket after setting down the tray on the desk.

"Well, well, look who's up," the grandma said, a smile on her face. But the cloud of nauseating something followed her in, filling the room and making Sarah Beth's stomach feel like she might heave. "I'm glad you're not afraid anymore, dear. That's good. You don't need to be afraid. No one will hurt you here, I promise."

The cloud in the room thickened and Sarah Beth felt it wrapping around her, almost choking her now like an invisible deadly gas. She shook her head, chasing the sensation away.

"I want to go home," she said. Her voice sounded strong, but as the words left her, she was overcome by fear and longing for her family, and the tears returned. "Please, won't you help me?" she cried.

"There, there," the grandma said and reached out a hand as if to pat Sarah Beth on the shoulder, but at the last moment she pulled her hand away quickly.

She's afraid to touch me. Why is she afraid?

She looked up, met the grandma's gaze, and for a moment thought she saw something—a faint, amber glow around the colored part of the old woman's eyes.

"I brought you some goodies," the woman said and held out the brown paper bag.

"Please help me," Sarah Beth said and grabbed the woman's extended right forearm. On contact, her mind filled with gruesome images, flashing too fast to make sense of individually, but together they filled her with terror. Then came a cacophony of voices, raucous and overlapping—like a loud party in another room—and she couldn't home in on a single one.

The grandmotherly woman jerked her arm away as if she'd touched a hot stove. The bag fell from her grip and hit the floor, where it barfed its contents onto the multicolored rug—candy bars and fruit snacks and a small bag of Cheez-Its. She felt rage and fear emanating from the woman, and the amber glow she thought might have been a trick of the setting sun flared to bright red before disappearing altogether. And for a moment, Sarah Beth thought the woman's face changed slightly, turning darker, losing all warmth.

Then, as if nothing had happened, the grandma's color and her sanguine smile returned. "Oh, my, look what I've done—I've dropped your snacks. Those were meant to be a surprise."

But instead of bending to pick them up, she backpedaled to the door, keeping her eyes fixed on Sarah Beth the whole time. Only after she'd stepped past the threshold into the hallway did she pull the key from her apron, with a hand that Sarah Beth thought looked years younger than the woman's aged face.

"You've never told me your name," Sarah Beth said, mustering her courage. "What should I call you?"

The woman's brow furrowed at the question, her expression equal parts perplexity and dismay. "I know this is scary, dear, but don't worry—you'll be with your family very soon. This ordeal is almost over." She shut the door with a resounding thud.

Sarah Beth heard the old-fashioned key rattle more than usual in the lock, and she couldn't help but wonder if the woman's hands were shaking. With her jailer's exit, the voices projecting from the woman's mind immediately receded, but one spoke clearly and above the din.

She's nearly ready, the woman announced. *We should start soon, before she figures out the power she possesses . . .*

Then all of the voices left—not suddenly, like a switch turned off, but slowly dying, like those last embers of a campfire up at the cabin they rented every spring break—as the grandma's heel strikes faded in the hallway outside.

Sarah Beth stood by the door a long time, wondering what had just happened. The noxious cloud the grandmother trailed dissipated along with the voices, and Sarah Beth's nausea left her. Feeling suddenly ravenous, she took the tray to her bed. She gathered up the spilled bag of treats and set them on her nightstand, then sat down beside the tray, her stomach aching with hunger as if she'd gone days without eating or had run ten miles like her mom often did.

But first she bowed her head.

"God, thank You for this food and please keep me safe. Be with Mom and Dad, and please let me go home."

Tell her . . .

She closed her eyes again.

Mom, it's me. I don't know if you can hear me, but if you can, please give me a sign . . .

CHAPTER SEVEN

VANDERBILT UNIVERSITY BOOKSTORE

2501 WEST END AVENUE

NASHVILLE, TENNESSEE

THURSDAY, 1645 HOURS LOCAL

As Jed eased the sedan into the narrow parking spot, it occurred to him that he'd driven all the way here from Maclin's apartment on autopilot, without ever consciously deciding to do so. He'd just let the car take him where it wanted to go and the car, apparently, wanted to go to the Vanderbilt University bookstore.

It wanted to go to the scene of the crime.

Some folks liked to call this kind of decision making going with the gut, but Jed knew that wasn't the mechanism at work here. As an operator—a *former* operator, he reminded himself—he knew all about gut decisions. In his experience that cerebral mechanism worked quickly, and the decision came with a hard bias based on experience. This probably happened by design—the brain's way of course correcting the ship the moment before it ran aground.

Don't go that way or you're gonna get shot.

Better swap magazines now, because in ten seconds you won't have time.

Kiss her now before she changes her mind.

This, however, was different. A slow, meandering, "feel your way through the dark" type of process. A process without words. Without numbers. Something very ancient and spiritual.

Intuition . . . or is it even more than that?

He climbed out of the rental car and shut the driver's side door. As he walked away, he pressed the lock button on his key fob. The car chirped compliance and the doors locked dutifully behind him as he stepped over the curb and onto the sidewalk. A sweet, aromatic breeze wafted over him. He inhaled deeply. Lemon verbena, his mother used to call the scent, when the magnolia trees bloomed. He didn't know what *verbena* was, but the fragrance brought warm feelings of childhood and home. It felt pure and feminine . . . the opposite of him, in every way.

"Hey, watch where you're going, mister," a smallish voice said directly in front of him, and he pivoted out of the way before sending the girl flying.

"My bad, sorry," he said, suddenly aware he'd closed his eyes in the moment of nostalgic rumination.

The girl, a Vandy coed, gave him the stink eye but seemed no worse for wear after the near collision that could have been traumatic, especially considering he had probably a hundred and twenty pounds on her.

He put Jed the daydreamer to bed and let the SEAL take charge. Despite knowing that his personal threat level walking along the sidewalk in broad daylight was low, if not nonexistent, he felt that old familiar tension creep into his muscles anyway. Every operator knew the sensation—that state of "preoperational" readiness cultivated from years of physical conditioning and training for battle. In the Teams, unless he slept at home in bed, his motor was always warmed up and ready to go from idle to redline in the blink of an eye. He took comfort in this ability; in some ways now it was a part of his identity. If an active shooter situation erupted right here, right now, 99 percent of the civilians milling about would react by either panicking or freezing. Some would find cover; others would run; the rest would either get shot or hurt others in their attempt to not get dead. But not him. The SEAL would take control and flip the script, turning the hunter into the hunted. With a seasoned operator in the mix—especially an armed operator—the event would be over in the blink of an eye, and not in favor of the bad guy.

Jed attuned his body to register the weight and feel of the Sig P229 in the holster inside his waistband, hidden under the drape of his Rubicon jacket. Without needing to touch the weapon, he did this little check multiple times a day because he was so accustomed to the feel of the Sig that it mostly faded into sensory background noise. As a kitted-up SEAL, his normal loadout was anywhere between twenty-five to sixty pounds depending on the op and the location. The thirty-two-ounce Sig was nothing to him.

Nothing appeared to have changed at the bookstore since earlier when he'd met David for coffee—a meeting that had taken on the surreal quality of something from another lifetime, though only a few hours had passed. The yellow-and-black police tape still stretched between barricade stands, one edge now loose and flapping in the breeze like a flag, but still cordoning off the sidewalk where the priest had been killed. The section of plate-glass window damaged from the collision was boarded over. He walked up to the tape line but did not cross or touch it and instead scanned the sidewalk and parking lot trying to re-create what went down based on the scant details he'd gathered.

The Vandy bookstore was one of several tenants in a small shopping center. A parking lot, landscaped median, and sidewalk separated the little strip mall from West End Avenue, and the entrance into the lot was offset from the bookstore.

"I don't get it," he murmured as he walked away from the crash site, retracing the vehicle's likely path.

After walking almost all the way to the entrance, he turned around and imagined being the driver of the car that hit the priest. To navigate the turn off West End into the lot, the vehicle had to slow, which means the brakes were working. To achieve the angle necessary to hit Maclin, the driver would have to make a left turn toward the bookstore, followed by a hard right without running into a knee-high brick wall around the café patio. Jed put his hands on his hips and screwed up his face.

"No swerve or skid marks, which means the driver didn't brake or even try to avoid Maclin," he said, scanning the asphalt between where he stood and the impact site. "In fact, he would have had to be accelerating."

Gooseflesh stood up on his neck as a terrible deduction solidified in his head.

This was no accident. No way. Maclin was murdered.

He turned and stared down the sidewalk to where Sarah Beth had been forced into a panel van.

Talk about the perfect distraction to draw attention away from a kidnapping operation . . .

Suddenly feeling eyes on him, Jed looked over his left shoulder. Like a targeting computer, his mind surveyed the parked vehicles and pedestrians in the vicinity, looking for new arrivals, possible threats, and anything that fit the category of "just ain't right." His gaze settled first on a gray Chevy Suburban with dark windows in the parking spot near Twenty-Fifth Avenue on West End. Other than the paint color not being black, it gave off a strong government vehicle vibe. Instead of lingering on the Suburban, his attention was drawn to a white metro police cruiser—lights off and idling along the curb just on the other side of a row of bushes. Jed's heart rate ticked up a notch as he locked eyes with a lone male officer staring directly at him from the driver's seat. The staring contest lasted several seconds, but Jed looked away first, turned, and headed for the bookstore. He resisted the urge to give the cop a backward glance and instead walked straight to the double-door entrance and let himself inside.

He's watching the crime scene, right? He's not watching me. I'm just being paranoid. No one but David and Rachel knows I'm here . . . well, and Mary from the apartment complex. But she wouldn't have called Nashville PD on me, would she?

He shook off the paranoid ramblings and walked into the café. Two college-age baristas were working this afternoon: a girl at the register and a guy making drinks. Half the tables and booths were occupied, and two coeds were ordering as he casually stepped into line behind them. After they'd paid, the girl at the register turned to him. Her name tag said *Nora*, handwritten in a loop-de-loop style.

"What can I get you?" she said with a "please don't flirt with me" smile.

"Large iced tea," he said.

"One Venti iced tea," she said, entering his order. "Sweet or unsweetened?"

"Sweet, of course," he said and with a chuckle added, "Is there any other way?"

"Not in Nashville," she said with a saccharine-sweet smile back. "Anything else with that? A pastry or one of our sandwiches?"

"No thank you," he said, and then the words just rolled out of his mouth unbidden. "So, Nora, you were working the day when the accident happened . . ."

"Wait, what?" she said, her cheeks blanching.

"The accident, with the man outside—you were working that day, right?" he said.

Jed had no idea how he knew his statement was true, but he knew it just the same, with the same certainty that the sun would rise in the east tomorrow morning.

"Are you with the police? I already talked to the police," she said.

He registered a sudden drop in ambient noise level and in his peripheral vision saw that the two girls who'd ordered ahead of him had stopped their conversation and were eavesdropping while they were waiting for their drinks.

"No," he said, speaking more quietly. "I'm a private investigator who's been hired to look into the—shall we say—goings-on that day." When she hesitated, he added, "It's okay for you to talk to me. There's nothing illegal about sharing information with private investigators. We work hand in glove with local law enforcement."

She chewed her bottom lip for a second and then said, "Yes, I was working that day."

"Did you know the man who was killed?"

"I didn't *know him* know him, but I've seen him around."

"Did you know he was a priest?" Jed pressed, curious to see how she would respond to the information, which, to his knowledge, had not been widely reported.

She shook her head, seemingly unfazed by the news. "No, I didn't know. I don't remember him dressing like a priest. I mean, I don't think he was wearing one of those white collar thingies. I just thought he was a tutor."

The girl referring to Maclin as a tutor now made sense and resolved one of the things bothering him. A priest might be a teacher at a Catholic school as part of his duties, but no mention had been made of an association to a Catholic school in the area. But a side hustle as a tutor made far more sense.

"Okay, so you'd seen him before tutoring students here?"

"Like I said, he wasn't a regular," she said, looking up for a second. "I recognized his face, but I don't remember ever having a conversation with him beyond taking his order."

"Sure, sure," he said, feeling eyes on him. He glanced around, expecting to see the cop watching him but didn't. There was something else, but he hushed it into the background and continued, trying to seem somewhat casual—or at least nonthreatening. His size always made that hard. "So, um, was he here alone that day, before . . . the accident?"

"No, he was with Corbin. I think he was tutoring her," Nora said.

"Corbin is a girl?"

"Yeah."

"Does Corbin go to Vanderbilt?" he said, committing the new name—and potential new lead—to memory.

"No," Nora said with a smart little smile and shake of her head. "She's, I don't know, fourteen or fifteen maybe. I think her dad is a professor in the engineering school. I'm not 100 percent. I used to see her here all the time, studying or getting tutored, but not lately."

"Venti iced tea for . . . the big guy," the male barista said, setting down Jed's drink on the counter with a definitive thunk.

"Thanks," he said, glancing at the dude's name tag, which said *CHAD* in bold, square letters. He turned back to Nora. "Do you happen to know Corbin's last name or the name of the school she goes to?"

"I'm sorry, I don't," she said and the tension in her voice hinted that Nora's patience at being questioned was wearing thin.

"Professor Worth," Chad said. "That's her dad. I'm pretty sure, anyway. I took his thermodynamics class."

"Thank you," he said. "Chad, were you working that day too?"

"Yeah," Chad said and looked at his hands. "Pretty messed up what happened."

"Yeah, I know." Jed felt a very thin but tangible connection with the male barista, sensing his unease and dread.

"Anything else either of you can tell me about that day? Anything about Corbin or Father Maclin that might help make sense of what happened? Anything at all . . . no wrong answers here," he said, feeling a strange gravity around him—as if things might fly off the shelves and come careening toward him like he suddenly had the gravitational pull of a black hole.

"Sir, I'm sorry, but there's people waiting behind you to order," Nora said, her cheeks getting their color back and then some.

"Sure, sure—sorry, folks," he said, turning to smile at the college couple who'd just stepped up in line behind him. The guy nodded and the girl flashed him a polite, albeit mirthless smile. He sidestepped along the counter but didn't disengage just yet. "Nora, if there's anything else you can tell me that might be helpful—like why Father Maclin got up to leave. Or what happened to Corbin after he did. Did she leave with him?"

"I don't know. It was really busy at the time. Look, I'm sorry, mister, but I already told the police everything I know." She turned to her new customers. "Welcome to the Barnes & Noble Café. What can I get you?"

Jed swallowed down his irritation and grabbed his iced tea from the counter, turning his attention to Chad, who he felt had something else to say.

"I don't know if it's true, dude, but I heard that a girl was kidnapped right out there," Chad said, pointing in the direction where Sarah Beth had been abducted.

"Yeah, that's what I understand," Jed said. "Do you think the two events were related?"

"The rumor is the tutor dude was running that way when he got smashed." Channeling his best Benedict Cumberbatch as Sherlock Holmes, he added, "Coincidence? I think not."

"Nora said that Corbin was being tutored that day. Did you notice anyone else who looked like they might be waiting to meet someone? An older man or woman with a middle or high school–age student, maybe?"

Chad laughed at this. "Yeah, like, half the people in here. Everybody's waiting for somebody. There were probably forty people in here last Saturday when it happened. It was packed, dude."

Jed nodded. "What about tutoring pairs? Is that unusual to see tutors and students?"

"Are you kidding me? It's the university bookstore—we've got tables, free Wi-Fi, and Starbucks coffee. There are study groups and tutors here every hour of the day."

"Understood. Thanks, Chad, for all your help," Jed said, accepting that he'd worn out his welcome, at least for now.

"Any day," the barista said and resumed making drinks.

Jed took a long pull from his iced tea, not realizing how thirsty and thoroughly decaffeinated he was until that moment. He walked over to the coffee prep station—with its abundance of sweetener packets, straws, and stir sticks—while surveying the café and bookstore. The cop he'd locked eyes with in the parking lot had not followed him inside, but he couldn't shake the feeling he was being watched. It was the same feeling he used to get when his team would walk into a village in Afghanistan or down city streets in Iraq.

Eyes in the shadows . . .

Jed took a handful of napkins and then settled into a two-top table where he could have his back against the wall and a view of the entire café and the entrance. Sipping his tea, he made a show of looking at his mobile phone, no different from all the other patrons glued to their screens. But his eyes ticked up briefly, again and again, clearing the space around him the same as if he were clearing a room—identify all figures present, designate as friend or foe, then decide whether to engage or not.

He swept his gaze left, to the far corner of the café seating area, where a man lowered his eyes just as Jed looked over. The man was seated with a woman, but they were both looking at their phones, not talking. The man wore jeans and a plaid shirt, sleeves rolled up on his forearms revealing sleeve tattoos common in Jed's line of work. He sat straight, his body like a coiled spring, despite an attempt to look casual. The telltale for Jed, however, was the left leg, tucked back behind him, foot flat on the floor, body slid to the left side of the wooden chair. From that position the man could be up and in the fight in an instant. Jed looked away and smiled as he realized his own body was positioned, instinctively, in the exact same position.

Takes an operator to notice an operator.

He shifted his gaze to the escalator bank that handled traffic to the textbook area upstairs. A man was descending on the escalator, phone pressed to his ear. Jed noticed him glance, almost imperceptibly, at the table with the seated couple Jed had just been watching. Just like the man at the table, escalator guy had the build, stance, and presence of an operator. *Neither of these dudes are Vanderbilt students*, Jed thought, *that's for sure.* Instead of looking away, Jed took a moment to burn the escalator guy's face into his memory: green eyes, freckled skin, shaggy light-brown hair, and a thin beard that needed trimming. His intent expression suddenly morphed into a casual smile as he stepped off the escalator.

"Yeah, sweetie, I'm just leaving now," the guy said and gave Jed a classic dude nod as he headed for the exit. "You need me to pick anything up from the store on the way home?"

And then he was gone without a backward glance.

Jed shifted his attention back to the couple at the table who were on their phones. He watched the woman show something on her screen to the man, and they both chuckled.

Okay . . . that's it. I'm completely paranoid and losing it. They're not operators. They're not surveilling me. Enough.

He sighed heavily, sipped his tea, and shifted gears from scanning the café to reconstructing last Saturday's events. In his mind's eye, he imagined Father Maclin sitting with the girl he now knew as Corbin, at one of the tables in the center of the rectangular café seating area. He imagined them happy and talking with a familiarity that suggested they'd known each other awhile—that they were not meeting for the first time and that the girl liked, even admired, her tutor. Abruptly, they stop. Something has happened. Something's changed . . . but what? The priest gets up—maybe in a hurry—but he says something to Corbin first. Instructions? Something stronger—an order.

Hide in the bathroom. Lock the door. Don't come out until it's safe.

With difficulty, Jed extracted himself from the theater in his mind. Satisfied he'd learned everything he could here today, he pressed to his feet and headed for the door. On his way out, he glanced at the dude with the tattooed forearms still sitting and chatting with the woman. *The guy looks more like a gym rat than an operator,* he decided and, in the absence of a compulsion, strolled out of the café.

CHAPTER EIGHT

The first thing Jed noticed when he stepped out into the parking lot was that the gray Suburban with tinted windows was gone. Same went for the Nashville Metro PD cruiser with the officer he'd been convinced was watching him. He shook his head and silently chastised himself for letting paranoia get the better of him.

It's David's fault—bringing up all that spooky fantasy stuff from our childhood. He's got me acting like a crazy person. It wasn't real then and it's not real now. These feelings are the product of a blooded and combat-weary Navy SEAL who has lost his purpose and walked into an emotional minefield. There's nothing mystical going on. There's no such thing as second sight. I need to get back to reality if I'm going to be any help at all to Rachel and her daughter.

He let out a long sigh and pondered his next move. He glanced right, back toward Twenty-Fifth Avenue, which stretched into the Vanderbilt campus. It would be easy to find the engineering department and look up Professor Worth. If the professor's daughter had been with Maclin last Saturday, then maybe he would learn more about the mysterious, dead priest. Perhaps, if he played his cards right, he might be able to talk the professor into an interview with Corbin.

Jed walked to his rental car, unlocked the doors with the key fob, and climbed into the driver's seat. He checked his watch—five minutes after five. It seemed pretty unlikely that Professor Worth would still be on campus, but it was worth the ten minutes of effort to check. After that, he'd go back to the hotel and find their fitness center. Exercise always cleared his head and gave him focus, especially when he was tense and nervous like he was now. With a workout under his belt, he would reach out to David. They needed to have another talk; the last one had been emotional and disjointed and less productive than it needed to be given the situation and the stakes. Hopefully David had done as Jed had asked and broached the subject of Jed stepping in as a family liaison with the lead detective on the case. In Jed's mind, that was the only way the investigators would be willing to talk to him.

He started the engine, checked his mirrors, and pulled out of the parking lot. He turned right onto Twenty-Fifth Avenue and entered the Vanderbilt campus. A half block in, he checked his rearview mirror and saw a police cruiser tailing him—not a campus police vehicle, but the distinctive white- and blue-lettered sedan driven by Nashville PD. Jed's chest tightened with irritation as he noted the driver, the same officer he'd locked stares with before entering the café.

"Of course," he mumbled.

He signaled and changed lanes, moving from the right lane into the left to verify this was what he thought it was. In his rearview mirror, he watched the police cruiser do the same.

Should I go back to the hotel or drive in circles until this guy pulls me over?

The tailing officer made the decision for him, turning on his flashers and giving a short whoop of his siren.

Cursing under his breath, he used his signal, moved cautiously back to the right, and pulled into the parking lot of apartments at the intersection of Vanderbilt Place. The cop pulled up behind him, lights flashing. Jed put the transmission in park and pulled out his paper copy of the rental car contract from the armrest and his driver's license and military ID from his wallet. After several minutes of making him wait, the uniformed officer stepped out of his cruiser and approached on the driver's side.

Jed lowered the window and said, "Good afternoon, Officer."

"License and registration," the cop said in a tone both humorless and superior.

Jed glanced at the officer's name tag, which read *Alexander*. He noted the two chevrons embroidered on the man's uniform sleeve, indicating his rank as a police corporal. Then he looked up to meet the policeman's gaze. Never in all his life had Jed met anyone with eyes so light blue they were almost white.

"It's a rental car," he said as he handed over his license, military ID, and the envelope with the folded rental car contract.

Flashing his military ID whenever he got pulled over—something that rarely happened these days—was just something Jed did to engender a little solidarity through shared service. Around

Norfolk, it didn't make much of a difference, but most places it could mean the difference between a ticket and a verbal warning. Although in this case it shouldn't matter, because he'd done absolutely nothing wrong.

Corporal Alexander gave the rental car paperwork a cursory once-over, looked at Jed's driver's license, and ended by studying Jed's military ID—which he held for an uncomfortably long moment before handing all three items back.

"Is the home address listed on your license current?"

"Yes," Jed said.

"What do you do in the Navy?"

"I worked with Naval Special Warfare."

"Worked, as in past tense? Your ID says you're active duty," Alexander pressed.

"I was—I mean, I am. Technically, I'm on terminal leave for the next forty-five days. Yesterday was officially my last day," Jed said.

"One day retired, and you're already a police detective," Alexander said with a combative edge to his voice. "Must be nice."

"Excuse me?" Jed said, sure he'd misheard the man.

"You think because you were a Navy SEAL, you can just show up here out of the blue, start snooping around a crime scene, and question witnesses you have no business questioning . . . huh?"

"Now hold on there," Jed said, raising a placating hand. "No reason to get upset and I do not appreciate—"

"I'm going to need you to step out of the vehicle, Mr. Johnson," Alexander said, cutting him off while at the same time taking a step back and moving his right hand to the butt of his sidearm.

"Whoa, take it easy, brother," Jed said. "I'm sorry if we got off on the wrong foot . . ."

"Step out of the vehicle, Jedidiah," the cop said. "Now!"

A surge of anger flared in Jed's chest. Something about this guy offended him on so many different levels. With great effort, he checked his temper and complied with the order. Moving slowly and deliberately, he unlocked the driver's side door, opened it, and climbed out of the car. Standing now, he towered over the uniformed officer by a solid six inches. Alexander scowled at him, and Jed watched the cop's fingers close around the pistol grip of his weapon.

"Shut the door; walk to the front of the vehicle. Place both your hands on the hood and spread your legs shoulder-width apart," Alexander said, his voice all business.

"You're arresting me?" Jed said, making no attempt to disguise his incredulity.

"Yes."

"For what?"

"Obstruction of an active criminal investigation," Corporal Alexander said, his voice more growl than speech. "Now put your hands on the hood of the car and spread your legs."

Jed swallowed hard and complied. "I have a licensed, concealed weapon in my waistband," he said, now concerned that the angry cop might be looking for an opportunity to escalate this encounter to something far more deadly. "My permit is in my wallet," he added.

"Of course you do." The cop reached roughly under Jed's jacket and pulled the Sig Sauer free, scraping it uncomfortably— and apparently intentionally—across Jed's side as he did. Then Alexander ran his hands roughly up and down his sides, front, and both legs. "What other surprises do you have for me, jackass?"

"None," Jed hissed, gritting his teeth and using every ounce of self-control to not beat this Deputy Fife unconscious with his own service weapon.

"Empty your pockets and put your palms facedown on the hood of the car," the officer repeated. "And we'll see."

Jed set his jaw and glared at the cop for a heartbeat before complying with the order. He placed his wallet, keys, pocketknife, and mobile phone on the hood of the car, then leaned onto his palms. "This is outrageous," he said under his breath as Alexander stepped up to frisk him again—this time more thoroughly, he supposed.

Jed's mobile phone buzzed and vibrated loudly against the sheet metal on the hood. He glanced at the phone and saw *David Yarnell* flash on the screen.

"I really need to take this call," he said.

"Don't touch that phone," the cop said as he patted down Jed's flanks.

The phone rang three more times and then the call went to voice mail.

"Get smart with me, tough guy," Alexander said as he hard-frisked Jed's legs, "and maybe you make the next part of your journey in an ambulance." He ended the "search" by driving a rigid hand hard up into the V of Jed's crotch.

Jed buckled at the waist and a nauseating burn roiled his abdomen. "What the hell was that for?" he said through a cough.

Alexander didn't answer and instead grabbed Jed's right wrist and jerked it behind his back.

"Oh, come on," Jed growled. "I hardly think that's necessary."

"I'm sure you don't," the cop laughed, then repeated the operation with Jed's left arm and completed the cuffing sequence by

wrenching on a pair of flex-cuffs so tight they cut off the circulation to his hands. He Mirandized Jed next, talking so fast he
sounded like a recording being played at 2X speed.

"I've treated terrorists better than you're treating me," Jed said
as Alexander marched him to the back seat of his cruiser, pulling
up on the flex-cuffs so that Jed's shoulders burned with pain.

The cop tried to ram Jed's bowed head into the top of the
doorsill, but Jed anticipated the move and ducked hard the split
second before impact. The cop made no effort to help him get
right side up in the back seat, just slammed the door, slipped into
the driver's seat, and drove away. Jed struggled to get upright, his
left hip screaming in pain and his hands throbbing from the cuffs
cutting into his wrists. He watched the angry cop in the rearview
mirror, but Alexander was wearing dark sunglasses, making his
gaze impossible to discern. They reached West End Avenue and
Alexander turned right, a smile suggested by the rise of his cheeks
in the mirror as he took the turn fast, tumbling Jed over. As he
pulled himself back up, Jed looked out the side rear window and
saw a gray Chevy Suburban pulling out of the Vanderbilt bookstore parking lot onto West End Avenue.

The gray Suburban had definitely not been there when he'd
left. He'd looked specifically for it.

There are probably tons of gray Suburbans in Nashville, he told
himself. *Probably second only to pickup trucks in popularity.*

Nonetheless, he looked over his right shoulder out the rear
window and saw the Suburban slip into a tailing position—
two cars back and matching their speed. He decided that it was
probably an undercover or unmarked detective vehicle working
with Alexander.

The drive to the station took no time at all. They circled around to the back of a low, white cement-and-brick building, with *Midtown Hills Police Precinct* emblazoned above the glass entrance. Once in the rear lot, Alexander put the cruiser in park, opened the back door, and pulled Jed roughly from the seat by his wrists.

A group of three uniformed officers walked out the precinct door just in time for Alexander to put on a show for all to see.

"Sir, if you would please stop resisting, it will be much more comfortable for you. Cooperate and I promise we'll sort this out. Fighting me just makes things worse."

Alexander stumbled at the top of the stairs, feigning that Jed had resisted, and pulled hard against his lead.

"Please, sir. This is your last warning," Alexander growled before shoving Jed roughly through the door, held open by another officer.

"Looks like you got a live one there, Nate," the other cop said with a chuckle.

"Yeah, but I can handle him," Alexander answered with a laugh. "These big guys are always pansies underneath."

Once inside, the police corporal marched Jed straight to an interrogation room without in-processing of any kind and slammed the door. Jed eased himself into one of two open chairs with a groan, his bad hip barking mad with hot pain. Thankfully, Alexander left him alone, giving Jed the time he needed to collect his wits. He closed his eyes and completed several rounds of four-count tactical breathing to calm and center himself. He leaned his chest against the table, which was apparently bolted to the floor as it offered enough resistance that he could press his whole weight into it in an effort to relieve the pain in his shoulders. His hands were throbbing and he felt pins and needles in all ten fingers. He watched the clock over the door, and with each circle of the second hand, the numbness in his hands increased. When he began to have concerns about permanent damage from lack of blood flow, he lashed out.

"I know you can hear me," he said, glaring at the video surveillance camera in the upper left corner of the room. "If somebody does not come in here and loosen these cuffs in the next sixty seconds, I swear I will have my CSO from Group Two of the Navy SEALs phone the chairman of the Joint Chiefs and tell him what's happened here. General McMillin will ask the president to make a call to the governor of Tennessee and have the chief of police of this precinct terminated for cause."

The door to the interrogation room opened thirty seconds later, and a handsome, early middle-aged woman, her jet-black hair pulled back tightly, entered the room with Corporal Alexander in tow. She nodded to Jed and then looked down at his hands. Then she screwed up her face and turned to the uniformed officer who'd brought him in.

"Oh, come on, Alexander," she said with disgust in her voice. "Get those Cobra Cuffs off him."

Jed saw the corner of Alexander's mouth curl into a malevolent grin at the order.

"Yes, ma'am, Detective," the police corporal said and removed Jed's nylon restraints.

Jed let out an involuntary groan with the release of tension in his shoulders and the pressure on his wrists. He brought both hands around in front for inspection and watched the bright-purple color slowly fade as the blood flow returned to equilibrium.

A burning pain accompanied the color, and he looked up menacingly at the uniformed cop.

"That was completely uncalled for," Jed said, shooting daggers with his eyes at Alexander but speaking to the detective.

"I apologize," she said, "but Corporal Alexander said you were belligerent and resisted arrest."

"Did he?" Jed said, aggressively massaging the pins and needles out of his hands. "I suggest you watch his cruiser's dashboard cam footage of the arrest. Or you can ask the two dozen college students who were all taking videos on their cell phones. I'm sure a quick search on social media will yield dozens of clips. And just so you know, I'll be directing my attorney to get that footage as part of the lawsuit I intend to file against Corporal Alexander and this department."

"Thanks, Nate," she said, looking at Alexander. "I can take it from here."

"You sure you don't want me to—" the cop said.

"I said I can take it from here," she said, her voice a hard line.

Seemingly unperturbed by the exchange, or Jed's threat of legal action, Alexander shot Jed one final look and walked out of the interrogation room.

"I'm Detective Perez," the woman said and took the seat opposite him at the table.

"Jedidiah Johnson," he said, relaxing a little now with Alexander gone. "Or just Jed."

"Nate tells me you're a Navy SEAL." She crossed her legs and angled in her seat a bit.

"Former SEAL," Jed said, hating the way the words felt as he spoke them. "Just retired."

She nodded. "My brother is a Marine. He's with the MARSOC group, I think it's called."

"Yeah, those guys are solid. I've worked with the Raiders many times."

"So, Jed . . . whatcha doing here in Nashville?" she said, dispensing with the small talk. "And why are you snooping around the crime scene of an active investigation and questioning witnesses?"

Jed blew air through his teeth.

No point in making things more difficult for myself than I already have, he decided.

"David and Rachel Yarnell are longtime friends of mine. They were supposed to have told you I was here, that they asked me to function as a family liaison for them and that I would be interfacing with the department for the remainder of this investigation."

"Which they did," Perez said, unfazed. "And I was looking forward to meeting you, Jed, but when Mr. Yarnell said you would be connecting with me today, I never imagined it would be with you arrested and cuffed in an interrogation room."

"Neither did I," Jed said with a self-deprecating laugh.

"And the Yarnells certainly said nothing about you trying your hand as an unlicensed private detective bent on interfering with my investigation," she added, leaning in on both elbows to meet his gaze.

"I wouldn't necessarily go that far—"

"My brother doesn't talk much about what he does," she said, "but I can read between the lines enough to know that I have no business trying to function in your world. If I went with you on some SEAL Team op, I would do nothing but get in the way—maybe get someone killed. Your interference here is no different and, I promise you, no less dangerous. Does that make sense? Am I speaking a language you can understand?"

"Yes, ma'am. You're crystal clear," Jed said, even managing a small smile. "And I can assure you that was never my intent."

Perez nodded but pursed her lips. "I'm good at my job, Jedidiah, and I care deeply about the Yarnells and their missing girl. I'm working around the clock to bring Sarah Beth home safely. What I don't understand is why you assumed otherwise."

"I didn't."

"Then why didn't you come to me with your questions first? I mean, if your motive is truly to support the Yarnells as their family liaison and be a rock for them in their time of need, why come to Nashville only to stir up trouble?"

"You're right," he said. "I should have come to you first. I apologize."

"So now we're on the same page," Perez said, her smile broadening. "Wanna tell me what you've really been up to, Jed?"

Jed smiled back. There was no sense in holding anything back, and the question might be a test. Obviously they knew what he'd been up to, or he wouldn't be sitting here with his cuffs off. He gave the detective a quick, abbreviated overview of the events of the past twenty-four hours, starting with the phone call from David he took in Virginia Beach and ending with his visit to the bookstore. He kept his personal backstory to a minimum and carefully left out his paranoid thoughts on the gray Suburban as well as his feeling that the apartment in Murfreesboro seemed for all the world like a safe house. While he spoke, Perez listened intently without interruption or judgment in her eyes. When he finished, she started fishing.

"What made you go to Maclin's apartment?" she asked, no tells of her true level of interest in her voice.

"Seems one heck of a coincidence that the daughter of a divinity student was kidnapped at the very moment a priest was murdered, don't you think?" he asked but decided to keep the information he gleaned from Nora and Chad about Maclin's tutoring activities to himself.

Perez laughed out loud. "That might be true, were there any evidence that Maclin was murdered. What happened at the bookstore was tragic, but rest assured, it was an accident. We did a deep dive on the driver, and his vehicle, and determined uncontrolled acceleration was to blame for the incident. That poor kid is an emotional wreck; he's going to have nightmares about this for the rest of his life."

"Uncontrolled acceleration?" Jed repeated, incredulous. "You mean the accelerator stuck? That just doesn't happen in modern vehicles."

She leaned in again. "You may be reading too many mystery novels, Jedidiah, or watching too much late-night TV. The floor mat shifted and caught the gas pedal. It's rare, but it happens. And moreover, who are you to question this department's findings?"

"I apologize," he said, keeping the rest of his thoughts to himself.

"I thought I was asking you questions," she said with a little heat.

"You were—sorry."

She adjusted her suit jacket flaps and said, "Did you find anything noteworthy at Maclin's apartment?"

"No, nothing at all."

"Us either," she said, "or we might have come to the same crazy conclusion as you."

"But the apartment did seem a little . . . unusual," he said, trying to lead her without being so overtly clumsy this time.

Perez cocked her head to the side. "In what way?"

"I don't know. Seemed Spartan to me, I guess. Not very homey in my opinion."

"Maybe it's a priest thing," Perez said.

"Maybe," Jed answered, trying to sound convincing and apparently succeeding.

"Is there anything else you think that I, as the lead detective and investigator on this case, should know?"

"No, ma'am," he said but then decided to press one more question. "But I am curious about the people the Yarnells were going to meet last Saturday when it happened—the alumnus and student. Did you guys find out if they were at the bookstore when it happened? Did they witness anything noteworthy?"

Perez looked at him oddly. "This is the first I've heard of it. The Yarnells were meeting someone at the bookstore?"

"Yeah, from what I understand they were considering a private school for Sarah Beth."

Perez flipped open her notebook and pulled a pen from the spine. "What's the name of the school?"

"Not sure," Jed said, suddenly wondering if he'd made a mistaking bringing it up.

"I'll check into it. I don't remember anything in the notes from the responding officers, but I know the Yarnells didn't mention anything about the meeting to me. Who can blame them with so much raw emotion and confusion at the time. There's nothing more traumatic than losing a child."

Jed nodded. "Detective, I just want to see the girl back home with her parents."

"Well, we all do," she said, her voice softening but gaze going to the middle distance, suggesting to Jed it was an outcome she didn't think was likely at this point. "And I promise we're doing everything we can. I take my job very seriously, Jedidiah."

"I know; you said that already," he said with a tight smile, regretting the comment as soon as it left his lips.

She fixed him with a stare and a tight smile of her own before drawing a hard line in the sand. "Okay, here's the deal. In the state of Tennessee, to work with law enforcement and engage in the types of activities you've been up to requires that you're licensed with the state's Department of Commerce and Insurance—or a similar license from one of the seven other states that Tennessee recognizes reciprocity with. Are you a licensed private investigator in Virginia?"

"No, ma'am."

"I didn't think so." She crossed her arms over her chest. "Look, Jed, I get it. Your childhood best friend's daughter is missing. He's asked you to help because he looks at your military pedigree and your accomplishments and thinks that if anybody can help get his daughter back, it's a Navy SEAL . . . am I right?"

"Kidnapped," Jed corrected.

"Excuse me?" she said.

"You said David's daughter was missing, but she was kidnapped. I mean, that's not semantics—it's a pretty big distinction."

"You're right," Detective Perez said with a defensive smile. "But did everything else I said register?"

He exhaled and tried to deliver his next sentence without any of the emotion he was feeling inside. "Is this you telling me, in your official capacity, to back off?"

She nodded. "Yes, Jed. This is me, in my official capacity, telling you that if you interfere again with this investigation, you will likely be charged with a felony and incarcerated. You won't be much help to your friends in their time of need then, will you?"

Jed shook his head. "So I take it that means you guys aren't going to talk to me?"

"I didn't say that," she said, meeting his gaze, and her look was soft and compassionate. "The Yarnell family has designated you as their official liaison, and there is no law against that. I could demand they give you legal power of attorney, but I don't see how putting administrative roadblocks in place helps anyone in this very tragic and difficult situation. The better the communication and cooperation between our department and the family, the smoother the investigation can proceed. But that being said, the message I want you to take away from this experience is that you putting on your junior detective hat and running around trying to do my job isn't going to fly. Now, if you want to get your private investigator's license, be my guest, and in four to six weeks we can have a different conversation, but for now why don't you let me do the police work and you can be the Yarnells' liaison."

"I understand," he said.

"You understand and you agree, or you understand what I said but still plan to do things your way?" she said, narrowing her eyes at him but with a slight smile on her lips. "Like I said before, my brother is a Marine, and when he says, 'I understand,' it means he hears me, but it in no way represents compliance."

Jed chuckled at this and decided he liked Detective Perez. She was a straight shooter, and, unlike Police Corporal Alexander, she didn't have an ax to grind with him. "I understand and I agree," he said, smiling, "so long as you're playing it straight with me and promise to take my calls."

"It's not a negotiation, but yes, I promise to answer your calls." She reached inside her suit coat and retrieved a business card, which she pushed across the table toward him. "Here's my card. It has my mobile phone number on it, which I don't just hand out to anyone."

"Thank you," he said, rubbing his wrists again as a subtle reminder to her that both parties had crossed the line.

She stood and took a step back from the table. "Do you have any questions for me?" she asked, her stance signaling for him not to press his luck.

Unfortunately for Detective Perez, pressing their luck was what Navy SEALs did for a living. "Several," he said, remaining seated.

Perez smiled, then sighed and took her seat again.

"Do you really believe that the death of Father Maclin and Sarah Beth's kidnapping are unrelated?"

"I've discussed all I'm willing to discuss with you regarding the Maclin case," she said. "Next question."

"Okay, well, what does the FBI say about Maclin's death as it relates to Sarah Beth's kidnapping? Have they looked at the apartment?"

"The FBI is not involved in either case," Perez said and momentary anxiety flashed across her face. Maybe it was just the trite

"I don't want the feds taking over my case" type thing, but Perez showed a genuine emotional reaction at the thought of the FBI being involved.

"Sorry," he said, watching her carefully. "I thought the FBI always got involved in kidnapping cases, but like you said, I'm way out of my element. Probably learned that from TV."

"There are pretty specific criteria of a case requiring FBI involvement," she said, but her tone now was as if reading from a cue card. "So far, none of those has been met."

"Do you have any leads you're pursuing on Sarah Beth's possible whereabouts? I know the department issued an Amber Alert—have any tips come in on the vehicle that took her or sightings matching her description?"

"Unfortunately, the few tips that came in from the public turned out to be dead ends. Anything else, Jed?"

He had more questions but sensed her mood souring and decided he'd pushed her as far as she'd let herself be pushed.

"No, that's it for now," he said. "Maybe we can schedule a follow-up meeting and include David and Rachel, at a time that's more convenient for you. I know they have many questions and their nerves are fraying. Everyone knows that the odds of finding Sarah Beth alive dwindle with each passing hour."

"I think that's a good idea," she said. "Now, it's getting late . . . You have my card."

"I do," he said, scooting back his chair and getting to his feet.

Her eyes went wide for a second. Maybe she'd misjudged his size while he was seated.

It happened a lot.

"Police Corporal Alexander will get you out-processed."

"So you're not pressing charges?" he asked.

"That depends on you, Jed," she said and opened the door for him.

"Understood," he said with a wry smile and walked out of the interrogation room to find Alexander waiting in the hall.

"Nate, if you could check Mr. Johnson out," Detective Perez said. "Thanks."

Alexander nodded at her, then turned his attention to Jed, staring at him with those unnerving frost-blue eyes of his. "You should count yourself lucky today, Jedidiah."

A half-dozen comebacks came to mind, but Jed resisted all of them and instead said, "If I could get my personal weapon back, please."

Alexander shook his head. "We have pending charges against you and precinct leadership has already gone home for the night. I'm afraid that's not going to be possible."

"Detective Perez is right there," he said, gesturing down the hall to the detective, who was walking away but clearly still in plain sight. "And she just told me charges were not being filed."

"Like I said," Alexander replied, a vulpine grin curling his lips, "I'm afraid returning your firearm tonight is simply not possible. Come back tomorrow and we can revisit the matter."

Having already challenged Alexander once today and paid the price, Jed decided to cut his losses and walk out of the station . . . without his gun, without answers, and without any illusions that Nashville Metro was on his side.

The police corporal led him down the hall, taking him to the front of the precinct building this time instead of out the rear

door. He felt anger more than irritation at the feel of the policeman's hand on his back. He kept the rage inside.

At the front desk, Alexander became pleasant and even
smiled. "Glad we straightened this all out, Mr. Johnson," the
police corporal said, then turned to the heavyset man at the
desk, a gold badge on his chest. "Sergeant, Mr. Johnson here is
all good to go."

"'Kay," the bored desk sergeant said. Then he looked up from
his paperwork at Jed. "You got a ride, son, or do you need Corporal
Alexander to give you a lift back to your car?"

Alexander raised his eyebrows twice and smiled.

Jed snorted softly and shook his head. "Nah, I'm good, thanks."

He took the yellow envelope from the desk sergeant, shook out
his wallet, keys, pocketknife, and cell phone. He signed for and
pocketed his personal items and then pushed out through the glass
doors and onto Twelfth Avenue—thirteen blocks at least from
where his car had been left.

Outside, the air had become cooler and the sky was growing
dark in the east. As Jed set off, he navigated to his call history to
click on David's number only to find his call history had been
erased. Anger flaring in his chest, he looked back at the precinct
house over his shoulder.

Next, he checked his contacts—blank. On closer inspection,
he realized that all but the factory-installed apps were gone too.

Alexander had wiped his phone.

He mumbled a string of salty Navy SEAL curses, questioning Alexander's maternal lineage, and slipped his phone into his
pocket. He'd not memorized David's number. In fact, he didn't
memorize anyone's number these days. When he got back to the

hotel room, he would try restoring his phone from a backup copy on his computer. Until then, he was dead in the water.

With his fists clenched, and another string of curses streaming from his lips that would make Davy Jones proud, Jedidiah Johnson trudged west—chasing the setting sun and waiting for his phone to ring.

CHAPTER NINE

JIMMY KELLY'C CTEAKHOUSE

217 LOUISE AVENUE

NASHVILLE, TENNESSEE

THURSDAY, 2310 HOURS LOCAL

"You can stay and finish your beer, but could I get you to close out your check?" the waitress asked.

Jed looked up to meet her gaze, then checked his watch. Somehow two hours had disappeared at the small high-top table in the bar, while he gorged himself and beat himself up for his first day's failures on the job.

"So sorry," he said, fishing out his wallet and handing her a credit card. "Time got away from me."

She tilted her head and flashed him what was meant to be an

understanding smile while she took his card. "You definitely seem like a man with a lot on his mind."

"Yeah," he said without elaboration.

"Well, take your time. I still have stations to clear, so there's really no hurry, 'kay?"

"I appreciate that," he said and took a pull from his gone-warm beer.

The dozen fried oysters and twenty-ounce cowboy steak—a monster-size, bone-in rib eye—had filled even his massive Team Guy appetite but had done little to satisfy his hunger for answers. Jed understood he was ill-equipped to investigate a crime like Sarah Beth's kidnapping. He also understood Detective Perez's very clear orders that he let her handle it, that for him to do otherwise could mean felony obstruction charges. But you didn't need to be a detective to see that the death of Father Maclin—assuming he was a *real* priest—and the simultaneous kidnapping of the daughter of a graduate seminary student had to be connected. Did Perez not find Maclin's sterile apartment odd, reminiscent of a covert operations–style safe house? And why didn't David and Rachel tell her about the private school alum and student they were meeting? He was making a mental note to ask David more about the school when an epiphany struck. What if Father Maclin and Corbin Worth were the alumus and student that the Yarnells were going to meet?

How could I be so stupid? Of course they are . . . because there are no coincidences.

"Here you go."

Jed startled and looked up as his waitress slipped a fresh cold beer in front of him beside a black folded check case with his credit card sticking out at the top. "I don't need another," he said.

"On the house," she said. "You barely touched this one, and after two hours it can't be very good."

He chuckled. "That's very kind of you, Lisa," he said, sneaking a covert glance at her name tag.

She glanced over her shoulder at the bar and then, making sure the bartender wasn't eavesdropping, added, "I'll be done in like twenty minutes, if you want to talk. You look like you could use a friend, and I'm a really good listener."

She hasn't had a date since she broke up with Brad.

The information came to him unbidden and a chill chased down his back.

"You're the best," he said. "Can I get a rain check? I'm exhausted and gonna head back to my hotel and crash hard."

"Sure," she said, disappointment on her face. "I get it."

I'm so stupid. I should never have asked him. Her voice sounded clear in his head, and he stared at her pursed lips, hoping she'd said it out loud but confirming that she hadn't.

Why does this keep happening? he thought. *Is this what it feels like to slowly go insane?*

He pulled his credit card receipt from the check jacket and saw she'd written her number on the receipt. "I appreciate the offer," he said, folding the receipt and tucking it in his wallet. "I had a pretty rough day, and your kindness tonight was the one good thing that happened to me. I'll be in town for a while, so, um, maybe I could swing by and try to catch you another time."

"I work all weekend," Lisa said, her smile back. She touched his shoulder and then hurried off.

After leaving Lisa a 30 percent tip, Jed departed. He descended the brick steps beneath the long red awning and turned onto Louise

Avenue, heading south toward West End Avenue. A weary exhaustion settled over him, and the five blocks back to the Marriott suddenly felt like a five-mile beach run after an ocean swim when he was with the Teams. He needed to rest his racing mind and stop imagining people's thoughts and making connections that didn't exist.

As he strode the sidewalk beside West End United Methodist Church, a wave of nostalgia swept over him. He'd come to this church during the summer between his sophomore and junior years for a youth group festival and to hear a Christian band play in the church parking lot. Rachel had been his girlfriend then. They'd held hands and sat on a picnic blanket, back to chest, and swayed together while listening to the music. The memory was twenty years old but felt like it happened yesterday. He could practically smell the floral notes of the shampoo she used.

The streetlights flickered and he heard a soft, electric hum as he approached the parking lot. Just before he reached the corner of the building, Jed tensed, his "spidey sense" suddenly on fire. If this had happened to him as an assault team leader in Iraq, he'd be holding up a closed fist for the SEALs in line behind him to take a knee and search for an enemy ambush ahead. His spidey sense had never let him down before, and he wasn't about to ignore it now.

He didn't take a knee, but he did stop to survey and listen.

The streetlight closest to him flickered again and went out. Perhaps the hum was just a bad transformer box? When the rest of the lights in the parking lot ahead went dark a heartbeat later, his right hand flew instinctively to where his assault rifle would normally be slung on his chest over his body armor . . . but it wasn't there, of course, because tonight he wasn't a kitted-up SEAL on patrol with his team. He was a civilian, alone and unarmed. Thanks to Corporal Alexander, even his trusty Sig Sauer P229 was unavailable to him, locked up at the police precinct downtown.

It took a moment for his eyes to accommodate to the darkness, but he did not fear it. As a SEAL the night was his ally, a reliable partner who'd never let him down, and he took comfort in that knowledge. He scanned the street on both sides but saw no figures waiting in those shadows. To his left, the bright lights of West End Avenue glowed behind the tall financial building on the left corner. A quick glance behind him confirmed that light still streamed from the front of the church complex, where the main sanctuary sat.

Whatever this was, it was certainly no power outage.

Jed strained to hear movement or a converging threat but heard nothing beyond his own pulse in his ears. *Time to move,* he decided and set off at a jog toward the corner of West End Avenue. His hip protested, stiff and uncompliant from sitting too long at Jimmy Kelly's. As he approached the second gated entrance to the church's darkened parking lot, movement to his left caught his peripheral vision and he whirled, then froze in surprise at the sight of a motionless figure across the street.

Jed squinted at the uniformed, male figure standing in a dull sliver of moonlight.

"Corporal Alexander?" he called, recognizing the man's build and features even in the dim light. "What are you doing here?"

The cop didn't answer, just stared at Jed with arms crossed over his chest. Then a strange prickle washed over Jed's skin, and Alexander smiled.

An arm wrapped around Jed's neck from behind and jerked

him violently backward and off-balance into the dark parking lot. Years of close-quarter combat training kicked in. Jed turned his head left, tucked his chin to his shoulder, and thrust his right arm sharply up beside his own ear, threading the newly created gap between his neck and the bony arm attempting to crush his windpipe. The defensive maneuver worked, and Jed broke the choke hold, dropping to the ground. He hit hard, landing on his left side, but he was operating at reflex speed and immediately rolled clear of his attacker. Having achieved separation from the dark figure who was repositioning just out of arm's reach, Jed popped into a combat crouch and raised his forearms. The attacker, who was wearing an oversize black hoodie that kept his face completely in shadow, drew a long, curved blade that glinted silver in the moonlight.

With preternatural speed, the figure attacked—closing the gap and slashing at his midsection. Jed spun right, dodging as the blade whisked across his shirt. He didn't feel contact, but with a razor-sharp blade, flesh could be opened without pain. He reset his stance just in time for the knife fighter's second strike, a thrust. This time, however, Jed was ready. Using a Krav Maga technique, he sidestepped, blocked at the wrist, and captured the attacker's forearm. With devastating effect, he twisted and drove the arm up and back. Ligaments popped as he hyperextended the assailant's joints, and the knife clattered to the pavement. He finished the counteroffensive with a punishing left elbow to the man's temple.

But instead of screaming in agony or falling unconscious to the ground—the response Jed expected after having unleashed the full power of his six-foot-four, 230-pound frame—the hooded figure uttered only a single grunt and charged him. Incredulous, Jed pivoted and shoved the assailant with a double palm strike in the back, sending the man flying. Like a ninja, the hooded attacker executed some bizarre quasi backflip and landed on his feet facing Jed. With an inhuman howl, the dark figure charged, closing the gap between them so quickly Jed could barely get his arms up. The cloaked fighter was on him, striking and kicking with speed and fury the likes of which Jed had never encountered before, and it was all he could do to shield his face. The grunts and shrieks coming from the attacker made Jed wonder if he was fighting a wild primate, not a man.

A voice echoed in Jed's mind with savage, singular malice—*kill, kill, kill, kill, kill*—and Jed felt himself losing the battle against his attacker both physically and mentally. The next thing he knew, they were on the ground, Jed on his back in the guard position and the hooded animal on top of him. At this face-to-face distance, Jed could now see his opponent's features. The man beneath the hood was middle-aged, unkempt, and emaciated, yet he attacked with the power of someone half the age and double the weight. In the calculus of Jed's mind, he registered that the body on top of him could not weigh more than a hundred and fifty pounds, but he could not seem to throw the man off. It was like wrestling with a rabid wolverine.

And how is he fighting with a hyperextended arm? he thought as the hooded maniac tried to bite him.

Jed clutched the man by the bony shoulders and rolled in a tangle of thrashing arms and legs. As he did, he spied the blade on the pavement a few feet away. He felt a sharp pain in his left forearm as his attacker succeeded in clamping his jaws down on a cord of muscle. Fresh anger dumped a bolus of adrenaline into

Jed's bloodstream as they completed the roll with Jed ending up on top. As if sensing his intention, the hooded freak released his bite and turned his head toward the knife. Both men reached for it with lightning speed, but Jed's arm was longer and his fingers found the grip first. The man beneath him shrieked and lunged upward to bite Jed's throat, but not before Jed drove the blade into the side of the man's neck up to the hilt.

Jed yanked the blade free and a geyser of arterial blood sprayed from the wound. The hooded fiend hissed, air escaping his severed trachea in a mortifying sputter. Jed met the man's gaze, and then he saw it: a faint amber ring glowing in the eyes.

"No, no, no," he stammered, leaping off his attacker. "It can't be."

Despite the growing puddle of dark blood accumulating on the pavement beside the man, he righted himself and scrambled toward Jed on hand and knees like some sort of crab. Jed leapt aside and drove the blade into the base of the man's skull, severing the brain stem. The hooded attacker collapsed in a heap, unmoving.

Seriously freaked out, Jed whirled, looking for Alexander, who had decided not to intervene on Jed's behalf while this rabid homeless man tried to murder him. Beneath the darkened streetlight where the cop had been standing, he saw only shadows.

"Alexander," he hollered, walking out of the parking lot and onto the street, where he scanned in both directions.

As he looked right, he glimpsed taillights disappearing onto West End Avenue. The car was a white sedan but it was gone before he could be sure if it was a police cruiser or not. Jed felt his pulse beginning to slow post conflict. He rolled his neck and did a four count of slow tactical breathing, as he'd done countless times in far more dangerous combat all over the world. In his hand he still clutched the knife, a knife he'd used in self-defense but one that could also be called a murder weapon for a crime committed with no witnesses.

The electric hum returned, and behind him the lights of the parking lot flickered back to life. Jed turned and looked back at the lot where the hooded figure lay dead on the pavement . . . except there was no body anymore. The lot was empty. Confused, he jogged to the scene of the fight and found that not only was the body gone, but no trace remained of the battle he had just won. Instead of blood, he saw a pool of bleach—the noxious fumes flooding his nostrils.

Jed spun in a slow circle, scanning again the empty lot and nothingness around him.

How had he not heard a car or footsteps or scraping and heavy breathing as the corpse was dragged away? What was going on? And where did Corporal Alexander disappear to?

Jed looked at the blade in his hand—a Cold Steel six-inch mega folder—the only proof remaining of what had just happened. If not for the knife, and the throbbing human bite wound on his forearm, he would have no choice but to conclude he'd completely lost his mind. But there it was, bloodstained and heavy in his hand. He depressed the Tri-Ad lock, folded the blade into the handle, and slipped the weapon into a thigh pocket on his cargo pants. He looked down at the cut in his T-shirt and, with a weary sigh, lifted the fabric to confirm that his abdomen had not been sliced open with a mortal injury masked by adrenaline.

Profound paranoia washed over him, hitting him like a rogue wave in a surf set.

Alexander's coming for me. There are probably cameras all over the place here. He's going to show up at my hotel and arrest me for murder.

He turned and started walking, out of the church parking lot and toward West End Avenue. His mind went immediately to Detective Perez. She was a straight shooter, and his gut told him he could trust her. He remembered the business card she'd given him and was about pull it out and call her when his phone vibrated in his pocket. He retrieved it and looked at the caller ID. Thanks to Alexander, no name showed up, but he recognized the digits as David's number.

"Hello? Jed?" came David's anxious voice.

"David, listen—someone just tried to knife me in a parking lot," he said, slowing down, his head on a swivel, searching in all directions for the next attacker.

"What? Are you okay?"

"Yes, but the man who attacked me is not. Something very strange is going on. Other things have happened today too. We need to talk—you, me, and Rachel. The three of us."

"Okay, I agree. When and where?"

Jed had no idea. The hotel would be watched by Alexander and probably others from metro PD. He didn't want anyone to follow him to the Yarnells' house. "Somewhere near Vandy and West End Avenue," he blurted. "Somewhere safe and not obvious."

"Okay, let me talk to Rachel . . ."

Jed waited through a painfully long pause, aware of a muffled conversation happening between David and Rachel. When he finally got tired of waiting on them to hash it out, he said, "David, ask Rachel if she remembers the Thursday snowstorm years ago and the heart-shaped piece of glass."

"What?" David said. "What are you talking about?"

"Just ask her," he insisted.

The memory gripped him by the throat—the emotion associated with that day almost crippling. January 16, 2003, Nashville had been pounded by a once-in-a-century blizzard dropping seven inches of snow in an hour. They had been on a class trip to a play—the name of which he couldn't remember now—and they'd been caught in the storm. It had been barely snowing when they'd left school but had become a blizzard by the time they arrived downtown. The bus had gotten stuck in the snow, after being stalled by gridlock, and so they'd sought refuge inside the big Catholic church. In the sanctuary, he'd found a piece of ruby-red stained glass on the floor beneath the scaffolding of a window being repaired. It was small, the size of a half dollar, but ironically shaped like a heart, and he'd given it to Rachel . . .

I doubt she remembers such a silly thing.

David's voice was muffled even more, his former friend perhaps placing his hand over the microphone.

"She remembers," David said, coming back to the line. His voice suggested displeasure at the meeting place or Rachel's reaction to the memory or maybe both.

Jed looked at his watch. "Let's meet there in one hour," he said. "If I can get us inside, we'll talk in the sanctuary. If not, the parking lot."

Another muffled pause followed.

"She says she can make sure we get inside—I'm not sure how, but that's what she said. Just go to the front door."

"And I need *things*," he said. "Do you understand what I mean?"

"I think so," David said. "Things related to . . . what you do for a living?"

"Yes," he said. "And that includes a new phone. Preferably a prepaid burner."

"Then we're going to need more time. Let's make it two hours."

"Okay," Jed said with a tight grimace, not sure how he was going to kill two hours wandering around the city without getting rounded up by Nashville PD. One hour was already pushing it in his book.

"Jed, one more thing: we think we have some new information to share with you," David said, a hint of excitement bubbling through his anxiety.

"You better," Jed growled. "Two hours. Don't be late—and you won't be able to reach me until then."

He disconnected the call and then dropped the phone into a garbage can at the corner. Mobile phones could be traced, and there was no point in making it easy on whoever was pulling the puppet strings here. Shoving his hands deep in his pockets, he vectored away from West End Avenue with its bright lights and late-night traffic. Despite the allure of that perceived safety, he would need to walk the backstreets and keep a low profile for the next two hours.

"I'll probably get mugged . . . *again,*" he growled.

An image of the hooded man's twisted, maniacal face appeared in his mind's eye like a waking nightmare. It was not the first time he fought off someone out of their mind with rage. A flash-bulb memory of Kenny Bailey's basement, Rachel on the floor and . . .

No, don't go down that bunny hole. Stay focused, the SEAL in his brain barked. *Remember the mission. There's a little girl out there who needs you. She's terrified and she's alive.*

He had neither the time nor the desire to ponder how or why, but he knew Rachel's little girl was still alive. It wasn't hope. It wasn't wishful thinking. He could feel it in his bones. In his soul.

She was alive.

He just *knew.*

I will find you, Sarah Beth, he thought, looking east. *No matter who took you, no matter how far away, I will find you . . . and that's my promise.*

CHAPTER
TEN

In her dream—and Sarah Beth knew it was a dream because of that weird, disconnected awareness that somehow fails to make the situation any less terrifying—she walked through the large, ornate doors beneath a stained-glass window of a soaring white bird. The doors, heavy and substantial with their oak frames and lead glass panes, opened gracefully and in unison without her touch.

"Dreams are like that," her mom's voice reminded her.

Sarah Beth stepped tentatively inside the church. She didn't recognize the dimly lit sanctuary—it was nothing like the aesthetic of her church at home with its folding chairs, modern stage, and concrete walls embedded with glass mosaics. But despite her certainty that she'd never been here before, this place felt comfortably familiar.

Twin rows of dark-stained wooden pews divided by a center aisle stood in stark contrast to the cream-colored walls, columns, and highly stylized ceiling overhead. Her gaze followed the aisle to the front of the sanctuary and swept up—up to the incredible painting that decorated the domed ceiling above the altar. In the painting, brightly colored angels flanked Mary, who was dressed in a red gown and gazing down on the crucified Savior carved in white marble below, His arms stretched wide on the cross. Her expression was perplexing—sadness and wonderment interwoven. The large and impressive sculpture of her Son was positioned behind the altar and the undeniable focal point of the church.

The altar, a long white table on which the sacraments sat, was draped in green silk and had been moved to the very rear and placed nearly at the feet of the Jesus statue. Even she, a newcomer to this place, understood this was not its usual position. Room had been made for microphones, chairs, and music stands. Twin stacks of black speakers three high stood behind the pulpit with cables snaking off to a sound-board unseen.

Hesitant to proceed any further, she stopped short of the last pew. The congregation was packed with people—standing room only, her dad might say—and she felt an electric energy inside. They were waiting for something . . . something joyous and exciting.

"Watch," a voice whispered.

For a moment, nothing happened.

Then gunfire—deafening, mechanical rage like she'd seen in war movies—erupted all around her. The noise echoed in the church, amplified and twisted by the cavernous space with its marble surfaces and towering ceilings. She covered her ears and cowered, but the people in the pews just sat quietly, eyes forward, waiting for whatever show was supposed to begin. It seemed like the soundtrack from one dream had been mistakenly dubbed onto the video of another.

Dreams are like that . . .

The altar was torn apart before her eyes, splintered wood revealed beneath the high-gloss white paint as the bullets shredded the heart-wood. It sagged in the middle and collapsed; the sacraments tumbled in slow motion to the floor, bleeding their contents into the gold rug. Then the people in the pews began to turn and look at her—one at a time at first and then en masse.

A white-haired woman just ahead of her, near the aisle, showed her only half a face, the left side missing above a stark white and flesh-stripped jawbone. Each face that turned was as horrible as the last, mutilated and blood-soaked. A boy had a small hole just above his right eye, but when he turned to look at his mother beside him, her throat was ripped out and bleeding all over her pink blouse. She hugged her son, pressing his head to her chest, and Sarah Beth saw that the back corner of the boy's head was missing, exposing white bony edges and something pink and bloody inside.

She screamed and tried to run, but her feet acted like they were bolted to the floor.

Figures, clad in black and holding assault rifles, swarmed from the transepts on either side of the altar, gunning down the congregation. At first, she thought them monsters or demons with skulls for faces, but then she noticed they were wearing black hoods and skeleton masks. Their torsos shook and the muzzles of their guns spat fire as the killers razed the congregation . . . sparing not a single man, woman, or child.

"You can stop this," the whisper said. "It's not too late."

Then another voice—a strong, confident baritone—spoke over the first.

"I will find you, Sarah Beth. No matter who took you, no matter how far away, I will find you . . . and that's my promise."

Sarah Beth's eyes sprang open.

Panting and drenched in sweat, she stared at the ceiling. The blades of the ceiling fan cast dancing shadows and whispered a relentless *whip—whip—whip*. Her mom said she was a pro at nightmares—she'd been having them since she was a little girl—but the horror show she'd just witnessed would take time to unpack and bury. She swallowed hard, took several long, controlled deep breaths, and tried to slow her pounding pulse. Then she set about the business of forgetting it.

But should I? The voice said I could stop it . . . Maybe I need to remember that church? Maybe it's important.

She closed her eyes and tried to burn the image of the cathedral into her brain. She focused on the unique details—the wooden pews, domed ceiling, the painting of Mary, and the white marble statue of Jesus—knowing somehow these things were important. Then, satisfied she could remember what the church looked like, she forced the icky, bloody imagery out of her head. Feeling a little better, she opened her eyes, released her death grip on the sheets, and swung her legs out of the bed. Barefoot, she slipped to the floor and walked to the barred window. As she stared out into the moonlit night, she thought about the voice that had woken her. Not the whispery voice that she'd grown accustomed to over the years, but the other one—the man's voice. He had called her by name. He had promised to find her. Was it real or just her dreaming mind telling her what she *wanted* to be true?

Wishful thinking is wasted thinking, she thought—something her mom loved to say.

She gazed at the red lights that formed a circle around the giant bowling pin thing on the next hill over, wondering for all the world what it was. *If Dad were here, he'd know. He knows everything.* She felt tears brim in her eyes but immediately blinked them out with annoyance. *Too much crying,* she told herself, *I just wish I was home. I just wish someone would find me . . .*

Wishful thinking is wasted thinking, she heard again, but this time in her mom's voice.

A chill snaked down her spine.

Mom? Mom, is that you? Can you hear me? Mom . . . Mom?

No answer came.

With a heavy sigh, she looked at the five little gouges on the wall between the headboard and the edge of the window. She would add another when the sun came up, before Fake Grandma brought her eggs and oatmeal.

Five days.

I've been here five days . . .

Nobody's coming for me.

It was time to be honest with herself. The only way she was getting out of this place was if she got herself out. The idea of escaping was empowering but also terrifying. Feeling suddenly cold and vulnerable, she crawled back into her unfamiliar bed and pulled the unfamiliar bedspread up to her chin. Overhead the ceiling fan whirred.

Whip—whip—whip . . .

Fake Grandma is afraid of me . . . I know she is.

I wonder why.

She grabbed one of the stuffed animals, an oversize white bunny with pink ears, and dragged it under the covers. Hugging it to her chest, she started to make plans.

I need to get the key off Fake Grandma's neck, but to do that I'm going to have to trick her. Or fight her. She doesn't look very strong, but she is a grown-up.

A bad word popped into her head.

I'm sorry, God.

Whip—whip—whip . . .

As she watched the fan go around, she said a prayer for her parents, who must be losing their minds, and for herself, that she could be strong enough to do what she had to do, and also for the voice that had woken her from her dream . . . whoever he was.

Amen.

A wave of drowsiness washed over her like a tender kiss. Before sleep took her, she pushed out a thought, just in case it wasn't wishful thinking.

If you're coming for me . . . you need to come soon.

CHAPTER ELEVEN

In many parts of Nashville, the party was just getting started at 1 a.m., but Centennial Park was not one of them. The park was deserted and that was just the way Jed wanted it—wide-open and empty. If anybody decided to come at him, he'd see them from fifty yards away. This was his third loop around the Parthenon—a full-scale replica of the original iconic temple in Greece. Replete with a double row of Doric columns, sculpted pediment friezes, and a forty-two-foot-tall statue of the goddess Athena, the Centennial Park Parthenon gave anyone who visited Nashville a glimpse back in time at what the original in Athens looked like twenty-five hundred years ago. As cool as it was, architectural sightseeing was the last thing on Jed's mind.

He was not in a good headspace.

For the past hour, he'd been seesawing back and forth about whether he'd made a mistake ditching his phone and not calling Detective Perez. Both had been snap decisions driven by instinct. Right now, his brain was screaming at him to pull the detective's business card from his pocket, march straight back to his hotel lobby, and call her. He would tell her everything that happened and explain that Corporal Alexander had watched the whole thing and done nothing. More than nothing—Alexander had smiled, let it happen, and then driven away. For whatever messed-up reason, Alexander had it out for Jed.

Dude, you killed somebody. And like a moron, you're still carrying the murder weapon around in your pocket, the SEAL said, kicking off an argument in his head.

Wrong, I was attacked and acted in self-defense. I have the bite mark to prove it. And if there's security camera footage of the incident, the video will clearly exonerate me. Detective Perez is a straight shooter. Her brother's a Marine.

The SEAL laughed. *And she's a cop and so is Alexander. Bro, whose side do you think she's going to take by default? Whose verbal testimony is she going to give the benefit of the doubt? Imagine if some chump you didn't know accused Captain Jared of a crime. Whose word would you trust?*

Jed shook his head. He hated arguing with himself. It just added kindling to the growing pyre of firewood in his brain. One ill-timed spark and *whoosh*, he was a bonfire of insanity.

Check your six . . .

Head on a swivel, he scanned the park for threats. Forty yards away, a homeless dude pushing a shopping cart was making his way toward Twenty-Seventh Avenue.

I'm gonna have to keep an eye on that guy, he thought.

Jed kept trudging east, but instead of vectoring around Lake Watauga, he headed toward the water's edge. As he walked, his thoughts circled back to the aftermath of the attack. It didn't make any sense.

Alexander had to have taken the body . . . but how? How did he do it without me seeing? Nobody moves that fast. And if he disappeared the body, what did he do with it? Is it on some coroner's exam table right now? My DNA has to be all over it. Oh, man, I gotta get rid of this knife.

The whole incident was insane—like the plot from some B movie that people only watch when they have insomnia. B movie plots might suck, but he had new respect for the characters. They were not the idiots everybody assumed they were. Circumstance conspired against them, just like it had with him. Tonight, he'd killed a man in a parking lot in self-defense and run away. He was still holding the would-be murder weapon, and he had no proof to counter whatever case Alexander was building and no witnesses to dispute any "evidence" the cop was gathering.

I'm royally and completely screwed.

Jed crossed the sidewalk that looped around the perimeter of Lake Watauga—a pond that really had no business being called a lake—and stood on one of the limestone blocks at the water's edge. He reached into his cargo pant pocket, fully intending to wipe down the knife and toss it into the pond.

How do you know you're not on camera? the SEAL asked. *And how guilty will you look when they fish the knife out of this pond and show the jury footage of you throwing it in? Don't be a chump. Get your head in the game.*

He stared down at his moonlit reflection in the water and barely recognized himself.

"What am I doing?" he murmured. "What did David get me into?"

He had half a mind to hail a cab and head to the airport right now. He could buy a ticket on the first flight home to Virginia Beach tomorrow and put this whole mess behind him. His gut told him that David, and Rachel by way of complicity, had not been completely honest with him. Either lies had been told or, at a minimum, truths had been withheld. He owed nothing to these people. He'd already walked away from them once; he could do it again. He'd gotten over Rachel before, and he could get over her again.

So you're just gonna quit? the SEAL asked. *Ring the bell and walk away—that's your solution?*

Jed blew air through his teeth.

His guts felt leaden and queasy.

Quitting didn't come naturally to a SEAL, no matter the mission or the cause, and since the day he'd been accepted to BUD/S, he'd never walked away from a challenge. But this was different. This time he was standing on the edge of the abyss and they were asking him to jump. Sirens wailed in the distance, spiking his heart rate, but after a few seconds he concluded they were fading rather than heading in his direction.

He felt something shift in his left outside cargo pocket.

Remembering what was there, he reached his hand into the pocket and pulled out the picture David had entrusted him with. He held the photograph up into the light streaming from the lamppost behind him. Sarah Beth's glacier-blue stare caused his heart to skip a beat. She truly was Rachel's clone. The same heart-melting, carefree smile. But there was something haunted in those eyes—a look he remembered seeing so often in his first love's eyes. An untold story? A secret insight only *she* was privilege to?

Whatever had happened, whatever lies had been told or truths had been omitted, this little girl had been kidnapped and was waiting to be saved. She was alive. This much he was certain of. He slipped the picture back into his pocket, tightened his jaw, and summoned the words he had relied on hundreds of times to give him strength and courage.

I will draw on every remaining ounce of strength to protect my teammates and accomplish our mission . . .

The SEAL creed was the only Bible he'd embraced since he'd left Tennessee more than sixteen years ago. Honor, commitment, and courage his only religion.

I am never out of the fight . . .

He didn't know where *they* had taken Rachel's daughter.

And he had not the foggiest idea who *they* were.

Maybe it was time to find out.

Balling his hands into fists, Jed steeled himself and set off for the Cathedral of the Incarnation at a brisk walk. It was high time for David and Rachel to read him in on what was really going on. And after that, once he was armed with the truth, maybe he could finally get down to the business of rescuing the scared little angel calling to him in his head.

CHAPTER TWELVE

Jed surveyed the intersection of West End and Twenty-First Avenues, looking for threats. To anyone watching him, he must look crazy suspicious—skulking around, glancing over his shoulder every thirty seconds. But he couldn't help himself. His paranoia was maxed out, and making it to the church without another incident was all that mattered. With a grimace on his face, he crossed the street and did another scan before approaching the pale-yellow brick facade of the modern Roman Catholic church in the heart of Nashville.

I'm safe. No one's tailing me, he thought as he walked up the short steps to the heavy wooden double doors of the Cathedral of the Incarnation.

Incarnation . . . such a powerful concept.

Thought corporeal. Love born into life. Spirit made into flesh . . . Deity become man.

He had not thought of such things in a very, very long time, but arriving at this place at nearly two o'clock in the morning, his mind excavated old and unordinary thoughts. *"The name of a church is important,"* he remembered Tobias once saying. He could almost hear his onetime mentor's voice in his head.

"It imparts a certain character to the building and an ethos to the congregation. If you close your eyes and touch the stone, you can feel a resonance, Jed . . . like a single pure note, reverberating from a struck tuning fork."

Feeling foolish, but driven by compulsion, he pressed his right hand against the decorative stone framing the wooden doors. He closed his eyes and listened for a musical resonance . . .

A metallic *ka-chink* snapped him out of his fugue as the lock mechanism shifted on the inside of the door. Jed took a step back and his right hand automatically went to the cargo pocket with the knife he always carried there. The left-hand door shifted and then opened inward, stopping at an eight-inch opening. A weathered, bespectacled priestly face appeared in the gap.

"Ah, you must be Jedidiah," said the man of God with a weary smile.

"Yes, I'm Jed," he said. "And I'm sorry to bother you at such a late hour. I was supposed to meet—"

"Come in, come in," the priest said, opening the door wide enough for Jed to pass. "You're the first to arrive."

Jed stepped inside and then helped the priest shut and lock the heavy wooden door.

"Thank you. That door's a handful for me," the priest said with a self-deprecating chuckle. "I'm Father Newman. Welcome to the Cathedral of the Incarnation."

Jed paused to look around the nicely appointed lobby—*narthex,* a voice from another lifetime corrected. His gaze was immediately drawn to a beautiful arch window in the door leading into the sanctuary, with a stained-glass inlay—a white dove, wings spread wide in soaring flight set upon a circular, swirling background of royal blue. The image felt both iconic and familiar to him.

"A simple but magnificent piece of work," the priest said, following Jed's gaze to the stained glass. "You're not the first to marvel at it."

"A dove's wings are not supposed to be that wide," Jed said, studying it. "It's soaring, like an eagle—keeping watch from above."

"Maybe the artist intended as much," the priest said with an almost-imperceptible curl of his lips. "What is art, if not metaphor?"

"Yeah," Jed said, nodding. "I suppose you're right."

"Follow me, Jedidiah," Father Newman said.

Jed followed the priest through the beautiful sanctuary with its marble columns and neo-Italian renaissance architectural style. They walked up the center aisle between rows and rows of wooden pews, and as they approached the altar, Jed's gaze was drawn to the Crucifixion statue—which in this sanctuary was carved entirely from white marble and slightly elevated behind the dais. Over the years he'd seen countless depictions of Christ on the cross, but no matter the arrangement or the artist's skill, the Crucifixion always moved him. A sacrifice that transcended race, gender, language, and time . . .

Father Newman led him out of the sanctuary via a side door, then down a hallway and to a nice little reading room with a collection of books and comfortable club chairs.

"Wait here, please," the priest said.

Jed nodded, but instead of taking a seat, he walked to the wall of books and perused the spines and covers. He recognized very few of the collected works and had read even fewer, but one collection caught his eye. He was just about to pull out a copy of *Spiritual Warfare and the Discernment of Spirits*, one of a dozen titles by Dan Burke on the shelf at eye level, when he heard footsteps in triplicate approaching. Jed turned . . . and there she was.

His breath caught in his throat, time slowed, and everything but her face faded into a blur. Seventeen years had passed since he'd last seen her, and although hers was a face he would recognize anywhere, she had changed. When he'd left, she'd been a girl—vibrant, pretty, and naive. *This* Rachel was a woman—composed, beautiful, and hardened.

He opened his mouth to greet her, but the words caught in his throat.

"Thank you, Father," she said to the priest with a gracious smile, dismissing him quickly and decisively. Then, still not looking at Jed, she said to David, "Let's just get this over with."

Seventeen years and this is how you greet me?

During his time in the Teams, he'd been punched, kicked,

stabbed, shot, blown-up, and knocked off a roof . . . and none of those injuries held a candle to the blow she'd just dealt him. He felt his jaw tighten, borne of equal parts anger and ignominy. He looked at her and waited for her to meet his gaze.

"How 'bout we all take a seat," David said, playing arbiter.

Not until after she'd slipped into one of the reading chairs did Rachel finally lock eyes with Jed. And for a fleeting instant—no more than a millisecond—he caught a glimpse of the old Rachel.

"I want to be clear," she said, her voice taking on a disconnected, administrative tone, "that I was against your coming from the beginning. It was David who insisted on contacting you."

Jed, who since joining the SEALs had always been judicious with his words, said simply, "I understand."

We don't need you . . . not anymore, he thought he heard her say next, but her lips were not moving.

"Yes, okay, well, I don't see how rehashing the past does us any good. Let's just try to keep our eyes on the objective and focus on next steps," David said.

"I'm not rehashing anything. I'm simply stating for the record that Jed being invited here was a unilateral decision. I think it's important for him to understand that," she said.

"Okay, then for the record, should he also know that you taking Sarah Beth to the Vanderbilt bookstore that day was also a unilateral decision—a unilateral decision that you acted on despite my objections? I wanted to do more research on St. George's Academy," David fired back.

"So you *do* blame me," she said, her voice oozing with venom. "I knew it."

For the next several seconds, they all just stared at one another in what had to be the most uncomfortable moment in Jed's adult life. It was David who broke the three-way standoff by doing something that took Jed by surprise, extending both his hands—his left to Rachel and right to Jed. While the idea of taking David's hand was repulsive, Jed realized it was perhaps the only way to regain their forward momentum. As impossible and unlikely as it was, David had somehow become his only ally in the room.

David waited patiently, head bowed, until both of them took his hand in their own. Rachel did not extend her hand to Jed.

And neither did Jed to her.

"Dear Lord, we ask that You please be with us," David said, his voice tight. "We need You, Father. We need You with us to comfort and guide us. We need the Holy Spirit to light the path that takes us to our little girl and brings her safely home . . ."

Jed opened his eyes and glanced over at David, certain he had never heard him pray before.

"We need You to restore our faith and trust in each other and remind us of our capacity for understanding and empathy. We need You to help us to communicate in a productive manner so that together we can do what we must do for Sarah Beth . . . for our little girl, Father, who has been taken by wolves," David spat these words out—a flash of the angry, impetuous David of their youth. "And we ask You, Lord, to help Jed find her and bring her back. We pray this in Jesus' name. Amen."

"Amen," Rachel said.

Amen, Jed thought but did not say.

David gave Jed's hand a firm squeeze and then released it.

Jed glanced from David to Rachel and saw her smile at her husband, and a heartbeat later that chiseled expression she'd been wearing softened just a little. Like an exhale into frozen winter hands, Jed felt a warm, soothing energy envelop and relax him. He brought his hands together in his lap and knit his fingers together, perplexed by the power and poignancy of what had just happened. The reading room was not the same place it had been just minutes ago.

Scripture came to him . . .

"And I will ask the Father, and he will give you another advocate to help you and be with you forever."

He recognized the passage from John 14:16 but had no memory of the verse until it appeared there, as if sent from another.

The Holy Spirit . . .

Still holding Rachel's hand, David fixed his attention on Jed.

"Jed, despite what you just heard or might be thinking, please know that we are both truly grateful to you for coming and agreeing to help us. We know that what we've asked of you is both emotionally uncomfortable and . . ."

"Dangerous," Jed said. "I think that's the word you're looking for. All the more dangerous for me, when I don't have all the information that's available. And that's why we're all here at two o'clock in the morning having this conversation."

"Yes, I suppose it is."

"But you knew how dangerous this would be when you contacted me, didn't you?"

David and Rachel looked at each other, and then David nodded slowly. "Yes, but not in the way you think. We don't know important things that would help you or keep you safe—not in the material sense. But we do feel strongly that there are evil forces at work. And I'm sorry if that topic is out of bounds for you these days . . . but I think it's something that needs to be discussed. Even if it's uncomfortable."

Jed flashed him a wan smile. "You know what's uncomfortable? Getting arrested by Nashville PD, having my sidearm confiscated, and then having someone try to kill me on my walk back to the hotel while the arresting officer stood in the shadows and watched."

"What!" Rachel said, showing the first inkling of concern for him since this little reunion began. She shot an accusing look at her husband. "When you told David there'd been an incident, I didn't realize you'd been attacked."

Jed blew air through his teeth and leaned forward so that his elbows were on his knees. "Guys, whatever is going on here is bigger than just Sarah Beth's kidnapping. It sounds crazy saying it out loud, but Nashville PD is somehow involved. Now, I don't know if it's just that we're dealing with a crooked cop or if something more insidious is going on, but for whatever reason, Police Corporal Nate Alexander wants me out of the picture. And I'll tell you something else—what happened to that priest outside the Vandy bookstore was no accident. It doesn't take a homicide detective to recognize that a car traveling on West End Avenue couldn't *accidentally* lose control and execute the S-shaped maneuver necessary to hit Father Maclin on that sidewalk. To navigate the parking lot and hit him at speed would require purposeful action and intent. So as my former CSO was fond of saying, it's *open kimono* time. If there's anything either of you is holding back, it's time to lay it bare. If you don't . . . then I'm walking."

Jed touched the cargo pocket with Sarah Beth's picture. He didn't know if his heart had gone so cold that he could leave her to the wolves, but bluffing as much was the only leverage he had. To succeed, he needed them to read him in.

Rachel looked at David and they held each other's gaze for a long moment, until David gave her a tight-lipped nod. She let out a heavy exhale, turned to Jed, and said, "I don't know how else to say this but to just say it. Sarah Beth is . . . special. Which is why, we believe, she was taken."

"Special how?"

Rachel hesitated a moment, as if second-guessing herself, before saying, "Sarah Beth has a gift, Jed. . . . She has the gift of second sight and sees and hears things others can't."

The words hit Jed like a slap in the face.

"Oh no, not this again," he said, popping to his feet. "Don't tell me that after all these years, the two of you are still indulging in that stupid childhood fantasy. We're not kids anymore. There's no magic or miracles in the world. No supernatural creatures, abilities, or powers. No angels. No demons. There's just people and their imaginations. The only monsters in the world are men, and if anyone can speak with authority on that subject, it's me because I've spent the past seventeen years hunting those monsters. They are vicious and they are evil, but they are just men."

Are you trying to convince them or yourself? You know what you saw in the hooded man's eyes. You know the voices you've heard in your head.

A newscaster's smile spread across Rachel's face and she turned to David. "See, I told you this was a waste of time."

"We just need to give him time to process all of this," David said.

"Time is the one thing our baby girl doesn't have," she said, her voice beginning to strain. "I'm telling you that Sarah Beth has reached out to me and she's alive. She believes that the people who have her will do something terrible to her soon, and when they do, it's over. We'll never see her again."

"You don't know that," David said softly. "I know you guys have a connection. I've felt her gift too, but with all that's going on—"

"I do know it," she snapped, pressing her right hand hard against her chest. "Because I feel it like a dagger slowly piercing my heart, David, millimeter by millimeter with each passing hour. She's alive, but the sand in her hourglass is running out."

"Then Jed can still help us," David said. "We can get her back before whatever you believe is coming—"

"What I *know* is coming," she said, exasperated. "And Jed can't help us if he doesn't believe. Without faith, he'll never find her."

David nodded, took a deep breath, and turned to Jed—his eyes asking the only question that mattered. *Please . . . please will you help us?*

Jed looked from David to Rachel and then slowly sat back down. What he was hearing from Rachel seemed to be little more than a desperate mother's wishful thinking. She knew the statistics about missing children, and she needed this to cling to. But what if? For a moment he was back in high school, and it was the night of the bonfire . . .

He shook his head.

I can't do this again. I can't . . . I just can't, he told himself.

Yes, you can, another voice said. *I believe in you.*

His gaze snapped to Rachel. "What did you say?"

She cocked an eyebrow at him. "I didn't say anything."

His heart, which had taken half a lifetime to heal, felt like it was being ripped in half along the same old fissure. What was it about the three of them that created such an atomic situation? For twenty-five years now the combination was like a chemical reaction—sometimes magical, sometimes explosive, but always volatile.

And how can it be that I so desperately want to love and to hate them in the same breath?

"Jed, I could try to make some eloquent speech to inspire you, or I could tell you for the hundredth time how desperate we are and that you're our last and only hope. I'm not above getting down on my knees and begging, if I thought it would do any good," David said, "but the time for speeches and begging has passed. You need to follow your heart. If you want a moment, we can step out so you can think. I know that you, of all people, understand the stakes. Because you've seen the face of evil—and I don't mean in Iraq or Afghanistan or whatever other places evil lives these days. After that night at Kenny's house, we took different paths. You chose to walk away from your faith; I chose to embrace it. A part of me doesn't blame you—"

"I told you I don't want to talk about that!" Jed snapped, cutting him off.

"You asked us to be honest with you, Jed," Rachel fired back. "Well, this is us being honest. We need you. There, I said it. We need you. Sarah Beth needs you. Please don't walk away from us. Please don't walk away from Sarah Beth."

Just take the mission, frogman, the SEAL inside him said, speaking up for the first time. *Do what you do best and go save their little girl.*

Jed let out a long, rattling sigh through pursed lips. "I'm not going to walk out on you guys. I'm not capable of walking away from a mission once it starts. It's just something that gets grafted into the DNA of a Navy frogman. But I'm begging you to please leave the past in the past."

David and Rachel nodded. "Okay," they said in unison.

"And don't start talking about stupid Muggles, the Dark Lord, and how Sarah Beth got an invitation to Hogwarts . . . deal?" he said, breaking the tension and forcing a smile.

"Deal," David said. When Rachel didn't respond, he shot her a look.

"Deal," she said grudgingly, but for a fleeting instant Jed thought he might have seen the slightest curl in the corner of her lips.

"All right," Jed said. Even if he was tempted to believe in Rachel's desperate fantasy, they still had no idea where Sarah Beth was, so what difference did it make? If Rachel was wrong, the math said their daughter was likely dead already. If she was right, they had little time left and no target for him to hit. If he was going to do this, he needed everyone on the same page. "In the Teams, before every mission we had what we called a pre-op brief. This is our pre-op brief for retrieving Sarah Beth. First and foremost, every mission is given an operation call sign—like Operation Crusader or Operation Bright Falcon. Rachel, what do you want to call this mission?"

"You're serious?" she said.

"Dead serious. It's important."

"Okay, then I want it to be Operation Daniel," she said, crossing her arms and raising her chin. "Because it won't be us, alone, who rescues our little girl from this lion's den. This rescue can only be done with God's help."

Jed smiled. She wasn't going to give it up, and maybe he shouldn't try so hard to make her. Rachel needed to feel like God was on their side, and that was fine.

"Okay," he said. "I like it. Operation Daniel it is. And now that our operation has a name, the next, absolutely critical piece of information is a location. Without a location, there is no mission. So unless God Himself has seen fit to tell you where on Earth—"

"We know where she is," Rachel said.

"What?" Jed gawked at her. "Since when?"

"Since about an hour ago," David said. "We've been working on it together."

"That's incredible," Jed said, both his voice and expression dubious. "How?"

David reached down into his backpack and pulled out a notebook computer. Jed rose and walked to stand behind David. Looking over David's shoulder, Jed watched him open a browser window, pull up Google Maps, and load a saved location using satellite view. David zoomed the image to full screen, revealing a small compound on a tree-cleared hillside somewhere in the Smoky Mountains. The tactician in Jed immediately began to plan what a covert assault on the compound would look like.

"We believe she's in the main building . . . here." David moved an arrow over the large, two-story house in the center of the acre or so of cleared area. The house was flanked by smaller buildings: To the north, a long, narrow, flat-roofed structure that could be a barn—or a bunkhouse for an army of shooters. To the south, a building that looked like a multivehicle garage. "We believe she is in this room, on the second floor, looking east."

Jed tore his eyes away from the screen and looked back and forth between Rachel and David. "But how?"

"We just know," Rachel said simply. She stared at him defiantly from beside her husband, the computer open between them.

Jed pursed his lips and crossed his arms on his chest, nodding. "Knowing the source of intelligence is crucial in decision making when planning an op like this. I believe you," he said, trying to sound as if he actually believed her, "but I need to know *how* you know."

David and Rachel looked at each other, silent communication occurring with their eyes—like married couples who were intimately connected, he thought with an internal grimace. Then Rachel gave a slight nod and looked down at her hands.

David spoke for them. "Rachel and Sarah Beth—because of Sarah Beth's gift—have a very powerful connection. At times, they can have entire conversations in their minds. This is most powerful when they're in physical contact, and we worried it may not work at all from a long distance. But Rachel believes she received . . ." Rachel looked up abruptly, shooting him a sharp look, and David held up a hand in surrender. "Rachel *did* receive very clear images from Sarah Beth that allowed us to determine where she is."

"Go on," Jed prompted, exasperation creeping in.

David zoomed out from the compound and Jed watched it shrink away to a small green patch in the middle of the woods. He now saw it sat on the face of a forest-covered mountain, and to the north was a valley, checkered with small farms and a few small buildings. A winding road, like a service road that Jed doubted was paved, wrapped around the mountain containing the compound, heading south, and then climbing the next mountain peak in a series of switchbacks.

"See this?" David asked, using the mouse pad to manipulate the arrow to the top of the more southeastern mountain, where the switchback access road ended in a square field, significantly smaller than the compound they had shown him. A tiny white dot, surrounded by a circle, sat in the very middle of the square cleared of trees.

"Yeah?" Jed said. "Strange-looking. Another little house?"

"No," David said and zoomed in.

Jed now saw that the structure was a conical white tower, like a beacon, in the center of a circle of fencing and post lights. He leaned in for a better look. As he did, he felt a bark of pain in his left hip, which he shooed away.

"What is that?" he asked. "Some sort of signaling device? Or an antenna of some kind?"

"It's a VOR station—a very high frequency omnidirectional radio beacon. Pilots use them as a navigation tool in aircraft. About ten years ago I got my private pilot's license, and flying around Tennessee, Kentucky, and North Carolina has become a real passion for me—" David waved away the unnecessary rambling. "Anyway, there's a VOR station on the field I fly from, and I recognized this immediately from her description."

"Okay," Jed said, intrigued now. "But there must be thousands of these all over the country if they're used for aircraft navigation, right?"

"Yes, of course," David said. "And that was the challenge." He reached into his backpack again and pulled out what looked like a map. "From Sarah Beth's images in Rachel's mind, we could tell she must be within a mile or less of the VOR and was looking slightly up on it, and Rachel saw mountains like those we're familiar with—rolling Tennessee-type hills. Of course, we also wanted her to be close, so we put that bias in." He had spread out the map on the table now. "This is an aviation sectional chart where you can see landmarks on the ground, which appear on the chart. We began by finding mountains like what Rachel saw in all directions from Nashville. These—" he tapped a finger on a symbol on the chart, a sort of circle with three nubs on it, making it appear somewhat triangular—"are VOR stations, and the rectangles beneath them give the names and frequencies for tuning them in."

Jed saw now that there were VOR stations, especially east and west of Nashville, in the rolling mountains, which had been highlighted in yellow. Each then had a penciled circle around it. "I still don't see how you could have determined that it was this station you were seeing. Don't they all kind of look alike? And it looks like you've circled a bunch of them here—in all directions."

"We had another data point," David said, beaming and gesturing to Rachel.

Rachel looked up at Jed, crossing her arms before she spoke. She used to do the same thing when they were dating in high school and she would lecture him about letting David get him into trouble. Jed shook the memory away.

"Sarah Beth showed me other imagery as well," she said. "Pictures out her window and of the shadows of her building and those around her. From that we sketched a rough guess of what the property must look like."

Jed smiled now and nodded, impressed. He saw where they

were going with this, and it was actually quite brilliant. Though it did begin with the crazy premise that their twelve-year-old girl could beam visions to her mom from hundreds of miles away.

Still . . .

"With that," David said, "we picked the VOR stations you see highlighted here. Then we turned to Google Earth, zoomed in, and scoured the mile radius around each, searching for something resembling what Rachel had seen."

"We found it," Rachel said softly. "With God's help."

"Amen to that," David agreed. "The soft whisper of the Holy Spirit guided us." The couple locked eyes again and smiled. Then David turned back to the computer. "Most of the VORs were easy to exclude because they had little or nothing in a one-mile radius. We found a few possibilities, but this one—" he pointed at the compound he had scrolled back over to—"looked right."

"It's exactly right," Rachel corrected. "And based on the angle of her view of the station, we can tell she is in the rear of the main house—facing east—and on the second floor. This . . ." She looked up at Jed, her finger pointing toward the computer, her face desperate for signs he believed her. "This is where my little girl is."

"Okay," Jed said, not sure what else to say. He'd decided, no matter his skepticism about the method, to show no hints of his doubts. And frankly, once you got past the hard-to-accept, supernatural way the images were provided, the rest was truly genius and fit perfectly. "So where is this, exactly?"

David scrolled out, shrinking the image of the compound and the VOR tower until they were swallowed up in the rolling mountains. To the north, the valleys became small towns, and he saw a large highway to the west and another, running east and west, to the north, perhaps twenty miles or so. David tapped the screen and the image changed from a satellite view to a map view.

"The VOR is here—" he showed him with the arrow—"right on the Tennessee–North Carolina border. The compound is here . . ."

"In the middle of the Cherokee National Forest," Jed finished, recognizing the map features now. "That's a stone's throw east of Pigeon Forge and Gatlinburg—maybe only four hours or so from here."

"That, Senior Chief Johnson," David said, "is the target compound for the mission you are planning. The place the hostage is. The target for Operation Daniel."

Jed paced away, tugging at his chin and ignoring the burning pain in his hip. He allowed himself, almost as if on a dare, a short, concise prayer, his eyes still open.

Is this real, God? You gotta give me something here.

There were no words, no flashes of light, and definitely no burning bush, but he was instantly filled with a sense of peace, confidence, and purpose. He felt—he believed—that the compound was real and that Sarah Beth was there just as David and Rachel claimed she was.

"I believe you," he said.

"Oh, thank God. What are our next steps?" David said with more hope and enthusiasm on his face than Jed had seen since that first meeting in the Vandy bookstore.

"I swap vehicles, gear up, and head east," Jed said.

"Aren't you going to rest?" David said.

"Yeah, but not here. Like I said, I don't know what's going on with Nashville PD and this case, but I want to put some distance between me and this town first. Don't worry; I'll find a place to rest before . . . before I get her out."

"Okay, well, let me use the restroom real quick, and I'll meet you both in the parking lot." David started to leave, but Jed grabbed his arm. "I know, I know; we got the things you need and a vehicle."

"David, you get that I'm going alone, right?"

"Absolutely not," Rachel answered for them both. "This is our daughter. We're coming with you."

"Look, I get it, I do—you want to save your little girl. When David and I first spoke, I told him I didn't know if I could help because as a Navy SEAL I'm an operator, not an investigator. Point me to the door and I'll kick it in and capture the high-value target, kill the bad guys, and rescue the hostage. That's what I do, and I do it better than anyone in the world. This isn't me being a lone wolf or trying to be some hero. The complete opposite in fact. They call us Team Guys for a reason. If you were brother SEALs, we would do this together—as a team—but you're not operators. You'll only slow me down and risk getting everyone killed, including Sarah Beth."

"Wait one minute," David said, his face flashing with hot emotion. "Okay, you want Rachel to stay behind, fine—we need someone here to interact with Nashville police anyway. But I'm not some pansy who will get in your way. Maybe you think you trade in your manhood when you accept the call to the ministry, but you're wrong. I was more of a man than you when we were kids, and I'm more of a man now than I was then." Then, nearly shouting, he said, "She's my daughter, Jed. And I'm going."

"This is not me questioning your manhood, David," Jed said, fresh irritation blossoming at the man who had stolen his girl, usurped his dream of ministry, and now was trying to tell him how to do *his* job. "Being a man and being an operator are very different things."

Jed moved with lightning speed—knocking David off-balance and then locking him up in a standing choke hold. He applied pressure to David's carotid artery and felt pity as his onetime friend flailed helplessly in his grip. Before David blacked out, Jed released him and shoved him aside. He pulled the Cold Steel mega folder from his pocket and opened its six-inch blade still covered in dried blood.

Rachel gasped and David's eyes went wide.

"Are you trained to take a life? Because I am," Jed said, dropping into a combat stance with the knife. David backpedaled as Jed advanced on him. "Take the blade from me, David. Do it . . . show me what you've got."

"Jed, stop it!" Rachel said, her voice hard but also ripe with fear.

He whirled to face her, showing her his warrior's soul. "Do I frighten you? Do I?"

"Yes," she stammered.

"This is nothing. Nothing!" he snapped. "You have no idea what this task you've begged me to undertake requires. Neither of you are physically, tactically, or emotionally prepared for combat. And make no mistake, into combat is where I am going."

Husband and wife stared at him, slack-jawed and cowed.

"I didn't realize," Rachel said, looking from his eyes to the blade and back again.

"David, you're no shooter. If you come on this mission, you'll be baggage I can't afford to carry. That's not an insult; it's a fact. Our best chance of saving your daughter is for me to go alone. And I think now you understand that."

"But she's my daughter," David insisted but with less zeal.

"I know, and for the record," Jed continued, his irritation rising instead of falling, "I have never felt that ministers weren't men. Pastor Tobias was a mentor and friend, and I never thought he was soft or weak or anything other than a real man—not just when I was a kid, but now, as a Navy SEAL. But if you want me to get Sarah Beth, I'm doing it alone," he said, putting the knife away.

David nodded and walked out of the library, leaving Jed with Rachel in a cloud of suffocating awkwardness.

He looked at her, and she met his gaze.

"That was unnecessary, what you just did," she said, narrowing her eyes at him.

"I disagree," he said, straightening his shoulders and staring down at her. "The two of you have no idea what you're asking of me."

"I can say the same about you," she fired back. "You still don't get it, do you?"

"Oh, I think I do, and more than you know," he said with a tight smile. "But what I don't get is you. You won't even look me in the eyes."

"What did you think would happen, Jed?" she said with a pitying laugh, her eyes suddenly glossy. "That you'd show up here and everything would be okay? That *we'd* be okay? That everything would magically click back into place, and all would be forgiven? We'd be the three musketeers?"

"The truth is . . . I didn't."

"You didn't what?"

"I didn't have any expectations. I just figured what needed to happen would happen."

"Unbelievable," she said, shaking her head. "You haven't changed a bit. I'll see you in the parking lot. I'm going to go thank Father Newman."

"Hold on," he said, catching her by the arm and stopping her as she tried to walk away. "Maybe I don't get it . . . How can you still hate me after all these years?"

"Because you left us, you selfish bastard," she said, pulling her arm free from his grip. "You left us both, and you took all your light with you."

PART II

THE SEARCHING

The Lord has made everything for its purpose,

even the wicked for the day of trouble.

PROVERBS 16:4, ESV

CHAPTER THIRTEEN

Jed was on mission.

And it wasn't just the fact that he had a righteous objective, a target location, and a plan that put him in a jacked, mission state of mind. He felt a sense of task and purpose that seemed to come from somewhere else . . . a higher authority than just some head shed. He could try to run from that belief—and when this was over, he might do just that—but he couldn't deny the peace he felt inside. The meeting with David and Rachel at the Cathedral of the Incarnation had been difficult and yet cathartic at the same time.

He glanced at the duffel bag on the passenger seat of the old brown pickup truck he navigated eastbound on I-40. His confidence level would kick up a few more notches if magically that bag could somehow be filled with a SOPMOD M4 assault rifle, ten extra magazines, grenades, flash-bangs, night-vision goggles, and an MBITR radio linked to a Predator drone giving him real-time ISR and fire support from on high.

And you can throw in a couple of SEALs for good measure . . .

But he didn't have any of those things.

He let out a whistling breath. He had eight hundred dollars in cash, a small backpack, a widemouthed water bottle, energy bars, a portable charger for the iPhone David had given him, which he was using to navigate from a cup holder phone mount, a Sig Sauer P365 pistol, a butane lighter, an emergency mylar camping blanket, binoculars, and ammunition. A gorgeous Mossberg 500 Centennial Edition hunting shotgun—that apparently belonged to Rachel's father—hung in a truck gun rack behind the bench seat. Great for a close-in dogfight, the Mossberg was hardly tactical. It had no long-distance precision, carried only a five plus one load, and was pump-action—each round needing to be advanced manually by the shooter. He had plenty of extra shells, but reloading after every five rounds during a gunfight was not ideal.

It is what it is.

He stayed in the right lane as the eastbound highway split, the left lane continuing east toward Virginia and his lane bending south toward the Great Smoky Mountains. As he piloted the pickup south, the sun rotated to his left and he flipped up the visor, grateful for a break from hours of squinting.

If only I'd thought to ask for sunglasses.

With no adrenaline from the hunt and nothing to generate a heightened state of readiness, exhaustion was creeping in and he could feel it dulling his alertness. He knew sleep was a valuable weapon, knew he needed that edge, but with no idea what awaited him in the Smoky Mountains, he couldn't risk getting picked up by the state police, asleep in some rest area, so he'd chosen to forge ahead and rest when the opportunity presented itself. His plan was to hit the compound under the cover of darkness and exfiltrate Sarah Beth at night, which meant he had twelve-plus hours to burn on the hike in. As a SEAL, sleeping during the day was something that had become second nature to him, and he couldn't imagine not finding shelter in woods as vast as the Cherokee National Forest.

But first, I gotta make a pit stop.

The town of Hartford was little more than a swell between I-40 and the Pigeon River as the highway cut through the Cherokee National Forest. He was only ten or fifteen minutes from the small burg and decided it was probably his last and best chance to refuel and take care of business. *I don't suspect I'll run into Corporal Alexander, murderous street bums, or Suburbans with blacked-out windows here,* he decided with a chuckle. He zoomed in on the map by spreading thumb and finger on the screen and then smiled as dining icons began to populate the screen. The Pigeon River Smokehouse would be the perfect place to cure the hunger gnawing a hole in his stomach. But when a little coffee cup icon materialized with the name Bean Trees Café, he got really fired up. A huge plate of barbecue and a giant cup of coffee was the fuel his body desperately needed. Also, he needed a break from the road so he could study the satellite imagery with fresh eyes and finalize the plan for his one-man assault on the compound where Sarah Beth was being held.

Jed growled out a yawn as he exited the highway a few minutes later. He saw the sign for the Pigeon River Smokehouse, boasting "The Best Pork Bar-B-Q Around," but couldn't resist heading for the Bean Trees Café first—all the while imagining he could see the aroma trail leading to the coffeehouse, like in a cartoon. With a smile on his face, he pulled the beat-up pickup into a parking spot in the coffee shop's small gravel lot and turned off the ignition. He rolled his head and stretched his back, twisting his shoulders right and then left, both earning satisfying pops while stretching his aching muscles. His left hip screamed in protest as he unfolded his six-foot-four frame out of the too-small truck cab. Balancing on his right foot, he raised his left knee and pulled it toward his chest to stretch out his hip flexors and hamstrings—the burning pain in his cramped muscles strangely comforting. While he stretched, Jed scanned the parking lot and street behind for any eyes that might be on him. Finding no persons or vehicles of concern, he limped his way to the entrance of the log cabin–style café, all the while cursing under his breath as he waited for his hip to loosen up.

He pulled open the door and to his surprise was hit by the aroma of a short-order grill, which almost, but not quite, overpowered the roasted coffee. As he scanned the chalkboard menu behind the counter, he noted the joint had an impressive sandwich and burger lineup in addition to coffee and baked goods. He considered his options while a young couple dressed in full-on hiking gear—all brand-spanking-new and no doubt bought online—ordered. While he had no doubt that the Pigeon River

Smokehouse's barbecue would be as good as the sign advertised, one particular offering on the menu caught his eye.

And why not kill two birds with one stone at this quaint café?

"Help y'all?" the woman at the register asked when it was his turn.

"I'll have a Venti double-shot latte, please," he said, defaulting to Starbucks ordering lingo.

"Extra-large double-shot latte—got it," the barista said, smiling at him in her brightly flowered dress. "What else?"

"I'll have the Kohlen burger, please," he said, the pun not lost on him as the burger had a fried egg on top, along with jalapeños, cheese, bacon, and fried pickles. "With fries," he added. "And a sweet tea in a to-go cup."

"You got it, darlin'," she said. "Eatin' on the patio?"

"Yeah," he answered.

"What's y'all's name, sugar?"

He froze for just a second, then shook off the paranoia. "Jeff," he said.

The girl wrote *Jeff* in flowery cursive on a card and pressed it into a card holder stand, which she handed him. "Wait a sec and I'll get your coffee now."

He watched her make his order with practiced efficiency, the whole time his body practically aching for the caffeine. The smell of the espresso and the sound of steaming milk was pure torture that lasted until he had the double latte in his hands. Grinning with anticipation, he headed out the side door. Once outside, he spied the perfect spot on an expansive deck dining area that looked down onto the scenic river behind the café. Positioning himself strategically, he took a seat at the corner table where he had a view of the café, the entire deck, and the street entrance to the parking lot on the north side of the building. His back to no one, the location also afforded him the ability to keep an eye on Hartford Road through the trees.

The coffee worked its magic almost immediately, and he felt renewed energy that had to be at least partially a placebo effect since most of the caffeine was still in his cup and not yet coursing through his veins. He casually scanned his environment and couldn't resist a broad smile when he locked eyes with a little boy at a picnic table where he sat with his two sisters and parents. The boy gave Jed a salute. Jed winked and saluted back. *I probably should have changed clothes,* he thought, suddenly and acutely aware that his coyote-gray T-shirt, Group Two ball cap, slick BDU-style cargo pants, and hiking boots screamed *operator chic.* The kid's dad gave him a "thank you for your service" nod, and Jed nodded back.

Moments later, the girl from the counter arrived carrying a basket with a steaming, egg-topped burger and fries. The aroma lifted his spirits almost as high as the coffee. His first bite was an eyes-closed, carnivorous celebration in his mouth—savory charbroiled beef, salty bacon, creamy melted cheese, spicy jalapeño, and sweet fried pickle. *Heaven in a bun.* He devoured it in what felt like seconds and soon found himself scavenging the last french fry from under the white paper of the red plastic basket. He dragged it through the drippings of the best burger he'd ever had in his life and popped it in his mouth.

With a long, contented sigh, he opened the mapping app on his phone and zoomed out from his location. He needed to get to Grassy Fork Road to start his infil. From here, he could either take local back roads or hop back on I-40 south and exit at Green Corner Road. The latter option not only looked like it had fewer switchbacks, but it took him through a much more remote stretch of the mountains, where he was less likely to encounter any prying eyes. Next he studied the terrain and identified a series of waypoints for the hike out and entered them into the map application.

Preparations complete, he tapped off his phone screen and scanned the area before departing. This time, his heart rate shot up, and not from his double-shot latte. In the corner of the post office parking lot next door, he spied a parked gray Suburban. He forced himself not to stare at it directly and instead made a long, painful show of being unperturbed—returning his attention to his phone and burning time by scrolling through the news feed. After a couple minutes, he rose slowly, gathered his coffee, and headed back inside the café. He resisted the urge to touch the Sig Sauer P365 in the small-of-the-back holster he was wearing. The compact Sig was a smaller, thinner, and far more comfortable carry than his P229, and he imagined far less noticeable to even the trained eye. The inside of the café had two patrons, neither of whom he identified as a concern. With a tip of his gray NAVSPECWARGRUTWO ball cap to the barista in the flowery dress, he headed out to the parking area.

He saw no other suspicious vehicles in the Bean Trees Café parking lot, but that was little comfort. The Suburban next door could easily contain as many as seven or eight heavily armed men. Behind those darkened windows, he had no way to tell what or who was waiting for him. He unlocked the door of his pickup and folded himself into the driver's seat. Tapping his fingers on the steering wheel, he made a decision.

I need to know for sure . . .

Jed started the truck's engine and casually piloted the pickup back onto Hartford Road heading north. He watched in the rearview mirror and hoped he was mistaken. The Chevy Suburban was a hugely popular SUV, and gray was probably the most popular color. Surely this one belonged to a family on a camping vacation in the Cherokee National Forest. But when he spied a second identical gray Suburban parked behind an RV in the Pigeon River Smokehouse parking lot, he could no longer pretend away their presence as coincidence.

Jed accelerated toward the highway, but at the last second, he jerked the wheel and made a right turn onto Big Creek Road before the on-ramp. He passed the smokehouse, drove under the I-40 overpass, and turned in to the Citgo gas station and food mart. Instead of pulling up to a pump, he parked in front of the food mart and glanced in his rearview mirror.

I should have just enough time to make this work, he thought as he grabbed the Mossberg and stuffed it into the bag. The duffel was big, but not big enough to swallow a shotgun, and the buttstock stuck out the end of the zipper run. Cursing, he zipped it closed as best he could and climbed out of the pickup. Ditching here was going to delay his timetable for sure. On foot, it was five miles as the crow flies to the target compound, but these were the Smoky Mountains and he was no crow.

Plan for twice that, he told himself.

Disappearing into the woods was his only play now that he'd confirmed he was being surveilled by the crooked cops, the FBI, or whatever evil cabal was behind this. Jed slung the handles of the duffel over his shoulder, pulled open the glass doors of the food mart, and stepped inside.

"Morning," he called with a cheerful smile to the long-haired boy at the register, while angling his broad torso to hide the butt-stock of the Mossberg.

The kid just gave him a chin nod.

"Restrooms?" Jed asked.

"In the back," the kid said.

Jed nodded a thank-you and headed down the short hall. The men's restroom was located on his left. He tried the door and found the single-stall restroom unoccupied. After stepping inside, he turned on the water tap at the sink and then looked for a window to crawl out. Finding none, he did the next best thing and used the push-button lock on the handle to lock the bathroom door from the inside.

"This ought to buy me a minute or two," Jed murmured as he stepped out into the hall and closed the door behind him. He swiveled left, toward the emergency exit, and saw no wires or alarm box near the door. Praying there was no siren, he pushed the beater bar and slipped out—silently—into the sunshine behind the food mart.

Not wasting any time, he sprinted across the shallow back lot and into the woods abutting the service station. He figured he had five to seven minutes before the SUVs arrived. Hopefully, the imaginary dude camped out in the bathroom would keep them guessing awhile before they figured out he'd escaped on foot into the woods. Even with his nagging hip, he could run for miles flat out. Unless they were elite athletes or had ATVs, they wouldn't be able to catch up.

He was a Navy SEAL after all.

CHAPTER FOURTEEN

SOMEWHERE

AFTER DINNER

PROBABLY FRIDAY, EARLY EVENING

Sarah Beth could hear Fake Grandma coming. Well, not so much *hear* but rather feel the woman's thoughts rumbling closer and closer. Like a thunderstorm. After spending most of her childhood trying to ignore the thoughts and voices randomly invading her mind, now Sarah Beth was trying to harness them. She suspected that in this place, the "gift" she never wanted might, ironically, be her salvation.

Despite the darkness of her situation, things were looking up. She'd had a huge breakthrough yesterday and connected with her mom. At first, the connection had been weak and muddy, but as they both zeroed in on each other, it had become strong. Sarah Beth didn't know much about radios, but her dad had once tried to explain the concept of tuning to different frequencies. She was beginning to think her gift might work something like that, where each person's mind had a different frequency and the trick was figuring out how to dial in.

If only I had somebody to teach me.

Fake Grandma was close now. Sarah Beth had gotten so calibrated to the woman's aura that she could predict when she'd hear footsteps on the stairs, followed by the sound of the creaky board in the hall outside her room, and finally the key in the lock.

Like right now.

In three, two, one . . .

The board groaned and a moment later, the heavy key rattled loudly in the lock.

Sarah Beth sat on the edge of the bed, hands in her lap, as the woman let herself in. Fake Grandma greeted her with a saccharine sweet smile and the malodorous cloud of negative emotion she exuded everywhere she went. Hatred floated to the top of that toxic stew the woman called a mind—hatred not only for Sarah Beth, but also for some larger, unfortunate group that this woman loathed and named Sarah Beth a member of.

"And how are you this evening, sweetie?" Fake Grandma asked from the doorway. "Did you enjoy your dinner?"

"I want to go home," Sarah Beth said flatly.

"I know, dear, but today you get to meet someone very special instead—someone who is going to help you understand all of this.

I know this must be quite confusing, but Victor will help you see why your visit here is for your own good."

I hate you. I hope you drop dead.

Fake Grandma cocked her head to the side, reminding Sarah Beth of the look her grandparents' goldendoodle, Grace, used whenever she didn't quite understand a command.

"I'm sorry, dear. Did you say something?"

"I said I want to go home," Sarah Beth repeated, getting to her feet. She had an experiment she was desperate to conduct, but she was also deathly afraid of what could happen when she did. If it went wrong, she risked losing the only advantage she had.

"Well, that's not going to happen tonight," the woman said after a rather long pause. "Come along. I want you to meet my friend. You'll really like him . . ."

A chilling image flashed in Sarah Beth's mind but disappeared too fast for her to make out the details.

A face? A cruel and terrible face . . .

With the image came a profound sense of dread. Suddenly her insides felt like they were filled with black slime, but she mustered up her best little-girl smile and obediently walked toward the door. As she reached Fake Grandma, she glanced at the woman's left apron pocket—the one that held the key. A brass chain grew out of that pocket and wrapped around the woman's skinny, drooping neck. In the right apron pocket, Sarah Beth spied a little notebook and three different colored pens.

It's now or never, she told herself, gathering her courage.

"I'm scared, Nana," she said, using the term of endearment for the very first time. "I miss my mommy and daddy."

Before her keeper could respond, Sarah Beth reached out and

touched the woman's hands, which were knit together in a tight bony knot resting against her stomach. At the same time she made contact, Sarah Beth pushed a simple thought into Fake Grandma's head.

Put a pen on the dresser. Put a pen on the dresser . . .

The woman recoiled at the touch and shivered, and for a moment something scary—like an animation special effect—rippled across her face. It was as if a new face were superimposed on top—something twisted and snarling and not human. It flashed momentarily and then disappeared, leaving only a faint amber glow around the woman's eyes that faded slowly until it was gone too.

Fake Grandma shivered once more and quickly summoned her fake smile.

"It's okay, my dear," she said and stepped past Sarah Beth toward the dresser. "There's no reason to be frightened."

Sarah Beth said nothing, just watched with amazement as the woman reached into her apron pocket and, with trembling bony fingers, retrieved the green pen clipped to the right pocket flap.

"I know this is confusing, little one," Fake Grandma continued without missing a beat while gently placing the pen on the dresser, "but it will all be over soon. All's well that ends well."

Stupefied, Sarah Beth did her best to conceal her shock and amazement at what she'd just witnessed. Did Fake Grandma know she'd left the pen behind? It almost looked like she'd done it subconsciously, without bodily awareness.

Or what if she's trying to trick me?

"Okay, Nana," she said softly, looking at her feet, a five-year-old cowed to obedience. "I trust you."

"That's my girl. Now come along," Fake Grandma said, stepping aside and gesturing with her left hand to the hall outside the open door.

Sarah Beth padded into the hall, eager but frightened to take her first steps out of her pretend little girl's room prison since her arrival. She paused, letting Fake Grandma lead the way down the hall with its dark wood floor and ugly flowered wallpaper.

This looks like an old person's house, she thought, *not a summer camp.*

A board creaked its familiar groan halfway down the hall. Not until they reached the staircase did Sarah Beth realize she'd gone barefoot. She made a mental note not to make that mistake when she tried to escape later. As she trudged down the wooden steps, she was careful to keep to the middle of the bloodred runner carpet, hands clasped in front of her like Fake Grandma did. For some reason, Sarah Beth was afraid to touch the dark wood of the ornate banister. With each step she descended, her heart rate climbed. Anticipatory terror clawed at her throat and made it hard to breathe. She tugged at the neck of her T-shirt to keep it from touching her skin.

She felt cold and small and weak.

Who is Victor and what is he going to do to me?

She began to shiver as her imagination took a dark turn. Her parents kept her sheltered, but she wasn't stupid. She could imagine what happened to girls like her who got kidnapped . . .

At the bottom of the staircase, she followed Fake Grandma across a nice foyer. Sunlight streamed in through rectangular beveled-glass panels in an enormous, heavy-looking door. Dust motes danced in three distinct yellow rays, giving the foyer a strange and otherworldly look. Across the space, a cased archway revealed a long dining table that appeared to be carved from a single piece of thick, chunky wood. At the far end sat the man she assumed must be Victor, elbows propped on the table and long, sallow fingers pressed together like the steeple of a church. He had a thin face and smiled at her through a neatly trimmed goatee. His onyx-colored eyes met hers as she hesitated under the wooden archway. Seeing no amber glow in those dark eyes, she tried to read him, but she got absolutely nothing from the man.

"Ah, Sarah Beth," he said, his voice a cello's moan.

What a weird thing for me to think.

She said nothing while her heart pounded like a bass drum in her chest.

Victor sat frozen and unblinking; had his lips not moved, she might have thought him a statue.

"It is lovely to finally meet you, my dear," he said and then finally moved, his right arm indicating that she sit in the high-backed wooden chair beside him.

"I want to go home," she choked out, her voice cracking. This time the little-girl quality was anything but an act. She felt a sudden urge to conform, to obey his invitation to sit. Then, as if sleepwalking, she moved slowly along the table and settled into the seat beside him.

Is he doing to me what I did to Fake Grandma with the pen?

A chill ran down her spine at the thought.

"Please let me go home," she said, this time not looking at him.

"I know you want to go home, Sarah Beth," Victor said, his voice no longer a low, sad note. Now it felt warm, almost comforting, and that realization frightened her even more. "I know you miss your parents—Rachel and David—and that is normal. But don't you sometimes feel like they're holding you back?"

"Holding me back?" she echoed. "I don't understand."

"I can only imagine how frustrating it must be for a young woman like you to be treated like a child. Always being told where to go, what to do, how to think. That's not how you deserve to be treated. . . ."

He's right, she realized. *They're always trying to control me. Always bossing me around . . .*

"And they don't understand your gift or appreciate how talented you truly are, especially David."

She looked down at her hands, which she was surprised to see were balled into fists. It was true—her parents did treat her like a child. Like a baby. Her father was unable, or at least unwilling, to even discuss her gift.

That judgy look he always gets on his face. He even claimed I was making it all up. And Rachel . . . She shook her head. *No, it's Mom. I've never thought of her as Rachel . . .*

"Rachel treats you like a fragile little girl instead of embracing the woman you know you're becoming."

They don't understand you.

They don't understand me . . .

Panic gripped her. She looked up at him and found confirmation in his smile. Victor was in her head, violating her thoughts. A wave of nausea swept over her and she buckled at the waist.

Get out of my head! she screamed in her mind. Then, as if a switch had been flipped, her fear and nausea disappeared.

"I won't treat you like that here. I will respect and cherish your gifts," he said, and she realized he was now standing on the opposite side of the table from her, shadows and light from the breaks in the heavy curtain behind her dancing across his face.

She exhaled an unsteady breath, wondering if she'd stopped him or if he'd taken pity on her and released her.

"Where was Rachel taking you last Saturday when we rescued you, Sarah Beth?"

"My mom," she said, clutching tight to the word, "was taking me to meet some people. I'm interviewing for a private school. It's for special kids like me."

"They want to send you away," Victor said, nodding. "That's because they're afraid of you. Afraid of the gifts that David refuses to talk about, aren't they? They want to send you away because you scare them. But what they didn't tell you is that once you go to the special school, you become a slave. They'll make you use your gift for their own purposes until you've burned it up. And after that, nobody will want you. You don't want that to happen, do you?"

Her brain screamed that the words were lies—she *knew* they were lies because the school had been her idea . . . hadn't it? But she felt the crush of sorrow. The weight of abandonment.

What are you doing to me?

"That's not true," she whispered breathlessly.

"What's that?" Victor asked, cupping his hand to his left ear. "I'm sorry; I can't hear you."

"Nothing," she whimpered, her gaze in her lap.

Victor paced back to the head of the table, his feet making no sound, almost as if he glided across the dark-red-and-gold area rug instead of walking.

"We believe in you, Sarah Beth, and that's why we rescued

you—rescued you from parents who don't appreciate or understand you and a school full of bad people who want to use you."

"You kidnapped me! You stole me from my parents." She looked up, powered by a flash of anger. The skin on Victor's face rippled, not like the weird special effect thing that happened to Fake Grandma, but like an undulating nest of snakes. She was about to tell him, *You are the bad people*, but what she was watching made her reconsider.

He circled behind her and her inner voice screamed alarm. Time to leap from the chair and run . . . run to the forest, where the creatures were far less terrifying than this man—or whatever he was. But she was paralyzed; her backside felt glued to the chair. She bowed her head as if in prayer, or perhaps some other form of submission, and began to sob.

Long, sallow fingers slid onto her shoulders like icy serpents and squeezed.

With his touch, her mind filled with horrifying images—images of demon-masked killers massacring children, women, men, in the cathedral she'd seen in her dreams. But then the images were sucked out of her—vacuumed from her mind by the cold skeleton hands on her shoulders. New images flooded her brain, and she heard herself cry out in anguish and pain as they harassed her mind's eye, like oncoming traffic zipping at speed on a two-way street. She wanted to stop them—to block them—but she was powerless to do so. Imagery of unspeakable evil, of executions and beheadings, children killed in a dusty desert town and people nailed to walls, men in orange jumpsuits kneeling on a beach with black-clad figures butchering them from behind, one by one . . .

Image after image filled her mind and all she could do was scream.

When she couldn't take it anymore, the cold, bony fingers released her shoulders.

She felt herself pitch forward as if she'd lost all muscle control, and her forehead smashed painfully onto the heavy wooden table with a dull thud. Unable to lift her own head, she stayed in that position and cried, uncontrollable sobs racking her body.

Victor returned to the chair at the head of the table. "Oh, Sarah Beth," he said, his voice warm oil. "It seems I overwhelmed you. I am sorry; that was not my intention."

Her strength returning, she raised her head. Tears chased down her cheeks and then hung, in hesitant little drops, from her chin. She didn't want to look at him, but she was unable to resist the compulsion.

"You're a monster," she heard herself say, and where the words came from, she did not know.

"So that is how you thank me?" He fixed her with a mirthless, closed-lip smile. "Did you not feel me taking the nightmares from your mind? I only want what's best for you, Sarah Beth, but I can't help you if you won't let me." He looked past her and snapped his fingers, summoning Fake Grandma. "We'll try again tomorrow. Hopefully, after a good night's sleep and in the fresh light of a new day, you'll see me differently."

"Come, dear," Fake Grandma called to her. "Time for bed."

She rose, but weariness dragged her down like an anchor chained to her soul. The weight was almost too much for her to walk, but she shuffled away from the table and Victor. She would have crawled over broken glass to get just a few feet farther away from him. Shoulders slumped, she followed her keeper out of the dining room and into the foyer. But with every foot of separation she put between herself and Victor, she felt a little bit better, a little bit stronger. By the time she'd reached the top of the stairs, she felt like herself again.

Be not afraid; I walk beside you, a voice said in her mind—the old, familiar voice she knew and trusted.

Hope sparked in her chest—lighting an ember she knew she must fan into a raging fire. Because tomorrow would be too late. She understood that now.

The massacre at the cathedral wasn't a nightmare; it was a premonition.

I have to stop it, she thought and then quickly boxed the thought in case Victor was listening.

A groan echoed in the upstairs hallway as she stepped on the noisy floorboard. She made a mental note of its location, picking out a particular flower on the wallpaper and matching it with the third wood panel under the chair rail. Just ahead, Fake Grandma stopped at the threshold to Sarah Beth's room and gestured for her to go inside.

Swallowing down her disgust, Sarah Beth threw her arms around the woman's waist. "Thank you, Nana," she said and squeezed the bony figure tight.

Don't lock the door . . . Don't lock the door . . . Don't lock the door . . .

Recoiling as if she'd touched a hot stove, Fake Grandma jerked herself free from the embrace and defensively clasped her hands against the front of her apron.

"There, there, dear," she said with a painfully fake smile. "It's almost over. Everything will be okay. All's well that ends well."

Sarah Beth summoned a weak smile, nodded, and dutifully stepped into her prison. The door swung shut behind her, closing loudly. She whirled and dropped to her knees in front of the heavy wooden door. Pressing her hands to the wood, she projected her will.

Don't lock the door . . . Don't lock the door . . . Please don't lock the door . . .

She closed her left eye and peered into the keyhole. Her stomach sank as she watched the light disappear and the key enter the lock.

Don't lock the door . . .

She heard a dull click and a scrape.

Don't lock the door . . .

The key started to turn.

Sarah Beth realized in that instant that it wasn't *her* power that mattered. It wasn't her will.

God, it's me—Sarah Beth. Please, God, please. Don't let her lock the door. I'll be brave and true, but please don't let her lock me in tonight.

Still staring into the dark keyhole, she heard the key rattle. Fake Grandma's hand was shaking. Then it went still. Her keeper pulled the key without engaging the bolt, and the dim light shone through the keyhole again.

She listened to fading footsteps and the groan of the board and then silence.

Depleted, Sarah Beth exhaled and with great effort got to her feet. She trudged to her bed, hugged the oversize stuffed bunny tight to her chest, and fixed her gaze on the dresser, where the green pen sat near the corner, the tip hanging just over the edge.

Thank You, Father God. Now please . . . one last thing . . . make me strong.

CHAPTER FIFTEEN

As soon as he saw the fallen tree, Jed knew it was time to stop. The sun was already setting and this was the best cover he'd seen on his trek through the woods so far. The odds of finding something better were slim, and he was exhausted. After ditching his pickup at the Citgo station, he'd pushed himself hard—racing through the woods, backtracking frequently to clear his six, and maintaining a maximum alert level to detect anyone hunting him. Either the mysterious crew that had been tailing him in the Suburbans had not pursued him on foot or he'd outrun them. With darkness falling, it was time to rest. Like all elite operators, Jed considered sleep a weapon, and he needed to lie down before he fell down. He circled the fallen eastern hemlock, a massive specimen with a trunk that even he, with his mighty wingspan, could reach only halfway around. A ten-foot diameter root disk had been unearthed in the falling, and much of the tangled mass was still packed with earth.

Perfect, he thought and knelt to inspect a canoe-shaped depression under the trunk.

Tucked in there he would be well-hidden by the root disk on one side, the trunk above, and dense underbrush on a third side . . . leaving only the entry side he'd need to conceal. He spied a large branch ripped off from a neighboring tree during the fall, and he dragged it over, laying it propped up at an angle so that the foliage blocked his impromptu dugout. Satisfied with the coverage, he shrugged off his pack, lifted the branch with one arm, and slid his pack and the Mossberg shotgun into the hollow. The Sig Sauer P365 now lived on his right thigh—secure, accessible, and out of the way—thanks to a drop holster that David had impossibly located. Unburdened, he shimmied underneath and lowered the branch back into place. He wiggled about until he found a reasonably comfortable reclined position for his extra-large frame and used his pack as a headrest. Outside, dusk settled over the Great Smoky Mountains and the tree frogs and crickets already warmed up for their nocturnal chorus.

Jed grabbed the Mossberg and clutched it to his chest in a relaxed but ready posture. About the same time, a mosquito found him—announcing its arrival with a shrill buzz near his left ear before going silent. "Enjoy your dinner," he murmured, not feeling where the bloodsucker had landed and too tired to care. Sleep found him quickly after that, and his mind transported him back to the place and time of the event he'd spent the vast majority of the past seventeen years trying desperately to forget . . .

The instant Jed stepped out of the car, he could feel the heat.

For years Jed had heard stories from the annual, unofficial "Senior Bonfire" but now they were finally here, just a few months from graduation. Rachel, unwilling to ride tonight with David, who she felt was getting more and more out of control these days, had agreed to meet the boys at the bonfire on the Bailey farm, not far in fact from where Rachel's family lived. Her concern had been well-founded—David was already sipping from the large thermos filled with a horrible combination of liquors he had pilfered from his dad's cabinet—a little of this and a little of that to keep from taking a noticeable amount from any one bottle.

"Whoa, now that's what I call a fire," David said, tipping back his thermos and marveling at the tepee-shaped tower of flames leaping fifteen feet in the air.

"I'm going to go find Rachel," Jed said, shutting the driver's side door.

"Of course you are," David muttered. "Talk about whipped."

Jed ignored the comment and headed toward the upwind side of the raging pyre. Most of the gathered kids were maintaining a wide standoff, but a few fearless idiots were attempting to run up and roast marshmallows on long sticks—only to be repeatedly rebuffed by the heat from the inferno. Gabe Meacham's F-150 seemed to be the focal point of the activity. He had the doors open, radio blaring, and at least a dozen people dancing in the bed. Beer and soda cans littered the ground where the not so recently mowed grass had been trampled flat from the teenage herd.

"Yo, Jedidiah," a familiar male voice called. "Y'all made it. I was startin' to think you might sit this one out."

"No way," Jed said, clasping hands with one of his football teammates, Scot. "You know how I like to roll—always fashionably late."

"I got a longneck Bud in the cooler with your name on it," Scot said. "Feel free to help yourself."

"No thanks, bro. I'm good."

"That's cool," Scot said, then turning to David. "Hey, Dave."

"Scot."

"Looks like you're already good fer," Scot said, nodding at David's thermos.

"Yeah, I brought all my friends," David said with a grin. "Mr. Daniels, Mr. Smirnoff, Mr. Beam, and Captain Morgan."

The comment got a laugh out of Scot and everyone else within earshot. Except Jed, who had tried without success to stop David from raiding his father's liquor cabinet.

"Hey, Scot, have you seen Rachel?" Jed asked, scanning the faces in the firelight and not finding her.

"Yeah, man, she's here," Scot said and made a quick survey of the crowd before adding, "I saw her talking with Stacy. I think maybe they went over to the house. Kenny might have gone with them."

"Okay, thanks." Jed turned to David. "You wanna walk with me over to the house? See if we can find her?"

David exhaled with feigned irritation, took a swig from his thermos, and said, "Sure, maybe Kenny's dad smoked some ribs. Kenny's been bragging about it all week."

"Yeah, cool," Jed said and the two best friends set off toward the house.

"That's kinda weird," David said when they got to the back

patio and found the sliding door wide-open and all the indoor lights turned off.

"No way Kenny's parents are asleep with all this noise," Jed said.

"Kenny told me they went out and promised not to come back till midnight," David said. "I guess that's the same deal they did for his older brother at the bonfire two years ago."

A girl's scream inside the house raised the hair on the back of Jed's neck.

"What was that?" David said.

"That was Rachel!" Jed cried and ran toward where he thought he'd heard the scream coming from. "Rachel . . . ," he shouted, spinning in a circle. When no reply came, he stopped in the downstairs hallway and called again, "Raaaachel!"

David grabbed Jed by the arm, giving him a start.

"Dude, I think I heard something from behind that door," David said and pointed to a closed door behind Jed

Jed whirled and flung the door open, revealing a set of stairs down to a basement. A faint red light glowed at the bottom of the steps, and a wave of dread, fear, and nausea washed over Jed all at once. Despite every primitive instinct in his mind and body telling him to run away, he sprinted down the stairs with David in trail. As he neared the bottom, he heard a pained whimper—like the sound a wounded animal might make—but it was quickly drowned out by another noise . . .

Something carnal and terrible and wicked.

At the bottom of the stairs, he turned, and what he saw defied logic—Rachel, on her back and pinned to the ground beneath a broad-shouldered torso, her skirt hiked up and her blouse ripped open. The male figure on top of her was struggling to pull down his pants with one hand while holding her by the throat with the other. Rachel's eyes were glazed and tears streamed from the corners. Shell-shocked by the scene before him, Jed stood frozen, watching her squirm helplessly under her attacker.

Her gaze ticked to meet his own, and he heard her whisper in his mind—"Help me."

Something snapped inside him and rage took control.

"Get off of her!" Jed shrieked, dragging Rachel's attacker off by the hair.

The man—wait, no, the boy—turned and looked up at him. What Jed saw made his blood run cold. The face in front of him wasn't human. In some part of his brain, he registered that the face belonged to Kenny Bailey, the host of tonight's party and someone Jed had known since kindergarten. But Kenny's face was consumed by another—a grotesque, ghostly visage superimposed on top. The demonic face snarled at Jed, eyes glowing the color of flame. A prickle washed over him and gooseflesh stood up on his arms and legs.

"What the hell?" David stammered behind him.

Rachel screamed and crabbed backward across the cement floor on hands and feet to get away from the monster.

And then Jed was on top of the thing.

Hatred, anger, and homicidal rage exploded from somewhere deep and dark inside him, and he became something more terrifying than his foe. Jed's first blow knocked his classmate's face hard to the left. Kenny's eyes widened in fear, but the other face snarled and laughed with a deep, mocking vibrato. Jed's second blow broke Kenny's nose. He found a rhythm in the beating—right fist, left fist, right fist, left fist. Harder and faster and harder and faster the blows rained down, turning Kenny's face into a bloody pulp. A carnal roar echoed in the basement, and he didn't even register that it was his own.

And then someone was on his back, hammering his shoulders with butterfly blows.

"Stop it! Stop it, Jed; you're killing him!" Rachel screamed.

He whirled and shoved Rachel away, sending her skidding across the floor. Undaunted, he turned his attention back to the creature, closed his hands around its throat, and squeezed. As he did, he watched the twisted demon face peel off the bloody human one and float in the air, dragging a twisted, wiry body with it. The ethereal being, hellish and billowing like smoke, hovered over Kenny. It laughed victoriously, its demon eyes boring into Jed. Then, with a burst of red light, it streaked across the basement, smashed into the far wall, and disappeared, leaving behind a faint orange glow on the cinder block that faded slowly to dark.

"Please, Jed," Rachel begged. She was back again, tugging feebly on his arm while sobbing in lurching, breathless gasps.

He ignored her, consumed with rage and hatred which, instead of fading, seemed to be building to a crescendo inside him.

A raspy voice whispered in his ear, "Do it. Do it with your own hands. It will feel good to watch his light go out . . ."

Jed tightened his grip on Kenny's throat. But as he resumed the choking, another voice, soft and comforting, spoke to him: "Enough, Jed. Let go. It's gone. It's over."

The voice in his mind sounded like that of Pastor Tobias, his youth minister, but Jed knew that was impossible. Still, the words quenched the inferno of violence inside him and he could think clearly again. It was a struggle to unclench his hands from Kenny's throat, like overcoming an alien will trying to control the muscles in his hands and burning forearms, but he did it.

As he released his grip, a slow, wet hiss escaped the boy's purple lips.

"Is he dead?" Rachel asked through a sob from where she knelt beside him.

"What was that thing?" David said over his shoulder.

"Answer me, Jedidiah. Is he dead?" Rachel repeated, her voice frantic now.

Jed turned to look at her. She was barely recognizable—with black mascara tear streaks down her face, bloody teeth from a split upper lip, and an angry bruise on her left cheek swelling her eye shut. He stared at her, jaw slack and mouth open, not sure what to say. Then he looked back at the mess of Kenny beneath him. A rattling hiss of a breath went in and out of the boy's battered face.

"What did you do, Jed?" Rachel said, eyes wide.

"Seriously, Jed, you almost killed him," David said and his voice sounded funny.

Jed reached to comfort Rachel, but she recoiled.

"What?" he said but realized it was him. She was terrified of him. He looked at his hands, his knuckles raw, swollen, and covered in Kenny's blood, and he understood what he'd done . . . understood what he had become.

"God," he said, consumed by fear, anger, and confusion, "God, where were You?"

Jed jerked awake, heart pounding, clutching the Mossberg in a death grip. For a split second, he wasn't sure where he was or, more accurately, *when* he was. Was he teenage Jed or old Jed? He blinked and the scenery did not change. He might as well have had his head in a box it was so dark, but the sounds of tree frogs and crickets sang him out of his stupor.

You're in the woods, under a tree, and on mission to rescue Sarah Beth Yarnell, the SEAL silently reminded him.

He exhaled, swallowed, and closed his eyes.

Now I remember . . .

The fallout after the event, at least for Jed, had been just as traumatic as the incident itself. The nightmares, the gruesome flashbacks, the whispers in the hallways at school . . . all amplified the paranoia that had taken root in his mind that night. Then came the police investigation, the breakup with Rachel, the court case, and him enlisting in the Navy without telling anyone. He clenched his jaw as the many-headed Hydra of regrets started gnawing at his brain. If only he could go back in time—there were so many things he'd do differently.

Don't go there, Jed, not now . . .

The sound of a twig cracking nearby sent a jolt of adrenaline into his bloodstream, instantly cleared his mind, and ramped his muscles from *at rest* to *combat ready*. He shifted his right index finger from the trigger guard to the trigger, kept perfectly still, and listened. For several long seconds, he heard nothing, but this was telling too. The tree frogs and crickets in the immediate vicinity had gone quiet.

He waited.

Not moving.

Pulse pounding in his ears.

He heard a soft crunching sound. And then another. And then another . . .

Footsteps.

He estimated the distance at fifteen yards plus or minus five. Based on the singular, evenly spaced nature of the footfalls, he was 90 percent confident he was listening to a single party moving through the woods alone—either a patrol from the target camp or a hunter. He ruled out the possibility of a lost hiker or camper; in either case, he'd certainly have seen the glint of a flashlight beam.

His time in the Teams had reinforced the power and proof of Occam's razor: *with all unknowns being equal, the simplest explanation is the most likely one.* In this situation, the simplest explanation was that a roving patrol from the target compound was conducting a wide perimeter sweep. But was that really the simplest explanation or his paranoia talking? He was still a few miles from the camp. Did a roving patrol at this range really make sense? He was in the Cherokee National Forest, not Taliban country in the Hindu Kush mountains.

What I'd give for night-vision goggles . . . and my kit with body armor, grenades, and my SOG Bowie, he lamented to himself. *But I'd trade all of that for my SOPMOD M4, with extra magazines and an infrared laser target designator.*

Three more footsteps crunched nearby, each getting successively louder, and then the movement stopped.

If this guy has night vision, I'm probably okay. But if he's using thermal, I'm dead, Jed thought and immediately began to visualize how he would conduct his counteroffensive if shooting started. He would roll out the backside of his hollow, sweep right while ducking low and moving behind the root disk for cover. From a crouching firing stance, he would engage the patrol with the Mossberg and—

A handheld radio crackled, and a static-ridden male voice said, "Four, Base—check in?"

Jed heard a shuffling sound and then a nearby voice, in the clear, answered, "Base, Four—on the northern perimeter, sweep in progress."

"You're five mikes late checking in," the caller came back.

"Yeah, well, sorry. Nature called."

"Understood," the radio voice replied. "Next time, check in first, then take your dump."

The patrolman cursed his colleague on the other end of the radio, then said, "Roger that, will do."

The crunching resumed and Jed listened, finger still tense on the trigger of his shotgun. The footfalls eventually got quieter with each step as the patrolling shooter moved on into the woods. But only after the tree frogs and crickets started singing again did Jed relax and blow out a long, victorious exhale.

Dodged a bullet, he thought but immediately wondered how many perimeter guards they had and what sweep frequency they were using. Like all close calls in tactical environments, the incident had been informative. That the camp was running coordinated perimeter patrols this far out, with radio comms managed by a vigilant commander, told Jed a lot —and none of it good. Any hope that tonight's face-off would pit him against a bunch of hapless hillbilly Bubbas in the woods was now thoroughly and completely dashed. This crew was organized, paranoid, and had resources.

Infiltration was going to be a challenge with this level of vigilance, but executing a successful exfil with a twelve-year-old girl in tow . . . well, that might just be impossible. He shook off the thought and told himself to worry about that problem later. For now, he needed sleep. Even if the camp ran another perimeter patrol, he figured he had at least two to three hours to sleep virtually risk free.

He closed his eyes and tried to ignore the dull, throbbing ache in his hip. At home, he'd have already popped 800 mg of ibupro-fen. Out here, he'd have to manage the pain the old-fashioned way, by trying to ignore it. He performed three rounds of four-count tactical breathing to relax his body and calm his spirit. Feeling marginally better, he gave his mind just enough leash to let it wander without falling back into the abyss of reliving the night of the bonfire again.

Eventually his mind went to Rachel.

No surprise there.

For seventeen years, he'd felt as if there was some invisible tether tying his thoughts to her. No matter where he was or what he was doing, he always felt that tug. He was like a dinghy, tied to a ship at sea—dragged along, forever bouncing in her choppy wake.

After a while, he began to get drowsy.

He drifted to the Cathedral of the Incarnation and replayed Rachel's parting words to him. And as the phrase echoed in his head, the guilt he carried began to throb painfully with each and every heartbeat.

"You left us, you selfish bastard. . . . You left us both, and you took all your light with you."

CHAPTER SIXTEEN

CHEROKEE NATIONAL FOREST

APPROXIMATELY TWO MILES WEST OF THE TARGET COMPOUND

FRIDAY, 2340 HOURS LOCAL

More than two hours of sleep under a toppled tree was no eight-down in the Ritz, but Jed felt energized and ready to go after the short respite. In the Teams, he'd had to learn how to fall asleep on command—no matter the location, no matter the weather, and no matter the creature comforts. Truth be told, he'd gotten pretty good at it over the years. He'd slept under the belly of a helicopter in the desert with sand scorpions, on a rack next to a torpedo on a submarine, even on a narrow mountainside ledge at ten thousand feet in the Tora Bora without fall protection. But tonight he'd gotten all the sleep he was going to get. Operation Daniel was underway. His mission: to single-handedly extract twelve-year-old Sarah Beth Yarnell from a fortified compound in the woods, with inadequate gear, no QRF, and no real-time surveillance . . .

Hooyah, frogman.

In the movies, action heroes made it look soooo easy.

Well, this ain't Hollywood, he mused.

Thankfully, he had the night.

For a SEAL, the night—like the ocean—was a reliable partner. A silent ally. A weapon he understood and knew how to deploy. As an operator, he learned how to leverage the darkness and the deep to his advantage. Places that others feared, he embraced and found refuge in. For nearly two decades, Jed had been a creature of the night.

As a SEAL, he owned the darkness.

But as Jedidiah Johnson, civilian traipsing through the woods alone, not so much.

With no night-vision goggles, no eyes in the sky, and spotty mobile phone coverage, he was operating blind. He didn't even have a paper map, and every time he looked at his iPhone's navigation app, he sacrificed light discipline—trashing his organic night eyes and risking counterdetection. Of all the times for his old ally to abandon him, this was the worst. He shook his head at the ridiculousness of it all and could almost hear the night laughing at him.

Hey, Jed, remember that previous agreement we had? . . . Yeah, well, consider that null and void. You're on your own, brother.

With a cleansing exhale, he pulled out his iPhone. He tapped to open the compass app and oriented himself to the proper heading. After getting his bearings, he switched apps to the map. His current position was roughly where he thought he was, an earlier detour around an unexpected loose rock face having slowed his progress without deviating him too far off course. Jed found the target compound waypoint on the map and zoomed until its red dot and his blue dot were both visible on the screen. The most direct route to the target took him up and over an exposed ridge that would require him to climb down what—as best he could tell from the satellite view—was a pretty steep descent. That would be noisy, slow, and the risk of falling was much higher in the dark. It might look direct, but the devil was in the details.

Lips pursed, he planned an alternate route on the screen that would take him around the ridge. This new route, which involved taking a switchback down into a ravine, appeared to add an extra mile. The ascent out, however, looked more manageable and shouldn't involve any climbing. Provided the actual terrain he encountered looked anything like it did on the app.

With a long, ragged sigh, he leaned his back against a tree and slipped the phone into his pocket. Using his left hand, he massaged deep pressure into his bad hip. A hot burn flared as he kneaded the knots out of his muscles—muscles that were seizing up in an effort to protect the damaged joint. But despite the pain, he had to get things loosened up or he'd pay the price later. After a full minute of deep tissue work, he straightened out his leg for a few quick stretches, rotating the leg around in an arc as the Team physical therapist had taught him to do. Feeling marginally better, he adjusted the Mossberg by its sling to the ready position and set off.

Squinting into the darkness, he slowly made his way in the dim shadows, navigating the descent into the ravine. He moved as swiftly as stealth would allow in the dark, careful to avoid holes and twigs with each footfall. He didn't get far before the path became rocky and started descending steeper and faster than he expected.

Did I miss the switchback?

He couldn't be more than two hundred yards from the last waypoint he'd used to orient himself, and already the path didn't match. Using his dimmed iPhone screen as a low-lumen flashlight, he spun 180 degrees and backtracked to look for a path he could take as the switchback. To his right, he saw what looked to be a narrow but well-worn deer path, weaving up toward him with what appeared to be a gentler slope than the path he found himself on. And at thirty inches wide, it seemed cleared enough that he wouldn't risk his stealth brushing into branches every few feet. To the left he spied another trail, narrower and rockier than the first, but potentially viable. It disappeared into a dense grove of forest which, if it persisted, would slow his progress.

From a purely cardinal heading perspective, the left path should be the better choice, but he needed to consider stealth and speed over ground too. He was burning more time than he wanted on this infil, and if he took too much time to reach the compound, he wouldn't have enough night remaining to get Sarah Beth out.

Frustrated, Jed took a knee and opened the map again in satellite terrain mode. Using his finger and thumb, he zoomed in as close as the app would let him, right on top of the blue icon representing him. For all he knew, the satellite picture being accessed could be ten years old. For sure the imagery didn't match what his eyes were showing him. And neither of the two new trails was visible, even at maximum zoom.

He closed the app and held the phone tight in his hand, barely suppressing the compulsion to hurl the blasted thing into the woods. As a SEAL, he'd always been equipped with the right tools for the job. But tonight felt like amateur hour. He stood, frozen in indecision. God only knew where these paths snaked off to. Either path might work as the switchback or, alternatively, could veer off in the wrong direction.

He hesitated.

As a special operator, his had always been a world with no time for debate or rumination. In the Teams, a bad decision was always better than no decision, and as an NCO he'd always been a decisive leader.

So why am I hesitating?

Just be a SEAL—make the choice and go.

He glanced at the wide, inviting trail to his right and then at the other more ambiguous option on the left. *They both seem wrong*, he thought as he blew air through pursed lips. Bathed in uncertainty, he decided to do something he'd not done in over a decade . . . bowed his head and prayed.

Lord, I know I've been pretty quiet lately . . . okay, absent . . . okay fine, completely absent. The truth is, I don't know what I believe about You. Do You really work in our lives, or are You just up there watching us act out some play You wrote a million years ago? But, God, I do know You're up there somewhere. So here goes . . . God, this little girl needs me. I just want to get her out and bring her back to her parents safely. After that, I don't know, but right now I need You. God, please show me the way. Guide me here on the path that will take me to Sarah Beth. In Jesus' name . . . amen.

Jed let out a long, quivering sigh and felt his eyes going wet. For reasons he didn't understand, a tight sob caught in his throat. *Why am I getting emotional? I'm a SEAL. I don't do emotional.*

A tear ran down his cheek as if in counterpoint.

Closing his eyes, Jed steeled himself with a round of four-count tactical breathing. Then he swallowed all the doubt, negativity, and emotion he was feeling down deep into his gut. After two more rounds of controlled breathing, he felt better, his head clearer.

He looked left. There was no clap of thunder, no light radiating down from above, no voice from heaven, but he knew. Flush with the same confidence he used to feel when God had been a presence in his life, he knew which way to take. Scripture filled his mind, one he was pretty sure came from Psalms, but it had been a very long time since he'd read his Bible:

"I will instruct you and teach you in the way you should go; I will counsel you with my loving eye on you . . ."

If the passage came from God and wasn't something he'd resurrected from his youth via subconscious wishful thinking, then the message couldn't be more clear.

Setting his jaw, he went left.

As he hiked, his thoughts turned to the mechanics of his upcoming compound infiltration—mechanics he'd yet to fully flesh out. So far, he'd "cowboyed" this thing, and if he kept on that way, it would be a recipe for failure. *The devil is in the details,* he reminded himself. If his time in the Navy had taught him anything, it was how true this adage was. Military men learned this lesson with blood, especially those within the special warfare community. It was for this reason that the planning and preparation phases that preceded every operation dwarfed the *actual* time on mission by a factor of ten, if not a hundred. Unfortunately, unlike a SEAL mission where extensive intelligence, surveillance, and reconnaissance operations were conducted on the target in advance, for this op, the only ISR Jed had to leverage was what Rachel had collected in her head.

He chuckled. *I've never run an op off visions before. So this oughta be interesting.*

He didn't know how many shooters he'd be facing and it was imperative that he not find out. In other words, the key to his success tonight was maintaining stealth; it was that simple. Get in, find the girl, and get out without being seen or heard. If he was counterdetected at any phase of the rescue, odds were he'd be KIA due to their superior numbers and superior firepower.

Looks like I'm just going to have to conduct my own ISR the hard way, he thought with a sigh, *once I'm on target.*

Over the next forty minutes, he descended the switchback with relative ease and quiet while making good time. God had apparently answered his prayer, because the path he'd chosen had not only taken him down the ravine but also continued up the final hill he needed to cross. At the summit, he found the perfect spot to surveil the compound where Sarah Beth was being held. Grateful for the guidance, he bowed his head in reverence.

Thank You, Father. Now just one more ask—please help me save this girl.

The moon, which had been hiding out behind the clouds all night, chose that moment to finally make an appearance—illuminating the countryside well enough for him to survey the compound with his binoculars. He found a nice boulder to use as a backrest and sat down in the dirt. Bringing his knees up to support his elbows, Jed pressed the compact binoculars to his face and began his scan.

"Well, I'll be . . . ," he murmured, bringing the buildings into clarity with the focus dial adjust. "This place is real after all and laid out just like Rachel said it was."

From his vantage point, the compound layout resembled a crescent, with three separate structures arranged in a shallow arc on a tree-cleared, rectangular plot of land. At the bottom of the property sat the main house—two stories with the front facade oriented exactly as Rachel had described. The upstairs bedroom where Sarah Beth was supposedly being held would have a clear view of the VOR antenna, which he could see clearly from his vantage point—a circle of red lights around it atop the next mountain beyond the compound. Next to the main house stood a simple, rectangular prefab, single-story building. The sides and roof were constructed from standing-seam metal panels. It had no windows and the entry door was positioned dead center on the east side.

"That's a bunkhouse," he whispered with a disappointed sigh. "Awesome . . ."

He swept his binoculars to the right and focused on the final building—a barn that, from the tire tracks in front, was clearly being used as a garage. Multiple antennae on the roof and a yellow glow from the single window on the second story strongly suggested that it might also be their security and comms center. He dragged his field of view across the grounds, looking for a roving sentry.

"Just please don't have dogs . . . Anything but dogs," he murmured.

It wasn't that he had a fear of dogs per se—although a well-trained shepherd or Malinois could certainly mess a brother up.

It was that canine patrols operated with a completely different level of sensory awareness compared to their human counterparts. While the odds of him silently evading a human sentry were better than 50 percent, he placed the odds of slipping past a human-canine pair at around 10 percent. If they were using dogs, he'd have to abort and come back in a few days with a suppressed AR with optics, and Sarah Beth didn't have a few days. He exhaled through pursed lips while mentally crossing fingers as he systematically scanned the entire property for guards.

Gotcha, he thought as he spied a single sentry walking the tree-lined perimeter. He was already zoomed to the maximum magnification of his binoculars, which wasn't enough to provide the level of detail he would have liked, but it was enough to tell the guard was male, not overweight, and carried a pump-action shotgun and not a rifle, which surprised him.

He surveyed the property for another thirty minutes, watching the roving sentry's level of attentiveness and noting the man's routine. During that half hour, he observed no changes in alert level on the compound—no vehicles coming or going, no lights turning on or off, no additional sentry personnel interacting with or augmenting the single roving guard walking the tree line. Based on his near-miss encounter earlier in the evening with the long-range sentry, Jed knew he could not let himself become complacent on the approach. There was no telling how many perimeters these guys walked and how many patrols they ran. What he did know, however, was that the dude he'd been watching was not the only roving sentry out there, so he'd need to be hypervigilant during the approach.

After noting that the compound sentry completed his perimeter sweep in fifteen minutes, he returned the binoculars to his pack and pulled out a bottle of water and an energy bar. He ate, drank half the water, and then—despite his protesting hip—got to his feet. He shrugged on his pack, adjusted the Mossberg sling, and emptied his bladder. Bodily demands managed, he set off through the woods on a vector that would take him to the rear of the main house. As he advanced, he reminded himself a final time that stealth was the key to survival. He kept an eye out for snares, trip wires, and camera boxes on tree trunks. He paid attention to each and every footfall, managing his noise.

Be the night.

Be the night.

Be the night . . . went the mantra in his head as he made his way down the side of the mountain and through the woods. Eventually it happened, and he slipped into the zone—a zen-like state where his senses, mind, and muscles were hyperconnected and unified. Like laser-guided ordnance, he followed what felt like an invisible glide slope to the compound, and the next thing he knew, he was hunched in a tactical crouch outside the tree line behind the target house. Carefully and quietly, he retrieved his binoculars from his pack. First, he scanned all the windows, looking for watchful eyes and also identifying a pair of windows on the second story where he decided Sarah Beth was most likely being held, due partly to the lace trim on the curtains but mostly to the presence of bars on the window.

Just like Rachel said she saw in the images "sent" to her from Sarah Beth . . .

Next, he scanned the eaves, roofline, and window ledges for security cameras.

Surely these guys have electronic surveillance, he thought, spying nothing suspicious and suddenly worrying about what he *couldn't* see more than what he could.

He checked his watch: 0217.

The dead of night—the perfect time for an op.

Most likely, their sentries had six-hour watches, probably changing at midnight and 0600. Usually watches turned over at either the top or bottom of the hour. Based on his observational calculations, the sentry should be passing Jed's location on perimeter walk sometime in the next four minutes. A critical decision begged his attention . . .

Do I try to eliminate the sentry now and then breach the house, or should I wait until after he passes and breach while he's roving the opposite side of the compound?

Each option had its pros and cons.

He glanced back at his watch, managing the time: 0219.

I'll do what feels right, he thought and decided to let intuition be his guide.

He retrieved the Cold Steel mega folder from his pocket and rotated his slung Mossberg around to his back. With a flick of the thumb, the six-inch steel blade locked into place. Gripping the knife, he settled into a deep crouch and waited. His quads soon began to burn, but he embraced the pain—just one more sensory input he had to manage. He calmed his breathing and listened . . . Barely audible footsteps, boots on turf, pricked his ears. Slowly he turned his head in the direction of the converging sentry who'd just come into view, rounding the southeast corner. At this range, Jed could make out details he could not before. The patrolling guard was younger than Jed had anticipated, not a day over twenty-five, if that. He was tall and lean and moved with a lazy confidence, gripping his shotgun in a two-handed carry.

Gooseflesh stood up on Jed's skin as the young sentry closed inside thirty feet—the same prickle he'd felt right before he'd been attacked in that parking lot in Nashville. The memory of the incident last night made him anxious and angry at the same time. The hooded man had possessed superhuman strength for his size. Was this sentry cut from the same cloth? On a normal day, Jed wouldn't think twice about going toe-to-toe with a dude he had forty pounds of muscle on, but something about this roving guard felt off.

Deferring to his gut, Jed made the decision not to engage unless his hand was forced.

The sentry scanned right and left as he closed on Jed's position, not letting his gaze linger too long on any one particular thing. Jed's spidey sense was pinging like crazy as the armed guard closed within fifteen feet of where he was squatting in the heavy underbrush along the perimeter of the tree line. Heart pounding, Jed watched the sentry walk three paces past his hide and stop.

The guard lifted his chin and, to Jed's bewilderment, sniffed the air.

Jed watched the young man turn and his expression morph into a malevolent sneer. The sentry brought his shotgun up, and then, sighting over the barrel, he swiveled to point the muzzle directly at Jed.

CHAPTER SEVENTEEN

Crouching in shadow, Jed stared down the muzzle of the night sentry's twelve-gauge shotgun. At this range, the blast would probably kill him. Even if he survived, he'd be severely incapacitated and unable to complete the mission. He stilled his breathing, froze every muscle in his body, and imagined himself dematerializing.

I am vapor.

I am the night.

An owl hooted from a nearby tree and the sentry turned his chin to look in the direction of the call. Then something rustled in the underbrush off to Jed's right, and the young guard spun counterclockwise thirty degrees, readjusting his aim in that direction. The owl hooted again, as if taunting the armed patrol as he scanned the woods for a target. Suddenly the tree frogs that had gone silent since Jed's arrival began to trill, joining the owl.

So now the forest decides to wake up, he thought with an eye roll.

Whatever had moved in the brush scuttled around for a second before going still again. The young patrol scowled and marched toward the tree line, sighting intently over his shotgun. Jed tracked the sentry with his eyes but didn't dare reposition. His Mossberg was slung behind his back, which meant his best option was to take the guard with his blade—providing the geometry worked out.

The thing in the brush scurried again, but this time, not without consequence. In the corner of Jed's eye, he saw a ghost-gray shape descending on silent wings, talons bared and silver dollar eyes reflecting moonlight. And as the owl executed his kill, so did Jed—closing the gap between his hide and the distracted sentry. Like his winged night hunter companion, Jed struck with lethal, silent precision. His knife found its mark, driving into the junction where the neck connects to the base of the skull. He wrenched the blade back and forth, severing the brain stem from the spinal cord, and then pulled the knife out. His adversary dropped like a marionette whose strings had just been cut. Jed caught him under his armpits and quietly lowered the body to the ground until he was staring at the other man's face from above and upside down. An amber ring flashed around his vanquished adversary's irises, and then something biologically impossible happened.

The guard spoke.

"God can't help you here," the sentry said, his voice perfectly clear and articulate despite an open mouth pooling with blood. And then the thing that should have been a corpse began to laugh. "You're dead . . . ha-ha-ha . . . You're dead . . . ha-ha-ha . . ."

Jed stumbled backward, almost falling over a tree root.

Snap to, frogman! the SEAL barked in his head, pulling him out of his funk like a slap to the face. *We're on the clock now. Check the body and go . . .*

Heeding the call from his inner warrior self, Jed returned to the body.

Don't look at his face. Whatever you do, don't look at his face, Jed told himself as he took the black nylon shotshell case clipped to the dead man's belt, but the compulsion was overpowering, and he looked anyway.

"You're dead . . . ha-ha-ha . . . You're dead," the corpse taunted once again, but this time Jed was positive the sentry's lips were still and only the eyes were moving.

"What the hell is going on?" he murmured as gooseflesh stood up on the back of his neck.

But in the deepest, darkest corner of his mind he knew the answer.

He'd always known.

Steeling himself for what lay ahead, he stowed his knife, and then he brought his slung Mossberg around, checked a cartridge in the chamber, and moved with purpose toward the back of the main house, where Sarah Beth was being held. He crossed the lawn in seconds, quick-stepping in a tactical crouch while scanning over his shotgun. When he reached the back door, he stopped and quickly contemplated the best method to break in. In the Teams, they breached hard and fast with overwhelming force—typically with an explosive called a "breacher charge" or by busting down the door. Unfortunately, he was alone and needed to avoid "waking the neighborhood" at all costs.

He looked at the handle and lockset, which was a standard variety two-piece unit with a keyed knob below and a dead bolt cylinder above. The door itself appeared to be made of painted wood but, unlike a typical rear entry door, was windowless. Unfortunately, he couldn't just break a windowpane, reach in, and unlock the door from the inside. He blew air through his teeth. He could try to pick the locks, but lock picking wasn't something SEALs practiced every day. With a grimace, he repositioned, ready to put his massive shoulder into the door. Hopefully it didn't take multiple hits to splinter the jam.

It's unlocked, a voice suggested in his head, stopping him a millisecond before the charge. He screwed up his face at the idea but stepped forward and reached for the handle anyway. To his astonishment, the knob twisted freely, and the door swung open. Sighting over his Mossberg, he stepped into a darkened kitchen. He cleared left and right and then advanced toward what he presumed was the hallway leading to the front of the house and staircase to the upper level. An old, freestanding grandfather clock ticked loudly in the hallway, reminding him of the grandfather clock his parents had inherited from Gran-Gran and Pop-Pop. He hated grandfather clocks—always chiming and ticking and making their presence known at all hours of the night. He stepped quietly past it, resisting the overwhelming compulsion to pull his gaze away from his gunsight and check if it was the same model that his parents kept.

He crept past it into the foyer, which had two cased openings, each leading to a room on opposite sides of the rectangular entryway. Jed went right first, clearing a dining room before rotating 180 degrees to cross the foyer. He cleared up the flight of stairs as he crossed and then stepped into a formal living room on the other side of the second cased opening.

Clear.

He swiveled and retraced his steps back into the entry, sighting up the staircase before ascending. Carefully placing his feet, he took the steps two at a time with feline stealth and precision. At the top of the stairs, he cleared left and advanced down the dark and narrow hallway. He noted three doorknobs on the right and one on the left, with his gaze settling on the second door on the right, the one with bars on the windows outside. He advanced, heart pounding—hyperalert for any sounds that would indicate he'd been detected.

He quietly and steadily closed the gap to the door.

Ten feet . . . seven feet . . . five . . .

When he was one stride away, as he shifted his weight from his rear foot to his lead foot, the floor creaked loudly. He cursed silently to himself and carefully lifted his right foot, relieving the pressure but causing an almost-as loud countercreak. He froze, holding his right foot in midair . . .

When nothing happened, he exhaled and stepped around the offending spot, giving it wide berth until he was standing in front of the target bedroom door. Only then did he notice that the door was not fully closed. Instead, the slab was resting against the jamb and unlatched. Still sighting over his shotgun, he dropped lower in his crouch and eased the door inward and open with his left shoulder, the creaking of the hinges horribly loud in the still night air. He shifted forward, peering in only to find the room empty, or at least apparently empty. Based on the juvenile-themed decor, the girlie bedspread, and the stuffed animals scattered about, he was confident he'd picked the right room. So where was Sarah Beth?

When kids are scared, they hide . . .

He nodded at the timely advice from the ether and slipped into the room. Quickly and methodically he checked the obvious hiding locations—under the bed, in the closet, in the bathroom—but he found no cowering, trembling little girl.

C'mon, Sarah Beth, where are you?

A surge of anger blossomed in his chest as possible explanations for her absence populated a list in his mind:

Maybe she's in a different room.

Maybe they knew I was coming and moved her.

Or . . . they killed her.

A lump the size of a golf ball formed in his throat.

No, no, no—this is not how it was supposed to go down!

With gritted teeth, he turned to exit the bedroom, resigned to the dreadful fact that he'd now have to check all the rooms in the house for the girl before he could exfil. Leading with the Mossberg, he moved into the hallway. The instant he crossed the threshold, he saw a figure standing motionless on his left. He swiveled, bringing the shotgun around to point center mass at a late-middle-aged woman, small and thin in stature, dressed in nightclothes, a robe, and slippers. She'd not made a sound in the hall, apparently well-wise to the creaking floorboard. Most remarkable and disconcerting of all, however, was the way she maintained her composure. Despite staring at the business end of his twelve-gauge, she just stood there in the dark, fingering an antique brass key hanging from a long chain around her neck.

"Naughty, naughty boy," she said with a grimace reminding him of a face his Gran-Gran used to make whenever she caught him with his hand in the proverbial cookie jar.

"Where's the girl?" he asked, instinctively taking a step back to open the space between them to a proper tactical standoff.

She ignored the question. "You're not invited here," she said, her voice oozing with venom and completely out of sync with her placid expression and unthreatening posture.

"I'm going to ask you one more time, grandma," he said, putting tension on the trigger. "Where is Sarah Beth?"

"Dead," the woman said, holding his gaze.

His heart skipped a beat.

Dead? No . . . it can't be.

A shadow rippled across the old woman's visage and for an instant he saw two faces—one marcid and grotesque superimposed upon another, mild and numinous. His mind flashed without warning to the same image nearly two decades ago—a demonic face flickering across the soft features of his classmate, Kenny, after Jed had caught him trying to rape Rachel in the basement.

He squeezed the trigger.

The Mossberg kicked and spit fire, and a thunderclap shook the walls of the narrow hallway. The blast knocked the old woman backward and she hit the floor like a sack of wet cement. Jed pumped the forestock—ejecting the spent shell and chambering a new cartridge—as he stepped up to look at the thing he'd just shot. The blast had hit her midchest and done considerable damage. The hand she'd been fondling the brass key with was now a mangled stump and a bloody gaping hole was open in her sternum. And yet despite this, she was still alive and lucid.

Fixing her gaze on him, a vulpine smile curled her lips and then she screamed a single word—her voice a harpy's cry so loud it rattled his skull.

"Shepheeeeeeeeerd!"

He squeezed the trigger again, this time silencing her for good.

A switch flipped in his head and years of training took over, his muscles and mind synchronized and ready to do what he knew how to do better than anything else in the world. He slung the Mossberg and pulled the Sig P365 from his drop holster, trading brute force for precision and a fifteen-round extended magazine. The gun's motion-activated Romeo Zero red-dot optic powered on the instant he drew the weapon and was illuminating by the time he brought the weapon up.

He had one shot at this, and that window was closing rapidly.

"Sarah Beth Yarnell," he hollered, turning his head right and left as he did to project up and down the hallway. "Your parents sent me to rescue you. If you hear my voice, come out now." When no reply came, he tried again. "Sarah Beth Yarnell, I'm here to rescue you. Come out now or I'm leaving without you."

She's alive but she's gone, Jed. . . . Get out of there. The thought came to him like one of his own, but from outside. Like the prompt he'd gotten earlier that the back door was unlocked.

Rachel? he asked in his mind. *Is that you?*

Go now, the voice commanded. *Hurry.*

Jed stepped over the grandma's corpse and moved toward the staircase. The instant he reached the landing, the front door flew open and two shooters entered. Because he was already sighting the foyer when they crossed the threshold, he had both a half-second advantage and the high ground.

Trigger squeeze. Trigger squeeze.

He dropped both tangos with head shots.

Feeling a presence behind him, he checked his six but found

the hallway empty. He swiveled to the front and rapidly descended the stairs, then stepped over one of the fallen shooters and took a knee behind the open front door to take a quick peek outside. The crack of rifle fire outside echoed in the night, and a bullet slammed into the doorjamb, inches above his head. He snapped back, taking cover behind the slab. He glanced at the two dead sentries and a smile curled his lips. One had a shotgun, but the other had a Smith & Wesson M&P 15 with a thirty-round magazine.

"Oh yeah, come to daddy," he said, holstering his Sig to liberate the Magpul Spec Series semiautomatic rifle from the dead man. "Now we're in business."

Unlike his Sig, the M&P 15 didn't have red-dot optics, but that was okay. He'd fired tens of thousands of 5.56 rounds over the years. The weight and feel of the weapon were good in his hands, and the iron sights would do him just fine. He squeezed off a couple of "think twice" rounds out the front door and then popped to his feet to exfil via the hallway and out the back the way he'd come. As he passed the grandfather clock, this time compulsion got the better of him and he glanced at the clockface.

Yep, same stupid one . . .

He entered and cleared the kitchen, swiveling right, then left, sighting over the M&P 15. With nobody to shoot, he advanced to the back door, which he'd left hanging wide-open. He took a knee at the threshold and then popped his head out for a look right . . . *clear*, then left . . . *clear*. He was about to sprint out into the night, but the thought of getting sniped in the back from a second-story window popped into his head.

But what choice did he have?

This is going to suck, he thought, but he knew what he had to do. Like his first NCO, Scab, used to say: *Always be hard to kill.*

Teeth gritted, he charged out the door. After ten feet, he spun around 180 degrees and sighted up. With robotic precision, he put a round in the center lower pane of each and every upstairs window, working from right to left.

That'll give 'em something to think about, he thought as he squeezed off the last round.

He was just about to turn and sprint into the woods when a light turned on in the middle bedroom, freezing him with indecision.

Sarah Beth?

A figure stepped up to the window, creating a backlit shadow on the still-drawn curtains. To Jed's surprise, the figure was not holding a weapon or dropping into a sniper posture. Instead, the tall, square-shouldered form stood motionless, brazenly vulnerable, but its face hidden from Jed behind the curtains.

Definitely not Sarah Beth.

He brought the iron sights of his M&P 15 to bear on the figure, but when he tried to squeeze the trigger, his right index finger refused to budge.

"What the hell?" he muttered, suddenly terrified.

Then, as he tried to flex his frozen trigger finger, Jed felt something else . . . something new and terrible and world-changing. The sudden and overwhelming compulsion to drop his rifle, pull the Sig P365 from its holster, press the muzzle under his chin, and squeeze the trigger.

No, he said in his mind.

But the compulsion was so overpowering. It felt *right* to kill himself. It was the proper thing to do. It was the fate he deserved for all the horrible things he'd done as a SEAL. Penance for all the people he'd killed. This was what God wanted. This was what God demanded of him . . .

He lowered the M&P 15 and let it hang from its sling.

The world would be a better place without him in it. Yes, he was a failure. He'd abandoned his God and his family and his friends. Nobody loved him and nobody ever would.

His right hand found the pistol grip in the drop holster.

I don't want to do this . . .

But it was the right thing to do. The noble thing. The proper thing.

He pulled the Sig and jammed the muzzle into the soft, fleshy triangle under his chin between the V of his jawbones. His finger shifted from the trigger guard to the trigger.

Jed, we need you. . . . Come back to the light.

Don't listen to him.

You are loved, Jed. Come back to the light.

He squeezed his eyes shut and mouthed a prayer, "Jesus, save me from this evil trying to end me. God, chase away these evil thoughts . . ."

Jed gasped as the compulsion evaporated. Where a second ago it had felt like he was clutched in an iron fist, now he felt liberated. The murderous intent he'd had for himself redirected to the figure in the window, and he fired six rounds at the silhouette. The slugs flew true, shattering the window and ripping holes in the curtains, but the figure did not shudder. It did not sway. It did not fall.

Run, Jed! Run as fast as you can . . .

Rifle fire cracked to his right and a bullet screamed past his ear.

He dropped to a tactical knee, put his red dot center mass on the converging shooter, and dropped him with a double tap to the chest. Then he holstered the Sig and brought the M&P up. Instinctively, he swiveled left and sighted another tango rounding the other side of the house. They were trying to catch him in a cross fire, but the first shooter had lacked the discipline to wait for his partner to get into position. Jed dropped the second tango with a head shot. He scanned the rest of the left quadrant, then swiveled right to check the other side. The first shooter was squirming on the ground, trying to bring his rifle up. Jed put two more 5.56 rounds in him, turned toward the woods, and ran.

Lungs heaving.

Hip on fire.

Jed ran . . . ran like he'd never run before.

CHAPTER
EIGHTEEN

Lungs on fire . . .

Legs churning . . .

Sarah Beth ran . . . ran like she'd never run before.

Her footfalls were noisy—dead leaves crunching and twigs breaking with every step—and her hard panting seemed to echo in the forest. She was so very, very loud. Somewhere in her mind she recognized this was a problem, but fear drove her heedlessly, like a pack of wolves nipping at her heels. She tired quickly and desperately wanted to stop and rest, but the voice in her head wouldn't let her.

Keep running, Sarah Beth, it said. *Run as fast as you can for as long as you can and don't stop. Whatever you do, don't stop.*

And so she ran.

The first steps, the ones crossing her bedroom and into the hallway, had been the hardest. After that, she'd just taken them one at a time until she'd somehow made it down the stairs, through the kitchen, and out the back door of the house without waking a soul . . . if her captors even had souls. And all the while, she'd imagined herself as young David facing Goliath—undaunted and unafraid, with God on her side.

But everything changed when she got to the woods. At first, she was overcome with euphoria at her escape, but that feeling of victory eroded with every footstep she took deeper into the forest. Then she heard a gunshot behind her and panicked, sprinting again without direction away from the sound. But with no flashlight, no map, and no smartphone with GPS, she had absolutely no idea which direction to go or where to run to. Then more gunshots echoed, and she wondered if they were shooting at her. After that, a very simple strategy governed her escape plan: put as much distance between her and the house with Victor and Fake Grandma as possible. Now, with the cramp in her side and her breathless lungs, maybe it was time to—

She didn't see the tree root and face-planted hard on the forest floor.

She heard herself yelp at the sharp flares of pain that hit in multiple places at once: her left shin, her right wrist, and her tongue, which she'd bit. She tasted blood in her mouth and a part of her wanted to cry, but then another part of her said no.

Help! she shouted in her mind. *Help me. Please, someone help me!*

She rolled onto her back and clutched her left shin, which definitely hurt the most.

Mom . . . Mom? Can you hear me? Mom!

Panic consumed her as she realized her thoughts weren't going out.

It's not working . . . Why is it not working?

A rustle in the woods snapped her out of her own noisy head. Fresh fear sobered her mind, dulled the pain in her shin, and pricked her senses. Holding herself very, very still, she listened and heard the rustle again. It was close and it sounded like someone, or something, walking and pausing . . . walking and pausing.

She scanned the dark spaces between the tree trunks for movement, but in the static-filled inky black, her eyes registered nothing.

What if it's one of Victor's guards, one of the men I saw walking around the yard with a gun?

Her heart was pounding so hard she could feel it against her ribs.

The rustle happened again, and this time she scampered to her feet and ran. Her shin and her wrist instantly began throbbing, but she tried to ignore them. She ran for several long minutes, until exhaustion forced her to slow.

I don't know how much longer I can keep this up, she thought as she jogged past a big fallen tree. *I could hide and rest here . . . for just a little bit.*

She slowed and circled back to inspect the possible hiding place she'd found. Panting, she took a knee and inspected a hollow that was just big enough for her to crawl into. It seemed perfect, unless it was full of spiders, ants, and centipedes. Bugs gave her the heebie-jeebies. *You can do this,* she told herself with a grimace and climbed into the dark little hole. Inside, it was damp and smelled like dirt. She had the sensation that bugs were already crawling on her, but she confirmed that was only her mind playing tricks on her by scratching at one of the spots and finding nothing on her skin.

I can't stay here. They're going to find me—but I'm so tired and scared.

She shuddered and felt tears pressing.

Then, not sure what else to do, she said a prayer. And then another and another. They were simple prayers, straight from the heart. The first was a prayer of gratitude for God helping her during her escape from the house. In the second, she asked Him for His continued help, and lastly, she prayed for guidance so that she might know what to do next. With each prayer, she felt a little stronger and a little less afraid, and by the end of the third, a warm calm settled over her, like she'd just been wrapped up in one of her mom's world-famous hugs. In that calm, she felt her connection to the strange and ethereal world of other people's thoughts suddenly renewed. And she felt *him*—the gruff-sounding man from her dream who she now felt certain had been sent to help her. She couldn't intuit his name, but that was okay because she felt his goodness.

Also, she felt him searching for her, in all the wrong places.

You're going the wrong way, she said, pushing her thoughts out . . . connecting and pushing . . . pushing and connecting.

I'm over here. . . . This way, mister . . . over here.

I'm waiting for you, over here.

I'm here.

I'm here.

CHAPTER NINETEEN

CHEROKEE NATIONAL FOREST

ONE MILE NORTH OF THE TARGET COMPOUND

SATURDAY, 0305 HOURS LOCAL

In Afghanistan in 2014, Jedidiah had rescued a badly wounded teammate holed up in a makeshift hide in the heart of Taliban country. While dozens of Taliban fighters scoured the woods looking for the SEAL in the dark, Jed had led a rescue operation. He thought about that night because, despite denying it at the time, a supernatural influence had guided him to his fellow SEAL. It had been as if Mike Arnette—Mikey—was a radio beacon and Jed the sole receiver, drawn to the signal. He'd found the wounded SEAL under a large rock in a depression the SEAL had dug using only his hands and knife. Mikey had been so well-hidden, Jed couldn't see him on NVGs, but he'd homed in on the right spot anyway. After killing a Taliban patrol with his bare hands to maintain stealth, Jed had carried Mikey back to the rest of the team. He'd been awarded a Silver Star for the rescue but never told a soul the truth about how he'd really found his teammate.

Searching for Sarah Beth felt the same, but her beacon was much stronger.

And unlike with Mikey, she was calling him . . .

He'd not had time to properly unpack what had happened to him at the compound, but one thing was certain: It was time to stop denying the cold, hard truth that was staring him in the face. Tonight's event was not the first or second or even the third supernatural horror show he'd found himself in the middle of. Kenny Bailey in the basement, the bomb maker in Anbar province, the hooded man in the parking lot, the roving guard at the compound, the grandma in the hallway, and the shadow figure in the window . . . these people were not *people*. He shook his head. Yes, they were people, but also not . . . And it was time to stop denying the voices in his head. Since he'd arrived in Nashville, it was happening with increasing frequency. It was insane and impossible and defied all explanation, but it was happening. Which meant that either he was certifiably nuts and needed to be locked in a padded room, or the phenomenon was real.

I'm here, said a tiny voice in his mind, adding a metaphysical exclamation point.

Just go with it, dude, the SEAL weighed in, *and focus on completing the mission.*

Taking his own advice, Jed shut down his internal monologue

and focused on the job at hand—weaving his way through the dark while carefully navigating roots, rocks, and sticks he could barely see without making noise. Two guards from the compound were hunting him. He'd had one close call already, where he'd hidden behind a large tree just in time to avoid being seen. He'd been forced to wait, delaying his search for Sarah Beth, for five minutes after their footfalls had disappeared. The last thing he wanted to do was lead them to her. But now, as he made the final push toward Sarah Beth, he sensed that threat closing in on him once again.

I'm here . . .

He pressed on through the forest, scanning over the M&P 15 rifle for threats and placing each footstep with care.

I'm here . . .

Fifty more yards covered.

I'm here.

Ten more paces. He should be close now.

"I'm here . . . ," a tiny voice said, and this time it was not in his head.

He stopped, low in the crouch that made his left hip scream in painful protest, rifle still raised and at the ready. He surveyed the forest. The beacon that was Sarah Beth was hitting a fevered pitch, but he still couldn't see her. This girl was hiding like a SEAL.

"Sarah Beth?" he whispered, daring to call out to her.

"Here," she whispered back. "Hurry; the bad men are coming."

Jed eased forward and then he saw her—sitting inside the hollowed-out trunk of a fallen oak, her legs crossed.

Crisscross applesauce.

He smiled and shook his head, then took a knee beside her. "Hi, Sarah Beth," he whispered. "You okay?"

She nodded. "You're the gravelly voiced man," she said softly. "And you came for me."

Jed cocked his head and raised an eyebrow, not at all sure what the girl meant by that, but grinned at the miracle of the moment.

"I'm Jed," he whispered. "I'm a friend of your parents. I'm going to take you home, Sarah Beth."

She smiled at him and held out her hands. He set down the M&P and leaned into the hollow to help her out. She wrapped her arms around his neck, and she was all little girl, clinging to him and sobbing, her tears wet and hot on his neck. He held her tight, her body shaking in his embrace.

"I got you. . . . Everything is going to be okay," he whispered awkwardly.

Suddenly she pulled away, looking over his shoulder and past him into the dark. "They're coming," she hissed. "Two of them."

Still kneeling, he turned and looked into the blackness, straining to hear some sound of approaching men. He heard only her breathing beside him and his own pulse in his temple.

"I don't hear them," he whispered, his voice nearly inaudible.

She screwed up her face and shook her head, like he'd said the most ridiculous thing and she was being rescued by an idiot. She touched his arm, clutching it with her small hand, and now her voice was loud and clear, making him jump to silence her until he realized she was talking in his head.

Two of them are coming from the left. I think when I talk, they can hear me.

Jed started to reply, but she raised a finger to her lips to silence him, fear in her eyes.

He nodded and pointed a finger to her and then raised his hand in the universal "stay here" gesture.

Please don't let them take me back, Jed. I'd rather die than go back, she said in his mind.

He'd experienced the evil that lurked in that house. The only way those monsters were getting her back was over his dead body, and he had no intention of dying tonight. He smiled and touched her chin. Then he repeated the "stay" gesture and watched as she folded herself back into her hiding spot.

Jed picked up the M&P and moved silently, the pain in his hip just background noise. He stayed low, his feet light and silent, as he circled around the tree trunk with his prize tucked inside. Then he accelerated, vectoring away from Sarah Beth's hollow. He wanted separation for when the shooting started. The last thing he needed was a stray bullet ending Operation Daniel in tragedy. As he advanced, silent and deadly, he thought of what Rachel had said when she'd named this mission after the Old Testament book of the Bible.

"This rescue can only be done with God's help."

Jed bowed his head for the second time—in both a day and a decade—and asked for the Lord's help to complete his mission.

Kindling crunched underfoot nearby.

Jed froze, his body a coiled spring ready to unleash stored-up potential energy into violence of action. He pivoted left, toward the sound, and strained to see through the darkness. The moon was playing peekaboo with the clouds and presently the forest was dark as pitch. He couldn't see the enemy yet, but he could smell them—laundry soap and something else it failed to mask . . . the sweat of their fear.

They witnessed what I'm capable of at the compound and they are afraid.

He waited, frozen and listening.

The slightest hint of silver moonlight began to stream through the canopy of branches overhead, casting night shadows if one knew how look to for them. He saw the first shadow creeping slowly and cautiously through the maze of trees—identifiable because it was moving at steady pace and not swaying like the shadows of branches in the gentle breeze. Once he knew where to look, Jed's brain filled in the rest—a man, clad in black, materialized beside a tree trunk. He held an assault rifle, cheek pressed into the stock, as he scanned through what Jed assumed was a night-vision sight.

That's a problem, Jed thought as he lowered himself slowly and silently into a kneeling firing position.

The assaulter raised his left fist, signaling a stop to a second shadow Jed now saw trailing at an offset behind the first. The lead shooter turned slowly toward Jed, rotating in a counterclockwise arc, searching for a target. Jed raised his rifle and used the subtle green light from the assaulter's optics, which illuminated the right side of the shooter's face as a target for the iron sights of his M&P. The man continued his slow turn, then came to a sudden halt—undoubtedly spying a kneeling Jed aiming at him in the darkness. Jed didn't give him time to do anything about it, however, because he'd already squeezed the trigger. The shooter's head jerked and his body crumpled to the forest floor as Jed shifted aim to the other shadow. He squeezed off two rounds that hit center mass. The loud retorts of the M&P reverberated in the hills, followed by the dull thud of the second body hitting the ground.

Jed was on them in a minute, validating both kills. After confirming the threat was neutralized, he traded his M&P for the first shooter's Sig Sauer MCX with a night-vision scope and slung it over his shoulder, then patted over the body for other useful tools. He found an optics case on the man's belt and pulled night-vision binoculars from inside. He couldn't help smiling as he pulled a two-way radio from the man's vest and an earpiece accessory that had been dislodged from the shooter's ear when the bullet hit him in the face. Now he would be able to eavesdrop on their comms. *Hooyah.*

He pressed the earpiece into his ear and dropped the brick into his shirt pocket. He quickly searched the second body, finding nothing else useful.

Armed with the Mossberg, the P365, the MCX with night vision, and a radio, he finally felt like a SEAL again. Invigorated, he moved swiftly back to the hollowed-out tree trunk and knelt beside the opening.

Bright eyes looked up at him.

"Did you kill them?" she asked, surprising him.

Jed hesitated. "They can't hurt you anymore," he answered finally.

"I knew you'd win," she said, extending her hand to him, "because you're the warrior God sent to save me."

"You're going to be okay, Sarah Beth," he said, taking her hand and helping her out of the tree, trying to reassure her.

She shook her head, annoyed. "It's not just about me, Jed. I saw things . . . terrible things. He has something planned. Unless we stop it, people are going to die."

Jed stared at her, confused, but there was no time to get into whatever this was right now.

"I just made a lot of noise, Sarah Beth," he said. "I don't know how many more shooters they have, but however many there are, they're coming for us. We need to get moving."

"Before I ran away, I watched them load a truck with men and guns," Sarah Beth said, unable to let it go. "They're going to kill people . . . a lot of people. I have to tell you—"

"And you will later," he said, cutting her off. "But first we need to get out of here and find somewhere safe. We can't help anyone if they catch us first."

"Okay," she said, looking up, her head barely reaching to his chest. "Where do we go now?"

Jed pointed at a rise in the forest to the north. "We head up and over that ridge," he said. "We keep the high ground, and eventually we'll break out into a valley with farmsteads and houses. One Good Samaritan is all we need and then we can arrange transportation home."

She nodded.

"Can you run?" he asked, looking her up and down for injuries. She nodded again.

"Good. We have to move fast, but we also have to try and be quiet, okay? I'll lead, but if you need me to slow down, just tell me . . . in here," he said and, with a crooked grin, tapped his temple.

"Check," she said with a grin of her own. "That's what you guys say in the Army, right?"

"Consider me impressed," he said and meant it. "Now let's go."

They set off with Jed in the lead, heading north and east, his feet gliding smoothly over the forest floor. As they ascended the slope, the tree cover seemed to thin, and silvery moonlight lit their path, making it easier to navigate through the trees. They weren't silent, but Sarah Beth moved softly enough. The radio he'd taken had been quiet, which bothered him as he'd expected to hear chatter and check-ins, so he stopped them every few minutes for a listen and a scan.

Twenty minutes passed without incident.

They crested the ridge and started their descent into the valley. His spirits buoyed, he considered calling Rachel on the mobile phone. He'd promised to keep her in the loop, but he didn't want to stop, make noise, or have his attention distracted. Discipline was the key. He needed to get Sarah Beth somewhere safe first; then he could communicate with David and Rachel and work out the logistics of getting back to Nashville.

A click froze Jed in his tracks.

The sound was so soft, so quiet, that only someone intimately familiar with firearms would recognize it—the sound of a thumb rotating the safety-selector switch on an M4 rifle. He pulled Sarah Beth in tight to him, his left arm reaching back for her as he raised his rifle with his right.

"Stay behind me," he whispered and stepped between her and the direction he thought he'd heard the sound.

He scanned through the night-vision sight on the Sig MCX, seeing the woods around him in the otherworldly green-gray monochrome palette. He'd spent so much of his life on NVGs in his war against terror, it looked as familiar and natural to him as daylight. He didn't see the shooter at first. Instead, he picked out the soft-yellow glow of the man's night-vision goggles, barely visible through the thick brush beside a tree ten yards away. Then he saw him, the bearded face under the helmet holding the NVGs, looking past him and slightly to his left.

A twig snapped behind him, and Jed knew they were dead—caught in a kill box created by shooters front and back.

I'll shield her and maybe she'll survive, he thought as he whirled, pulled her to his chest, and took her to the ground, creating an envelope of protection for her with his body.

Then the stillness of the night was shattered by a loud voice. "Jedidiah Johnson—we're here with you. The threat is behind you—protect the girl!"

Suppressed fire poured from the operator in the bushes. At the same time, return gunfire—unsuppressed and much, much louder—exploded from behind. Trace rounds screamed overhead in both directions, streaking through the night forest like a meteor shower. Jed pushed Sarah Beth into the dirt and tented his torso overtop her as the woods transformed into a battlefield. Fresh fire poured from multiple spots where he'd seen nothing just moments ago.

He would have returned fire, if only he had some idea who the good guys were, who the bad guys were, and who was shooting at who.

The battle raged for what felt like an eternity, but he knew from experience and the hundreds of gun battles in his SEAL career that *eternity* in combat spanned mere seconds. He exhaled and it was over.

"Clear," a voice called out to his right.

"Clear, four tangos down."

"Clear."

He popped into a combat crouch, weapon up and scanning over Sarah Beth, who was curled in the fetal position in the dirt, palms pressed to her ears. Like specters materializing from the ether, kitted-up operators emerged from the forest in pairs.

"That's close enough," he hollered, sliding his rifle sight from one figure to the next to the next. It was not lost on him, however, that no one was sighting on him, their weapons held in a relaxed carry across their chests.

He felt a tug on his cargo pant leg, but he kept his focus and didn't look down.

"It's okay," Sarah Beth said from her knees. "They're the good guys."

"We'll see about that." He hovered the dark dot of the gunsight center mass of the closest operator walking toward them. "I said that's close enough. Stop or I shoot," he shouted.

The operator in the middle held up a closed fist, halting the advance.

"We're here to help, Senior Chief Johnson," another voice called, and Jed turned, setting his gunsight now on the taller figure walking up from the rear, a slight limp in his step. "Sarah Beth, are you okay?"

Sarah Beth popped to her feet beside Jed and said, "Check."

"How do you know our names?" Jed hollered, still not lowering his weapon.

"Because we have the same objective as you: to find and bring Sarah Beth home safely." The man flipped his NVGs on top of his helmet so Jed could see his eyes. "If you'd lower your weapon, I'll walk over and shake your hand."

Jed looked at Sarah Beth and cocked an "are you sure?" eyebrow at her.

She nodded. "It's okay. I feel like we can trust them."

I can't believe I'm taking tactical instruction from a little girl, he thought and grudgingly lowered his weapon.

"Hey, I'm twelve, almost thirteen," she said, hands on hips, and shot him the stink eye.

"Sorry," he said with a shrug. "I don't really know kids' ages and stuff."

The operator resumed his approach and walked up to Jed.

"You're a very hard man to get an audience with, Jed," the kitted-up team leader said with a lopsided grin, and Jed realized the man looked strangely familiar. "We were hoping to help you rescue Sarah Beth, but you kept shaking us every time we tried to get close enough to have a chat."

"So you're the guys in the gray SUVs who've been surveilling me, huh?"

"Yeah, that's us." He snapped his chin strap off and removed his helmet. Running a hand through thick, dark hair, he turned his attention to Sarah Beth. "Looks like you didn't need our help, though. Got her out safe and sound all by your lonesome. *Hooyah,* right, Sarah Beth?"

"My mother sent him to rescue me," she said. "Well, and God."

The man laughed at this and gave her shoulder a paternal squeeze. Jed looked closer at the face he still couldn't place. Somewhere deep in his memory banks there lurked a name that he couldn't quite dredge up.

"Do I know you?" Jed asked.

The man extended his right hand and Jed shook it.

"Ben Morvant," the man said, jump-starting Jed's memory.

He felt his mouth drop open. *Ben Morvant . . . now that's a name I haven't heard in a long time.*

"I get that reaction sometimes," Morvant said with a chuckle. "We have a lot to talk about, Senior, but first let's get you and Sarah Beth somewhere safe."

Jed nodded and followed the legendary former SEAL toward the cluster of operators waiting for them in a tight, tactical security perimeter.

"I have things to tell you," Sarah Beth said, desperate urgency in her voice as she jogged to catch up to Morvant. "Important things. Something terrible is going to happen."

"Okay, Sarah Beth," Morvant said as he passed through his men, who now fell in on him and formed a loose diamond tactical formation as he led them through the forest to the east. "As soon as we get you somewhere safe, you can tell us all about it. In the meantime, why don't you keep close to Jed."

"Check," she said and turned back to look at Jed with a "c'mon, slowpoke," expression plastered on her face. Jed chuckled and trotted to catch up to her as the group exfilled down the hill. To his surprise, he felt her kid-size hand slip into his as they walked.

And to his even greater surprise, he held it.

CHAPTER TWENTY

As soon as they were underway in the caravan of gray Suburbans, exhaustion settled on Jed like a lead blanket. The effort required to keep his eyes open seemed to grow exponentially with each mile they put between themselves and the target compound and woods. He looked down now at the girl—who slept, legs pulled up to her chest, and her head on Jed's thigh—in the back bench seat of the Suburban. He gazed at her face in profile.

You look so much like your mother . . . it's uncanny.

He pulled the jacket, given to him by one of the operators, up

235

onto her shoulder, but she didn't stir. She was out like a light, crashing not thirty seconds after the driver had put the SUV in drive.

A smile curled his lips.

Mike Charlie . . .

Mission complete.

Jed looked up and studied the man in the captain's chair of the middle row in front of him. Ben Morvant, the former Navy SEAL, was a legend in the Teams. While deployed to Africa as a young operator, the SEAL medic had single-handedly saved his entire fire team during a battle against an overwhelming force of terrorists. Much of the operation and battle remained highly classified, even within the special warfare community, and the SEALs who survived the operation never talked about it. But according to the rumor mill, something strange had happened on that operation. Yes, it wasn't uncommon for legends to be built around men who'd served on highly classified operations, but this was different. What Jed knew for sure was that Morvant had been awarded the Navy Cross for his heroism, every Team guy on the op made it home alive, and that Morvant himself had been badly wounded. Reports that Morvant had been medically retired and confined to a wheelchair from injuries sustained were either exaggerated or complete garbage. Morvant had a perceptible limp, but he'd moved through the woods with the fluid power of a seasoned operator.

Jed's mind was swimming with questions.

But why ask? His years of experience interfacing with these ultrasecret, special task force guys said that they never shared anything about who they were or what they were up to. Any info they did share was contrived from whatever NOC—or nonofficial cover—they were operating under. Why bother soliciting the lies?

He'd learned long ago that when an operator type stared at the middle distance and said, "I'm with a joint, blah, blah, blah, task force," nothing could be gained by asking for more.

These dudes are clearly joint task force guys.

Jed's hip barked, for the tenth time, for attention, begging him to shift position and ease the growing pain from sitting still. But the kid was using his quads as a pillow and she desperately needed sleep, so he was just gonna have to tune out the pain and focus on something else.

"So," he said, interrupting the hushed conversation between Morvant and one of his guys as they talked over a laptop screen. "I need to know when it would be appropriate to let Sarah Beth's family know she's okay."

Morvant turned and smiled over his shoulder. Even in the dim light cast on him by the screen in his lap, there was no doubt in Jed's mind that this guy really was the legendary Ben Morvant.

"I think it's okay to do that anytime now, Jed," the former SEAL said. "I assume you'd like to make the call?"

"If it's okay," Jed said with a glance down at Sarah Beth. "I don't want to violate your OPSEC. I know you guys can be pretty tight about security and especially signals." He chewed the inside of his cheek and then, unable to resist, added, "Obviously y'all are task force guys."

Morvant's smile broadened. "Something like that. But I doubt you would have worked with this task force before, or at least you wouldn't *know* that you did." The operator beside him chuckled at that. "How about you call the Yarnells, but do you mind using one of our encrypted phones?"

"Yeah, of course," Jed said and accepted the boxy, flip-style satellite phone from Morvant's outstretched hand. "Anything I should—or should not—tell them?"

Morvant considered the question for a moment and then said, "You can certainly tell them that you have her and she's safe. You can also say you were aided by a task force, but no names or any other details."

"I don't know any other details," Jed pointed out, aware that he was fishing, as he entered David's mobile number.

"Right," Morvant said, still with that charismatic smile. "Well, when we get secure, I'd like to change that . . . if you're interested in learning more."

Jed arched his eyebrows in surprise but also felt a paranoid caution sweep over him. Information always had a price, always, especially when it came from guys like this. He thought to point that out, but instead the only thing that came out of his mouth was "Sure—of course."

"We have a safe house just east of Sevierville. That's where we're headed now. We'll decompress, check our kits, and check in with our higher authority and also get an ISR update. We'll get the girl—and you—something to eat and drink and make sure our doc checks her over. Don't mention where specifically we are, of course, but let them know that we hope to have her home and in their custody by this afternoon. We have air assets that can pick us up at the Gatlinburg Pigeon Forge Airport in a few hours, and then it's just a short hop back to Nashville. No need to share any of those details, but we want to keep you in the loop—since for now you're embedded on the team."

"Appreciate that," Jed said and then, narrowing his eyes, asked, "So you're really Ben Morvant."

"Yeah, I'm Ben Morvant," the operator answered with a good-natured chuckle. "Better-looking than you expected?"

Jed laughed at the warmth of the familiar Team Guy banter. "Hardly, but you're sure less banged up and hobbled than I would have expected—from the stories, I mean."

Morvant nodded, his eyes gleaming with something more than Team Guy repartee now. "We can get into that later, if you like." Then with a soul-gazing stare he asked, "How's the hip doing, Jedidiah? You five by, shipmate?"

Jed swallowed down the uncomfortable feeling he got from that look and simply said, "Still in the fight."

"Aren't we all," Morvant said cryptically and turned to face front.

Jed stared at the side of the man's face a moment, then shook his head to clear it and pressed the call button on the satphone. It rang only once before Rachel answered.

"Hello?" she said with the voice of a woman carrying the weight of thousand worries.

"It's Jed," he said. "She's safe, Rachel. I got her out."

Rachel said something impossible to decipher though the sudden explosion of sobbing. In the background he heard David, pressing for information.

"Thank you, Jedidiah," Rachel finally managed between sobs. "Thank you, thank you, thank you."

He heard shuffling noises and imagined the phone sandwiched in the embrace of husband and wife. Any guilt-inducing bad feelings the image gave him were dwarfed by the warm feeling of a mission completed and a young girl rescued and headed home to her parents. He looked down at Sarah Beth and felt flush with gratitude—gratitude he felt compelled to share.

Thank You for Your help, Father. I couldn't have done it alone.

He opened his eyes to see Morvant staring at him again over the middle seat, with a knowing look on his face. The man gave a short nod and turned back to the front. Jed wanted to feel embarrassed for being caught in the silent prayer, but he wasn't.

"Jed? Jed, are you still there?" David said, snapping Jed back to the call.

"I'm here, David."

"Is she okay, Jed? Is she . . . hurt? Did they *hurt* her?" David's voice cracked.

"No, she's fine, David. And you can be very proud of her. She's strong and *so* brave. She's passed out asleep now or I would let you say hello, but she'll be back in your arms by this afternoon. We've got a few more boxes to check before we head back to Nashville. As you can imagine, the outfit that took her are not the type of people you want to underestimate. We just need to make sure it's safe to travel."

"I understand," David said. "But you said *we* . . . are you with other people?"

"Yeah, I ended up getting some last-minute assistance from some folks with experience in my line of work."

"Tell me what happened, Jed. I want to know everything."

Jed understood, but now was not the time. "When we get back, David. Not on the phone. And one more thing . . . don't tell anybody she's been rescued. Not even Nashville police, okay?"

"Understood," David said. "When can we talk to her?"

"As soon as we get to the safe house. It won't be long."

"Thank you, Jed. Thank you for saving my baby."

"You're welcome," he said and broke the connection, an enormous smile still on his face.

Sarah Beth shifted in the seat and mumbled something in her sleep. He looked down again at her and gently swept a tussle of hair back that had fallen across her young, pretty face.

"It's not just about me, Jed. I saw things . . . terrible things. He has something planned. Unless we stop it, people are going to die."

He shuddered as her words from the woods came back to him and decided her warning was something he needed remind Morvant about.

"Do you remember what Sarah Beth told you on the exfil?" he asked, tapping the former SEAL on the shoulder.

Morvant nodded. "I do."

"What do you think she meant? Is it real? I think the people who took her might be planning something." When Morvant didn't respond, Jed said, "You know something, don't you? You know what it is she was talking about."

"Maybe . . . Look, Jed, Sarah Beth has been through an incredible ordeal and she's been subjected to . . . things."

"That's a little vague," he complained. "What kind of *things*?"

"We'll talk more about it—and everything else—when we get to the safe house," Morvant said, ending the discussion. "For right now, you can take comfort in the fact that this is not the first time we've dealt with the group that kidnapped Sarah Beth. We're familiar with, shall I say, their modus operandi."

Jed gave a little snort at Morvant's dodge but dropped it for now.

Task force guys . . . they're all the same.

And yet something was different with this group. They'd been surveilling him since the Vandy bookstore the same day he arrived in Nashville. Why? More importantly, why was some direct-action element from a secret government task force interested in the kidnapped daughter of a seminary student in the first place? Wasn't that the FBI's wheelhouse?

He shifted his gaze out the window and watched green hills roll by as he mulled over the one and only thing he was certain of:

There's more to this story than everyone is letting on.

Way more.

And come hell or high water, I intend to find out what it is.

PART III

THE BATTLE

Put on the whole armor of God, that you may be

able to stand against the schemes of the devil.

EPHESIANS 6:11, ESV

CHAPTER TWENTY-ONE

SOMEWHERE VERY, VERY DARK

The man called Jed—her rescuer, her white knight, her avenging angel—stroking her hair and serving as a makeshift pillow, was far more reassuring than any down comforter or fluffy pillow, and for a respite she felt safe. Sarah Beth remembered the sudden silence of the truck turning off and his strong arms lifting her, holding her to his broad chest, and him carrying her into a house. He'd tucked her into a bed, smoothed her hair, and left, closing the door with a quiet click.

Then the darkness came and engulfed her.

She felt not *in* the dark, but rather *of* the dark. As if the dark somehow originated from inside her—growing from a tiny shadow in her mind and flowering out of her to fill the room. To fill the world. The feeling both disgusted and terrified her.

She swallowed hard and decided to be brave—what other choice did she have?—and set off swimming through the darkness, looking. If she was in the dark, of the dark, then it must be because the light wanted her to see or know or find something there. She knew with certainty that her gifts came from God . . . from the light and were of the light.

She opened her eyes.

She sat at a table—not unlike the table where she'd met Victor, but not the exact same one either—and looked across at a man fidgeting nervously in his seat.

"We can't proceed," the man said. A bead of sweat peeked out from his hairline at a thin part, saw the coast was clear, then sprinted down his temple and cheek, leaving a little wet stain behind. "We don't know what she told them. The Shepherds might be waiting for us."

"Had you not let her escape, we wouldn't be having this conversation."

The voice, oily and familiar, had come from her—from deep inside her—and she watched the eyelids, which somehow were not her own, blink twice. With the voice came a sense of vertigo and a wave of nausea so severe she felt certain she would puke, if she'd only had any food in her stomach. Somehow, Victor was inside her, or she in him or something . . .

"How could we have known he was such a threat?" the nervous man said.

She looked down, but not of her own volition, at her—his—bony hands, with their long, narrow fingers and long, sharp fingernails. She clutched a single fig, turning it over and over. The hand with the fig came up and disappeared beneath her line of sight—presumably into Victor's mouth.

"And yet here we are . . . and they have her now."

"Yes, but she is but a girl, with no training or mentoring. I think you grossly overestimate her abilities, Victor. She knows nothing . . . useless fragments at best, and those she will keep to herself out of fear and embarrassment."

The hands were back, or the right hand at least, blurry at the edge of her vision on the table; brown-pink juice dripped from the fig on the pad of flesh beneath the thumbnail.

"What do you know of her capabilities?" Victor's voice said, and she could feel his malice and judgment. "You were charged with the security of the compound. This is your failure, and I do not suffer incompetence."

The other hand abruptly came into view, holding a shiny silver pistol. The long barrel with the little fin at the tip moved through space and came to rest pointing at the bridge of the sweating man's nose.

"Mercy, please . . ."

She tried to close her eyes, but she couldn't. These eyes were not hers to close. She had no choice but to watch.

The gun spit fire and a cloud of smoke swirled around the bony hand. Through it she watched as the bullet split the man's forehead open above his left eye, taking a large chunk of the top of his head and spattering it against the wall. The one remaining, lifeless eye stared at them through the cloud of smoke, and then the face pitched forward with a horrible, wet splat onto the wood table.

She screamed.

And when she did, everything froze.

Suddenly the world became dark again—though she didn't see the eyelids draw closed like before when Victor had blinked. Instead, she was plummeted with great velocity into the inky black. But from the black, Victor's skeletal face appeared in a halo of red, parading itself in front of her mind's eye. His eyes glowed a deep crimson that made all other shades of red seem pale by comparison. His thin gray lips split into a smile over dull, dead teeth.

"Well, hello there, my dear. Did you miss me?"

Terror choked her, like someone had just stuffed a sock in her mouth. She clawed at her throat.

I need to wake up, *she told herself. She pinched a hunk of flesh on her left forearm and twisted it with all her might, begging the pain to revive her to consciousness. But nothing happened.*

Why is it not working?

"Oh, it's not as simple as that with me, my dear," he said through thin, bloodless lips that didn't move. "Now, where are you hiding?"

She twisted her flesh harder and harder and then, somehow finding her voice, unleashed a bloodcurdling scream.

CHAPTER TWENTY-TWO

Jed fidgeted in his seat at the kitchen table, willing himself not to dig his knuckles deep into his aching hip. He had a thing about not showing weakness in front of fellow operators. Was it childish machismo?

Yes.

Did he care?

No.

Morvant set his rifle against the wall in the corner of the eat-in kitchen and then struck up a hushed conversation with the operator who Jed had decided was second in command. Jed narrowed his eyes and tried to place the familiar face of the man Morvant had called Eli. Suddenly it came to him—the shaggy brown hair, the thin beard, the emerald-green eyes . . .

"I know you," he said, interrupting them and fixing his gaze on Eli. "You were at the Vanderbilt bookstore the other day. You were coming down the escalator and talking on the phone."

Eli grinned and shrugged his shoulders. "Guilty," he said.

"The couple at the table who were eyeing me—I assume they're also with your task force?" Jed asked, shifting his gaze to Morvant.

"Yeah. In retrospect, we should have made contact with you then. I'd planned to have a sit-down with you over a beer, but then you went and got yourself arrested and—yada yada yada—life got complicated," Morvant said, combing his fingers through his hair.

"*Complicated* is probably an understatement, don't ya think?"

Morvant chuckled. "It's the world we live in."

A hair-raising scream came from upstairs. Jed heard it, but he also felt it like a hot saber, searing his insides. He sprinted across the kitchen to the bottom of the staircase, assault rifle in his hands and at the ready.

"Jed, wait," Morvant called, stopping him before he charged up the steps.

"Who else is up there?" Jed asked through gritted teeth.

"Only Sarah Beth, Jed," Morvant said, his voice calm and unperturbed. He put a hand on Jed's shoulder, seeming to understand his state of mind. "You check on her. . . . We'll stay here."

Jed grunted and ascended the stairs quickly, moving sideways so as to keep eyes on the group of operators at the bottom of the stairs as well as the seemingly empty landing above. His mind was suddenly a thunderstorm of conspiratorial thoughts: *Can I really trust these guys? How do I know their motives are pure? They surveilled me, show up in the woods after I hit the compound, and I hand Sarah Beth over without any proof of who they are or who they're working for. How could I be so naive—so stupid?*

Right cheek pressed against his rifle stock and shoulders rolling forward into a combat crouch, Jed slid into the slipstream of combat readiness. He took the last six steps two at a time, ignoring the fire in his hip, just as a second bloodcurdling scream ripped through the silence as well as his heart. With renewed urgency, he cleared the upstairs hallway left and right, while a voice in his head pointed out that if Morvant and his team were not allies, it was too late already. The door to Sarah Beth's bedroom at the end of the hall stood partially open. Jed plowed into it, entering the room like a freight train. He cleared left and his blindside corner, then scanned the right corner before surging forward toward the bed, where Sarah Beth sat bolt upright, fists balled at the ends of arms so stiff they looked as if they might snap in half. Her eyes were shut painfully tight, but her mouth gaped wide-open as she gasped for air.

Jed unslung his rifle and leaned it against the nightstand. He took a seat on the mattress and reached for her. She pushed him away, terrified, flailing her arms and swatting him as she made a "nuh . . . nuh . . . nuh . . ." sound. He saw a fresh, dark bruise on her left forearm he'd not noticed when he put her to bed.

"Wake up, Sarah Beth. It's me, Jed, your mom and dad's friend," he said, his voice calm and soothing. "You're safe, Sarah Beth. . . . No one can hurt you here."

Her eyes sprang open so wide he thought they'd pop from

their sockets, and for a moment he thought he saw a faint amber glow. He shook the irrational thought away and reached for her again, the light in her eyes a trick of the morning light streaming in through the picture window behind him.

"J . . . J . . . Jed?" she stammered.

Before he could answer, she collapsed into his arms and wrapped her own tightly around his neck.

"He was here," she said, then repeated it over and over again until it sounded less like words and more like the wail of a wounded animal.

"It's okay," he said, holding her tightly. "Everything's going to be okay."

During his tenure with the SEALs, he'd had hostages—both men and women—cling to him tightly after being liberated from their captors, but never anything quite like this. He rocked her gently and shushed her. Eventually she relaxed and her sobbing ebbed.

When she was ready, she let go of his neck and pulled back to look at him. Fresh worry furrowed her brow and she scanned the room. "Where am I?"

"In a safe house," he said, taking her hand in his. "You were having a nightmare, but it's over now."

"It wasn't a nightmare," she said. "He was here—or I was there, or I was him . . . I don't know. I don't really understand, but I don't ever want that to happen again," she said, wiping snot unceremoniously from her face with the back of her hand.

"There're no bad guys here, I promise. It's just me and you and the men who helped save us."

"No," she said, shaking her head with a resigned certainty that gave him goose bumps. "Victor *was* here."

"Who's Victor?" he asked, but the electric dread in his gut was proof he already knew the answer to that question. He'd had his own run-in with Victor, only he'd not known the name of the shadowy figure behind the curtains at the time. He shuddered at the memory of being compelled to take his own life. "At the compound, did he . . . did he hurt you, Sarah Beth?"

She shook her head, this time almost as if annoyed. "No . . . I mean, yes. He didn't torture me or rape me or whatever you're thinking, but he hurt me inside—like in my soul. He can get inside my mind and I was inside his mind. I saw things—horrible things—and I know he is the one doing it." She fixed him with a wet, pleading stare. "Please, Jed. You have to stop him. Don't let him kill all of those people. Don't let that little boy die."

"What people, Sarah Beth?" he asked, increasingly frustrated and confused. "What little boy? Did this man have other kids in the house—a little boy? Does he have other hostages? Who is Victor?"

"I know who Victor is," a voice said from behind him.

Jed turned to see Morvant in the doorway of the bedroom. He was alone, standing with his arms folded across his chest.

"I saw people being murdered. We have to stop it," Sarah Beth said to Morvant. "Can you help us, mister? Can you stop it?"

"We're going to try," Morvant said. "I know how terrifying those images and voices can be, Sarah Beth, believe me. Especially at first, when they come at random and you don't know what they mean. It's really scary, isn't it? I've had it too."

Once again, Sarah Beth looked annoyed, and Jed thought maybe he got it. She had something important to say, and she needed to be taken seriously. She thought—and he wasn't sure how he suddenly knew this—that when grown-ups were trying to make kids feel better, they practiced listening without hearing.

"I think we really need to hear what she has to say, Ben," Jed said, hoping the familiarity of using Morvant's first name might help strike a chord.

"I agree completely," Morvant said. "Which is why we have some special friends en route who are going to help us sort this all out. You'll really like them, Sarah Beth—especially Pastor Dee. She's awesome. And there's a girl, not much older than you, who you can talk to. Would it be okay if we go downstairs now? We'll figure this all out, get you some breakfast, and then call your mom and dad."

"I'm starving," Sarah Beth announced and slipped out of bed. Smoothing her shirt over her jeans, she walked to Morvant, all her fear apparently evaporated. "What do you have to eat?"

"Well, one of my guys is making a bunch of bacon and eggs as we speak. How's that sound?"

Sarah Beth looked at him as if considering. "I've been trying to go vegan," she said but then sniffed the air, and Jed noticed the smell of bacon wafting up for the first time. "But I guess that can wait until this is all over." She looked back at Jed. "You coming, Jed?"

"Yeah," he said, pressing to his feet. "I'm starving too."

Sarah Beth smiled, slipped past Morvant, and headed down the hall.

Jed looked Morvant in the eyes, searching for any clue at all that he could trust this man, this legendary SEAL. "I think it's about time you and I had that talk," he said, his voice hard but even.

"Agreed," Morvant said. "But let's hear what the girl has to say, eat some breakfast, and get her on the phone with her parents. After that, you and I can go for a walk and I'll tell you anything you want to know. C'mon, let's go eat."

Jed was about to acquiesce but then shook his head. "No, I'm done putting this off. I want to know what's going on now, *before* your shrinks start interrogating that scared little girl. Start with who you guys really are, why you're interested in a kidnapped girl from Nashville, and whoever this *Victor* is." He folded his arms on his chest, mirroring Morvant's stance. "It's time to talk frogman to frogman," he added. "For the brotherhood."

"All right, Jed," Morvant said with a conciliatory smile. "For the brotherhood—past and present."

CHAPTER
TWENTY-THREE

Jed knew from the look on Morvant's face he wasn't getting a full read in. He'd been on the other side of these conversations in his prior life enough to know how this would go. No matter how demanding the curious party was, task force guys knew to give just enough information to scratch the itch. The most widely held misconception about the intelligence community was that it was an impenetrable vault, when in reality it was a giant onion—protected by an infinite number of layers. Crack a vault and the thief wins access to all the contents in one fell swoop. Peel one layer of an onion, and all you find is another layer. For most folks, one layer was all it took to satisfy their "need to know" because they were stuck in the wrong metaphor.

"We call ourselves the Shepherds," Morvant began.

Jed's mind flashed back to the upstairs hallway in the target house, where he'd faced off against the *thing* that looked like a grandma. *"Shepherd,"* she had called him, seething with both fear and hatred. *Shepherd* was the word she'd screamed, sounding the alarm.

". . . we're part of a joint task force that prosecutes both home-grown domestic threats as well as international plots against the homeland . . ."

This is how you're going to play it, Jed thought, already starting to tune out. *So much for the "brotherhood past and present" promise.*

His face must have betrayed him because Morvant abruptly stopped talking.

"Not working for you?" the former frogman said with a curl of the lips.

Jed shook his head. "Nope."

"All right, that's fair," Morvant said through a laugh, "but you can't blame a brother for trying. You know how these things go."

"I do."

The two men stared at each other, standing on the opposite sides of an invisible chasm. It was Jed who broke first. "So you're not going to read me in?"

Morvant gave a little shrug. "Well, Jed, that all depends on you . . . and whether you're ready to take the next step."

"And if I say I am?"

"Then I'll call your bluff. We both know you think you're ready to peel this onion, but you ain't quite there yet."

Jed blew a little puff of air through his nose and tried to figure out what to say next to this annoyingly prescient sage of an operator. Coming from anyone else, that line would have been infuriatingly smug, but from Morvant it simply felt fraternal.

"Tell you what," the man said, clapping a hand on Jed's shoulder. "Why don't we head downstairs and you break bread with the guys at the table. Hang out with us for a little while and you'll see we're not hiding anything from you. You're already inside the SCIF, Jed. All you have to do is pay attention."

Jed contemplated the comment and followed Morvant downstairs. He ducked his head at the bottom, where the combination of the low-sloping ceiling and offset final stair tread created the perfect head-thumping hazard for someone his height. He rounded the corner and stepped into the kitchen, where he found Sarah Beth sitting at a long, rectangular wooden table with four of Morvant's operators. To his surprise, she was laughing at something one of the guys had just said. Her plate was loaded up with eggs, bacon, and two slices of toast slathered in butter. The kid had as much food on her plate as the men who laughed along with her.

The moment they noticed Jed, the conversation stopped and the assembled diners all turned in unison to look at them.

"Make some room, fellas," Morvant said, and everybody scooted and shifted to accommodate.

Morvant slipped into the empty chair at the head of the table, while Jed walked to the end of the long bench seat and sat next to Sarah Beth. His hip flared with pain as he brought his leg around and under the table, but he just grinned and shouldered the agony.

The operator called Eli worked in the kitchen—happily filling the role of short-order cook—and called out to Jed with a smile. "What can I do you for?"

"I'll have what she's having," he said with a wink at Sarah Beth. "But drown my eggs in Tabasco if you have it."

"The works with heat," Eli said, spinning the spatula around in his raised right hand like a drummer helicoptering a drumstick.

"Make that two," Morvant said.

"You good?" Jed said, turning to Sarah Beth.

"Check," she said with a mouthful of eggs.

A mobile phone vibrated and a clean-cut operator seated across the table fished a phone out of his pocket and took the call. "Grayson," he said and then listened. "Yeah . . . appreciate the heads-up. Y'all can just pull in the garage, shut the door behind you, and come on in. We're having breakfast in the kitchen. . . . Yep, see y'all in a few." He ended the call and looked to Morvant. "That was Pastor Dee. They're pulling into the neighborhood."

"How'd she sound?" Morvant asked.

"Five by."

"Just to be sure, why don't you spot for me and make sure they don't have a tail."

"Roger that, boss," Grayson said and pushed back from the table. Jed watched the operator grab a rifle and head toward the front of the house.

"Order up," Eli said and delivered a warm plate to Jed with a mound of scrambled eggs—drenched in Tabasco—along with four pieces of bacon and two slices of buttered toast.

"Thanks, brother," Jed said and immediately started shoveling the eggs in. Seeing everyone staring at him, he said, "What?"

"Just a little game we play," Morvant said. "We call it First Bite."

"Huh?" Jed said, cocking an eyebrow.

"You never thought about that before? When you get a plate of delicious food, what morsel do you eat first?" Morvant explained as Eli slid a plate identical to Jed's in front of him. Morvant bowed his head for a quick blessing, and then he picked up a piece of bacon and bit it in half. "You went for the eggs first. Me, I can't resist the bacon."

"Is it some sorta psychology test?" Jed said, self-conscious now. "What does it mean?"

Morvant hesitated. Then with deadpan delivery he said, "It means you really like eggs."

A beat later, everybody busted up laughing, including Sarah Beth. Jed shot her his best *"Et tu, Brute?"* look but couldn't stop from smiling as he did.

"I went for the buttered toast first," she said. "I loooove bread."

Jed heard the sound of the garage door drive mechanism operating through the back wall of the kitchen. The operator called Grayson returned, still armed but holding his rifle in a relaxed carry. He nodded to Morvant—*all good*. A moment later, the house door from the garage opened and two figures stepped inside: one, a well-dressed middle-aged African American woman, and the other a thin white teenage girl wearing blue jeans and a navy-blue hoodie.

A wide, warm smile lit up Morvant's face and he pushed back from his chair to greet the newcomers. Wrapping the woman in a bear hug, he said, "Pastor Dee, thank you for coming. I'm sorry to have to wake you in the middle of the night, but you know how these things go."

"Oh, don't start with that, Benjamin," she said. "You don't need an excuse to get me out of bed. Besides, I could smell Eli's cooking all the way back in Murfreesboro." Pastor Dee returned the hug and patted him on the back. They whispered in each other's ears briefly before releasing from the embrace. Her attention shifted to her young companion. "This is Corbin, everyone, one of our most wonderful and talented young Watchers."

Corbin blushed and cast her eyes down.

Jed felt his mouth drop open. "Corbin? Corbin Worth?"

"Yes," the girl said, her gaze coming back up with a fire that reminded him a bit of Sarah Beth.

"I'm sorry about Father Maclin," Morvant said to the girl. "He was a good man."

Jed felt his pulse quicken and his mind spun in furious circles for a moment.

"Wait—you mean Father Maclin from the bookstore?" he asked.

"Yes," Morvant said.

Jed felt a wave of vertigo as the puzzle pieces finally clicked perfectly into place. From the beginning he'd known the two incidents were connected. Now he had confirmation. But there was one more question to ask. "You were the private school people that the Yarnells were meeting that day?"

Corbin looked at Morvant and he fielded the question.

"Yes, Jed," Morvant said with a tight-lipped grimace. "You were on the right track."

"So you go to St. George's?" Sarah Beth interjected, awe in her voice. "You were the student I was supposed to meet?"

"Yes and yes," Corbin said, a sad smile on her face as she looked at Sarah Beth. "I'm so glad you're okay, Sarah Beth. I can't even . . ."

"Thanks," Sarah Beth said and then looked at Jed, admiration in her eyes. "Jed got me out."

"Is the picture coming into better focus for you now?" Morvant asked Jed.

"So . . . Maclin was a Shepherd," Jed said, nodding, his words more statement than question.

"Sort of," Morvant said. "Father Maclin worked with the Watchers. He was a Keeper."

"He was my Keeper," Corbin said, the words catching in her throat. "And he was my friend."

"I know . . . and his memory lives on in everything you do," Morvant said, putting a comforting hand on Corbin's shoulder before adding, "Thank you for your service, Corbin."

"Thank you for your service"? What a strange thing to say, Jed thought as his mind went to Morvant's comment in the hallway upstairs: *"You're already inside the SCIF, Jed. All you have to do is pay attention."*

Pay attention indeed!

Morvant shifted his gaze to the operator sitting on Sarah Beth's opposite side from Jed and gave him a wordless signal. The operator immediately picked up his dishes and vacated his spot.

"That's all right, sugar," Pastor Dee said to the operator. "You don't have to leave on account of us."

"It's fine, ma'am. I've already cleaned my plate," the warrior said with a gracious smile. Then turning to Morvant, he added, "I'm gonna start organizing air assets."

"I'll help," Grayson said and they both disappeared.

"Can I get you a plate of something?" Eli called from behind the range.

"I'd love a pair of eggs over easy on toast," Pastor Dee said. "Thank you, hon."

"What about you, Corbin?" Eli asked.

The teenager scanned the table to see what her choices were and then said, "Just some toast and jam. Thanks."

Pastor Dee sat on the bench seat beside Sarah Beth, but with her back to the table and knees out, so that when Sarah Beth turned to look at her, they could talk more easily face-to-face. "I'm Pastor Dee," she said, her voice like a cool summer breeze. "What's your name?"

"Sarah Beth . . . Sarah Beth Yarnell," Sarah Beth said, her glance darting from Dee to Corbin and back again. "But I can tell you already knew that."

"Well, very nice to meet you just the same, Sarah Beth," the faith leader said with a warm smile. "I'm sorry for the horrible and frightening ordeal you've been through. It must have been very scary."

"Yeah," Sarah Beth said. "It pretty much sucked every second."

This comment garnered well-meaning laughter from Morvant, Eli in the kitchen, and the remaining two operators at the table.

"I bet it did," Pastor Dee said, giving Sarah Beth's back a pat. "Everyone in this room has had a run-in of their own with the Dark Ones. You're in good company."

"I can tell." Sarah Beth smiled and took bite of her toast.

"Hey, fellas," Morvant said. "Why don't we clear out and give our young Watchers some alone time with Pastor Dee."

The remaining operators pressed to their feet, nodded respectfully, and began to exit.

Jed, uncertain whether Morvant's order was meant to include

him or not, decided to remain put. Eli, for his part, delivered a plate of eggs and toast to Pastor Dee and placed a plate with toast and bacon for Corbin at an empty seat, along with two glasses of orange juice; then he hung up his apron.

"Thank you, Eli," Pastor Dee said, taking her plate around to the opposite side of the table so she could face Sarah Beth.

"You're welcome," the laid-back operator and short-order cook said. "Just holler if you need anything else."

Morvant nodded his thanks to Eli and returned to his previous seat at the head of the table. He turned to Corbin, who was still standing awkwardly off to the side. "It's okay, Corbin. Please join us," he said, gesturing to what was clearly meant to be her plate of food.

The teenager nodded and quickly took a seat next to Pastor Dee. The woman reached her hands out in both directions, and eyebrows up, Jed watched as Corbin and Morvant took her hands, extending their own around the table. Jed took Sarah Beth's small hand in his bear paw.

They bowed their heads.

"Father God, we thank You for being here with us. We thank You for delivering our sister Sarah Beth from the evil that took her and for Your protective mercy on us all. Bless this food and as always bless the work we do for You. Help us to be Your light in the darkness. In Jesus' name, amen."

Hands dropped all around, and Jed felt a warm calm sweep over him. Across the table, Pastor Dee smiled and winked at him, then, taking her first bite of yolk-drenched toast, proclaimed, "Mmm-mmm . . . so good."

The young girls chimed in their agreement, and Morvant

made a joke about Eli's culinary prowess eclipsing his tactical one. It felt good, Jed thought, breaking bread with these people. Real good.

"I understand we have you to thank for Sarah Beth's rescue, Jedidiah," Pastor Dee said, her gaze settled on Jed.

Jed pressed his lips together and then said, "Nah, she did that all on her own. I just, uh, helped her the last mile."

"Well, at least he's humble," she said with another wink, this time aimed at Morvant. "More than I can say for the rest of your boys."

Jed looked from Pastor Dee to Corbin, who was slathering raspberry jam on her toast, the bacon left untouched and pushed to the edge of the plate. Despite her diminutive posture, the girl had an acute presence he couldn't quite describe—like the thought beacon Sarah Beth had been in the woods, only many times more powerful. Pastor Dee had called the girl a *Watcher* and he wondered what that meant.

"So, Sarah Beth," Pastor Dee said. "Corbin here is just like you, only she's a few years older and has had training to help her use and control her gifts."

Jed watched Sarah Beth's attention abruptly shift from Pastor Dee to Corbin and then both girls burst out laughing as if at some inside joke.

Pastor Dee chuckled and glanced sideways at Jed. "Takes a while, but you'll get used to it."

Jed looked at Sarah Beth and, for the first time since he'd found her in the woods, felt like her anxiety had been lifted. An instantaneous connection between these two girls had formed, and he marveled at how such a thing was even possible.

Sarah Beth turned to Pastor Dee and said, "I'm ready to talk about my dream now. Corbin says I can trust you."

"I'm relieved to hear that," Pastor Dee said, setting down her fork. "All you have to do is tell me what you saw. It doesn't matter if it makes sense or not. It doesn't matter if you can't remember all the details. You don't have to be embarrassed or shy or worry about offending me. We're just talking."

Pastor Dee exuded a calm empathy the likes of which Jed had never felt before. This woman was like a rock in a river, immune to the currents, eddies, and rapids raging and swirling around her.

"Okay, but, um, some of the stuff is not nice—like, really not nice."

"That's okay, Sarah Beth. I'm used to that. But if you want, Corbin can help you through it," Pastor Dee said and looked at Corbin.

"Sure," Corbin said, giving a cautious smile. "I'm down with that."

Sarah Beth looked confused. "I don't understand. What do I do?"

"It's easy," Corbin said, extending her hand to Sarah Beth. "Just take my hand, close your eyes, and remember your vision. When I ask, all you have to do is invite me in."

"Invite you in?" Sarah Beth echoed with a knit brow.

"You'll see. Say a little prayer asking God that we can share the moment. The power all comes from Him, Sarah Beth, from the Holy Spirit. These are gifts of the Spirit that God decided we needed to do His work." She looked over at Pastor Dee, who smiled approvingly. "If you don't like it, we can stop anytime. But the Shepherds need us. We're their ears and sometimes their eyes. Without us, the battle would be over before it begins."

"All right," Sarah Beth said with a nervous smile. She took Corbin's hand and closed her eyes.

The first thing Jed noticed was that Sarah Beth's smile disappeared. Then the color drained from her face and her breathing picked up. He glanced at Morvant, who was also watching but did not appear at all concerned. The Shepherd must have felt Jed's eyes on him because he lifted a hand as if to say, *"Just watch and learn."*

Corbin closed her own eyes and then smiled.

"Oh, hi," Sarah Beth said, relief in her voice. "This is cool . . ."

Jed watched their faces—the expressions suggesting a conversation, but whatever was being exchanged was definitely in their heads. He wanted desperately to be in on the conversation, but no one else seemed bothered at all.

Sarah Beth kept her eyes shut, but Jed saw her lips moving ever so slightly, mouthing words. A minute or so passed, with both girls transfixed. They murmured now and again and often their lips moved, but no sound came out.

"It's okay, Sarah Beth; take my hand. . . . They can't hurt you," Corbin suddenly said out loud, her voice clear and at normal speaking volume, undoubtedly for the adults' benefit. "You wanna see something cool?"

"Whoa," Sarah Beth murmured. "This is like, crazy . . . like pausing a show on DVR."

Corbin's lips moved in silent reply and then her eyes popped open. She fixed Pastor Dee with a creepy, hollow stare that made Jed's heart skip a beat. She started speaking very quickly, her voice detached and distant. "Wooden pews under an arched ceiling. A domed ceiling over the white marble statue of Jesus on the cross. There's a painting in the dome over the crucifix—brightly colored angels flanking Mary; she's dressed in a red gown, looking down on the Savior. Five shooters in black, armed with assault rifles unloading on the congregation. They're fanned out in a semicircle, walking from the front toward the back. It's not a church service; it's something else . . ." Corbin's eyelids snapped shut and her voice changed back to its previous conversational style, presumably with Sarah Beth. "Hey, let's walk up to the front. . . . Looks like they're set up for a concert or something."

The imagery Corbin described of the marble crucifixion depiction and the fresco of Mary sparked a memory in Jed. He cleared his throat to get Pastor Dee's attention, and she turned to look at him, her eyes urging him to speak.

"I think I know where they are," he said. "Ask her if they see a stained-glass window above the lobby doors—I mean narthex—showing a white dove, wings outstretched against a royal-blue circular background. If this is the cathedral I'm thinking of, this particular window is at the back of the main sanctuary."

Pastor Dee nodded and said, "Corbin, can you go to the—?"

"I heard him," Corbin said, eyes shut, voice all business.

Her lips moved silently again.

Jed watched both girls, their eyes closed, holding hands across the table. Somehow, impossibly, Corbin was visiting Sarah Beth's headspace and seemingly participating in Sarah Beth's remembered vision. He took a mental snapshot, knowing this was one of those handful of watershed moments he'd experienced that he'd think about for the rest of his life.

Corbin opened her eyes first and turned immediately to look at Sarah Beth, who swayed a little and had a dreamy look on her face. Sarah Beth smiled at Corbin, and the older girl pulled her in for a hug. "You did so good, Sarah Beth, especially for your first time."

"Thanks," Sarah Beth said. "That was so cool having you with me. How did you do that?"

"Actually, you did it," Corbin said. "I was just along for the ride."

"Shut up! That was me doing that?" Sarah Beth said, almost giddy.

"That was God doing that," Pastor Dee corrected with a smile and a glance at Corbin. "And what an honor to be able to serve Him, isn't it?"

"It was scary . . . and hard."

"Most things worth doing are, in my experience," the pastor said. "God doesn't only call us down easy paths, girls, but He equips us for the paths He wants us to take."

In the corner of his eye, Jed saw Morvant shift in his chair, a cue that Pastor Dee instantly picked up on.

"I'm so proud of you, Sarah Beth," Pastor Dee said, her voice honey. "So it sounds like you saw an attack at a church?"

Corbin nodded and pulled a sketch pad and pack of colored pencils from the messenger bag she'd brought with her. Jed watched with intense curiosity as she flipped through the pages for a clean sheet. The drawings inside were unlike anything he'd ever seen before—beautiful and macabre. Spectacular and mortifying. Like scenes from a graphic novel, Corbin's sketchbook contained dozens and dozens of vignettes, sometimes one large scene covering an entire page and sometimes seven or eight different images forming a collage. Most of the sketches were of places or people—featuring men, women, and children of all different ages and ethnicities—but she also sketched symbols, alphanumeric sequences, and bizarre patterns. Among these, however, other things caught his eye—dark, twisted, and inhuman things. Gooseflesh stood up on his forearms as one of the fleeting images sparked a visceral reaction: a kindly woman of late middle age with a demonic ghostly countenance superimposed atop. A shudder chased down Jed's spine as the sketch hit home. He glanced at Morvant, but the man's gaze was clinical and fixed on the sketch pad.

Upon finding a fresh white space, Corbin began to sketch. She worked at ludicrous speed, her hand practically a blur as a dove materialized on the page—its wings outstretched like an eagle's, soaring against a royal-blue sky.

"Amazing . . . ," Jed said through a breath, awestruck at the girl's talent. "That's it, that's the dove in the stained-glass window at—"

"The Cathedral of the Incarnation," Morvant said, cutting him off as he locked eyes with Pastor Dee. "Is there mass today or a special event scheduled soon?"

"I think it could be today," Jed interjected, a lump forming in his throat. "Sarah Beth, didn't you tell me you saw men with guns loading into a truck that left the compound before I got there?"

"Yeah, a lot of them. I couldn't see their faces, but I know they're the ones who are going to attack."

"There's a community concert this afternoon—Join Hands in Praise and Peace," Corbin said, looking up from her phone, where she'd just run a web search.

Morvant turned to Jed. "Join Hands in Praise and Peace is the first of its kind nondenominational concert series in Nashville. It moves from venue to venue, to bring people of all faiths together to celebrate community and caring through music."

"It starts at four thirty," Corbin said.

"Okay, we still have time," Morvant said, glancing at his watch and then looking back at Pastor Dee. "I was wondering if you and Corbin would be willing to escort Sarah Beth on her homecoming?"

"Even if you hadn't invited me, I was gonna go anyway," Pastor Dee said with a wink at Sarah Beth.

"We're going to roll out of here in a helo, but I'd like two of my guys to stay with you as escorts, if you're okay with that?"

"Are you asking or are you telling?" Pastor Dee said with feigned indignation.

"I wouldn't dream of telling you what to do," he said, scooting back from the table. "Mama didn't raise no fool."

They both laughed at this and she said, "Well, as long as Jeremy is one of them. That boy makes me laugh. And I sure do love to tease him."

A wicked smile curled Morvant's lips. "He was already on my short list."

"Hey, Sarah Beth?" Corbin said, closing her sketchbook and swapping it for a deck of cards from her bag. "Do you want to play Speed until it's time to go?"

"I don't know how to play," Sarah Beth said.

"No problem. It's easy; I'll teach you," Corbin said and got up from the table. She locked eyes with Pastor Dee for a split second, and the older woman nodded with approval. "C'mon, let's go in the family room and play on the coffee table."

"Okay," Sarah Beth said but then shot Jed a tentative look.

"Sure," he said, not that she needed his permission. Then awkwardly he added, "I'll be right here if you need me."

She smiled happily at this, popped to her feet, and followed Corbin out of the kitchen.

Jed looked down at his empty plate, not sure where he fit in the equation, and decided the least he could do was clear his place. He went to get up from the table and his hip seized. A stab of pain flared in the joint, like someone had just stabbed him with a samurai sword, and the muscles locked up in spasm. Wincing, he collapsed back onto the bench seat and used the table to steady himself—shaking everything and causing a partially drunk glass of orange juice to tip over.

"Oh, dear," Pastor Dee exclaimed. "Are you all right, Jedidiah?"

"Fine," he said, the strain in his voice suggesting otherwise. "Sorry about that—old hip injury acting up."

"All you Navy SEAL types put your bodies through the wringer," she said, getting up from her seat to grab a roll of paper towels. "You think you're invincible, but the flesh is mortal, young man."

"Yes, ma'am, it is," he said, forcing a smile as he awkwardly tried to move his left leg into a position where the muscles would unclench.

"Lay back on the bench, Jed," Morvant said, walking around to stand beside him. "Let me take a look at that hip."

"All right." Jed complied, wondering what Morvant could possibly do to help.

Oh yeah, he's an 18 Delta, he remembered, the information percolating up from somewhere in his memory. In the Teams, Morvant had been a special operations combat medic—a designation known as 18 Delta.

"I noticed you limping earlier," the old SEAL said. "That exfil must have been rough for ya?"

"Yeah, I'd normally be popping ibuprofen and muscle relaxers by now, but circumstances being what they are and all . . . ," he said through gritted teeth as he tried to straighten his leg on the bench.

"Jed, stop," Morvant said, his voice serious now as he took a knee beside him. "Just leave it alone."

"But the docs told me—"

"Let's not worry about what the docs said," Morvant said. "Close your eyes . . ."

Jed shut his eyes, feeling the same compulsion as if the order had come from his old CSO.

"What I want you to do, Jed, is imagine all the angry inflammation in your hip calming down. Imagine all that scar tissue you've accumulated becoming pliant and cooperative. Imagine all the pocks and pits from the arthritis in the joint filling in and becoming smooth and slippery . . ."

As Morvant spoke, Jed could feel him pressing and probing around the outside and top of the joint. Next, he felt gentle pressure as the man pushed down with the palms of both hands, again in two perpendicular planes—from the top and the side.

"Are you visualizing like I told you to do, or are you obsessing about my hands near your groin?" Morvant chided.

"Sorry," Jed said, while the voice in his head shared its opinion about how absurd this was. What good would three minutes of massage do for an injury that three years of PT couldn't fully repair? He shook off the negative thoughts and grudgingly tried to visualize his angry hip cooling down and knitting itself back together. Several long seconds passed and the spasm began to subside. He felt Morvant reposition his hands and press in two slightly different spots before letting go, and each time, his mind imagined a warm energy around his hip—like a glow he could feel, and he thought that if he opened his eyes, he might actually see a faint glow from Morvant's hands.

He made a *tsk* sound at how ridiculous that sounded even in his head. Jed lay there for a moment longer before opening his eyes.

Morvant was now standing, staring down at him. "How's it feel?"

"Spasm's gone . . . ," he said, gingerly swinging the leg off the side of the bench. But when he sat up and pressed to his feet, a stab of pain returned, this time accompanied by a deep, dull ache in the joint. He took pressure off the leg and said, "But the pain's about the same."

"Well, healing is a two-way street, Jed," Morvant said with a hint of fatherly disappointment. "It doesn't matter what I do if you don't do your part."

"Right," Jed said, not really sure what else to say.

Morvant seemed to sense his confusion. "Healing isn't something I can force on you," he clarified. "You have to be willing to receive. You have to be open to it and believe it's possible."

The light bulb came on, and Jed felt cynicism wash over him. "Ah, so you're talking about spiritual healing here. Not some slick 18 Delta stuff. You can—like—*heal* me?"

Morvant laughed at that. "No, Jed. Don't be ridiculous. This isn't some Jedi trick. I don't have superpowers or something. I can't heal anyone." The leader of the Shepherds sighed. "But God can. And I'm grateful He sometimes uses me for that purpose."

"Hey, boss," a voice called from the other side of the kitchen, saving Jed from having to formulate an awkward reply. "Got the air assets heading our way. Ready to start putting together a tactical plan."

Jed turned to see Eli standing in the doorway, fully kitted up.

"Thanks, Eli. I'll be right there," Morvant said; then he turned to Pastor Dee. "Thank you for coming. We couldn't do this without you."

"We're a team. No thanks required." She walked over to him and gave him a hug. "You be safe now, Benjamin. I've got a bad feeling about this one."

"That's what you always say," Morvant said with an operator's smile. "So long as we've got your kids watching our six, we're golden. Ping me when Sarah Beth gets home, will you?"

"Of course, and the same goes for you after you've stopped the attack."

He bowed his head and they clasped hands together while she said a short but powerful prayer of protection.

"Amen," she said when she was finished.

"Amen," the Shepherd leader said. "If either girl shares any new tactical details about the attack, let me know."

"Always." She turned to Jed and stuck out her hand. "Nice to meet you, Jedidiah."

"You too," he said, shaking it.

"Will Jed be coming with Sarah Beth?" she asked Morvant with an expectant look on her face.

"It's your call, Jed," Morvant said. "If you want to tag along with us and help stop the attack at the Cathedral of the Incarnation, we'd welcome an extra shooter. If you want to stay with Sarah Beth and escort her home with Pastor Dee and Corbin, that's fine too."

"You're sending a couple of shooters with her as a protection detail?" he asked, double-checking.

Morvant nodded.

Jed tugged at his chin, unsure what to do. "I still don't really know who you guys are," he said, as much to himself as to Morvant.

"I told you, we're the Shepherds," Morvant said as if that explained everything. "We're part of a multinational task force commissioned to combat evil forces in the world."

"Sounds a little James Bond to me, Ben. Combating evil forces . . . ?"

Morvant smiled. "We're on a short fuse here or I'd give you the full brief, Jed, but here's the skinny version. You've seen things in your travels that prove real evil exists in the world—like all the operators on this task force have before finding their way here. And Victor is part of that evil cabal. You've wondered yourself how men could do the things you've seen them do to other human beings and felt that cold hand of evil. There is spiritual warfare raging in the background around the world, invisible but not unseen, if you catch my drift. That's where the Shepherds come in. The Dark Ones are this world's fifth column, Jed, bent on undermining the Lord's peace and prosperity, and they do it by flying below humanity's collective radar. It's our job to root them out. If you want to come with us and see how we work and finish the mission you started when you agreed to rescue Sarah Beth, we'd love to have you. If you'd rather stay with the girl and see her safely home, I respect that too. But either way, you have my word we'll finish this conversation."

In Morvant's gaze, Jed saw neither judgment nor expectation. A part of him felt obligated to stay with Sarah Beth, but another part felt a powerful compulsion to continue down this bunny hole and see where it went. At his old unit, he'd been read in on all kinds of spooky intel about one terrorist group or another, while foiling attacks that never made the news, with the average citizen none the wiser to the threat lurking right next door in the shadows. But what Morvant's task force was doing felt different. The stuff he'd seen at that compound in the woods where Sarah Beth had been taken was some supernatural badassery, the likes of which he'd never encountered before.

That's what you keep telling yourself, a voice said in his head, *but you* have *seen it before, haven't you? And that's why you ran away . . .*

"If it's all the same, I wouldn't mind riding shotgun on your op," he said finally.

Morvant clasped a hand on his shoulder. "Good, I'll let the guys know."

Jed nodded. "Thanks for the opportunity. Give me a minute to tell the girl and help her call home. Then I'll be ready to roll."

With that settled, he walked toward the common room, pausing at the doorframe to watch Sarah Beth playing Speed with Corbin. Both girls' hands were flying, each trying to match cards faster than the other. They were smiling and laughing, but at the same time their concentration levels were off the charts, playing at a pace he knew would leave him in the dust on his very best day.

Yes, something very, very strange was afoot in Tennessee . . . and the time had come for him to accept the fact that he had a role to play in it all, whether he liked it or not.

CHAPTER
TWENTY-FOUR

Jed leaned against the bulkhead behind the bench seat next to the open port-side door of the helicopter. Wind whipped at his booted left foot, which he dangled above the skid, while his hands moved expertly over the kit checking his loadout. As he watched the blue water of the reservoir below zip by, he felt like a SEAL again. He rotated his leg in a slow circle and smiled as the old nagging pain in his hip was all but gone. Was the healing real or a placebo effect born from wishful thinking? Did it matter? He'd not fully appreciated the level of disability caused by the pain until it had evaporated under Morvant's touch. *Evaporated* wasn't the right word, truth be told—*dissipated* was a more accurate word, as it had taken several hours before the full effect had taken hold. Had he met Ben Morvant six months ago, he might be in workups with his old unit's next deployment instead of riding along with this crew as a *former* SEAL. Of course, then he wouldn't be here and Sarah Beth would not be on her way home to her parents . . .

He smiled as Scripture filled his head:

"'For I know the plans I have for you,' declares the Lord, 'plans to prosper you and not to harm you, plans to give you hope and a future . . .'"

"Hope and future," he murmured, wondering why he suddenly remembered that verse from the book of Jeremiah in the Old Testament.

Does it apply here? Is this the future that God had planned for me all along?

"Five minutes," Morvant announced in their Peltor headsets and raised his left hand with five fingers spread wide.

On that cue, Jed's fellow operators began doing as he had done, checking their kits and gear. Jed, for his part, chased away thoughts of spiritual healing, Bible verses, and his future and forced himself to focus on the mission at hand. When the gun smoke cleared and the sheep were safe, that was when the sheepdog could entertain such ruminations. Right now, he needed to put on the familiar, mental armor of battle.

Distractions led to bad outcomes in this business.

And undisciplined minds got people killed.

If Sarah Beth was right, then they were about to stop a terror attack on US soil and save dozens if not hundreds of lives. *That was why he'd enlisted as a SEAL in the first place.* Despite the lies he'd told himself over the years, his military service had not erased his belief in God. And despite how far he'd drifted from his faith, it hadn't changed his perception of evil. He'd seen things over the years in the dark places of the world that would emotionally scar the average person for life. As a SEAL, he had empirical evidence to validate the existence of pure evil. He remembered Pastor Tobias talking openly about spiritual warfare, about the battle of good and evil raging all around them. Was it really that hard to swallow that dark forces whispered temptation and lies into the ears of man, just as God and the Holy Spirit directed man on the path of good? You couldn't have one without the other, right?

"Two minutes," Morvant announced on the open channel.

It's game time, Jed. Enough with the philosophy of good and evil. Whether I'm a soldier for God or for country, it doesn't matter. Right now I need to be a badass operator.

Jed watched out the side door as a second helicopter drifted into formation with them. His thumb found the safety-selector switch on his assault rifle and rotated it one click clockwise to the single-round detent. He could feel the rest of the team bunching in beside him, in preparation for the fast rope in. With Morvant as rope master, Jed would be number two on the slide port side, following Eli, the other Shepherd, out of the helo. Eli had already taken a knee beside the big yellow rope bag. Morvant would follow Jed out after the last of the three operators fast roping out the starboard side made the ground.

"One minute," Morvant said. "Shepherd One . . ."

"Two," came the voice from Eli, the second in command.

"Three," Jed chimed, calling out his assigned number in the chalk.

"Four."

"Five," replied the man he now knew as Grayson.

"Six."

"Chapel, Shepherd One is on approach," Morvant called to the control team coordinating the operation from a TOC—tactical operations center—at a location Morvant had failed to disclose to Jed.

"Shepherd One, Chapel—you have the green light," the radio talker at the TOC replied.

"One," Morvant said, uttering his call sign in acknowledgment as was common protocol.

The other helicopter would orbit nearby, the four operators aboard serving as a quick reaction force for the assault team if things went south; they were also the CASEVAC platform if the Shepherd squad took any casualties. That helo was designated by the call sign "Sword," and the operators, Sword One through Four, were all 18 Delta special operations combat medics, according to Morvant. Jed's assumption that this was a government-sanctioned black ops team—a detail Morvant had conveniently left out—was confirmed in his mind when they'd briefed that the CASEVAC plan was to activate "Raphael protocol" at the Baptist Ambulatory Surgery Center and the adjacent Ascension Saint Thomas Midtown Hospital. Morvant explained they had a protocol to insert military-trained trauma teams to area hospitals under a government contract during combat operations in the US. It was not lost on Jed that the medical centers were both faith-affiliated, nor were the obvious political questions raised by even saying "combat operations in the US" out loud.

As the UH-1 slowed its descent toward the parking lot on Twentieth Avenue South at Terrace Place, just a block south of the cathedral and directly behind the University Catholic Student Ministry building, Jed moved in tight behind Eli, ready for his turn on the rope. He looked down and saw that the parking lot below was over half-full with cars, but the south corner was still relatively open and a good spot for their fast-rope infil. The lot one block north, just behind the Cathedral of the Incarnation, looked packed full, and Jed felt his chest tighten at the number of people already inside the cathedral for this afternoon's concert.

"Let's get some," he murmured, a phrase he'd said on the approach to each of the hundreds and hundreds of direct-action missions he'd conducted over the years.

"*Hooyah,*" Eli said over his shoulder, confirming himself to be a former SEAL as Jed had suspected. Jed had worked with special operators from every branch over the years, but the brotherhood he shared with fellow frogmen felt deeper and more familiar. It was, perhaps, why he'd trusted Morvant enough to come on this op in the first place.

At twenty feet above the ground, the pilot flared the helo into a perfect hover. Morvant used a foot to kick the large yellow bag out the side door and it fell, trailing three-inch-thick green rope from a stanchion above the door. While it was still uncoiling, Eli grabbed the rope in both hands, twisted his grip, and stepped out into the air. Using his feet below and hands above to control his descent, the operator slid down the rope toward the ground. Jed followed, allowing only a second of spacing to minimize the time the helo was on station in a vulnerable hover.

Heat built up in Jed's hands through his double gloves as he braked near the ground. He landed hard—but without the familiar scream of protest from his left hip—and moved off to the right, clearing the drop zone for Morvant's descent. He took a knee and scanned his sector carefully as Morvant landed behind him. A moment later, Morvant gave a squeeze on his shoulder and he advanced with the team, aware of the huge rope falling to the ground behind him as he did. He leaned in on his rifle, settling into a familiar fast forward motion in a combat crouch, as another verse filled his head.

"The Lord works out everything to its proper end—even the wicked for a day of disaster."

He felt a grin spread out on his face as the words floated through his head. Whether this was Scripture or from a poem he learned once and forgot, or from the Lord Himself, Jed intended to make the words true in the coming minutes. The men who had taken Sarah Beth and planned this massacre were wicked indeed, and he meant to make this their final day of disaster.

CHAPTER TWENTY-FIVE

Sarah Beth smiled, snuggled in tight between her parents in their king-size bed. Her dad was breathing heavily with his eyes closed, on the brink of sleep if not dozing already. Her mom was awake, though, gently stroking her hair. A week ago she would have *died* before letting her parents cuddle her like a toddler between them, but today she needed it as much as she sensed they did.

I love you, Mom and Dad.

Jed and the other soldiers were off to stop the terrifying attack she'd foreseen—except for two guards Mr. Morvant had assigned to watch over her and her family. She said a soft, silent prayer that they would succeed. If anyone could stop Victor's plan, it was Uncle Jed.

"Are you asleep?" her mom whispered so softly she barely heard it over the clunky ceiling fan spinning overhead.

"No," she whispered back.

"Are you okay?"

Sarah Beth pulled her mother's arm tighter around her waist with one hand and touched her father's forearm with the other, pulling them both in around her.

"I am now," she said through a breath.

She felt like her mom might need more, but she didn't know what to give her.

"Did they hurt you?" Her mom's voice cracked and a tear, warm and tickly, dripped onto Sarah Beth's shoulder. Her mom wiped it off and sniffled.

"No, Mom," she said, her own voice tight, the feel of Victor still so fresh and terrifying. She pictured his thin, skeleton-like face and recalled the feel of his oily serpent's voice. She swallowed hard, willing the memory away. "They scared me really bad, but no one hurt me. They kept me in a bedroom and gave me food. They mostly left me alone, except . . . except . . ." Her own tears spilled onto her cheeks and she wiped them away roughly, annoyed. She needed to be strong so her mom could stop worrying. "No one laid a hand on me, I promise," she said and squeezed her mom's arm tight. "It was just scary. And then—I don't know—I prayed really hard and Uncle Jed just found me and now I'm home."

She felt her mom tense.

"Uncle Jed? Did he ask you to call him that?"

Her mom's voice sounded funny for some reason, but she just felt too tired to ask her why or to sneak in with her gift and find out why on her own.

"No," she said, feeling her eyes grow heavy suddenly. She yawned, which made her shudder, and her mom pulled a blanket over her bare shoulder. "I decided it just now. It just seemed to fit. He's amazing. He's my white knight, I think. Or maybe a guardian angel."

She felt her mom's lips on the back of her neck and then drifted slowly to sleep.

When she opened her eyes, she was standing, or floating maybe, over a big parking lot full of cars. She stared at the church—the "cathedral," she corrected herself. She watched as soldiers, all in black, moved forward in two groups of three, arranged in little arrowhead formations. One group crossing a courtyard beside the sanctuary and the other loitering there at a pair of doors to enter the cathedral. They paused, scanning over their guns, and then the first group crossed the brick courtyard just as the other group took position at the front doors. And then multiple explosions happened and the courtyard was swallowed by fire and smoke. The six men were gone—evaporated in clouds of blood and bone.

Sarah Beth sat up in bed, clawing her way out of the dream, drowning in the heat and the horror of what she'd seen, aware that the screams she heard came from her.

It's a trap. You must tell them. Hurry.

The vision was gone, and she was back in her parents' room under the ceiling fan, her parents wrapping her up in their arms.

"Bad dream, baby?" her dad said, trying to pull her back into their embrace.

She shrugged his hands off her shoulders and crawled to the bottom of the bed, then slipped off onto the floor.

"Wake up, Sarah Beth. It's me—it's Mommy. You're sleep-walking."

"No," she hollered back at them. "Where are the men? The Shepherds? Are they still here?"

"Yes, baby," her mom said, off the bed now, trying again to wrap Sarah Beth in a hug. "Tell me, Sarah Beth. What happened? What was your dream? You're safe, baby. We're here and you're safe."

Sarah Beth twisted out of her mother's arms and made a beeline for the door. "No, Mom. It's not a dream. There's no time. It's a trap and I have to warn them."

She sprinted from the room and down the stairs, aware of her parents' feet pounding the floor behind her, trying to catch up.

"You have to stop them," she hollered as she turned left at the bottom of the stairs. She fixed her gaze on the large man with the rifle and shaggy beard. "It's a trap—you have to tell them!"

He nodded and said, "Hey, Pastor Dee, you want to field this one?"

Pastor Dee looked up from the couch, where she sat beside Corbin. The teenager had her eyes closed, an earpiece in her left ear stretching to a radio-looking thing in her right hand, but her eyes sprang open at the racket. "Honey, can you tell us what you saw?"

Sarah Beth quickly relayed her dream.

Pastor Dee turned to Corbin, her voice thick with worry. "What do you see?"

Corbin squeezed her eyes shut again. Several seconds later, she opened them and shrugged. "I'm not getting anything, but don't take my word for it."

"You have to stop them," Sarah Beth demanded, in a full-on panic now. "There are bombs in the courtyard. It's a trap. They're going to get blown up."

Sarah Beth put a hand on Corbin's shoulder, closed her own eyes, and tried to go back to the vision. The images came back as she squeezed her eyes tight, her fingers digging into Corbin's bare shoulder.

"Oh, God," Corbin said, the word a prayer more than a swear.

Sarah Beth opened her eyes and stared into the wide eyes of the older girl. "Now do you believe me?"

Corbin didn't waste time answering, just pressed a finger against the transceiver in her ear and keyed her radio. "Chapel, this is Watcher. Get out of there! It's a trap!"

CHAPTER
TWENTY-SIX

Though Jed heard sirens screaming in the distance, local police were not on the premises yet. Jed's concerns about a compromised element inside Nashville Metro PD had inspired Morvant to plan the police call for the last possible second, to allow for maximum OPSEC—operational security. The clock was ticking. Morvant believed the attack would occur shortly into the music program, which had already started. In his peripheral vision, Jed noted the gape-mouthed expressions of pedestrians walking by at their kitted-up presence—an extraordinary sight in a town as safe as Nashville.

He entered the University Catholic parking lot running full speed in a combat crouch. Just ahead, Morvant led the Shepherd assault team with the speed and grace of a jungle cat—nothing resembling the wheelchair-bound, disabled veteran of operator lore. Morvant bent their fire team right, weaving around parked cars and then turning left at the sidewalk on Twentieth Avenue, while Eli led his three-man arrowhead formation of operators left across the parking lot toward the cathedral.

"Evacuate and find cover; terror threat here," Morvant called to a young couple holding hands as they stared at the six combat operators who must have looked like something straight out of an episode of *SEAL Team*.

The couple looked at one another and then bolted for safety.

Morvant surged right, toward the corner of the Catholic campus administrative building. It occupied the right side of a central courtyard, while the cathedral bordered the left. A primary school sat at the head position behind a breezeway connecting the sanctuary to the admin building. Eli and his two fellow operators, Bravo team, were already crouched beside the cathedral doors. Alpha team, comprised of Morvant, Jed, and Grayson, would breach the breezeway at the top of the courtyard and enter the cathedral on the east. The two fire teams would then converge inside on perpendicular vectors toward the dais.

"Chapel, One—Shepherds set. Eyes?" Morvant called in, reporting they were ready to breach and asking for a final surveillance update on the position of friendlies versus possible tangos.

Jed waited, wondering what kind of assets this task force had for eyes in the sky. Was there a Predator drone orbiting above them, or had a satellite been tasked for their operation? He had so many questions, but his curiosity was dwarfed by the joy and rush of operating again.

"Shepherds, hold one," came a calm voice, just like the cool voices Jed was used to hearing in his ear on countless SEAL missions. "We have new intel coming to us live. Stand by . . ."

Morvant looked back at Jed and frowned. Jed raised his eyebrows and Morvant shrugged his shoulders. Then he watched the SEAL close his eyes and let out a long exhale. A split second later, Morvant's eyes snapped open and he was on the mic.

"Shepherds—pull back to the parking lot immediately," Morvant barked.

The controller, in a TOC somewhere, talked on top of Morvant's call. "Abort, Shepherds! Abort, abort . . . pull back!"

Jed backpedaled, scanning over his weapon and clearing the courtyard behind them during their retreat. Beside him, Grayson spun around, clearing their path forward into the packed parking lot.

"What's going on, One?" Eli asked on the comms circuit, his voice thick with concern. "We've got a lot of friendlies inside."

"Get out of there! It's a trap!" a girl's voice said on the line—a voice that sounded no older than thirteen or fourteen to Jed. And as impossible as it seemed, the voice sounded like Corbin, the teenager he'd met at the safe house. The fear and panic in her voice contrasted sharply with the cool, professional controller previously on the line.

"The Dark Ones know you're coming and set bombs in the courtyard. You're the target and they're going to—"

If the girl meant to say "blow you up," Jed never heard it because a series of explosions—three in a row a half second apart—turned the brick courtyard into a war zone. Clouds of fire burped skyward and shrapnel rained. The side of the admin building where they'd been crouching only seconds ago imploded. The horseshoe-shaped layout of the buildings surrounding the courtyard amplified and funneled the blast straight at them. The pressure wave hit Jed like an F-150 and he felt his boots lose contact with the ground as he was thrown backward. He smashed into Grayson and together they traveled four or five feet through the air before being slammed into the side of a maroon four-door sedan. The windows of every car in a fifty-yard radius blew out, sending razor-sharp shards of glass and dust in every direction. In his peripheral vision, Jed saw Morvant get tossed like a rag doll over the hood of a car and disappear on the other side.

When the dust settled, Jed found himself in a heap on top of his fellow shooter, his left side and knee screaming in pain.

So much for my healed hip, he thought as he scrambled to a kneeling combat position.

He checked and raised his weapon, then scanned the parking lot for targets. In the Middle East, IED attacks were almost always followed by enemy shooters lying in wait to take potshots at the fallen. He expected as much here, but a sweep found no targets—just a civilian lying facedown in the street twenty yards away, struggling to get up.

"Shepherd Two, Three—sitrep?" Jed called reflexively. This was hardly his first ambush and he had no idea about Morvant's status.

"Two is good," Eli reported. "We're all three intact. Where's One?"

"Stand by," Jed said into the voice-activated boom mic he had to reposition closer to his mouth after readjusting his helmet and Peltors, which had been knocked askew on his head. He turned to the operator struggling to get up beside him. "You good, bro?" he asked, grabbing Grayson by the kit and helping his teammate to a kneeling position.

Grayson shook cobwebs from his head and then blinked a few times before nodding at Jed. "Knocked me loopy for a sec, but I'm good now," he said. "Still in the fight."

"Cover the corner while I check on One."

"Check."

Jed paused long enough for Grayson to get his weapon up in a scan and then jinked around the back of the car they'd been huddled beside. The damage to the vehicles in the lot was extensive. A silver BMW four-door nearby had windows strangely intact but a wrought iron park bench embedded in its hood. Jed crabbed his way to Morvant and crouched beside the Shepherd team leader, who had made it up onto hands and knees, but no further.

"Ben, it's Jed," he said, grabbing Morvant under the armpit. "I got you, brother."

He helped the former SEAL to a sitting position and noted the streaks of blood on the man's face, two fast-moving streams pouring down from either corner of a deep gash on his forehead, just below the brim of his helmet. Jed pulled a blow-out kit out from a cargo pocket and retrieved a dressing and pressed it against the wound with firm pressure.

"Two, Three—One is up but will need—"

"One is in the fight," Morvant said, cutting Jed's sitrep off midsentence. "Watcher, this is Shepherd One . . ."

"Watcher here. Is everyone okay? Was I too slow?" The girl's voice was trembling, and Jed wondered what in the world they were thinking, having a teenager involved in all of this. Then he remembered what Corbin had said to Sarah Beth back at the safe house.

"We're their ears and sometimes their eyes. Without us, the battle would be over before it begins."

"Watcher, you did great. We're all good," Morvant said, taking the dressing from Jed and pressing to his feet. He wiped blood from his chin with his sleeve and spit a glob on the ground with extreme prejudice, seemingly quite put out at having been blown up. "Do you still have good eyes?"

"Not really," she said. "The wall is up again. I can try, but . . . no guarantees."

Jed pursed his lips in confusion at the exchange. Was Corbin—and he was 99 percent certain it was her voice on the line—running the overwatch drone or satellite for the op? Did they really have a kid providing their ISR?

"Watcher, thank you. You saved us, kid." Morvant rolled his left hand in a circle over his head, calling Jed and the other operators to form up. "Two, One—feels like a dry hole after the ambush, but we need to sweep to be sure. Same breach plan, but obviously if they're here, we've lost the element of surprise. One, Three, and Five in position in one mike . . ."

"Check," Eli came back.

Morvant led them across the parking lot, this time moving full speed, toward what remained of the brick courtyard. Three black craters dominated the landscape; the only pavers still intact zigzagged along the outermost perimeter. The breezeway—a glass-enclosed, four-seasons promenade that stretched in front of the primary school and connected the cathedral to the admin building—had taken the brunt of the damage. A giant hole had been blown in the center, where Jed remembered seeing a beautiful set of double glass doors just minutes ago. He prayed silently that no one had been passing between the buildings when the bombs went off. The two buildings flanking the breezeway had suffered less damage, probably thanks to the funneling effect of the geometry. Corbin—the "Watcher"—had been right. The target had been the breacher teams because the courtyard itself had been the target. Jed cleared right as Morvant cleared left, and in seconds they were across the smoldering wreckage of the patio and poised to enter what remained of the breezeway.

Morvant took a knee at the threshold, where the double doors had been, quick scanning left and then right inside. "Clear."

Jed surged past Morvant, broken glass crunching underfoot, and entered the breezeway through the gaping hole. Sparks fell from the ceiling as exposed, live electrical wires popped and sizzled. The olfactory hallmarks of destruction filled Jed's nostrils—concrete dust, smoldering char, and VOC residuals—and it evoked a visceral reaction inside him. Jed reserved a special kind of loathing for bomb makers . . . the ultimate cowards who, instead of facing their enemies in combat, hid on the sidelines and unleashed mindless, uncontrolled destruction. A memory of Scab's smiling face popped into his mind, and he shooed it away.

Gritting his teeth, he swiveled left, clearing what little corner remained behind him and then down the long, smoke-filled hall. As he did, Grayson cleared his six to the right. A split second later, Morvant came in between them, chopping his hand forward toward their objective—the cathedral. Yes, the courtyard bombs had been meant for them, but a packed house of concertgoers were still trapped inside. From the comms, Jed had gathered that Corbin and Morvant had inconclusive intelligence and did not know if enemy insurgents were still hiding inside the church, seconds away from massacring the congregation. Which meant that it was up to Jed and the Shepherds to secure the cathedral and get those people safely out.

Jed fell in on Morvant's left flank, Grayson on the right, and the trio quick-stepped down the decimated breezeway toward the cathedral.

"Two, One—nearly in position. Breach on my call," Morvant said.

"Two," Eli came back.

Seconds later, Morvant made the call—"Go . . . go . . . go!"— and Jed followed him through a set of heavy double wooden doors leading into the cathedral. They entered the east transept; Jed vectored right and stepped along tiered risers that he imagined usually held a choir. He scanned through his holographic optical sight for threats but found the box of bench seats empty. In Sarah Beth's vision, she had described bad guys firing from this exact position, but he saw no threats.

The explosions outside had the crowd less panicked than Jed would have expected. The main body of the sanctuary was packed with concertgoers—not exactly pushing and shoving, but nervously jostling and huddled along the center aisle between the pews. He could sense they desperately wanted to exit the cathedral via the main entrance to the north, at the rear of the sanctuary, but had decided to shelter in place. Jed shifted his scan for threats to the opposite transept, just as Eli's element of three operators emerged from behind the altar, passing in front of the crucifix alcove and beneath the frescoed dome. The crowd breathed a collective gasp and began jockeying for position like a herd of panicked prey animals at the appearance of their team of kitted-up operators holding assault rifles.

"Shepherd One, Chapel—West End Avenue has been secured by local law enforcement. No threats detected," the controller reported on the comms circuit. "Safe staging at the Qdoba parking lot next door."

"Copy all," Morvant came back. Before things cascaded out of control, he boomed out an announcement: "Ladies and gentlemen, we're part of a joint counterterrorism task force and we are here to help. The building was targeted by domestic terrorists. You heard the explosion outside, but we have the area secure now. We are going to assist with an orderly exit onto West End Avenue. Please no pushing or shoving. Once you're outside, move west—to your left—toward the Qdoba parking lot next door. If you parked in the church parking lot at the rear of the complex, do not return to your vehicle at this time. That area is still being secured. Police officers are arriving to assist you."

Morvant summoned all his operators in front of the altar. The five Shepherds and Jed remained instinctively in combat crouches, but they held their weapons lowered to forty-five degrees. Jed continued to scan, but he was convinced that the bad guys weren't inside. Victor, to be sure, had not attended this party, or he would have felt a presence.

No prickle of gooseflesh—that's a good sign, he concluded.

Morvant looked at Jed and held his eyes a moment. "Dry hole," the Shepherd said.

Jed gave a curt nod.

They knew we were coming, but how? We didn't even know we were coming until just hours ago. How did they plant the explosives for the ambush without people noticing?

A new thought got his heart pounding.

Who detonated the explosives? Someone outside with a line-of-sight view of the courtyard prestaged and watching our approach?

He was about to share these thoughts with Morvant, but the former SEAL seemed to be drawing a simultaneous conclusion.

"Five and Six, coordinate the evacuation, then meet us in the church lot. Keep your head on a swivel. Someone detonated that charge, so they may still be out there watching. The rest of you on me. We need to sweep the parking lot behind the courtyard again." Morvant tapped the boom mic closer to his mouth with the back of his left hand. "Chapel, did you copy my last?"

"Roger, Shepherd One," the controller came back.

"Have my Watcher take another hard look along Twentieth and Terrace," Morvant added.

"Copy, One. She's on it."

Morvant looked at Jed with fire in his eyes. "C'mon, let's go see if we can find the guy who pushed the button."

CHAPTER
TWENTY-SEVEN

Jed fell into the number two position behind Morvant as he led their chalk out of the cathedral, retracing their infil route across the courtyard into the church parking lot. Once outside, Eli and his teammate peeled off left as a two-man element while Jed and Morvant vectored right to increase their search efficiency. Jed had an uneasy feeling, his spidey sense suddenly tingling despite no evidence of a lingering threat. In Iraq and Afghanistan, there was always a gun battle after an IED, and he found himself scanning windows and the rooftop of the apartment building across Twentieth Avenue. Seeing nothing, he dropped his scan back to street level, looking for a shooter or possibly the bomber, set to detonate another wave of explosives.

Then Jed saw *him*.

He recognized the cop immediately, even from a distance and with the glare of the sun setting behind—reflecting a thousand scattered rays off the field of broken glass like a spotlight on a mirror ball. Jaw tight, Jed reached forward and gave Morvant's left shoulder a pat with his left hand, prompting the Shepherd to freeze. The team leader raised a left fist signaling halt—but of course it was just him and Jed.

"See that cop standing at the corner—the uniformed officer? I think he's part of this. That's Police Corporal Alexander, the guy who arrested me and set me up for the attack two nights ago."

The Shepherd nodded, but Jed wasn't sure he got the urgency of the situation. Anger flaring inside, Jed hovered the red dot in his holographic sight on the center of Alexander's forehead while stepping around Morvant and surging forward.

"You there—do not move. We're federal agents with a joint task force and we need to speak with you," he said, parroting the vague identification Morvant had used in the cathedral when addressing the crowd.

"I'm a Nashville police officer," Alexander called while brazenly moving his right hand to the butt of the service pistol he wore on his hip.

"I said don't move!" Jed shouted and shifted his index finger inside the trigger guard. Alexander *had* to be the bomber. That the cop was here, right now, and at the back of the building with a clear line of sight on the courtyard was damning.

There's no such thing as coincidences.

As Jed closed the distance, Alexander's expression changed, his jaw dropping open and eyes going wide with recognition.

"You," the dirty cop seethed.

"Take your hand off your weapon, or I'll end you," Jed said, the venom in his voice much more than bravado. Besides trying to orchestrate Jed's own demise, Alexander had tried to shut down his investigation into Maclin's murder and prevent him from tying it to Sarah Beth's kidnapping. Catching him here, at the cathedral bombing, was the final domino to fall.

Alexander regained his composure, shaking off his surprise. An ugly sneer spread across his pale, homely face as he removed his hand from his pistol and crossed his arms defiantly across his chest. "Your partner here is wanted for questioning by metro PD in connection with a murder that happened just a few blocks away," the cop said, his attention going to Morvant. "Bet you didn't know that, huh?"

"You mean when I defended myself against the guy trying to slit my throat while you watched without lifting a finger? I'd say you're the one who has explaining to do."

Morvant held up a hand to stop the exchange. "My colleague is a member of a joint counterterrorism task force and has been involved in an ongoing operation that has culminated with this act of domestic terror we've just witnessed. He won't be subjected to any questions outside our chain of command," Morvant said, his voice relaxed and controlled. He turned to Jed. "Three, join up with Two and Four while I speak with this officer."

"But this guy—" Jed started to protest but stopped midsentence when Morvant held up a hand again.

Jed lowered his weapon and looked into the stoic eyes of the former SEAL, where he received a wordless message loud and clear: *I got this, Jed. . . . Please go.*

Grudgingly, Jed retreated, all the while watching over his

shoulder as he sideways shuffled down the sidewalk toward Eli and the other operator. When he arrived, he kept his body tense and his rifle still tight in his grip, ready to drop Alexander at a moment's notice if he made a move on Morvant.

"'Sup?" Eli said, sidling up beside Jed to watch the standoff. "What's the boss doing?"

"That cop," Jed said, thick tension in his voice, "is the guy who stood by and watched while a nutjob tried to slit my throat two nights ago. I think he may have detonated the bomb."

Eli arched his eyebrows in surprise. "Well, if he's with the Dark Ones, the boss will sort it out. Nothing gets past Ben. It's one of his gifts . . . or maybe one of his curses. Depends on your point of view, I suppose."

Jed screwed up his face at the peculiar choice of words, then shook his head. "Dark Ones? Is that y'all's code name for these bastards?"

Eli nodded. "Yep."

Jed watched as Morvant and Alexander chatted, too far out of earshot to hear anything. But he was close enough to see Alexander's arrogant demeanor begin to fade and real concern grow on the man's face. Alexander said something, and Morvant reached out with his left hand and grabbed the cop by the arm just above the elbow. Alexander shook Morvant's hand away and took a step back, his hand moving again to the butt of his pistol.

Jed surged forward, raising his rifle as he closed range.

Morvant let his rifle hang on its sling and this time clutched the police officer with both hands. Jed watched the cop's body go rigid, as if he'd just been hit with a jolt of electricity. Blood suddenly poured from Alexander's nose, running from both nostrils over his lips and down his chin, but Morvant did not release the cop from his viselike grip. Next, Jed watched in disbelief as Alexander's head tilted back, mouth open in a silent scream. A heartbeat later, the cop's knees gave out and he became deadweight in Morvant's powerful grip. Jed watched in shock as the former SEAL lowered Alexander to the ground, where the officer lay sprawled and motionless on his back.

"What in the . . . ?" Jed said, trotting up to Morvant's side and lowering his rifle.

The police officer's eyes were open but had turned a milky white. Alexander's lips were still locked open in a creepy O, and his complexion started turning a disturbing shade of purple-gray right before Jed's eyes. He saw a wet stain form around the crotch of the man's pants as his body let go control of any remaining functions.

"Is he . . . dead?"

"Looks that way," Morvant said.

"What happened?"

"I healed him," the Shepherd replied without irony or sarcasm in his voice.

"Healed him?" Jed asked, incredulous. "The dude is dead, bro, so what kind of healing was that exactly?"

"There's only one kind of healing, Jed," Morvant said, putting a hand on Jed's shoulder, a patient teacher talking to a child. "It all comes down to what ails you. Know what I mean?"

The corners of the man's lips curled just a bit, and then he turned and walked toward where Eli and Grayson were still waiting on the sidewalk. Jed looked down at the corpse, then back at Morvant sauntering away, then at the corpse again.

What in the name of all that's holy?

"Chapel, Shepherd One—notify metro PD we have an officer down at the rear of the building on the corner of Terrace Place and Twentieth," Morvant reported on the radio. "No sign of trauma. Looks like the gentleman had a stroke or a heart attack or something. I'll wait here for the officer in charge."

Jed jogged after Morvant, his head swimming. By the time he caught up, the team leader was giving orders.

"You guys sweep west through the alley and finish clearing the rear. Then meet up with Five and Six in front on West End. We exfil in less than ten by ground." Morvant then spoke again into his mic. "Chapel, we need exfil via ground in less than ten. West End Avenue at the northwest corner."

"Roger, One," Chapel came back. "And be advised, your NOC has been deconflicted with state and local police by Eagle. Should be smooth sailing for you guys from here out."

"Roger, Chapel," Morvant said and turned to Jed. "You're with me."

Jed nodded and they walked back to Alexander's corpse to wait for the police officer in charge to show up. They didn't have to wait long.

"Jedidiah Johnson," Detective Perez announced as she walked up, seemingly less taken aback by Alexander's demise than she was by the sight of Jed, kitted up and fully armed. "Why am I not surprised to find *you* here."

"Detective," he said in greeting, while trying to avoid looking at Alexander until she did. Jed watched her glance at Morvant before finally shifting her attention to the corpse. She pursed her lips almost as if passing judgment on her fallen comrade for having the nerve to die so unceremoniously.

"I suppose I should have guessed as much," she said, looking back at Jed. "You didn't really give off a retired vibe, come to think of it."

Jed shrugged, not sure how else to respond.

An ambulance, lights flashing, zoomed down Twentieth Avenue and pulled into the parking lot. Two paramedics jumped out and charged over to the body of the fallen officer. Jed, Morvant, and Detective Perez shifted their little conversational triangle to make room for EMS to check vitals and conclude the obvious.

"So," Perez said, turning to Morvant. "You're team leader of this DHS counterterror task force? Maybe you can tell me what happened to Officer Alexander."

It struck Jed that she didn't seem surprised to have one of her precinct corporals dead at her feet. He'd sensed during their chat in the interrogation room that she hadn't much cared for the man, but still . . .

"Afraid we're not sure, Detective," Morvant said. "We saw him at the corner and came over to coordinate our sweep with him, and he just dropped midsentence. It seemed like he was dead before he hit the ground—heart attack or aneurysm or something, I think. No gunshot wounds or anything—we checked for that right away. Do you know if he had any medical problems?"

"I didn't know him that well. He was kind of a loner and frankly didn't really get along with people, as I'm sure Agent Johnson, or whatever his real name is, can tell you," she said, gesturing at Jed with a thumb.

"You seem to be taking the loss of a colleague pretty well," Jed said, more confused than accusatory.

"I apologize," she said, melting a little. "Occupational hazard,

I suppose. I was with Army CID in Iraq. I think I just learned to compartmentalize more than is healthy. I'm sorry if I seem cold. I assure you I'm not."

Jed cocked an eyebrow at her. "You didn't mention that before. I remember you said your brother was with MARSOC, but I didn't know you served as well."

"Oh, did I not mention that?" she said with a shrug. "Probably didn't want you to think you had me in the bag that day. Anyway, you and I both know what it's like to lose people, Jed . . . if that's really your name."

Jed gave her the knowing smile of a fellow wartime veteran. "I get it. Sorry; I wasn't implying . . . ," he said and then hesitated to finish the thought. "And yeah, Jed's my real name."

"Well, Jed, I can't thank you enough for all you and your team did here." She eyed him carefully, as if trying to weigh some question on her mind, before looking down at her hands. "Now if only we could find the poor Yarnell girl."

"On that front, I have some good news, Detective," he said, glancing at the dead police corporal, who'd just proven himself beyond a shadow of a doubt to be the bad actor in Nashville PD. "Our team rescued the Yarnell girl from the compound used by this terror organization just a few hours ago. We've already reunited her with her family."

The look on Detective Perez's face was one of relief, but also anger, which he imagined was normal when you'd been cut out of your own investigation by outsiders.

"You mean you didn't think to—" The detective held up a hand and closed her eyes, getting control of herself. "Sorry. I'm sorry. You brought that little Yarnell girl home to her family when

I was failing, and for that I thank you. You'll never know what that means to me. I wasn't ready to lose this one. It's so different with kids . . ."

He watched her face cloud at some distant memory—maybe from the horrors she'd seen in Iraq, or maybe from some loss here as a detective, but either way he watched tears rim her eyes. She turned away as if embarrassed, wiped her eyes on a sleeve, and then turned back, a sad smile on her face.

"Anyway—" she put out her hand—"thank you for all you did. I wish you could have told me who you were working for so I didn't act like such a . . . Well, anyway, thank you."

Jed took her hand, small but strong, in his and shook it firmly. "Pleasure" was all he said.

"Listen, Detective," Morvant said, "I don't know if you or state police are in charge of the scene, but my team will be exfilling shortly. Our guys still run nonofficial covers, so we need to be gone before press descends. FBI will be on scene any minute, so they'll handle the domestic terror aspects of the investigation from here. I wish I could tell you more, but I know you understand."

"Of course," Perez said. "I was told by my chief you guys are handling the follow-on, so looks like I don't get to put away the bad guys. I do have a bit of paperwork to finish up on the Yarnell case, however." She shook her head again. "I still don't see how the Yarnell kidnapping helped their agenda . . . What they put that little girl and her parents through is just unforgivable."

"We're going to be heading to the Yarnells' later," Morvant said, and Jed turned to him in surprise. "We still have a few gaps to fill in before we can locate and round up the remaining members of this terror cell. If you want to pop in and be part of that discussion, we might all benefit from the information sharing."

"Oh, I don't mind waiting until tomorrow to visit," she said. "I wouldn't want to intrude."

"Suit yourself, but either way I'll be sure to keep you in the loop, Detective," Morvant said.

"Thanks again, fellas," she said. "I'm going to chat with EMS while you guys disappear—exfil back to your secret lair or wherever it is you types live."

They all shook hands in parting, and then Jed followed Morvant west, feeling Perez's eyes on his back the whole time. He waited until they were out of earshot. "Why did you tell her we're headed to the Yarnells' place?"

Morvant turned, his face all business. "Because this is far from over yet. Our Watcher is at their house and we'll need her, and maybe Sarah Beth, to sort this out. This chess match isn't finished; there are still pieces on the board and those pieces are moving as we speak. If I know Victor, they'll have a secondary target in place for just this contingency. If we don't find it, there will still be a massacre today."

"But why invite Detective Perez to the house? Seems better to keep her out of it—you're not going to read her in, so why risk it?"

"Not sure, honestly," Morvant said through a sigh. "I just have a weird feeling that she may have a role yet to play in all this. And that detective is going to be following up at some point; might as well have her do that when the Yarnells have a little backup on-site, if you know what I'm saying."

"I do."

"Do you trust Perez?"

Jed pondered the question for a moment. She'd been straight with him in every interaction and she seemed almost hopelessly dedicated to her job. The fact she was military and had served with CID made her righteous in his book.

"Yeah," he said. "I think so."

They turned the corner into the alley that cut through the cathedral complex and headed toward the Qdoba parking lot, where a half-dozen police vehicles sat, lights flashing against the backdrop of a darkening sky. Morvant picked up the pace to a slow jog as two gray Chevy Suburbans with tinted windows pulled up along West End Avenue and stopped along the curb.

"That's our ride," Morvant said over his shoulder.

"Oh, I know," Jed said through a chuckle. "And thank God I get to be on the inside looking out instead of the outside looking in."

CHAPTER TWENTY-EIGHT

Sarah Beth felt proud and relieved and irritated all at the same time. She felt so many pairs of eyes on her and it was starting to give her the creeps. She wanted her mom to stop asking what she could get her. She wanted her dad to stop looking at her like she was a wounded baby bird. She wanted Corbin to stop telling her good job, and Pastor Dee to stop asking how she was feeling, and the two Shepherds to stop nodding respect at her with their serious soldier faces.

And at the same time, she kind of didn't want them to stop.

"Sarah Beth, honey, can I get you anything?" her mom asked, her voice hopeful.

She squelched the reflexive urge to roll her eyes and snap off a no. Instead, she smiled at her and said, "I'd love a glass of water."

"Sure thing, sweetheart. Coming right up," her mom said, and Sarah Beth could see it made her happy.

"Thanks, Mom," she said, accepting the cup a moment later.

"You're welcome. I'm always here for you. You know that, right?"

She nodded and took a sip of the water she didn't want while looking around their crowded kitchen, suddenly wondering why everyone was still here.

I mean, we stopped them. I'm safe now, right?

Pastor Dee caught Sarah Beth's eye and then the woman's gaze went to her parents. "Hey, Mom and Dad, if we could all move into the family room . . . we need to have a little group chat."

Sarah Beth saw her mom and dad exchange that "parents only" silent understanding they seemed to use all the time.

"Sure, Dee," her dad said and gestured for the group to relocate en masse.

Sarah Beth sat on their sofa with her parents protectively bookending her—one sitting tight against her on either side—while Pastor Dee sat in her dad's recliner and Corbin sat cross-legged on the floor.

"I'm not sure where to begin, but in the immortal words of Julie Andrews in *The Sound of Music,* 'Let's start at the very beginning—a very good place to start,'" Pastor Dee began.

This garnered a chuckle from Sarah Beth and her dad. They

both had the same sense of humor about embarrassing and stupid stuff.

"Your family," Pastor Dee continued, "has been thrust into the middle of a battle that has been raging for as long as there have been folks walking this Earth—the battle between good and evil. Now I know that might sound a tad archetypal, but I can't think of a simpler way to say it. And both sides are fighting for the same thing: to win the hearts, minds, and souls of the people who call this planet their home. Everybody feels it, but most folks don't perceive it. That used to really bother me—kept me up at night—but I eventually came to accept that it's not their fault. It's like getting mad at somebody for not knowing what happened on your favorite television series, when they're watching a different program. But I'm getting ahead of myself . . . let's back up. Why don't you tell me what you know about St. George's Academy and how you got connected with Father Maclin?"

Sarah Beth started to answer, but she stopped herself when she realized the question was directed to her parents. She felt heat in her cheeks and looked down.

"It's all right, Sarah Beth. You can answer," her mom said, giving her leg an encouraging squeeze.

She looked back up, feeling unexpectedly grateful to her mom for that. "Well, I don't really like my school that much. I mean, it's okay—it's, you know, a school—but I've never exactly felt like I fit in. Anyway, one day my dad and I were at the grocery store and I saw this boy wearing a St. George's Academy sweatshirt and he smiled at me. I smiled back and then he said hi to me in my mind." She looked at Corbin. "Like you did this morning."

"What?" her mom said, a perplexed look on her face. "You never told me that."

She bit her lip. "I know. I was embarrassed because, you know, he was a boy. And you and Dad were already freaking out about my nightmares, so I just didn't . . ."

"I don't think *freaking out* is the right term." Her mom knit her forehead like she did when she was irritated but not sure she should be.

"Anyway . . . I told him I'd never heard of St. George's Academy and asked him what it was like. He said it was awesome. He said that it was a school for kids like us and that I should definitely check it out . . . and so that's when I started getting interested in it."

"Wait," her dad said, "You had that whole conversation with someone—in your head?"

"Sort of," Sarah Beth said through a laugh. "He's the only person I was able do it with before, you know except for Mom."

Pastor Dee smiled at them. "But just to be clear," she said, "is it fair to say that the two of you—Mom and Dad—were under the impression before the incident that St. George's Academy is a typical Jesuit preparatory school for boys and girls?" Pastor Dee said.

Sarah Beth watched her parents look at each other and then back at Pastor Dee and nod.

"At Sarah Beth's urging," her mom said, "I queried the school to see about a campus visit, but the recruitment liaison said they always like to start with a face-to-face meeting." Her mom looked at Corbin. "From what I understand, you were the student who volunteered to meet us that day."

"That's right," Corbin said, her expression drawn.

Pastor Dee took the reins again. "Okay, so had that meeting

actually happened, Corbin and Father Maclin together would have vetted Sarah Beth to make sure that she had the gift and was of the proper moral caliber to be considered for admission. You see, Rachel and David, St. George's Academy is a school for Watchers, to educate and protect our umbrella organization's most closely guarded secret. Which is why, on behalf of the headmaster and the admissions department, I would like to formally extend Sarah Beth an invitation to attend St. George's."

A smile spread wide across Sarah Beth's face. "Really?"

"Yes, really," Pastor Dee said, smiling back. "You are such a fearless and special talent, young lady. You would make a wonderful addition to our student body and the Watcher program."

A dark thought came over her—in Victor's voice:

They want to use you for their own purposes . . .

She chased the thought—the lie—away. She knew better now who and what Victor was. And she'd seen the power of what her gift could mean in action. There was no other path she could imagine taking.

"Wait a minute," her dad said, holding up a hand. "If she goes to St. George's, does that mean she has to become one of these Watcher kids who are being put in harm's way? Please don't take this the wrong way, but it sounds to me like you're using these kids as—"

"David," Rachel interjected, using that "don't mess with Mom" expression Sarah Beth knew all too well. "I think this is a conversation we need to have offline with Pastor Dee or the headmaster."

"I don't want our daughter in danger," her dad said sternly.

"I don't go to St. George's now and look what happened," Sarah Beth argued. "I was kidnapped."

"Sweetheart, Mom and I need some time to talk about this," her dad said.

Now Pastor Dee held up a hand, the moderator perhaps. "This is a big decision and not one that I expect—or more importantly want—you to make on the spot. But with recent events being what they are, I wanted you all to know that we have a place for Sarah Beth, a safe place that will offer her a level of protection and security that you cannot in her current environment. And I say this not to offend or disparage you folks. I say it because, for whatever the reason, the enemy's eye is fixed squarely on Sarah Beth. She's simply not safe here."

Corbin cleared her throat to get Pastor Dee's attention, but it drew looks from everyone. "We're running out of time," she said.

Pastor Dee nodded and turned back to the family. "Sarah Beth, I hate to have to ask this of you, especially after everything you've been through, but we need your help again. Ben believes the Dark Ones have shifted targets."

"I don't understand," Sarah Beth said, her excitement deflating like a balloon and her mind now filled with dread about what else they might want her to do. "In my first vision I saw the attack at the Cathedral of the Incarnation. In my second one, I saw the trap. They stopped the attack and avoided the trap, so we won, right?" she asked.

"It's not that simple," Corbin said. "The battle with the Dark Ones is kinda like a football game—both teams have offense and defense. We're like the defense and the Shepherds are like the offense. But the other side has offense and defense too, and they're making changes to strategy and calling different plays to compensate for our moves. When your vision spoiled their original plan to attack during the concert, they changed the plan to set a trap. Then you foiled the trap, so now maybe they're going to call an audible and try a different play."

"Does the game ever end?" She felt tired just thinking about it.

"Yes ma'am, young lady," Pastor Dee said with a warm smile. "The Bible tells us not only that the game ends, but that we are playing for the winning team. But right now it means we've got to suit up, head back on the field, and try to stop them once more."

"But I only had the two visions," Sarah Beth said, all the good feelings she'd had just seconds ago washed away by a vague sense of failure and guilt. "That's all I saw."

"I know," Corbin said, getting to her feet. "Which is why you and I are going to try something new. Are you willing to try?"

Sarah Beth shrugged. "I guess."

"Is that okay with you, David and Rachel?" Pastor Dee asked.

Her dad opened her mouth to reply, but Mom beat him to it.

"Yes, but only with us here," she said. Sarah Beth smiled nervously at her mother, who squeezed her hand.

I'm proud of you, Sarah Beth . . .

Thanks, Mom.

"Can I join you guys on the sofa?" Corbin said.

David immediately gave up his seat. "Take my spot."

"Thanks," Corbin said and sat down beside Sarah Beth and took her left hand. "What you're going to do is reach out and try to find Victor and then try to steal the name of the backup target the Dark Ones are going to hit."

"What?" Sarah Beth snapped, jerking her hand away. "Uh-uh, no way! No way in hell I'm doing that."

"Sarah Beth!" her mom said.

"I'm sorry, but I'm not even sure it's a swear because Victor is for real from hell—the actual place. He's . . . he's evil. . . . I just can't."

Corbin looked at Pastor Dee for guidance.

"It's okay, Sarah Beth; you don't have to do it," Pastor Dee said after a moment's consideration. "It was a lot to ask, I know. We will find another way."

"Corbin, why can't you do it?" Sarah Beth said, looking to her left.

"I tried, several times in fact, but I've never encountered Victor before. We have no bond, no link, so he's hidden from me," the older girl explained. "It's like trying to find someone in a crowd that you've never met—you don't even know what color their hair is, much less what they're wearing."

"Why can't somebody else do it then? There must be somebody else at St. George's who can try." Sarah Beth felt tears welling in her eyes. She pictured Victor, sitting at the long wooden table with his dark, dead eyes and long, bony fingers, his oily voice and the thick power she had felt violating her. No, there was no way she could possibly connect to Victor. The very thought terrified her.

God, please. I don't want to do this. Father, show me another way so I won't have to do this.

And then the memory of Victor was replaced by a cold black shadow that filled the room and crept over her. Gooseflesh stood up on her arms. "Something's happening to me . . . Corbin, what's happening to me?"

"What's going on?" she heard her mom say beside her, but her voice sounded like it was getting very far away. "What's happening to her?"

Dark clouds rolled in front of her eyes and she suddenly felt like she was falling.

"She's found him!" Corbin said in a panic, her voice also slipping far away. "Stop, Sarah Beth! You're not ready yet . . . Stop and let me come with you!"

Panic washed over Sarah Beth as her family room dematerialized around her and she felt herself being swept away to someplace else—as if she were caught in some invisible and powerful undertow dragging her out to sea.

"What's happening?" she screamed, unsure if her voice actually worked or not.

In the distance, she heard Corbin yelling for her to stop.

Stop? Stop what?

Then an epiphany struck. *I'm doing this!*

Like flipping an invisible light switch in her mind, she turned it off. She experienced an instant deceleration and suddenly she was hovering all alone. Something popped, a sound as if she'd just stepped on one of those air-filled packing bubbles, and Corbin was standing beside her. Well, not exactly standing, as there seemed to be no ground in this place.

"What happened?" Sarah Beth asked, her own voice echoing in a weird, annoying way. "Where are we?"

"We're still here but also halfway there. You were starting to make a connection with Victor," Corbin said.

"How? I didn't want to make a connection. In fact, I was telling you no when it started happening."

"That's because as much as a part of you doesn't want to, your heart wants to help. Your heart, apparently, is fearless."

"Oh," she said, knowing deep down what Corbin said was true, but not wanting to accept it. "I thought for a minute maybe you were forcing me to connect with him."

Corbin laughed. "Forcing you? Even if I wanted to—or could—I would never. These gifts we have are from God, Sarah Beth. That's the difference between us and *them*. Never forget that."

"How did you get here?"

"I prayed and asked God if I could be allowed to help you." She shrugged in the weird vapor world they floated in. "I guess He said yes, because here I am."

"So how do we find him?" she asked, steeling herself.

"All you have to do is what you just did a minute ago and we'll be drawn to Victor."

"But I don't know what I did. It just started happening and then somehow I turned it off. It felt more like reflex than a thing I consciously made happen."

"It's hard in the beginning. And I don't think it works exactly the same for every Watcher. Maybe for you it feels different than it does for me." After puzzling on it a moment, Corbin said, "How does it work when you push thoughts to your mom?"

"I just think of her and I find her."

"How do you know it's *her*?"

"Um, because it's just her. There's only one Rachel Yarnell out there who's my mom."

"Exactly, and there's only one Victor. You find him the same way, but—and this is very important—you're not going to push any thoughts into his head or ask permission to enter his mind. We want to be like mosquitos—silently sneaking up on him and taking a little drink without him noticing. We're looking for one thought and one thought only, the name of the next target. You gotta concentrate and hold on to that. Hold on to it very tight and hold on to me. Okay? Can you do that?"

"I think so."

"No *I think so*s," Corbin chastened. "Faith, love, and certitude are our only weapons here. Faith more than anything. We're God's soldiers, Sarah Beth, and knowing that is a layer of your armor."

Sarah Beth nodded but then said, "What does *certitude* mean?"

"The belief in your cause, in your friends and allies, in your values and morals, and most importantly in yourself and in God. The Dark Ones exploit fear and doubt."

"Okay, I can do it," she said, trying to find her certitude in the ocean of self-doubt that was her default state.

Sarah Beth took a deep breath with her body and then forced herself to do the very last thing in the world she wanted to do . . . find Victor. She tried to replicate what had happened by accident when she was sitting on the sofa—channeling her revulsion, her fear, and her loathing for Victor. And when she pictured him—in all his creepy, vile repulsiveness—then it happened. A cold, creeping chill that seemed to envelop her, followed by an acceleration, like she was being pulled toward some giant black hole. A terrible, terrible feeling of desolation and worthlessness washed over her, and she felt his presence.

Am I in his mind or orbiting outside it?

"He's close," Corbin said, her voice a whisper. "Now concentrate on wanting to know the next target. Focus only on that."

She did as Corbin directed, but the undertow was so strong . . .

"No!" Corbin said, her voice sharp. "Too much . . ."

"I can't stop!"

She heard a pop and then she was immersed in him and looking through his eyes like she had in her nightmare. He was talking to someone—a man dressed in black military-style clothing. She tried to look around, to get more information, but his gaze was fixed on the man. She felt anticipation and malice as he spoke and was immediately attuned to the paradox of how his calm, measured voice belied the hurricane of fury and hate swirling in his mind. How could anyone function with so much rage inside? She forced herself to ignore the negative emotions and do what Corbin had instructed, focus only on trying to learn the next target.

What is the next target?

What is the next target?

"Oh, hello, Sarah Beth. Isn't this a surprise—you dropping by after running off like you did," he said, his voice very loud and close and taking her entirely by surprise because she could still hear him talking to the soldier. "And look, you've brought a friend . . . a friend who I've heard so very much about but have never had the privilege to meet. Thank you, Sarah Beth, for solving that problem for me."

"We need to go, Sarah Beth," Corbin said, fear and urgency in her voice. "Now!"

"But you just got here," Victor said, and everything around her began to morph and change back into her bedroom at the compound in the woods where the Dark Ones had locked her up. "Why don't you stay for a little while? We have some unfinished business, you and I."

"Corbin, help!" she screamed and tried to flee but ran into him. She turned and tried to run a different way but ran into him again.

"You're choking," he said, looking down at her with a vulpine grin, and her lungs suddenly felt like they were filled with Styrofoam.

"Something's wrong," someone said, very far away.

"She's not breathing!" another voice said, also very far away. Her mother. Yes, that was her mother.

She tried to scream, scream with her body and with her mind, but she couldn't.

"She's turning blue!" her dad shouted.

"You were a very naughty girl, running away like you did," Victor said, scratching a fingernail across her cheek. "And naughty girls need to be punished."

The bedroom door flung open and Corbin burst into the room.

"Thank God I found you," the teenager said and stepped into an unusual bracing pose.

"You need to wait your turn," Victor hissed and assailed her with a black wind, trying to push her out of the room.

But Corbin held her ground and the wind parted around her, seemingly deflected by the golden aura emanating brighter than ever from her skin.

Help, Corbin, I can't breathe! Sarah Beth screamed in her mind.

"*Yes, you can . . . certitude, remember?*" Corbin shouted, but her lips were not moving. "*Breathing is a choice, Sarah Beth, and so is leaving. Just flip the switch, and we can go home.*"

I can't . . .

"*Yes, you can,*" Corbin said, eyes bright. "*I believe in you. Pray . . .*"

She glanced at the open door behind Corbin and it reminded her of her escape from the compound in the real world. That time she'd been alone, and she'd managed to find her courage and use her gift and her wits to escape.

I already did it once, which means I can do it again, she realized. *For my mom, for my dad, for Corbin, and for Jed . . . I can do this!*

Head swimming, she channeled her inner David and said a prayer—the one she imagined he said as he walked out alone to face Goliath on the battlefield.

God, make me strong. God, take me home . . .

With a gasp, she sucked in a lungful of air and flew out of the room, grabbing Corbin by the wrist on her way out and slamming the door behind them. Time and space blurred and pulsed and then her family room materialized into view, her parents and Pastor Dee crowded around looking down at her. Panting, she threw her arms around her mom's neck and squeezed.

"Are you okay, Sarah Beth?" her mom asked, rocking her ever so gently.

"That was horrible" was all she managed to get out. "Is Corbin okay?"

"I'm here," Corbin said beside her on the sofa.

"Um, Mom, you can let go," she said and gave her mom a final squeeze. "I'm okay."

"You gave us quite a scare there, baby girl," her dad said, his voice tight with emotion. "What happened?"

"Victor happened," Corbin said.

"Who is Victor?" he asked.

"A very powerful Dark One, but Sarah Beth faced him and did amazing."

"You call nearly choking to death amazing?" her dad said, anger now in his voice.

Corbin nodded. "Yeah, actually, I do."

The doorbell rang, interrupting the conversation.

"It's Ben and Jedidiah," Pastor Dee said, and Sarah Beth could feel that the woman was right.

"It's them," she said with a nod as her dad hopped to his feet and went to the front door. After checking through the sidelight, he unlocked the door and let the Shepherd boss and Jed inside. Sarah Beth immediately felt their eyes fixate on her.

"Is everything okay here?" the Shepherd boss asked.

Sarah Beth leapt from the couch and ran to the door, wrapping her arms around Uncle Jed's powerful waist.

Then she felt, finally, totally safe.

"We had a little scare there for a minute, but everyone's all right," Pastor Dee said. "These two brave young women just conducted a very harrowing recon mission for you."

"But we failed," Sarah Beth said, ending the embrace and looking up into Jed's gaze and then down at her hands. "I'm sorry."

"Actually, we didn't," Corbin said from the couch, and Sarah Beth turned to her, eyes wide. "While you had Victor distracted, I read one of the assaulters Victor was with and got the name—Cross Landing Church."

"Really?"

"Really," Corbin said, grinning large.

"Are you certain?" the Shepherd boss asked, his face very serious as he clutched the handle of the rifle slung across his chest.

"Yes, they're prepping to hit it now," Corbin said. "I don't know the time, but I assume Cross Landing must have an evening service."

"Good work, girls," he said with a soldier's nod. "That was very brave what you did, and I'm proud of both of you."

"Thanks," Sarah Beth said, smiling at Jed, who stepped up to give her a fist bump.

The Shepherd leader turned to Jed. "You up for one more?"

"Hooyah, brother," Jed said.

"What about you, Corbin?" he asked. "I'd like to bring you with—you know, have you in the helo in case we need to adjust real time if they try to pull another target change on us."

"Okay, I'll come," Corbin said, giving Sarah Beth's hand a final squeeze and pressing to her feet.

"Until we get her back to campus, where Corbin goes, I go," Pastor Dee said with a nod of her head. "And that's called commitment, people, because you know how much I hate helicopters."

"Excellent. All right, Yarnells, I want you to shelter here until this is over. I'm keeping Jeremy and Rob with you for protection until tomorrow morning when we can assess what kind of security presence you'll need going forward and for how long." He turned to the bearded warriors still in the family room. "No one comes inside—not Nashville PD, not the FBI. At least not tonight. If anyone shows up, they wait outside until we get back. Understood?"

"Roger that, skipper," one of her shaggy-haired protectors said.

"Thank you," her dad said, shaking hands with the lead Shepherd and also, awkwardly, with Jed. "Good luck and may God protect and keep you."

The two warriors nodded and then turned to escort Corbin and Pastor Dee outside to the waiting vehicles. As Sarah Beth watched them go, a desperate thought escaped her mind: *Please don't leave me.*

Corbin turned, gracing her with a parting look before stepping out the front door. *It'll be okay. I promise.*

And what if Victor tries to get inside my head? she asked.

Just lock the door and tell him to go to hell, Corbin answered with a wry smile. *Back to where he came from.*

CHAPTER TWENTY-NINE

MH(S)-60 STEALTH HAWK HELICOPTER

EN ROUTE TO CROSS LANDING CHURCH

GREEN HILLS AREA, NASHVILLE, TENNESSEE

SATURDAY, 1905 HOURS LOCAL

Jed stared out the open side door of the helicopter, his guts in knots.

"What's on your mind, Jedidiah?" Morvant said in his ear, his voice clear and loud thanks to the special noise-canceling headsets and the helo's remarkably quiet rotors. The bird definitely had some high-speed, low-drag tech at work. "I can see something's bothering you."

"I don't like it," Jed said, turning to face him. "You say the bad guys are already here, which means they're either already hidden in the crowd or set in sniper positions. Either way, that's not good. Even if we execute perfectly, a lot of innocent people are going to die tonight. There's no way we can find and drop every bad guy before they start shooting."

Morvant pressed his lips together and bobbed his head side to side, which Jed took to mean maybe or maybe not. "One life saved is one life saved. We do the best we can."

"Do the best we can?" Jed echoed, screwing up his face. "That's all you got?"

Morvant smiled at him but didn't take the bait.

Jed thought back to that moment at the compound in the mountains when the Dark One in the window—who he'd since learned was Victor—had penetrated his thoughts. Victor had tried to coerce Jed into killing himself and had nearly been successful at that.

"With everything I've seen, isn't there something else you can do?" he said, pressing. "Like get inside the shooters' heads and force them to . . . ?"

"Force them to do what?" Morvant asked. His tone was patient but also reminiscent of the one Jed had used countless times when training up some clueless nugget fresh out of SQT.

"To drop their weapons and surrender or turn their guns on each other or blow their own heads off—I don't know, something," he said, his voice sounding more desperate and exasperated than he wanted. "I mean, going in there old-school like a bunch of door-kicking SEALs with assault rifles scanning for targets seems so . . . so yesterday. Can't you and Corbin just use your mojo and handle this?"

Morvant laughed and then put a hand on Jed's shoulder. "You're new to this, and over the past couple days, you've seen and felt some things that would blow most people's minds. You took it in stride, and you're rolling with us like a pro. But here's the thing, Jed—what you've experienced so far is just the tip of the iceberg. What's important to understand is that there's a physical component, a psychological component, and a spiritual component to these engagements. The best analogy is that our operations are like a three-legged stool—remove one of the legs, the stool tips, and we land hard. I can't stop bullets with my mind, Jed, and I can't stop them with a hug either. I wish I could, but we both know it doesn't work that way. And that, my friend, is why the Shepherds exist. So long as our enemies strive to inflict physical harm, we have no choice but to counter with a physical presence. That being said, rest assured that when we go in, my psyche and my soul will be engaged in conflict simultaneously with my body. But I don't want you to worry about that right now, okay? All I want from you is to be the best operator you know how to be and let us worry about the other two legs of the stool. Can you do that for me?"

"Yes, sir," he said, the *sir* just coming out . . . whether it was born of respect or force of habit, he couldn't say.

"Good man," Morvant said with a final backslap. He leaned back into his seat and then proceeded to number off the operators in this stick—with Morvant one, Eli two, and so on down the list to Jed, who was six.

Jed looked from Morvant to the teenage Watcher, Corbin, who was crammed in between Pastor Dee and Grayson. The scene was so surreal, seeing this teenage girl who couldn't weigh more than a buck ten, dressed out in a Kevlar vest and helmet with a Peltor headset and a boom mic. The funny thing was, she wore it like a pro. He'd seen plenty of boys holding AKs in Africa and the Middle East during his tenure as a SEAL, but never a kitted-up teenage coed from a boarding school.

"Ninety seconds," the helo pilot said, shaking Jed from his thoughts.

"Check," Morvant said, then turned to address the group. "All right, Shepherds, we're going in as a trio of two-man fire teams just like we briefed. One and Two in the front entrance, Three and Four enter via the north exit, and Five and Six via the south exit. The service is already in session. We've got ushers standing by to let you in. Our Watcher is going to be coordinating targets and helping us direct traffic with Pastor Mike Boseman, who has been informed of the threat. We also have the campus coordinator on the line with Pastor Dee. The Kids' Zone is being quietly evacuated to their on-site tornado shelter. Our goal is to find the shooters and take them out before they can start hosing down the congregation. Any questions?"

Jed had a million questions but held his tongue and decided to have faith in the process and his teammates.

"Watcher One, do you have anything for us?" Morvant said, looking at Corbin.

"Keep minds open and stand by," she said.

Morvant extended his hands, and everyone crammed into the back of the helo clutched hands in a circle. He then recited what Jed took to be the Shepherds' creed—a warrior's prayer that felt familiar and instantly energized and fortified him.

"Father, help us to put on the full armor of God and prepare us now for battle, not only against flesh and blood, but against the rulers, against the powers, against the forces of darkness, and against the spiritual forces of wickedness in the heavenly places and here on Earth."

"Amen," the team responded in unison.

"Amen," Jed said softly.

The helicopter flared on approach for their drop on the green space behind the main sanctuary.

"With God, Shepherds," Morvant said and chopped a hand left and then right at the helo's wide open port and starboard cabin doors. Jed followed his fire teammate out of the helo, sliding down the thick green rope and landing with a thud on what he now recognized as a soccer field. He sprinted clear of the helo and toward the south entrance, hoping that the enemy did not have a roof sniper waiting to cut them down on their approach.

Corbin would sense that, he told himself and put the troubling thought out of his mind.

He moved in tandem with Grayson—call sign Five in the chalk—clearing left and forward as his partner cleared right. In moments, they were across the field and sprinting up toward the south entrance as the other two fire teams spread away from them left and right toward the corners of the main building. When they reached the door—an exit-only slab without a handle on the outside—Grayson rapped his gloved knuckles on it twice. The door opened and a middle-aged woman greeted them with a wordless, wide-eyed stare. It was clear she'd never seen a fully kitted-up operator outside of television and movies, but equally obvious that she'd been expecting them, manning the door to let them in.

"Everything is going to be okay," Grayson told her. "Stay here, and when the time comes to evacuate the sanctuary, I want you to be a beacon of calm and order. We don't want anyone getting trampled. Can you do that?"

"I think so," the woman said, trembling.

Grayson put a hand on her shoulder and murmured a quick prayer, and Jed saw the woman immediately relax and her posture straighten. "Let's go," he said to Jed over his shoulder and brought his rifle up.

How in the world is this supposed to work? Jed thought as they advanced.

Scanning over their rifles, they quick-stepped up the sloping exit lane, which was shaped like a chute running along the left-hand side of the large, elevated dais. The sanctuary building itself was huge—far more in common with a movie theater or concert auditorium than the formal Methodist church sanctuaries he'd grown up in—and Jed quickly estimated that it sat at least fifteen hundred people, maybe more, in arena-style seating that sloped upward in tiers. Like other contemporary Christian services he'd attended, this evening's service was a multimedia extravaganza—more reminiscent of a MercyMe concert than some stodgy old-world choir Mass. The main sanctuary lights were off, with the stage lit by professionally managed spots overhead. Multiple mega-displays suspended from the ceiling livestreamed the band rocking out on the central stage. From the sound of it, Jed guessed there were at least a dozen singer-musicians performing for a packed audience. The lead female's vocals instantly drew him in, like a siren's song, and he had to shake his head to keep his focus.

A quick scan of the audience confirmed he was not alone in this feeling. Almost the entire congregation was swaying and bobbing in sync with the rhythm of the music. Many had their eyes closed, heads bowed, and hands locked with their neighbor. And those who didn't had their tear-rimmed eyes transfixed on the lead vocalist as she sang the words to a slow and melodic praise song, welcoming the Holy Spirit into the church. In that moment, he finally understood. The Spirit was at work here. No one, not even the worshipers standing a mere ten feet away, seemed to notice the armed operators moving into their sanctuary.

Wait . . . Not no one.

Some people did notice, and Jed noticed them too.

He wasn't wearing night-vision goggles, nor was he looking through a thermal-imaging scope, but the effect was eerily analogous. Dispersed in the crowd, he counted five figures with distinct dark auras. How it was that he could see *darkness* in an already-darkened amphitheater, he didn't know, but they were impossible to miss.

"One, Five—I hold five tangos," Grayson said on the comms channel from beside him.

"Confirm, five Delta Oscars," a man's voice said and Jed recognized it as belonging to the controller from the Shepherds' TOC, wherever it was *Chapel* located.

"Copy," came Morvant's voice, and for an instant Jed couldn't tell if the lead Shepherd was talking on the comms circuit, in his mind, or both. He focused on the task and saved such questions for later.

Five dropped into a very low crouch and moved into the rightmost aisle—a sloping series of stairs and landings servicing the main seating area. Not one of the faithful looked in their direction as they ascended. He glanced at Grayson and saw the Shepherd sighting in on one of the dark figures fifteen or sixteen rows up.

Jed took a knee and selected a different target, a Dark One in a seat best described as "center orchestra."

"Check, Six," came Corbin's voice in his head.

Do you know who I'm targeting?

"Of course" came her clipped reply, and he suddenly understood she was spiritually deconflicting targets for them. The controllers in the TOC didn't have eyes on—that was left to Corbin.

The music reached a crescendo and ended with the final lyric: *". . . to be overcome by Your presence, Lord."* The auditorium fell quiet and the worship leader stepped aside as the head pastor, Pastor Mike Boseman, jogged out to the middle of the stage wearing a wireless microphone.

"That was beautiful, Andi," he said, "Thank you. Praise God! And now I would like everyone to take a seat. Bow your heads with me, but bow them low. Humble yourself to Christ, like Mary did when she sat at Jesus' feet and like Christ did to wash the feet of His disciples."

In the corner of Jed's eye, on the big monitor, the pastor dropped low and fast to his knees, prostrating himself on the stage. On this cue, three other things happened simultaneously. First, the congregation obediently mimicked him, leaving only the darkened figures standing exposed; second, a single sniper round streaked down from the center balcony, sailing through the place where Pastor Boseman's head had just been a microsecond earlier; and third, the Shepherds went to work.

Jed's full attention snapped back to his optical sight and he steadied the red dot on the dark warrior's temple. The evil one turned to gaze at him—irises flaring amber and a distorted double visage snarling at him. As he squeezed the trigger, four other muzzle flashes joined his own, popping in space around him. Five bullets, fired from five suppressed Sig Sauer rifles, streaked like miniature comets through the night and dropped five targets.

Pandemonium erupted in the auditorium a heartbeat later, but their work was done.

"I want everyone to evacuate the sanctuary in a fast and orderly manner," Pastor Boseman said over the speakers. "Help your neighbor. Do not push or shove. The SWAT team is here. They've neutralized the threat."

The announcement worked, sort of, as terrified parishioners streamed for the exits. Jed's nerves were on fire, however, because he'd dealt with enough jihadists to know that any one of the tangos could be fitted with a suicide vest. He fully expected an explosion—raining fire and shrapnel in every direction—to rock the amphitheater at any second.

Keying his mic, he asked, "Do we know if any of the tangos have S-vests?"

"There's one vest," Corbin said in his ear.

"I got this, Jed," Morvant said and Jed saw the Shepherd commander already sprinting toward the center of the largest seating section. Jed pushed past the fleeing faithful, making his way up the wing aisle until he was even with the row where Morvant had gone. And as he gazed down the line between the seats, he saw a middle-aged man with half his head missing draped unnaturally over the back of a seat. A teenage boy with tears streaming down his face clutched the dead man's right hand in both his own, while his stupefied parents looked on.

"Hurry, Ben," came Pastor Dee's voice on the comms channel for the first time. "Corbin's losing her grip."

"I know," Morvant said as he went to work cutting open the Dark One's shirt with a knife to reveal a suicide vest under the dead man's clothes.

Despite Morvant's warning, Jed jogged down the aisle to where the Shepherd commander was working. Up close, everything was made clear. The bomber had a dead man's switch in his hand, but somehow the young boy had known to clutch the bomber's hand and keep the trigger depressed even after the head shot had taken him out.

Corbin. It had to be Corbin somehow . . .

If she heard him, she must have been too busy inside the boy's mind, keeping him from letting go of the dead man's switch, because he heard nothing in his head nor in his Peltors. And from looking at the vest's electronic detonator setup, Jed instantly understood the threat was not neutralized. He watched Morvant's hands flying over the bomb, tracing wires and leads as he worked frantically to disarm the detonator.

So predictable, a voice said in Jed's head—a familiar voice full of malice, hate, and acrimony. *Goodbye, you fools.*

Jed whirled, and down by the north side of the stage he saw a lanky figure making a mobile phone call. "Remote detonator!" Jed hollered as he brought his rifle up to sight on the figure. But as he took aim, he had an overwhelming and powerful compulsion to turn his weapon on his teammates instead. It was the same voice in his head as before, at the compound. And like before, the drive to comply was so strong that it was all he could do to drop his rifle before he brought it to bear on a Shepherd.

Victor . . .

A mobile phone rang beside him, and Jed knew it was over.

We've lost . . .

But instead of being consumed by a thunderclap of light, heat, and pain, a profound stillness settled over the sanctuary. Only Morvant moved. He hurled the ringing remote detonator and then brought his rifle up to sight on the dark figure who'd made the call. Morvant unloaded a full magazine, but the figure moved with inhuman speed the likes of which Jed had never seen before and disappeared.

"Do you want us to go after him?" Eli called, bringing his own rifle up.

"No," Morvant said. "Victor's time is coming, but it's not today."

"We can take him," Grayson said, falling in beside Eli. "I know we can."

"I said no. Even if you could catch him, the price we'd pay is too high," Morvant snapped. "We need to secure the scene and make sure he doesn't have any more surprises for us."

The two Shepherds nodded and set off to do as instructed.

"Watcher One, sitrep?" Morvant queried on the radio.

"All clear," Corbin said but then added, "I'm sorry about missing Victor. He concealed himself from me."

"Me too," Morvant said with a wan smile. "You did a great job, Watcher One. Thanks for spotting for us."

"Anytime," she said.

Jed looked from the young teenager still clutching the dead bomber's hand to Morvant. "Are we good, or do you still have work left to safe that bomb?"

"Oh, sorry," Morvant said, taking a paternal knee beside the boy. "You can let go now, son. It's over. This congregation and my men all owe you our lives, young man."

"Uh, are you sure?" the terrified youth said.

"I'm sure," Morvant said and gently peeled the boy's fingers free.

Jed's heart skipped the requisite beat and then he exhaled with relief when he was not vaporized.

"Five, do you mind escorting this young man and his parents out to the parking lot?" Morvant said with that "dodged a bullet" look that only a fellow operator would know.

"Sure thing, boss," Grayson, who had just joined them, said. Then turning to the boy, he said, "That was a very brave thing you did, young man. What's your name?"

"Um . . . Robbie," the kid said, still shaking.

"Well, Robbie," he said, acknowledging the kid's parents with a nod and putting his arm around the boy's shoulders, "let me tell you a story about this time I was in Djibouti . . ."

Morvant's eyes fell on Jed, a smile on his face—not haughty or smug, but proud.

"Whatcha think, Jed?" he asked. "Is this something you'd like to be a part of on a more permanent basis?"

Jed chuckled and dropped his head, suddenly exhausted. "Maybe . . ." He still had questions that needed answering, but it had been a long time since he'd felt this whole and filled with purpose. "Maybe," he repeated.

Morvant clapped Jed on the shoulder and flashed a smile suggesting he knew there was far more to it than a maybe. "Tell you what, let's talk tomorrow. A real talk, with no distractions and a full read in—I think you're ready to peel back that onion."

Jed nodded. "I think so too."

CHAPTER THIRTY

If you're coming, you must come now. I can't wait much longer or I'll be seen.

We have only a few left, healthy enough for the mission.

Send them to her. This is a priority or we will lose many more.

What about the parents?

Do whatever you have to do, but leave no Shepherds alive. There are two inside. Both downstairs.

Sarah Beth woke.

Not bolt upright, instant and anxious, like she did from her nightmares; instead the return to consciousness was a slog. A swim to the surface, from a too-deep depth—clawing her way out of the dark water with weights around her ankles. She resisted opening her eyes, fearful that when she did, she would find herself still a captive, in her fake bedroom with Fake Grandma waiting at her bedside and Victor standing in the doorway with steepled fingers, and the entire rescue just a cruel dream.

Wishful thinking is wasted thinking . . .

She listened . . . listened for the sound of someone breathing nearby but heard nothing.

With a resigned exhale, she opened her eyes and took inventory.

She was in her bedroom, her *real* bedroom, surrounded by her things. She was clutching her cozy caterpillar around her like a shawl, and her favorite pink blanket enveloped her torso. The dresser across the room was her dresser with her jewelry box and her mirror and her hairbrush on top. Thank God.

She sat up and tried to clear her head. This one had not been like her other dream visions, not vivid and mercurial. This was like one of those dreams that you know was bad but that faded to smoke upon waking. She strained to remember details of the voices, maybe something she'd missed that could help place them in time and space. She rolled onto her back and stared at the ceiling. Why had there been no images? If this was something that would happen soon, why didn't she experience it in vivid, high-definition three-dimensional space? Why hadn't she been there—like the massacre at the Cathedral of the Incarnation?

While she had no idea the time that had passed since she'd fallen asleep, the calm quiet of the night told her that time *had* passed. There was no sound of adult chatter downstairs or of a TV on, and no sound on the street outside her window.

She shuddered.

Something was wrong. She could feel it in her bones.

Send them to her . . . The words came back to her like an echo.

Could that mean me? Are they coming for me?

She closed her eyes and tried to remember more, to collect more echoes.

Leave no Shepherds alive. There are two inside. Both downstairs.

Sarah Beth flashed instantly back to the conversation with the Shepherd commander, Ben. He'd promised to leave two soldiers here, to keep her safe, until it was all over. She'd been asleep for hours, perhaps. Were the two Shepherds still there, waiting downstairs?

"Oh, God, no . . . ," she said through a breath, the words a prayer as much as an expression of fear. Her heart began pounding in her chest; she could feel her pulse throbbing in her temple. Her breathing quickened and she sat up in bed, dropping her brightly colored caterpillar to the floor. She scanned her room, searching the dark corners and the partially open closet for movement, feeling suddenly and profoundly vulnerable. But she heard nothing and saw only the shadows cast by the reading lamp on her desk.

And then one of the shadows, the one on the wall beside her window, moved.

She turned her head, snapping it left toward the door so fast it caused a sharp pain, just in time to see the shadow move toward her—not a shadow at all, but a dark figure all in black including a hat and mask over the face. Before she could scream, an arm wrapped tightly and painfully around her waist, lifting her up, and a black-gloved hand clamped over her mouth. The smell brought back intense memories of terror, the glove having the same wet leather smell as the time when they'd taken her off the sidewalk in Nashville.

It's happening again . . . just like outside the bookstore. They're taking me again and this time Jed will never find me.

She struggled and thrashed, but her body was locked tight in the grip of the powerful man carrying her, and her legs and arms flailed uselessly, several feet above the ground. She tried to scream, but finding it impossible, she squeezed her eyes shut and screamed in her mind:

MOM . . . MOM . . . They're taking me! Please help me! Help . . . help . . . help!

She spun her left leg around the waist of her captor but succeeded only in smashing her knee painfully into the doorjamb. She writhed and thrashed, trying to break free or to set the attacker off-balance, but accomplished neither, and the extra energy it took made her brain scream for air. She sucked in a loud, snorting breath through her left nostril, her right blocked by the glove-covered thumb and her mouth locked closed under the rest of the leathery hand.

She felt her head go woozy and worried that she'd been drugged again, just like the first time they took her, but realized that was not it. She just needed more air and tried to calm her panicked mind to stop hyperventilating.

They were halfway down the stairs, and she tried desperately to reach a hand up to grab at one of the pictures on the wall. If it crashed to the ground, the sound would wake her parents or alert the two Shepherds if they were still in the house. But the man carrying her shifted his grip and pinned her arms to her sides so tightly she could barely expand her chest to get what little air she could suck in through one nostril. She opened her mouth, barely, and bit down hard—getting only sour-tasting glove and nothing else.

MOM!

They reached the bottom of the stairs, and new panic hit, rising inside her along with vomit, which she tasted in the back of her throat.

Beside the stairs, the two Shepherd bodies lay side by side, gashes in their throats so deep that it looked as if their heads would fall off the moment someone tried to move their bodies. Their lifeless eyes stared straight up at nothing. She saw now that an enormous pool of dark blood surrounded them, reaching all the way to the circular off-white area rug by the front door, which had soaked up some of the blood in a curious arch, making it look like some sort of sick, bloody smiley face emoji.

If they had killed the Shepherds, then what if . . . ?

The creepy dream voices replayed in her mind: *What about the parents? Do whatever you have to do . . .*

Tears spilled onto her cheeks as she said a silent prayer. *God, please, please, please. Don't let my parents be dead. Don't let them be dead.*

The Shepherds were dead and her mom wasn't answering . . .

Uncle Jed! Jed, please! They're taking me and I think they hurt my mom and dad! Hurry!

Her kidnapper turned to the left, cutting through the dining room, and headed toward the kitchen. She understood now that he meant to carry her out the side door, which led to the carport and driveway, where a black van was waiting to take her away. As he carried her, she felt things going gray. Perhaps he'd drugged her after all, or perhaps she was fainting out of panic. As the darkness pulled in from the corners of her eyes, she decided that she was probably just dying from a lack of air and realized that, compared to going back to Victor, she was okay with that.

She felt her body go limp, too weak to struggle. Too weak to do anything but watch . . .

They were in the kitchen now, and the lights were on, but still everything looked gray. As she hung there in his viselike grip, her thoughts turned to God.

I love You, God . . .

"Don't kill her, you idiot!" someone said. A woman's voice. But not her mom's voice . . .

The suffocating hand shifted off her nose and mouth and she slurped air into her lungs. Her foggy head cleared as they crossed the kitchen. The side of her bare foot smacked the cooking island and pain throbbed in the bone on the outside of her ankle. Color began to come back to the world as her brain soaked up the oxygen flooding her bloodstream.

"Let go of my daughter!" someone shrieked, and this time it was her mom's voice.

A scream echoed in the kitchen—wild, furious, and feline—and suddenly Sarah Beth was falling. She tried to use her arms to catch herself, but too late. She hit the ground on her left side and felt a crunch. A horrible pain shot through her chest and up the side of her neck and into her jaw. She gasped and rolled over onto her back, expecting to see the man with the leather gloves reaching down for her. Instead, he was spinning in circles, grunting and pawing at her mom who—dressed in gold-and-black silk pj's—was riding him like a rodeo bull. Her left arm was around his thick neck and both legs wrapped tightly around his waist, locked at the ankles. As Sarah Beth's vision cleared, she understood the reason the man was howling. Light flashed off a bloodstained carving knife in her mom's right hand. Sarah Beth watched her raise it high and plunge it into the man's meaty chest.

He screamed, arching his back and clawing over his shoulders at the banshee on his back.

The knife came up again and Mom bellowed a guttural roar unlike anything Sarah Beth had ever heard before. This time, she plunged the knife into the man's face, burying deep into his left eye. He collapsed almost instantly, twisting as he did, her mom going down with him. Time shifted into slow motion, and Sarah Beth locked eyes with her mom as she fell. Her mom smiled at her triumphantly, and in that moment Sarah Beth flushed with hope. A millisecond later the back of her mom's head slammed into the corner of the island's granite countertop and the light went out of her eyes. Her mother landed on the kitchen floor with a thud, not moving and pinned under the weight of the kidnapper's body.

"Mom!" Sarah Beth shrieked and started crawling toward her limp and lifeless mother.

"Sarah Beth! Come to me! Hurry; there's no time!" a female voice called behind her.

Sarah Beth looked over her shoulder and saw a woman in a business suit, a gold police badge hanging from a chain around her neck, standing in the kitchen. "Who are you?" she asked.

"I'm with the police. My name is Detective Perez," the woman said, opening her arms as if beckoning Sarah Beth for an embrace. "Come to me. I need to get you out of here!"

Sarah Beth squinted at the policewoman.

Something felt off.

"Uncle Jed's coming for me!" she shouted at the woman, not sure why she'd said it.

Then she bolted—running around the island, ducking under the policewoman's arms and into the darkened family room. Her foot caught on the edge of the thick oriental rug beneath the sofa and love seat. She stumbled but managed to stay on her feet and sprinted across the room. She turned left, into the dining room, fully expecting the next dark figure ready to grab her. A shadow moved across the wall. She screamed and bolted for the foyer, only to trip over the pair of dead bodies at the foot of the stairs as she rounded the corner. Her chest flared in pain and she yelped as she tried desperately to climb off the two dead men. Their sticky blood was already soaking through her pajama pants and she felt them looking at her. Gasping in horror, she pedaled her feet like a cartoon character, finally finding purchase on the shoulder of one of the dead Shepherds and launching herself up the steps. As she sprint-crawled up the staircase, a gunshot cracked and echoed behind her.

"Jed, help me!" she screamed, out loud, she thought, but it might have been in her head. The line between the two was non-existent now.

By the top of the stairs her feet were under her again, and she started toward her room but then stopped, unsure. She whirled the other way, sprinting toward the extra bedroom Dad used as his office. She heard footsteps pounding through the downstairs as she reached the office door. Unsure if they were from Mom, the lady cop, or another kidnapper coming for her, she slammed the door behind her, spun the lock, and searched desperately for a place to hide.

CHAPTER
THIRTY-ONE

Jed yawned.

He deserved it.

Then he blew the air out through pursed lips as he piloted the gray suburban Morvant had let him borrow through Saturday night traffic en route to the Yarnells'. Right hand on the wheel, he balled his left fist and, without thinking about it, went to work on his wrecked hip. Kneading deep with his knuckles, he rooted around for the familiar burn, but it never came. He raised his eyebrows in pleasant surprise. Despite the pounding his body had taken in the last twenty-four hours, his hip felt like it did the day he signed in at BUD/S—completely and utterly normal.

He pressed deeper—nothing.

A smile spread across his face. This wasn't a placebo effect.

This was faith.

Flush with good feelings, he said a quiet prayer of thanks—first for allowing him to help save all those people, then for helping him look again at his faith for the first time in seventeen years, and then for the healing of his hip. Lastly, he said a heartfelt thank-you that he had been part of bringing home Sarah Beth and that she was finally safe.

His mind went to Rachel, Sarah Beth, and David. He'd promised to check in before going back to the hotel for the night, but now he was wondering if that was really necessary. The whole family must be completely exhausted after a week on no sleep, and Morvant had left two Shepherds there as a protection detail. Jed chewed the inside of his cheek as he put his turn signal on before the turn into the Yarnells' neighborhood. Feeling torn, he braked and pulled along the curb, stopping short of the corner. He tapped his fingers on the steering wheel. Other than his own selfish need for reassurance, what did it serve to stop by the house and intrude? Maybe it was time for him to fade into the sunset and let David and *his* wife and *his* daughter begin to put the pieces back together.

And what about me? What am I supposed to do? Walk away . . . again?

What would Rachel think if he did? And what about Ben Morvant and the Shepherds?

It's different this time, he told himself. *It's different than it was before.*

He looked at the burner phone in the cup holder. The navigation app displayed a green arrow instructing him to turn left in two hundred feet.

I'll just call them, he decided. *And I can figure the rest out tomorrow.*

That's when the scream came—so loud and clear he whipped around in his seat, certain it came from the back seat: *Uncle Jed! Jed, please! They're taking me and I think they hurt my mom and dad! Hurry!*

Sarah Beth's scream tore a hole in his heart, and fresh adrenaline coursed through him like liquid lightning in his veins.

"Sarah Beth!" he hollered out loud. "It's Jed. Where are you?"

No answer came, just the *tick . . . tick . . . tick* of his turn signal and the sound of his own breathing and the pulse pounding in his temple. He waited for what felt like an eternity, but the little girl's voice didn't return. Instead of green zone tactical energy, he now felt panic begin to swell inside him.

"I'm coming, Sarah Beth," he hollered to the ether. "Hold on, sweetheart. I'm coming."

He slammed his foot on the accelerator and powered toward the intersection. At the corner, he hit an unexpected dip, and the Suburban bounced up out of it, then impacted hard enough to grind the lip of the front bumper molding. Jed's backpack slid off the passenger seat and onto the floor. He reached over to the right, stretching his neck to keep a view out the windshield, and heaved the backpack up off the floorboard and onto the center console. As he approached the next intersection, he unzipped the bottom of the bag and fished out the drop holster with the Sig Sauer and the two extra magazines. Steering with his left hand, he used his right to pull the pistol from the holster and shove it into his waistband.

He ran the next stop sign and took the turn at speed, the big ute's tires squealing as he did. After the turn, he transferred the two extra magazines to his left cargo pocket.

Jed, help me!

Sarah Beth's voice hit him again, this time more sob than scream, and Jed gripped the steering wheel in both hands and mashed down on the gas. The Suburban bounced and rocked as he barreled through the neighborhood streets at a maniacal pace.

"I'm coming, Sarah Beth," he hollered, uncertain how it worked or if she could hear him in her mind. "Just a couple of blocks away. Hang in there!"

He glanced at the navigation app and committed the next turn to memory. Then he picked the phone up and pressed Ben from contacts, grateful that they'd agreed to talk tomorrow and he'd added the number to the phone. As it rang, he pressed the button on the steering wheel to activate the mobile Bluetooth connection to the SUV's infotainment system. A female voice said, "Connected," and then the phone was ringing on the Suburban's speakers. After another ring, Ben answered, his voice as calm and relaxed as if he were sitting on his back deck sipping sweet tea.

"Missed me already?"

"Ben, listen," Jed hollered, bracing himself for the next intersection. "Something's wrong at the Yarnells'. Sarah Beth reached out to me. She's in trouble. I think they're trying to take her again."

Morvant's voice was serious now. "Where are you?"

"I'm just a couple of blocks away. Have you heard anything from your guys?"

"No," Morvant said. Jed heard him call to someone else, his mouth away from the phone. "We're checking in with them right now and we're on our way. But we're fifteen minutes out, maybe more."

"I'll be there in less than two," Jed said, fire raging inside. If someone hurt that little girl, after all she'd been through, he would rip the limbs from their bodies.

"Jed, listen, I can't get my guys on the radio," the Shepherd said grimly. "Do you have weapons?"

"I have a shotgun and a pistol," he said, remembering the Mossberg, which Eli had been kind enough to remember to bring on the last op and returned to Jed. "It'll be enough."

"Be careful. We're coming."

The line went dead.

He screamed through the next turn and glanced at the console screen, which displayed the GPS map.

One more block to go . . .

And God help whoever he found when he got there.

CHAPTER
THIRTY-TWO

There was nowhere to hide, not that would conceal her for more than two seconds.

The realization of this fact sent Sarah Beth's mind into a swirling panic as she frantically scanned the room.

There was her dad's desk, which she could hide under for barely a moment before they found her. There was a split, bifold door covering a shallow closet that she knew was crammed with junk that had nowhere else to go. Dad loved to laughingly complain about his office closet being the garbage can of the house. Even if she wanted to, she wouldn't be able to fit inside. And there was his recliner.

She cursed her situation and didn't even apologize this time.

A soft creak sounded outside the door, the sound of someone coming slowly up the stairs.

What do I do? What do I do? What do I do . . . ? she thought, flapping her hands up and down in panic.

She ran to the single window, set in the center of the wall behind the desk.

It looked down on the front yard, and she immediately spotted the black high-top van idling in their driveway with the parking lights on. A man stood beside it, dressed in all black like the man downstairs; he was staring at the front door and looked mad. She could open the window and try to drop to the ground—maybe even survive the terrifying drop without breaking both her legs— but even if she did, the man at the van would be on her in seconds and throw her in the back of the van just like before.

A sob escaped her throat and she swallowed hard. Somehow she had to get past whoever came up the stairs and run as hard as she could. Maybe she could make it out the back door and into the yard.

Why did I come upstairs? So stupid, so stupid!

She turned and looked at the locked office door. It wasn't going to stop anybody for long. Even she knew how to pick the dumb little handle locks using a paper clip.

I have to get to the backyard. That's my only chance. But what about Mom? I have to save her, too.

And where was her dad? She felt her chest tighten as she thought of *one* possible reason she hadn't seen him yet. She imagined him slumped against a wall like the Shepherd soldiers, his throat slit open.

Tears rimmed her eyes.

She squeezed her eyes closed and let the tears spill onto her cheeks, while trying to force her hands to stop shaking.

No, no, no, he's safe. I know he is, she told herself. *I've got to be strong. I've got to fight.*

She quickly scanned the room for anything she could use as a weapon. A glint of silver on the black leather blotter on her dad's desk caught her eye. She snatched up the long silver letter opener with *Vanderbilt University* etched on the handle. Clutching it like a knife, she moved quickly behind the office door and listened. Her mom always said she had ears like a fox, and true to form she could hear the soft encroaching footsteps in the hall. At first, she pressed herself against the wall at the hinge side of the door to her right but then bit her lip in indecision. The door would conceal her for a moment, but she'd have to maneuver around it to get out. Changing her mind, she slipped across to the other side and waited.

The doorknob rattled once—someone checking the lock.

Her legs began to quake.

The doorframe creaked as weight leaned against the slab.

A sob nearly escaped but she clamped her jaw shut and slid down into a squat, her knees knocking so badly she could barely stand. She changed her grip on the letter opener and clutched it in both hands for stabbing down like her mom had done with the knife in the kitchen.

God, please make me strong . . . please make me strong. Strong and FAST.

Everything went still and quiet, and for a moment, she allowed herself the fantasy that the killer had gone away, but she could still see the two dark shadows in the gap underneath the door where his feet would be.

With a terrible crash, the door flew open. A massive dark figure surged in, filling the doorway as shards of wood dropped to the floor from the wrecked doorjamb. Her head was at his hip level, and above, she saw him scanning back and forth inside the room, sighting over a pistol just as she'd seen Uncle Jed do. She knew she had but an instant, and with all her might, she sprang forward from her crouch and plunged the letter opener deep into the back of the man's right knee, driving it in several inches until it hit something hard. Hot, wet blood soaked the back of her hand. The man screamed in pain and dropped to the ground on his knees, his gun clattering beside him on the floor.

Sarah Beth released her grip on the blade and scrambled out the door as the man rolled onto his side, lunging after her. His large hand slipped off her left wrist, but his fingers wrapped around her left ankle, tripping her. She landed hard on her right side, her already-injured ribs on the other side shrieking in pain. New pain flared in her right elbow, which smashed into the floor this time. And then she was being hauled backward, sliding easily under the strong grip of the man who weighed at least one hundred and fifty pounds more than her. He was on his side, his body forming an L in the doorway. He reached for her with his other hand to get a better grip as he drew her in.

She rolled onto her back as she slid over the hardwood floor toward him. With every last bit of strength she had, she kicked her right foot square into the middle of the snarling face. She felt a crack under her heel. Blood gushed from the man's nostrils and he let out an animal scream, releasing his grip on her ankle and reaching instead for his broken nose.

Sarah Beth scampered away, making it to hands and knees first, then up onto her feet. At the top of the stairs she slipped, sliding into the corner of the wall face-first, feeling her bottom lip split under the impact. She ignored the blood that dribbled over her chin, corrected her course, and half ran, half slid down the stairs, bouncing up off her tailbone, making it to her feet, then sliding hard down on her butt again. She was aware, as if from far away, of a sound coming from her, a "nuh . . . nuh . . . nuh" with each step or impact of her tailbone on the stairs. She was somehow able to regain control as she made it to the last two steps. She leapt, this time clearing the two dead bodies in the foyer, and reached for the front doorknob.

She froze, two thoughts simultaneously stopping her. The first was an image of her mother, lying facedown on the floor of the kitchen in a pool of blood. The second was the man she'd seen out the window standing beside the van. She turned left, retracing the same path she'd taken only minutes ago while nearly unconscious in the grip of the first kidnapper, through the dining room. She slowed as she rounded the table, glancing first back over her shoulder and then craning her neck to see into the kitchen. Her mom was there, sprawled on her stomach, but moving her legs and moaning, beside the still body of the dead man lying with his arms spread wide, the butcher knife still buried in his head. Seeing no one else, and ignoring the gruesome sight of the corpse, she sprinted around the table and into the kitchen.

"I've got you, you little bitch," a man's voice growled as she ran into a wall of flesh and bone.

A heartbeat later, she was two feet in the air, feet kicking, looking down at her moaning mother. Another man came out of the living room, blood smeared over his lower face from his broken nose. He glared at her, limping toward them, and raised a radio to his mouth.

"We've got her. We're coming out, so be ready to move."

Sarah Beth went limp.

She had tried and failed. She was only a little kid after all. Her mom was dying on the floor. Her dad was probably dead too.

Even if they both lived, she would never see either of them again.

It's over.

They got me.

CHAPTER THIRTY-THREE

In more than a decade of nearly back-to-back combat deployments stacking up hundreds of direct-action missions, Jed had never once felt the urgency he did now, braking to a stop two houses down from the Yarnells' place. He cut the engine, leaving the key in the ignition, and slipped his kit over his head. It no longer held ammo, grenades, or a radio—all the fun stuff he had to return to the Shepherds before Morvant permitted him to take it—but it would serve as a ballistic vest against low-velocity pistol rounds and had a plate carrier with ceramic SAPI plates front and back capable of stopping high-velocity bullets. Mossberg in hand and pistol in his waistband, Jed stepped out of the vehicle and moved rapidly into the shadows of the large oaks lining the north side of the street. He spied a high-top van in the Yarnells' driveway two houses to the west. He briefly considered returning to the Suburban and using it to box the bad guys in, but surprise was his only ally now. The way the armed shooter standing beside the van was scanning the house was a pretty obvious signal they had not yet loaded up their high-value target. If they had Sarah Beth, they'd already be gone. His main concern was how many shooters they'd brought. Enough to dispatch two highly trained Shepherds . . .

No, I have to be smart about this, he told himself. *I'm not going to win a gun battle. I have to be the night and take them out one by one, just like I did at the compound the last time I rescued Sarah Beth.*

He surged forward, sprinting across the neighbor's front yard. His strides long and fast, he cut through the narrow stretch of lawn shared between two houses. His best option was to loop around to the backyard, enter Sarah Beth's house undetected, and take the infiltrators out one by one.

But what if they drag her out and load her into the van while I'm sneaking in? From the back I won't be able to see the driveway.

Indecisiveness and second-guessing crept into his mind, just like that night in the Cherokee National Forest.

Don't do it, the SEAL barked in his head. *Make the decision and commit.*

Teeth gritted, he hurdled the neighbor's split rail fence without even breaking stride, and a distant part of his brain marveled at the strength and lack of pain in his left hip. One house away now, he crossed the neighbor's backyard, temporarily losing sight of the van while praying the neighbor's dog wasn't out. He breathed a sigh of relief when he reached the other side without incident. He jumped a hedgerow without slowing or making a sound. On the other side, he took a knee and forced himself to stop and listen. From this angle, he could look up between the yards and still see the rear quarter panel of the van, but not the man pacing beside it.

He heard a scream, muffled but still loud enough to hear from outside the house. The sound cut through him like a lightning strike, and he felt Sarah Beth's anguish. He was about to sprint to the side door, which he knew led into the kitchen, but he held and reconsidered.

I'm alone, not part of a four-man assault team . . . I need more surprise than that.

Jed ran to a lower-level double-hung window, ripped the screen off, and quietly raised the bottom pane. Mossberg clutched in his right hand, he climbed silently over the sill and dropped onto the floor beside a dining room table. Looking through the cased opening into the kitchen, he saw a black-clad figure talking on a radio.

"We've got her," the man said with his back to Jed. "We're coming out, so be ready to move."

Sighting over the Mossberg, Jed crept around the table, closing range and into position behind the man. If he could get close enough without being heard, he'd snap the man's neck. If not, all hell would break loose. Five feet away, a floorboard under his right foot moaned.

The man with the radio spun, and Jed squeezed the trigger.

The shotgun roared, reverberating like a bomb in the close quarters of the house. Without the sound-dampening protection of his Peltor headset, Jed's ears instantly rang with pain, but he ignored it. The black-clad figure—now with a gaping hole in his chest—tumbled backward and fell. Jed surged forward, pumping the forestock of the Mossberg, ejecting the spent cartridge and chambering a fresh one. Dropping into a combat crouch, he crossed the threshold and cleared right.

A gunshot rang out and a bullet clipped the base of his neck where his trapezius muscles connected. Sparks of pain shot down his arm to his hand, and the Mossberg clattered on the ground beside him. A muzzle flash from the darkened doorway ahead lit up the kitchen. A second round whizzed past his head, shattering crystals on the chandelier that hung over the dining room table behind him. He dropped to a knee, pulled the Sig P365 pistol from his waistband, and sighted.

Beyond the kitchen island, another black-clad fighter emerged from shadow. He held Sarah Beth clutched in his arms and she looked despondent. The kidnapper shuffled toward Jed's left, where the back door stood partially open, all the while using her as a shield. The target was moving irregularly but managed to maintain only an inch or so of his face exposed behind the much larger target in front that was Sarah Beth's head. Jed put his ROMEO red dot on the sliver of face anyway, floating it just above the man's right eyebrow. He tightened his finger on the trigger, hoping she'd duck or tilt her head to give him the split second of separation he needed to make the kill shot.

"There's nowhere to go," Jed shouted, his eyes ticking left and right looking for other shooters. He thought there might be a shadow on the other side of the partially open door, but he couldn't tell. "We have a whole team outside, so this is over. Put the girl down. You don't have to die tonight."

He waited for a reaction, but apparently his bluff did nothing.

In the dim light, the man's single visible eye behind Sarah Beth's head began to glow—orange at first, then deepening to red. A shadow rippled across the man's face and a deep, animal growl ushered from his lips while he bared his teeth.

With sheer force of will, Jed slowed his pulse. He needed to have the steadiest of hands if the shot became available, because there was no way he would risk shooting Sarah Beth in the head. He swallowed hard and formulated his backup plan, which was . . . sprinting to the front door as soon as the kidnapper stepped out the back door leading to the carport? With a different angle of engagement, maybe he could squeeze off a shot before they got Sarah Beth into the van.

Maybe.

At least one more shooter, the driver, was waiting outside. There could be more men in the cargo compartment.

He blinked hard, waiting desperately for the shot.

The man reached the door, smiled a victorious smile, and said, "You lose."

A single gunshot rang out somewhere to Jed's right. The kidnapper's head snapped right and the skull above his ear exploded, spackling the wall beside with blood and gore. As the killer fell, Sarah Beth still in his arms, Jed advanced and swiveled right. As he stepped further into the kitchen, he gained the angle to sight through the cased opening into the family room. Standing in the exact spot he imagined was Detective Perez with her pistol still raised, smoke dissipating around her face. Instead of turning on him, she sagged against the side of the sofa, her knees seemingly going weak. The blood-soaked left side of her white blouse answered his unspoken question. She'd been shot, potentially by another tango still in the house. He was scanning past her, over her shoulder, to clear her six, when her eyes went wide.

"Behind you!" she hollered.

He spun 180 degrees, just in time to see a dark-clad figure snatch Sarah Beth from behind and disappear out the door leading to the driveway.

Jed surged forward in pursuit, rounding the island and nearly stumbling over two bodies he'd not seen yet, a man half-draped over a woman with chestnut-brown hair. *Rachel!* A part of him screamed to stop, to check and see if she was dead or alive, but the operator in him won the moment. He leapt over the bodies and made for the door.

As he kicked it open, Jed felt an impact just right of center beneath his shoulder blade, like he'd been hit with a baseball bat. Luck abandoning him, the round impacted just outside of his ceramic SAPI plate that would have completely saved him from injury. Instead, he felt a crack and a stab of pain. Odds were good the slug did not penetrate the Kevlar of his vest, but if his lung started filling up with blood or he developed a pneumothorax in the next minute, then he'd know that it had.

He stumbled through the door and into the attached carport off the kitchen. Too late, he realized the Sig had slipped from his grip, and as he turned to look over his shoulder to see who'd shot him, he missed the first step and lost his footing. As he tumbled down the short three-tread wooden staircase, the tactical computer in his mind tried to make sense of what had just happened.

The guy who shot Perez must have circled around behind me in the dining room, he thought. *Meanwhile the driver snuck in and grabbed Sarah Beth.*

He hit the ground hard, but he was a pro at falling. Muscle memory ruled the day and he rolled out of it like a bad parachute landing, popping into a squat. His head didn't feel swimmy yet and his breath came easily enough in and out, which meant the vest stopped the slug. Pain told a slightly different story, however, because it felt like someone had driven a samurai sword into his back beneath his shoulder blade.

Broken rib, dude, the SEAL in his head reported, *in the back where it connects to your spine. Now get up and save the girl.*

Like a linebacker after the snap, he launched out of his squatting stance. Head low, shoulder forward, and legs churning, he slammed into the dark figure carrying Sarah Beth. And just like a linebacker making a game-winning tackle, he wrapped his arms around his quarry. As they flew through the air together, Jed dropped his left shoulder, rotating so they wouldn't land on top of Sarah Beth and crush her.

It worked, but he paid a price. He landed on his back and the black-clad man came down on top of him, driving the wind out of Jed's lungs. Despite gasping for breath, he kept his wits and wrapped his right arm around the man's neck from behind, quickly fashioning a figure-four choke. In his peripheral vision, he saw that Sarah Beth had tumbled free, thank God, rolling just a few feet away where she sat dazed and shaking her head. Jed completed the grappling hold by establishing "hooks"—wrapping both of his legs around the man's midsection and locking his shins inside and behind the man's knees to give him complete and total control over his opponent. A gurgling gasp escaped from the much smaller man's throat as Jed used the "blood choke" to restrict circulation to the brain. In seconds, the man would be unconscious in his iron grip.

Then the impossible happened.

His opponent squirmed free, slipping from Jed's grip as if Jed had gone from grappling with a man to wrestling a serpent. He blinked and the man was on top of him, straddling Jed's mid-section with his gloved hands wrapped around Jed's thick neck. His opponent's small hands squeezed with supernatural strength, and Jed felt like a machine, not a man, was choking him. He felt his head grow swimmy as he grabbed at his attacker's wrists. He looked up into the man's face, which was twisted in a homi-cidal snarl. Amber halos around the man's irises flared and grew in intensity until both eyes glowed like bright embers beneath a rag-ing fire. Jed worried his larynx would crack under the pressure and he pounded his fists against the man's forearms, but it was like hit-ting twin pillars of cement. The color faded from Jed's vision, first at the periphery and then moving inward until the man strangling him looked like a character in an old black-and-white TV show.

Father, give me strength, he prayed, finding only those four words as the world went dark.

He heard a whooshing sound and a sudden surge of strength, as well as clarity of thought, filled him.

Jed stopped fumbling with the man's wrists and instead raised his arms, hands clenched together tightly over his head. With all his might, he swung down in an arc, landing a powerful blow on the man's left forearm. The loud, nauseating snap of bone giving way was drowned out by the howl from the man above him. The choke hold eased for only a fraction of a second, but enough that Jed saw the color returning to his vision. He crashed his clutched fists down a second time, and this time the bones snapped com-pletely in half, bending the forearm in an unnatural, ninety-degree angle. Jed bucked and rolled violently left, throwing his assailant clear like a bull tossing his rider before the eight-second clock. Jed scrambled to his feet, his head clearing, as he faced off against his supernatural opponent.

The man stood facing him, chin down, eyes glowing deep red beneath the shadow of his brow. Apparently oblivious to the excruciating pain from his mangled arm, the man raised his fists like a boxer, but the left one sagged and twisted backward and drooped toward his chest, twitching as the muscles spasmed. Jed dashed in quickly to finish him, but the man's right fist flashed out at lightning speed, smashing into Jed's left temple and bringing stars to his vision as he stumbled back. Jed countered with a right hook, punching through the floppy, broken arm and driving his fist into the left side of the man's jaw. Jed watched the dark servant's head snap right as blood and perhaps teeth splattered the driveway. The blow should have dropped the man to his knees, but instead, the maniac just turned, grinning a bloody smile, and advanced.

Jed hit him again, this time a jab, and felt the man's nose break and flatten; he followed it with a perfectly targeted knife-hand strike to the man's throat with his left hand. The man's neck swelled immediately, frothy blood bubbles forming at his lips, but still he did not fall. Like two gladiators fighting to the death, they circled. After dancing ninety degrees in rotation, he came at Jed, shrieking and clawing with his one good hand. Jed dodged right, like a bullfighter, and delivered a punishing front kick to his opponent's lower back as he passed.

Then he realized his mistake.

His attacker wasn't going for Jed; he was trying to go *through* Jed. His real target was the Sig Sauer P365 lying on the concrete floor beside the steps leading up into the kitchen. Jed lunged after him, grabbing the kidnapper in midair around the waist just as the man's right hand scooped up the pistol. Jed dragged him back and they battled, trading blows mercilessly—elbows, knees, and headbutts—all the while wrangling for control of the gun. And then somehow Jed found himself tossed aside like a rag doll. He landed in a painful heap on the front lawn.

The SEAL creed—*his* creed—popped into his head.

I will never quit. I persevere and thrive on adversity . . .

With a weary grunt, he pressed to his knees, but when he looked up, he saw it was over.

The demon warrior was holding Jed's pistol in a straight-arm grip, the barrel a dark eye staring at him. His mind reflexively went to Sarah Beth, the only life that mattered to him in that moment.

"Run, Sarah Beth!" he screamed.

A gunshot sounded and he squeezed his eyes shut.

When a bullet didn't slam into his face, he opened them, per-plexed how a man only ten feet away could have missed the shot.

Dark blood dribbled down the side of the shooter's face from the large hole just above the corner of his left eyebrow. At first, it seemed the dead man standing might try to raise the pistol one more time, but the red glow in his eyes faded and disappeared. His arm dropped. He wobbled for a second, then collapsed unmoving onto the ground.

Jed tore his eyes away from the mutilated corpse and looked right, where Ben Morvant stood in a firing position, sighting on the fallen kidnapper through the holographic sight of his assault rifle.

"Thanks, brother," Jed choked out, his voice raspy from the partial strangulation he'd just suffered. "I owe you one."

"I'll just put it on your tab," Morvant said as four other Shepherds charged on the scene, two securing the van and the corpse and the other two entering the house through the kitchen carport door in a two-man breach.

He struggled to his feet, his body feeling like a thousand pounds of deadweight.

"Uncle Jed!" Sarah Beth called behind him. He turned just in time for her to wrap her arms around his waist. "I knew you'd come. I called you and I knew you would hear me and I knew you would come."

She began sobbing. He didn't say anything, just took a knee, closed his eyes, and held her tight. The sound of charging footsteps pulled him out of the moment a beat later. His eyes snapped open to see David running toward them.

"Sarah Beth? Oh, Father God, please tell me she's all right," David said as he ran to them, bumping into Morvant as he passed. He dropped to his knees and joined them in their hug. Jed noted the purple softball-size lump on his former best friend's left temple. Blood had dried onto his neck and cheek where a gash in the center of the hematoma had bled, and the white part of David's left eye was swimming with red blood as well.

Sarah Beth pulled back and looked at her father. "Dad?" she said with incredulity as if seeing a ghost. Then she squealed. "Dad! Dad, are you okay?"

"I'm okay," David said, his voice cracking.

On that cue, Jed extracted himself and got painfully to his feet as father and daughter embraced.

"I couldn't find you," she said. "I thought you were dead, but you're all right. You're all right!"

"I was walking back from the mailbox when somebody hit me in the side of the head. I woke up in the neighbor's yard and saw Jed fighting just as Ben and his guys pulled up and—" David stopped midsentence, the color suddenly draining from his face. "Sarah Beth, where's your mom? Is she okay?"

The question hit Jed like a gut punch and he started for the house.

"She's okay, Dad. She's okay, Uncle Jed," Sarah Beth said, her voice ebullient. "She just woke up too and told me she's coming out."

Upon hearing that, Jed exhaled, sat down on the grass, and buried his face in his hands. A dam broke in his heart, and seventeen years' worth of angst, guilt, and regret flooded his mind, body, and soul. The sobs came hard and fast and racked his entire being.

"Are you okay, Uncle Jed?" Sarah Beth asked, laying her hand on his shoulder.

"Yeah," he choked out, feeling at peace. "Thanks to you, Sarah Beth, I will be."

I will be.

CHAPTER
THIRTY-FOUR

The relief Jed felt seeing Rachel walk out of the house under her own power ebbed as he watched her embrace David, her head pressed against her husband's chest. Jed took a calming breath, which triggered a cough. Pain flared in his right-middle back and he could still taste coppery blood in his mouth. But when Sarah Beth wrapped her arms around her mother's neck, and David began tenderly stroking both of their faces, shame replaced Jed's jealousy and a comforting thought occurred to him. Maybe everyone was where they were meant to be.

Had I not left, become a SEAL, and honed my skills over a decade and a half, perhaps David and Rachel would be mourning the loss of their daughter right now instead of celebrating life.

A hand on his shoulder made him start. He turned and looked at the Shepherd who'd walked up beside him carrying a med kit.

"Hey, Jed. I'm kinda the 18 Delta for the fire team. I should probably have a look at all you got going on," the wiry special operations medic said, waving a hand in a circle, indicating what Jed took to mean his battered, bruised, and oozing body.

"Check on the detective first," he said and gestured to the front stoop, where Detective Perez sat leaning against the frame of the wide-open front door, her pistol in her lap and the bloodstain on her white blouse much larger than before.

"All right," the doc said, obviously experienced enough to know it was pointless to argue with operators. "But as soon as I'm done with her, I'm looking at you."

"Deal," Jed said and they walked over to the front stoop together.

"Hey there, Jed," Perez said, leaning her head back. "You look terrible."

"Maybe, but I bet you feel worse." He took a knee beside her as the medic did the same. "You hangin' in?"

She nodded as the doc checked her pulse and then lifted the bottom flap of her blouse to peek at the gunshot wound to her abdomen.

"But it's worth it," she said, her gaze going past him to the Yarnells, who were still embracing each other in the front lawn.

"Yeah" was all he could muster.

"Looks like a scything wound," the medic said. "Can't be sure, of course, but your pulse is rock-solid and you're not diaphoretic—sweaty—so you don't seem to be in shock. They'll do a CT scan, probably, at the trauma center. Hurt anywhere else?"

"My pride," she said and with a wince added, "and the back of my head. Jed, I didn't see that other guy until he smacked me with something and then went after you. When I saw him shoot you in the back at point-blank range, I thought you were dead and . . . and . . ." A sob caught in her throat, and he watched tears rim her eyes.

"Vest," Jed said, tapping his kit.

"Sorry. Not usually a crier," she said, wiping her cheeks. "When you went down, I thought we'd lost the girl for good."

Jed flashed her his best cool-guy smile. "Takes more than a bullet in the back to shut me down. . . . Hey, by the way, what did happen to the guy that shot me? Did you take him out?"

"Tried," she said, "but he bolted out the front door. I assumed your friends finished the job?"

"I don't think so," Jed said and turned and swept the property for a black-clad corpse he'd missed. "Must have run away . . ."

"EMS will be here in a moment," the Shepherd medic said, touching his earbud. "We let them know we have an officer down, but that you're stable."

"Thank you," Perez said, wincing as the medic pressed a thick combat gauze onto her wound, wrapping the free ends around her waist.

"No charge," the medic said with a grin. He helped secure her weapon and lowered her to the ground, folding her jacket under her head as a pillow.

Sirens wailed in the distance—a lot of them. Jed pressed to his feet, gave the detective a two-fingered salute, and turned to go.

"Hey," Perez said, stopping him. "That mom, Rachel . . . she jumped that guy with the knife in his face. He outweighed her by more than a hundred pounds, but she killed him dead."

Jed pursed his lips, remembering the horror show on the kitchen floor. "Yeah."

"Mama bear thing, I guess," Perez said with satisfaction and closed her eyes.

"Right," he said, staring at Rachel and feeling flush with emotion. "Mama bear thing."

"Hey, Jed, we gotta get outta here, and that should probably include you," Morvant said, jogging up to him with an all-business look on his face. "We're gonna take the Yarnells with us. Got a safe house on a ranch south of Clarksville."

Jed nodded but felt worry creep over him. "What if the civilian law enforcement won't allow it?"

Morvant laughed. "I got a letter in my pocket that will trump any objections. I know a guy who knows a guy . . ."

Jed chuckled and shook his head. *Task force guys.*

"C'mon," the Shepherd leader said. "Time to saddle up. We gotta go."

Jed looked at his childhood sweetheart in the arms of his childhood best friend, cradling their daughter between them. "Nah," he said. "You guys go. I'm gonna head back to my hotel."

"Don't be bullheaded. We need to get you checked out. That neck of yours ain't looking so good, brother."

"I don't need a babysitter."

"Didn't say you did."

"Not my first rodeo, either," Jed came back, his pride getting the better of him.

"I know," Morvant said with a disarming smile. "Tell you what,

I'll send my medic by the hotel when we clear here. He can stitch you up there."

Jed nodded. "And then you and I can have our sit-down tomorrow. I still have a lot of questions."

"Monday," Morvant said and put a brotherly hand on Jed's shoulder. "Tomorrow is Sunday. We've got church and then a day of rest."

"Monday it is."

"I'm looking forward to it, Jed," Morvant said, turning to leave.

"Me too . . . oh, and, Ben?" Jed called, feeling suddenly and strangely comfortable calling the larger-than-life operator by his first name.

"Yeah?"

"Take good care of them," he said, gesturing to the Yarnells. "Or you'll have me to reckon with."

"I hear you Lima Charlie," Ben said with a crooked grin. Then he made a circle in the air with his right hand and hollered, "Time to boogie, people. On the road in three mikes."

Jed shifted his gaze from Ben to Sarah Beth, Rachel, and David. As soon as he did, Sarah Beth looked up from her mother's arms and met his eyes. He winked at her. She grinned and winked back.

With a tight smile, he turned and started across the lawn, heading east toward his borrowed SUV as the first police cruiser and ambulance pulled into the driveway.

"Jed!" Rachel called behind him.

He froze, afraid to turn around, afraid that the sight of her might just erase all the emotional progress he'd made. And maybe afraid that it wouldn't.

"Jed," she said again, and he summoned his courage and turned just in time for her to wrap her arms around his chest.

Pain flared in his back, but he didn't care and let himself get lost in their first embrace in a lifetime. She pulled back and looked up at him, her face a battered mess and beautiful at the same time.

"Thank you," she said.

"You're welcome," he replied awkwardly.

He squeezed her hand, then turned to go, the sight of her just too much in his exhausted state. But her grip on his hand was firm and she stopped him, tugging until he turned to face her.

"Do you even know what I'm thanking you for, Jed?" she asked, her expression that old familiar look—stern, professorial, unconditional love—that he'd both cherished and hated since they were ten.

He laughed.

"I assume for getting beat up—twice—and for getting your daughter back to you. She's special, Rachel. She's amazing and special and . . ." He stopped and realized that everyone *was* exactly where God needed them to be. Him. Rachel and David. And their little girl. "Anyway, you're welcome."

"That's all true," she said, smiling at him knowingly. "But that's not what I'm thanking you for. Not this time."

"Then what?" he asked, as bewildered by her as ever.

She took both his bear-paw hands in hers and squeezed them tightly. "Thank you for bringing back your light . . ." She glanced at David, who was standing by watching them, his arm wrapped around Sarah Beth's shoulders. "For bringing it back to all of us."

Jed's heart skipped a beat at her words, and he realized that he suddenly felt a little less weary.

"You're welcome," he said and meant it.

With a smile on his battered face, he let go and walked away— forcing himself not to look back with each and every step.

CHAPTER THIRTY-FIVE

Overwhelmed with déjà vu, Jed followed Father Newman through the narthex and through the double doors into the main sanctuary. His gaze was drawn up, for a second time, to the stained-glass panel with the soaring dove with wings of an eagle.

There's more to that dove than meets the eye, he thought as they walked up the center aisle toward the dais. Once again, Jed pondered the quiet beauty of the cathedral as Father Newman led him to the same reading library where he'd met with David and Rachel the night this all began. This time, however, circumstances could not be more opposite. Sarah Beth was safe and the Yarnells' ordeal was over. As if in acknowledgment of this fact, the priest was dressed more casually this time, wearing blue jeans and an open-collared yellow golf shirt beneath a gray sports jacket.

At the threshold to the library, Newman turned and looked Jed up and down through his round, wire-rimmed glasses. "You look terrible, Jedidiah," he said with a disarming smile. "It would seem our friends put you through quite the ordeal?"

"I guess you could say so."

"And knowing Ben like I do, I imagine whoever was on the receiving end of you gentlemen's efforts looks far, far worse for wear. Or they're dead," he said with an unexpected little chuckle. "The more likely outcome, I'd suspect."

"You know Ben?" Jed stammered, the priest's candid words of violence taking him completely by surprise. "Ben Morvant?"

"Yes, of course," Father Newman said, holding the door to the small library open for him with his left hand and gesturing inside with his right. "For many years. Ben is a very impressive man of God. We have the same boss, you might say," the priest added, stealing a glance heavenward.

Jed entered the empty reading room, more confused than ever.

He turned to ask a follow-up question but stopped when Father Newman shed his sports coat to reveal cut, athletically built arms not hinted at by his kindly round face. In the center of the priest's left forearm, Jed spied a tattoo—blue and white—a miniature replica of the soaring dove in the stained glass. On the other forearm, a United States Marine Corps eagle, globe, and anchor had been inked.

Since returning to Nashville, every person he'd encountered had surprised him and prompted more questions than answers.

"That ends today," he mumbled.

"What does?" Father Newman asked, smiling and gesturing toward the coffee and snacks set up on the sideboard between the towering shelves of books. "Or should I guess?"

Jed smiled. "Be my guest."

"Can I get you a coffee?"

"Coffee would be great—just black." He pointed at the priest's arms while he poured. "I like your tats," he said, probing.

"Ah." The priest turned and handed him a three-quarters full coffee cup as he gestured to the club chairs. "Which one?"

"Both," Jed said after settling into one of the comfortable leather chairs opposite his host. "I spent a few months in garrison with elements of the Second LAR from II MEF on one of my first deployments as a SEAL. That was my first real time in close quarters with Marines outside of a gunfight, and I was nothing but impressed. Gotta love the Marines."

"Oorah," the priest said, smiling and sipping at his coffee.

"And I'm also struck by the dove. I can't help but notice that your tattoo matches the stained-glass window at the sanctuary entrance. A dove with eagle's wings—I can't get it out of my mind, for some reason."

"You'll learn more about that tonight, I suspect," the priest said with a cryptic smile and leaned back in his chair. "If you choose to."

Jed started to respond, but before he could, a visitor appeared in the doorway.

"Ben Morvant," Father Newman said, getting to his feet. "As I live and breathe!"

389

Jed turned and watched Ben step into the library.

"And I see you still do," the Shepherd replied, embracing Newman warmly, "despite all prognosticating to the contrary."

They both laughed—some inside joke perhaps—and Ben walked to greet Jed.

He stood and shook the former SEAL's strong, weathered hand, while excitement and anticipation began rising in him not like anything he'd felt since pinning on his Trident.

"Great to see you, brother," Ben said as they broke the handshake and took their seats. "Your neck looks terrible, which I assume means it's getting better."

"My throat feels normal when I swallow or cough. What you see is just bruising. Your medic came by my hotel and did a great job closing up the laceration on my neck and shoulder. Turns out I did crack a rib, so that feels awesome, but hooyah, semper fi, and amen, it could have been worse. Thank God you let me take the kit with me."

"Yes, thank God indeed," Morvant said with that sage smile Jed finally felt himself getting used to. "And I thank Him also that He had you positioned to respond in time. Had you not been where you were, when you were, things would have turned out differently. I don't know, Father Newman—it's almost like Jed is a Shepherd already."

Jed watched Ben and the priest exchange a look.

"Indeed," Newman said.

"I suppose while we're thanking Him," Jed said, "we should probably say thanks for Detective Perez showing up when she did. If she hadn't, I might be dead and Sarah Beth taken all over again."

"Yes," Ben said, holding his eyes. "Another stroke of what some might be tempted to call luck."

"How is Sarah Beth?" Jed asked, his mind suddenly going to the girl.

"On the mend. She's taken to the ranch like jelly on peanut butter. She's also fallen in love with the horses, and we can't seem to keep her out of the stable. The whole family went riding this morning. I think it feels a bit like summer camp to her. Pastor Dee is there with her, handling all the important stuff outside my wheelhouse."

Jed nodded. He wanted to ask about Rachel but knew it would dredge up feelings he didn't want or need to wrangle with right now.

"So . . . ," he said instead.

"So," Ben replied and then folded his hands in his lap.

Jed sighed. He knew how these supersecret squirrel organizations worked. He'd have to ask to be invited into the club before anyone gave him the secret handshake and magic decoder ring. His mind was all but made up, and yet he still found himself dancing around the door.

He turned to the priest. "So you're a Shepherd too, I take it?"

The priest laughed. "That's flattering, but no. I loved being a Marine, but even when I was younger and thinner, I was never really Shepherd material."

"Coulda fooled me," Jed said, glancing at the priest's stout arms.

"I was a field artillery officer in the beginning, but I spent most of my career in intelligence. I was never recon, or what you call MARSOC Raiders now. Shepherds are operators; that was never my calling." The former Marine leaned in on his elbows now, his eyes sparkling. "I am honored, however, to serve in the Watchers program. I was a Keeper for a number of amazing young people over the years, and now I serve in a leadership role." He held up his arm again to show the soaring dove emblazed on his arm. "That's the meaning of this tattoo. The dove represents peace, but the elongated, soaring wings are a metaphor."

"Watchfulness from above?" Jed said.

Newman nodded. "Peace through vigilance."

"I've pieced together bits here and there, but what exactly does the Watcher program entail?"

"How about we talk about the Shepherds first," Ben said. "If you're still interested, that is."

Am I in or out? It's time to either jump feetfirst down the bunny hole or walk away.

He met the Shepherd's ridiculously patient stare. "Ben, I'm going to be honest. I've thought about this a lot over the last two days, and while I've managed to walk away from seventeen years of denial, I'm still finding it difficult to rectify the series of seeming coincidences that have brought me here today."

"In my experience, there are no such things as coincidences," Ben said quietly.

"In my younger life, I thought I had all that figured out. I was a true believer, until something happened to Rachel, David, and me . . ." He closed his eyes and shook his head, chasing the demons of that night away. He blinked and focused on Ben. "I was told to pray about this decision, and I did—the only prayers I've said in seventeen years have been over the last few days. I can't shake the feeling that I'm here, in this position and sitting at this table with you, for a reason—for a divine purpose—but I don't know . . ." He pursed his lips. "Could that be just wishful thinking? I was medically retired from the Teams; it wasn't something I chose. And when a Team Guy loses his team, he loses his purpose. I guess I want to be sure that I'm not forging ahead on some made-up sense of higher calling that's filling a void after a lifetime as a SEAL."

Ben nodded, and his face seemed sympathetic. "Wishful thinking is wasted thinking, Jed. Or so I believe, and based on the life you've lived so far, it would seem so do you. One day I'll tell you the story of how I came to be here, but for now, suffice it to say that everything you're saying resonates with me, because I went through the same exact emotions when the Shepherds first approached me. I was broken—emotionally and physically—from my . . . encounter. And I was crippled. Losing the ability to be a SEAL stole from me my purpose as well, just like you're saying. And I bet every operator in the Shepherds has struggled with the same feelings. But what I can tell you is that never have I felt my skill set used for a greater purpose than since I became a Shepherd."

Jed nodded, wanting to be convinced.

"How's the hip?" Ben asked, the real meaning behind the question not lost on Jed.

"Like new. Like it was a decade ago. But you already knew that."

"I hoped it was true," Ben corrected. "And I'm glad it is. It means you were able to receive something that came from God, not me. Maybe you're ready to receive this . . . new calling . . . from Him as well."

Jed could feel himself inching closer to the edge of the bunny hole.

"I'm confused about the whole God aspect of this," he said. "Don't get me wrong, I know some Team Guys and other soldiers with powerful faith that helps them in tough situations, but this is different. How does a government agency exist with such a religious component?"

"First, let me be clear: there is no institutional religion in the Shepherds, no doctrine. We are a cross-denominational organization that shares a love for and faith in God. God is whom we serve, not the will or whims of competing religious institutions. Second, we do not work *for* the government, but we do work *with* the government. And when I say government, what I really mean is *governments*. This is a secret order with a global footprint. Our spiritual counterterrorism operations are sanctioned by a number of governments across the globe, and we are given both aid and covert support when needed by our allies in positions to do so. We are not, and never will be, a government agency."

"I don't understand. How are you allowed to participate in counterterror operations without any government ties?"

"I didn't say we don't have government ties," Morvant said cryptically. "You've already seen that we do. It's a complicated and delicate dance, and yes, there are politics involved, but I don't want to get into *that* right now. What you need to understand and accept is that we are all fighting for the same thing here. As a SEAL, you've battled the brutal evil that is jihadist terrorism across the globe. But where do you think that evil comes from—I mean originally? How did a man of no import rise to lead Nazi Germany and oversee the Holocaust? How did World War I happen, or the Crusades, or any of the unspeakably horrific wars man has waged against his fellow man? What you think of as discrete and discon-nected incidents of geopolitical conflict throughout history, we think of as battles in one long, never-ending war—a war that has raged for thousands of years. A spiritual war, ever-present and all around us. Good versus evil, God versus Satan, however you want to think of it. When your eyes finally open to the real players in this war, you will be forever changed, and you become an infinitely more effective warrior."

Jed thought about Ben's words, trying to make sense of it. "And maybe that's why I still feel reluctant, Ben. It's that faith compo-nent I've seen in your team that makes me question whether I'm the right fit. When things changed for me, when I had my own—encounter, I guess—I turned my back on God. I walked away, not only from God, but from my friends, my family, and my life here in Nashville. And I walked away from love. That decision was mine. I left my faith behind and, until now, never really looked back. So I don't know . . ."

Morvant nodded. "Why you? Is that the question?"

"Exactly. If this is some kind of a God moment, then why me? Ben, you have a profound and powerful faith. I feel it in your every word. Your every exhale. Father Newman is a man of God, a man who took a vow and walks it out. Me . . . I mean, come on. I don't have what you guys have. So yes, why me?"

"Easy one," Father Newman chimed in. "Why Moses, who murdered a man and became a hermit in the desert?"

"Why Joseph, rejected by his family and sold into slavery?" Ben said.

"Why Jonah, who like you walked away from God but returned with work to do? Why David, after the mistakes he made, including sleeping with another man's wife and sending that man to his death?"

"Why Saul of Tarsus," Ben said, "who, before he became Paul and wrote the lion's share of the New Testament, persecuted Christians and led many to their deaths? Jed, the Bible is full of stories where God used flawed, seemingly unworthy people to fulfill His purpose. He doesn't call the perfect to His service, or there would be no servants at all. He calls the ordinary, the damaged, and the uncertain to faith. I've prayed about this, as I hope you have. I believe, with all my heart, God has called you to this mission. And so I ask you . . ." He leaned in on his elbows, his smile broadening. "Don't you think you've spent enough time in the belly of that whale?"

Father Newman chuckled at that.

Jed sat silently for a long moment, thinking about the list they'd laid out. But it didn't matter, really. Because he'd prayed too. And he also knew this was much more than an ordinary job interview. He felt the pull of something greater than himself at work here. When his country called, he'd answered. His Team called, and he'd never faltered. If God was calling him now, then maybe he should answer that call, and everything in his life could make sense for once.

"The answer is yes," Jed said, surprised how easy the word felt on his lips after years of consternation and soul-searching. Was surrender really that simple?

Ben and Father Newman smiled.

"What happens now?" he said.

"Well, if you're ready, I'll read you into the program—no secrets held back—and tell you the nature and scope of our work.

Then we can talk about how you come aboard, your training, and the mission. We would love to have you lead a direct-action unit of your own."

Father Newman looked over at Ben, the surprise on his face unmistakable, but he said nothing.

"Where would I be working?" Jed asked, not that it mattered, he supposed. He was tied to nowhere. Not anymore.

"Well, the Shepherds is a multinational task force, Jed," Morvant said, diving right in. "We maintain Watcher and Shepherd units all over the world, including offices in the UK, Morocco, Berlin, Tokyo, Seoul—the list goes on and on. Our main campuses in the United States are in Arizona outside of Prescott and here in Tennessee, just outside of Nashville. We would want to base you here in Tennessee, which is also where the command staff are located—sort of the Shepherds' version of WARCOM, if you will."

That took Jed by surprise, and he let air whistle out between his teeth. Was he ready to be here—to come home? He welcomed the opportunity to reconnect with his parents and family. He wondered, even, if Pastor Tobias might still be in the area. And Tennessee, with her rolling hills and rivers, really did feel like home. That feeling of homecoming had been overwhelming since he stepped off the Southwest jet, but he'd not been able to embrace it because of the tidal wave of chaos and violence he'd faced since his arrival.

But Rachel and David were here as well. The thought of Rachel and her husband and daughter being so close was disquieting to say the least. It wasn't picking at a healing wound but tearing open a well-healed scar. Raw and painful.

"Would that be a problem?" Ben asked, sensing his discomfort perhaps.

"No," he said, pushing the sophomoric pining for a lost love aside. "Of course not." He looked at Ben with a newfound confidence, shrugged his shoulders, and sat up straighter in his chair. "I'm ready."

The door behind Ben opened and a familiar face entered the room. Jed's mouth dropped open and a flood of raw emotions washed over him.

"Ah, just in time," Ben said as David Yarnell walked in, his face set and reminiscent of the fiery teenage boy he'd once been. "Have a seat, David."

When do I get to shake myself free of this weight around my neck?

"Are you okay?" David asked Jed, taking a seat and holding his eyes.

"Fine," he replied. "I've been through worse. How about you guys? Everyone holding up? How's Sarah Beth?"

"Better than expected, I'd venture," David said, his eyes now smiling at the thought of his daughter. "There's plenty of trauma that will need unpacking, but Pastor Dee said that will take time. The extreme violence she sees in her visions, the abduction, and the psychological abuse from Victor—these aren't things you can just sweep under the rug. She's only twelve, after all. If it was me, I'd be having PTSD right now. On the other hand, she's tougher than everyone gives her credit for. In many ways, this experience has answered a lot of questions for . . . well, all of us. And it's brought us closer together as a family. I think I did a poor job of being there for her—I tried to pretend away her gift or curse or whatever it turns out to be . . . but now I'm all in."

Of course—it made sense now. This was why David was here, but also why Father Newman, who already said he was a leader in the Watchers, was sitting in with them. Ben had gathered them all here, perhaps knowing the bond Jed had formed with Sarah Beth and thinking if David and Rachel knew that Jed—the man who'd saved their daughter twice—was becoming a permanent part of the Shepherds, then Sarah Beth would be easier to recruit.

"So is Sarah Beth going to be in the Watchers?" he asked gently, looking at David. He imagined this to be a very difficult decision for the man, and his wife of course.

"We haven't decided yet," David said, "but it seems likely. After everything, that's where she may be the safest at this point."

Morvant cleared his throat and Jed looked over.

"But that's not why he's here, Jed." Reading his mind again.

"Then . . ."

Morvant held up a hand. "Jed, as we'll describe more fully over the coming hour or two, the structure of the Shepherds' direct action units is such that there is a team leader over every squad and fire team, much like in the SEAL Teams. But here, that team leader is partnered with a nonoperator. Each team leader works in tandem with a spiritual leader, usually from one of many denominations of churches, and together they make tactical decisions for the team. Obviously the spiritual leader remains in the TOC during the direct-action missions and functions like a command-and-control element, and his focus is on the spiritual side of the house."

"Okay," Jed said, not fully understanding what that meant or how it could work, nor where Ben seemed to be heading.

"David is being recruited to join the Shepherds as well, as a tactical spiritual leader, or TSL. We've had our eye on him for a while, in fact, and not only because he's the father of one of potentially the most gifted Watchers to be born in a hundred years."

"A hundred years?" Jed asked, momentarily distracted from the more disturbing news of David's recruitment. "How long have the Shepherds been in operation? I assumed they were like other iterations of the task force concept, born of the war on terror."

Morvant shook his head. "The Shepherds have existed for hundreds of years, in one fashion or another, and this is all history you'll learn more about during your training. But this current iteration, and its blended, multinational and multi-denominational structure, was formed during the height of World War I."

Jed let that sink in a moment. He found himself in a position now where he could scarcely resist joining just to learn everything about this ultrasecret unit that had been operating under everyone's noses since long before the Twin Towers made such things commonplace and accepted.

That's how they get you—that irresistible pull to peel back one more layer of the onion and learn the next secret . . .

He jerked back in his chair, belatedly becoming aware that Ben had just said something vitally important. "I'm sorry; what was that?" he stammered.

"I said, our hope was to train you and David together, so that you could work side by side in the joint leadership role I described. You have a long history together and a strong connection, especially now with Sarah Beth."

Jed rose from his chair, shaking his head. "No," he said, unable to look at David. "You ask too much. There's a lot in that shared history that you don't know about, which makes this impossible."

A moment ago, he'd worried about being able to live in the same city with David and Rachel, and now Ben wanted them, after all that had happened, to be a *team*?

Impossible.

The Shepherd commander watched him a moment, saying nothing, and then turned to Father Newman, who nodded.

"A moment ago, you seemed to suggest you felt convinced that God was calling you to this new task," the priest said gently. "As is common in our Christian walk, you seem to believe that the Lord of the universe is wise enough to call you, but too ignorant to manage the details. It's funny how so often we are willing to trust God with eternity, but not so sure we can trust Him with next Tuesday." Jed looked at the man, whose eyes radiated a knowing, but also a deep passion and caring. "I'm not pointing at you here, Jed. I'm guilty of the same shortcoming from time to time. But it makes you think, doesn't it?"

Jed clenched his jaw and paced behind his chair.

How can they ask this of me?

"We're not prescient, Jed," Ben said, perhaps attempting to answer that very question, "but we feel very strongly that this arrangement is best, that it's what God is calling us to do. That being said, we make mistakes, and if this is one—if this doesn't work—we can split you two up into different teams."

Jed stopped, leaned with his hands on the back of his chair, and looked at Ben hoping his eyes conveyed to the Shepherd the enormity of what they were asking of him. Then he looked at David, who held his eyes with a strength Jed was pretty sure he'd never seen in the man before. There was so much he didn't know about him now—and about Rachel as well, he imagined. Was he going to reject what felt like his true calling because of what happened in a basement half his life ago?

"If you'll try, I will," David said, chin up, folding his arms across his chest.

Jed started to point out how unfair that was, how much easier what they asked of David would be compared to the burden he would carry, but then a voice—that other voice that speaks to people only now and then—asked him clear as day: *Is that really true? Do you know his walk and the burdens he carries from that same terrible night?*

Jed snapped his mouth closed. Surely it would be just as hard for David—being asked to work with Rachel's first love and his best friend who had abandoned them—as it would be for Jed.

He pulled out the chair and dropped back into it heavily. He smiled, then nodded at David before turning to Morvant.

"Okay," he said, hands up in surrender. "I'm in. You're right, Father . . . If it's God calling, then how can I refuse? If it's not, well . . ." He shrugged despite feeling a fire grow inside him that he didn't expect. "If it's not, I imagine we'll know soon enough."

They all looked at one another in turn, trading nods and finding communion in purpose.

Ben asked Father Newman to lead them in a short prayer, and when it was finished, Jed saw that his new boss's face was glowing with excitement and enthusiasm.

"Welcome aboard, Jedidiah. Let's begin."

EPILOGUE

VANDERBILT UNIVERSITY MEDICAL CENTER, DIVISION OF TRAUMA

1211 MEDICAL CENTER DRIVE

NASHVILLE, TENNESSEE

TUESDAY, 0955 HOURS LOCAL

Detective Perez grumbled as they rolled her in the wide blue wheelchair out of the elevator and then down the long hall toward the main entrance, to western Tennessee's only level I adult and pediatric trauma center. She'd been in the hospital much longer than she should have been. The trauma doctors had determined that there was what they called "violation of the peritoneum" by the bullet that had scythed across her abdomen and flank, necessitating a laparoscopic surgical exploration and an extra day of observation. Her belly ached, not from the bullet wound they had washed out, debrided, and closed, but rather from having the long metal tubes shoved into her belly to blow her up with CO_2 so the doctors could poke around inside her.

No matter—the more serious her wounds appeared, the better. It was only pain, after all.

The nurse pushing her down the hall was chatting away, but Perez didn't care what the woman had to say. She nodded and smiled, her mind on the little white bag with her personal effects—more specifically, the $250 pantsuit the ER docs had destroyed when they cut it off her with scissors after denying her request to disrobe. Her favorite pair of Tory Burch flats were, at least, still intact and even free of blood spatter. She felt for them in the bag as the nurse rolled her through the automatic doors and out of the hospital's drop-off–pickup entrance. The wheelchair thunked over a seam in the concrete, and she looked up and waved at the uniformed police officer standing by the cruiser waiting to take her home.

All worth it. I'm not only still alive, but I'm still of value.

As if on cue, her phone rang.

She reached for it—but it wasn't on her belt where she normally wore it clipped. Irritated, she stood and rummaged through the plastic bag only to realize it was her *other* phone ringing. She held up a finger to the waiting officer in the universal "give me a minute" gesture. She fished out the phone and tapped the green button to receive the call, holding the same finger up to the nurse, who looked increasingly put out to have to wait beside the chair. No doubt the lawyers had rules that required her to stand by until her ward was safely whisked away from the corner.

"Hello?" she said, keeping the fear and anxiety out of her voice as best she could.

Like that mattered.

"You are well, I hope?" the low, oily voice said.

"Yes," she said. "Heading home now."

"Excellent," he said, the word a hiss.

"Listen, about the house . . ."

"Enough," the voice snapped. "Your decision was sound. The situation became unwinnable and you preserved a valuable NOC, which we need now more than ever. Every hive sacrifices drones—is not that their purpose? Anyway, a small price to pay for your . . . survival."

"Thank you," she said and exhaled relief. For the first time, she allowed herself to believe she might be alive by week's end. "I won't let you down again."

"Oh, I know, my dear," the hissing whisper responded, an almost joy evident in the words. "Heal quickly and get back to your post. There is much work left to do. The battle may have been lost, but the war rages on. With each setback, a new opportunity presents itself. We now have new threads to exploit."

"And the girl?"

A long pause hung on the line before he said, "She is stronger than I foresaw, but we have someone on the inside . . . Time will tell. She may yet be mine."

Then the line went dead.

Perez let out a long, shaking sigh and closed her eyes, suddenly aware they were rimmed with tears—perhaps from relief or perhaps from the pain gnawing in her belly.

She turned to the nurse, an apologetic smile on her face. "I'm so sorry," she said, collecting her plastic bag and the paperwork the nurse held out to her. "You know how dads can be."

"Oh, I know," the nurse said, smiling for real now and rolling her eyes. "Got me one of them overprotective dads too. Thank you for your service, Detective. And God bless you."

Perez smiled her goodbye and then turned and headed toward the squad car.

Not likely, young lady. Not likely.

Maria Perez resisted the urge to run her fingers over the incision sites on her abdomen and focused on looking natural in the small but posh lobby of the boutique Parisian hotel. The stitches in her belly button were driving her crazy. So very, very itchy. She'd taken a bullet while managing an operation at the Yarnell home in Nashville—not in an official capacity as a metro police detective, but in service of her *other* job. The trick, however, was making sure everyone believed otherwise. Yes, she'd been on duty that night. Of course she'd arrived just in the nick of time to save the girl. She'd become quite the actress over the years, and it appeared she had everyone fooled, including the Yarnells.

This trip to Paris, which she'd played off as necessary for psychological reasons, was also in service of her *other* job. The order had been given and she was in no position to decline. Once you were in, refusing was no longer an option. *There's no reason to be paranoid,* she told herself. *I'm not the target of the manhunt . . . at least not yet.* If Interpol and French police thought that Nicholas Woland was hiding out in this hotel, it would have been obvious by now. If she knew anything, it was how to recognize a sting operation in progress.

She crossed the lobby, her low heels clicking on the tile floor, and smiled at the stern-looking woman behind the reception desk. The woman, whose hair was pulled back in an impossibly tight bun, gave a half smile and held up a finger as she finished on the phone. After ending her call, the receptionist rested her hands on the ridiculously Parisian, faux-gold inlaid desk, which was positioned in front of a wall covered with a matching gold foil.

"Oui, madame. Comment puis-je vous aider aujourd'hui?" the woman asked, tilting her head in a way that reminded Maria of a Labrador retriever.

"English?" Maria asked hopefully. She was bilingual and fluent in Spanish, but her French was only middling. This was Paris, after all, where the privilege of speaking French was reserved for Parisians.

"Of course, madam," the woman said, her lips smiling but her eyes suggesting this to be the dumbest question of the day. "How may I help you?"

"I'm Anna Mayberry in room 413. Have any messages arrived for me while I was out?"

At this the woman's face showed genuine surprise. Perhaps in the age of cell phones and tablets, no one left messages with hotel desks anymore. Nonetheless, the woman dutifully scrolled through a box with dividers labeled with room numbers, then looked up and smiled her saccharine-sweet smile again.

"No, madam. No messages."

"Thank you," Maria said. "Have a nice day."

The receptionist gave a curt nod but didn't answer, and Maria headed for the elevator, where she was met with more obnoxious gold leaf. Once inside, she pressed the number four and the doors slid shut. Had the surveillance team detected anything of concern, she would have been aborted with a message at the desk. Moments later the bell chimed and the doors pulled open on the fourth floor. She would be glad to be back on task in Nashville, hunting the Shepherds and prosecuting the latest threat—the Navy SEAL who from all evidence had not, as promised, returned to Virginia Beach after helping rescue the Yarnell girl. Multiple attempts to find him the usually useful, much more supernatural way had failed. Even Victor himself was having difficulty finding his way into the man's mind.

Until the Nashville Metro Police cleared her to return to duty—at least another few weeks from the looks of it—she had the flexibility to serve her master however he saw fit. It was flattering to be tasked to a high-profile operation like this one. Victor had taken a tremendous risk breaking this man out of La Santé. Whatever he was planning for Nicholas Woland must be big, and she wondered what skills the man possessed that other Dark Ones did not.

Maybe one day, the answers to such questions would no longer be above her pay grade.

She swiped her key card, heard the click, and let herself into room 413.

The room was small, comfortable, and annoyingly Parisian in that it had the same pretentious style as the lobby. As she walked to open the curtains, she paused at the door connecting to the adjoining room 415. She felt a flutter in her chest, which was out of place given her years of service. She'd been in many more dangerous situations than this. Her task was simple—escort Woland across the border into Switzerland while posing as his wife. If they were stopped, her presence would help bolster the validity of Woland's new identity. On paper it made sense, but she also suspected Victor had a secondary motive. He wanted someone he trusted to keep an eye on the freshly liberated Dark One—an asset Victor had left to rot in jail for far more years than anyone, probably including Woland himself, had anticipated.

As she tried to convince herself she had nothing to worry about, anxiety clawed at her. The assignment felt bigger than it should. Darker, riskier . . .

Staring at the connecting door, Maria felt a visceral unpleasantness—as if malice was seeping in from the room next door and somehow tainting the very air she breathed. She quick-stepped to the window and flung open the curtains to let in the light. Shadows fled and the room instantly felt cleaner.

Sanitized.

It's not the mission . . . it's the man, a second voice seemed to say, not hers, and she shivered.

Then she made an annoyed *tsk* sound and shook her head. She was acting like a schoolgirl new recruit. She'd been with *Victor* of all people—or whatever he really was—and there was no one more malignant and powerful. Nicholas Woland was but a man. She took a long, deep breath and then let it out through pursed lips.

Even after centering herself, the compulsion to retrieve the pistol from her luggage was overpowering.

It's okay, she told herself. *We're on the same side.*

With a resigned exhale, she walked to the connecting door and unlocked the dead bolt. After opening her slab, she rapped twice with her knuckles on its twin.

"It's open" came a relaxed and refreshingly American voice from the other side.

Maria pushed and sure enough, the door swung easily into the adjoining room that was the mirror image of her own.

Woland sat at the small table, legs crossed at the knee and a stub of a cigarette between the first and second fingers of his right hand, a thin tendril of blue smoke rising beside his chiseled jawline. Both forearms were wrapped in sleeves of tattoos. The left, an image of Lucifer, wrapped around the thick, sinewy forearm. The image was gorgeous; gray skin, glowing eyes above a gleaming smile on the thin face, gold scars covering the lean, muscular body, which was also studded with horns on the shoulders and arms.

"You like the art, I see," Woland's deep voice boomed, just a hint of east Texas accent around the edges.

"It's magnificent," she said, then tore her eyes from the mesmerizing tattoo, immediately regretting how her voice sounded like a fangirl meeting her favorite musician.

"It cost a fortune," Woland said, uncrossing his legs and stubbing out the remains of his cig. "It covers an old tattoo that no longer suited my life choices. A perfect recasting, I thought, considering my pedigree."

"I'm sorry, but I don't know what you mean," she said, her voice now back to normal.

He smiled, and it occurred to her how similar the smile was to the image inked on the man's arm, an image of Lucifer straight out of her mind when she'd read Dante's *Inferno*.

"Lucifer was the ultimate fallen angel, don't you think? God's right-hand man. There's a saying—the bigger they are, the harder they fall. Well, that's a far fall and one that led to his incredible power. Kinda like me, right?"

He rose and she noted how his broad chest and shoulders tugged at the seams of his dress shirt, which he wore untucked over black jeans, the denim also stressed to contain the muscles beneath.

She forced herself to hold his penetrating gaze.

"I'm afraid I'm not fully read in," she said, searching for control over this conversation. *She* was the handler here, not the other way around. "I don't know your pedigree, nor do I care. My job is to get you safely to Bern. We're to pose as a married couple for the trip, a half-day's drive on the A6. I'm just filler for your NOC. Six hours—that's all we are to each other."

"Mmm-hmm," he said, stepping toward her. She felt her pulse quicken with both fear and desire as he did. "This is not my first rodeo. I know you work with Victor, and if he sent you, then you must be good."

He took another step, closing the interpersonal gap, and his scent flooded her nostrils. An unsettling and almost-uncontrollable lust flooded over her as she held her ground.

"After the Paris attacks when you were arrested, we were all shocked," she said, forcing herself to breathe through her mouth. "I'd never seen Victor so angry . . . I have to confess I was surprised he orchestrated your escape. So much rests on the success of your next mission."

She hoped the comment knocked Woland down a peg. At the same time, she also wanted to suggest she had knowledge of the upcoming operation for which this man had been freed from La Santé, but in reality she had no idea what Victor was planning.

The imposing operator took another step closer.

This time, Maria had no choice but to take a step back, but her heel hit the wall, leaving her nowhere to go.

"I never doubted Victor would come for me," he said, placing a hand on the wall behind her, leaning in as he did. She closed her left hand into a tight fist to stop the trembling. "You see, like Lucifer, I am a fallen angel, sweetheart," he said and used his free right hand to sweep a wisp of hair that had fallen onto her face and tuck it behind her ear. "That's why Victor needs me."

She placed both hands on his chest and shoved him hard enough to make him stumble. He caught himself, then looked her up and down, surveying her like one might a new car on a lot while deciding whether to take it for a test drive.

She crossed her arms. "We're all fallen angels of one sort or another. I can promise you that whatever you imagine your value to Victor is, you have miscalculated. If you die here, he has plenty of other fallen angels ready and willing to serve the cause. And I also promise you this . . ." She leaned in toward him. "If you touch me again, I will kill you."

He surprised her by laughing—a deep, genuine laugh—before returning to the table to take a sip of whatever cocktail he'd been drinking.

"I apologize," he said, eyes suggesting he regretted nothing. "Incarceration takes a toll on a man."

She gave a curt nod. "We leave in two hours. Have another drink if you like; I'll be doing all of the driving, so no issues there."

"Two hours." He raised his glass in toast to her and then drained the remainder of his cocktail.

She'd turned to head back to her room—where she fully intended to lock the connecting door, though she doubted that would prevent anything with this man—when he called after her.

"Young lady," he said, the honorific both demeaning and inscrutable as he looked no older than she was.

"Yes?" she said, turning to find him tugging his left sleeve up over a bulging bicep to reveal yet another tattoo.

"Victor doesn't have another fallen angel like me."

Her mouth dropped open and her eyes went wide at the iconic inked symbol—a Christian cross, with a sword and a shepherd's crook behind, surrounded by laurel. Speechless, she forced her mouth closed and met his lascivious gaze.

"That's right, sweetheart," he said, eyes glowing like the image of Lucifer on his forearm. "I was a Shepherd."

GLOSSARY

18 Delta—special operations medic

AR—augmented reality

BUD/S—basic underwater demolition/SEAL training

CAG—Combat Applications Group (First Special Forces
Operational Detachment-Delta—aka Delta Force, the
Unit), the Army's elite special operations force under
operational control of the Joint Special Operations
Command

CASEVAC—casualty evacuation

CIA—Central Intelligence Agency

CL or CTL—combat lead / combat team leader

CO—commanding officer

CONUS—continental United States

CSO—chief staff officer

DNI—director of National Intelligence

DoD—Department of Defense

exfil—exfiltrate

FOB—forward operating base

HUMINT—human intelligence

HVT—high-value target

IC—intelligence community

indoc—indoctrination

infil—infiltrate

IR—infrared

ISR—intelligence, surveillance, and reconnaissance

JSOC—Joint Special Operations Command

JSOTF—Joint Special Operations task force

KIA—killed in action

MARSOC—Marine Corps Special Operations Command

MBITR—multiband inter-/intra-team radio

NOC—nonofficial cover

NSA—National Security Agency

NSW—Naval Special Warfare

NVGs—night-vision goggles

OGA—other government agency; frequently refers to the
    CIA or other clandestine organizations

OPORD—operations order

OPSEC—operational security

QRF—quick reaction force

PT—physical training

ROE—rules of engagement

RPG—rocket-propelled grenade

SAPI—small-arms protective insert

SCIF—sensitive compartmented information facility

SEALs—sea, air, and land teams; Naval Special Warfare

SecDef—secretary of defense

SF—special forces; refers specifically to the Army Special
    Operations Green Berets

SIGINT—signals intelligence

sitrep—situation report

SOAR—special operations aviation regiment

SOCOM—special operations command

SOF—special operations forces

SOPMOD—special operations modification

SQT—SEAL qualification training

SWCC—special warfare combatant-craft crewmen; boat
    teams supporting SEAL operations

TAD—temporary additional duty

Trinity Global—the official cover entry for the Shepherds
    organization

Trinity Loop—the headquarters facility for Trinity and
    operational command of Shepherds North America

TRP—thermoplastic rubber

TS/SCI—top secret / sensitive compartmented information;
    the highest-level security clearance

TSL—tactical spiritual leader

TOC—tactical operations center

UCAV—unmanned combat aerial vehicle

UAV—unmanned aerial vehicle

USN—United States Navy

ACKNOWLEDGMENTS

We want to thank our families for their never-ending support during this crazy roller-coaster ride we've dragged them on. None of our books would see the light of day without the unconditional love and support you give us. Thank you, Gina Panettieri, our intrepid and tireless agent, for lifting us up and finding new homes for our creative efforts.

Thank you, Karen Watson and the entire Tyndale House team, for giving us this incredible opportunity to finally blend our military careers, our love of storytelling, and our faith in one wonderful place. The support, encouragement, and insights you have given us are inspiring.

Thank you, loyal readers, our wingmen and -women, who always have our backs. Your thoughtful reviews, kind emails, and word-of-mouth campaigns are the rocket fuel that keeps this ship flying. Thank you for starting this, yet another, journey with us!

And to those of you still out there, serving on the pointy tip of the spear, who have been a constant source of inspiration and support for us—thank you and God bless.

You know who you are . . .

ABOUT THE AUTHORS

Andrews & Wilson is the bestselling writing team of Brian Andrews and Jeffrey Wilson—the authors behind the Shepherds series, the Tier One and Sons of Valor series, and *Rogue Asset*, the ninth book in the W.E.B. Griffin Presidential Agent series. They write action-adventure and covert operations novels honoring the heroic men and women who serve in the military and intelligence communities.

Brian is a former submarine officer, entrepreneur, and Park Leadership Fellow with degrees from Vanderbilt and Cornell. Jeff worked as an actor, firefighter, paramedic, jet pilot, and diving instructor, as well as a vascular and trauma surgeon. During his fourteen years of service, Jeff made multiple deployments as a combat surgeon with an East Coast–based SEAL Team. Jeff now leads a men's military ministry for a large church in Tampa.

To learn more about their books, sign up for their newsletter online at andrews-wilson.com and follow them on Twitter: @BAndrewsJWilson.

BOOKS BY BRIAN ANDREWS AND JEFFREY WILSON

THE SHEPHERDS SERIES

Dark Intercept
Dark Angel

SONS OF VALOR SERIES

Sons of Valor

TIER ONE SERIES

Tier One
War Shadows
Crusader One
American Operator
Red Specter
Collateral
Scars: John Dempsey (a Tier One Origins novella)

W.E.B. GRIFFIN PRESIDENTIAL AGENT SERIES

Rogue Asset

THE NICK FOLEY SERIES (AS ALEX RYAN)

Beijing Red
Hong Kong Black

OTHER TITLES BY BRIAN ANDREWS

The Calypso Directive
The Infiltration Game
Reset

OTHER TITLES BY JEFFREY WILSON

The Traiteur's Ring
The Donors
Fade to Black
War Torn

STAY UP-TO-DATE ON NEWS FROM ANDREWS & WILSON AT

andrews-wilson.com

TYNDALE HOUSE PUBLISHERS IS CRAZY4FICTION!

Fiction that entertains and inspires

Get to know us! Become a member of the Crazy4Fiction community. Whether you read our blog, like us on Facebook, follow us on Twitter, or receive our e-newsletter, you're sure to get the latest news on the best in Christian fiction. You might even win something along the way!

JOIN IN THE FUN TODAY.

 crazy4fiction.com

 Crazy4Fiction

 crazy4fiction

 @Crazy4Fiction

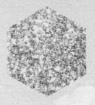